Praise for Mark Harril Saunders and *Ministers of Fire*

"Mark Harril Saunders's first novel, *Ministers of Fire*, is a brilliant, exciting and profound spy tale about, among other things, what it means to have faith. . . . This is a classic CIA novel, thick with political and moral complications . . . an incredibly rich reading experience."

——*Washington Post*

"Veteran cold-warriors confront the post-9/11 world in Saunders's impressive first novel, a complex spy-thriller. . . . While the intricate plotting and vivid action scenes are sure to please genre fans, more general readers should also find plenty to enjoy, from Saunders's meticulous prose to his closely observed characterizations."

——*Publishers Weekly* (starred review)

"What separates Saunders's work from much of the espionage field comes in two rewarding areas; first, he creates fully fleshed characters, and second, his writing soars above the pedestrian, not only in his characterizations but also in his lucid descriptions of life in contemporary China and his intelligent take on the perils of clandestine efforts in a dangerous world where loyalty can be a liability."

——Jay Strafford, *Richmond Times-Dispatch*

"*Ministers of Fire* can be compared to a John le Carré classic, with its complexity, atmosphere and deft use of language. Although it's a thriller, the varied pace, character development and ethical quandaries make it equally a 'thinker.' . . . [Saunders's] foray into book-length fiction is a great end-of-summer read."

—— *Virginian-Pilot*

Ministers of Fire

MARK HARRIL
SAUNDERS

MINISTERS *of* FIRE

a novel

SWALLOW PRESS
Ohio University Press • Athens

Swallow Press
An imprint of Ohio University Press
Athens, Ohio 45701
www.ohioswallow.com

To obtain permission to quote, reprint, or otherwise reproduce or distribute material
from Swallow Press / Ohio University Press publications, please contact our rights
and permissions department at (740) 593-1154 or (740) 593-4536 (fax).

Printed in the United States of America
Swallow Press / Ohio University Press books are printed on acid-free paper ⊗ ™

First paperback printing in 2014
ISBN 978-0-8040-1154-9

HARDCOVER   20 19 18 17 16 15 14 13   5 4 3 2
PAPERBACK   21 20 19 18 17 16 15 14   5 4 3 2 1

Library of Congress Cataloging-in-Publication Data
Saunders, Mark Harril.
 Ministers of fire : a novel / Mark Harril Saunders.
     p. cm.
 ISBN 978-0-8040-1140-2 (hc : acid-free paper) — ISBN 978-0-8040-4048-8
(electronic)
 1. International relations—Fiction. I. Title.
 PS3619.A8248M56 2012
 813'.6—dc23
                           2011053333

R.A.S.

In love we are incapable of honor—the courageous act is no more than playing a part to an audience of two.

—Graham Greene, *The Quiet American*

prologue

WHEN APRIL WAS GONE, DISAPPEARED INTO THE CENTER of the world, her voice in his head would still insist that he had planned everything—not just the night in Samarkand but all that surrounded it. It was in the Burling character, she said, using his name as she did in the third person, to engineer things according to his own mind, to will them into existence while keeping his distance at the same time. The problem, Burling thought, was people. He was never any good with them. Whether that failure was due to a flaw in his makeup, or just a hedge in case things went to hell, April—the tall, abundant woman with the narrowing gaze that seemed to hide a sly yearning that Burling, in the short time given them, had not been able to fulfill—never had a chance to tell him.

February 14, 1979: to this day no one marks it as significant. November 9, 1989, September 11, 2001, but not the last troubled months of the seventies, when the world we know was born. On that Wednesday, Wes Godwin, survivor of the Philippines, Korea, and the Ia Drang Valley in Vietnam, left the Embassy Residence in Kabul by the rear gate to attend a practice of the Afghan national basketball team, of which April's husband, Jack, was coach. Lucius Burling, deputy chief of mission and the Agency station chief, rode with Ambassador Godwin in his dusty black car. Plush seats, smell of cigarette smoke, milky sun smeared across the glass. Their route took them through an unpaved lane along walls the color of sand, punctuated at intervals by ancient wooden doors that opened onto courtyards shaded by fruit trees, where dark-eyed children with café-au-lait faces played solemnly in the dust. Burling had been a starting forward at Princeton, at a time when that meant something, but in retrospect he had to admit that his success at basketball had more to do with his natural size and a determined drive than with any great skill as an athlete. Slow-footed but strong, Burling would wait for the quick ones to feed him the ball, then lower his head, make a halting feint one way or the other, and take it to the hole.

Bull, they called him, which was ridiculous and probably in fun.

"More like Ferdinand," Amelia had teased him.

"I worked harder than they did, that's all," Burling said, a bit stung. At that time in their courtship, he was still getting used to her and couldn't really tell if her tone was affectionate or cutting.

"It's your big blond head, darling," Amelia said, reaching up to touch his hair, "with all those big thoughts inside it. The thinking man's bull."

He was not much interested in basketball now, not in the kind they had going at home, anyway. He had taken his son to see George-town play, but John Thompson's game had not appealed to him, partly because he knew he wouldn't have lasted a season in that fre-netic kind of scheme. The game in Kabul was not for him either, but some of Jack's players had ties to the northern tribes, and Burling had a plan to go up there that was lately gaining traction at Langley.

"Going through with this, are you?" Godwin said, face still turned to the world outside the car. At noon the alley was deserted except for a street dog that lapped at the gutter and perked up warily at the sound of the Cadillac, springs complaining as it shouldered through the ruts.

"I don't look at it that way," Burling told him.

The ambassador faced him, lips the color of bricks. He still wore his white hair in a military cut, in spite of his civilian appointment.

"We need friends up there," Burling said.

"He-ell." Godwin drew two syllables out of the word. "The tribes aren't anyone's 'friend.' They know Taraki is weak and the Russians are just waiting for an excuse to come across."

Burling watched him quietly, acknowledging the obvious. Godwin was southern military royalty and therefore, in Burling's estimation, lacked nuance in the extreme.

"You're not thinking far enough ahead, Lucius. What about the Chinese? You don't think they aren't already in there? Deng Xiaoping's got his own Moslem problem, and this is his backyard. Mark my words, this'll blow back, maybe not tomorrow, maybe not for twenty years."

"By then I hope we're all in a better place," Burling said.

The Cadillac reached a crossing ten blocks from the compound. Across the intersection, wires hung from a rusted box mounted on a pole. The place seemed unnaturally quiet under the white sky, and Burling had a vague foreboding, like waking in the morning and not remembering what you'd done—something not in your character, apparently—the night before. Perhaps it was just a case of misplaced respect for a superior. Godwin was only ten years his senior, but the Second World War made the space between them feel wider. In spite of the ambassador's greater experience, Burling was convinced that he, the younger man, was right.

"How's your bride feeling?" Godwin asked.

"Better, thanks."

The ambassador rearranged himself uncomfortably and chuckled deep in his chest. "Some women aren't made for this life. Doesn't appeal to them."

Burling's heart had begun to flutter. He was aware that he was about to reveal more than he should. "Sometimes I think I wasn't meant to be married, Wes. I seem to enjoy isolation more than . . ." Lately Burling had begun to leave sentences undone, as if his own thoughts could be read aloud. The habit worried him. "More than the alternative, I guess. At one time Amelia thought she wanted this."

3

"Women are changeable. Worst mistake you can make is try to stand in their way."

"You take Jack's wife," Burling began.

Godwin laughed aloud. "No, you take her, man. Too much trouble for me."

Burling smiled involuntarily, and a deep flush came to his face. Two nights before, in the Residence garden after drinking red wine at a dinner, he had done just that. Or not taken her, exactly, in the way that Godwin meant. The logistics of that he could not imagine. But he had kissed her, surprising himself if not, apparently, April. At first he had stammered an apology, but she had smiled at him as if he were a boy, then kissed him back, one palm placed tenderly against his chest. He couldn't tell if she was stroking him or pushing him away, and he was trembling slightly as she drew toward him, lips parting on his; he could feel the cleft of her lower back beneath his hand.

"It's almost as if this country makes sense to her," he said.

Godwin's face compressed in a wolfish expression, concentrated around the eyes. A lot of things seemed clear to April, dimensions of how people lived in the world that for Burling were surrounded by a haze of uncertainty. That seemingly amused capacity for taking things as they came was what had drawn him to her. And he was, he realized now, deeply attracted, on a level and in a way that had been working in him since she and Jack had arrived in Afghanistan more than a year ago. "She's a hippie anthropologist, Lucius. *The Wretched of the Earth*, all that. I've seen her type before in Vietnam. Comes over for the soft stuff, but what she really wants is to get in the shit."

The prospect thrilled and terrified him.

"You should take her up north, Lucius. Involve her in your little scheme. She's the one who speaks the languages."

A sound like a rock hitting glass caused both men to strain forward into the deep space between the seats. A star had formed on the windshield, and Godwin's driver—a thin, graceful Afghan with delicate fingers that could palm a basketball—slumped against the wheel. Slowly, with a smooth motion, the car rolled across the intersection, and its hood rose up, the radiator exploding behind it, emitting a wicked hiss of steam.

"Holy shit," Godwin said, sounding deeply perturbed.

Men in police uniforms were grabbing at the handles, and Burling fumbled with the strap of white vinyl on his own door, fighting to keep it shut. Behind him they pulled Wes Godwin from the car. Burling heard the singsong of Pashto or Dari—he couldn't tell which. The man at his window was gone, and he whipped around, expecting a blow from behind. Through the opposite door he could see Godwin's midsection, the starched white shirt and navy tie too short on his belly, his naked arms grappling with the men. His sleeves were rolled at the cuffs, and his hands tried to keep his assailants away from him, bobbing like a fighter, grasping at anything. The street outside was bright.

"We're going to the Serena," one said in heavily accented English, referring to the Kabul Hotel. "You are going to give us the *mujahedin*."

"We're not going anywhere," Godwin told them, breathing hard now, still fighting. "We're not holding any soldiers of God."

"Wes," said Burling. "It's a kidnapping, an exchange."

"Hell with that." Bullets began to hit the car again.

In spite of his position, Lucius Burling was a peaceful man. An intelligence analyst, not an ex-soldier like Godwin, or Jack Lindstrom, spoiling for a fight. He had come to this country, as he had more than a dozen years before to Vietnam, to assess the situation and to offer help, a way forward. A man had a few things to lean on or comfort him in life, and the integrity of this position was one of Burling's.

"Get down, Wes!"

Burling ducked, and the back window shattered. One of the kidnappers' bodies was flung against the trunk. Automatic fire came from three sides, and the men dressed as police crouched down and returned it with pistols and shotguns. Burling began to crawl across the seat, intending to pull Wes to safety. He was unprepared for how loud the firing was at close range. The man who had struggled with Godwin was hit in the back and thrown against the tufted leather of the door, his chest ripped open like a suitcase.

Wes was unprotected now. Burling watched him trying to push the dead man off his legs, but he couldn't do it without leaving cover. Godwin turned a quarter of the way toward Burling; his shirt bloomed red, and he fell on his side across the seat. Burling's ears were plugged. The rattle of gunfire sounded far away. A bearded face in a *keffiyeh* appeared in the space where the windshield had been. Burling thought briefly of Amelia, and a great, lonely sadness overwhelmed him. That he would die now, could die, with so much silence and distance between them. I really didn't know this could happen, he thought.

Wes Godwin's life left his body in a spasm.

Burling swallowed and his hearing returned to him, like a train approaching from far away. The broken car was running with a tick, then a rasp. He closed his eyes to squeeze out the water. When his vision cleared he realized that he was alone.

IN THE DAYS AFTER THE KILLING, THE ORGANISM OF THE CITY broke down and its hungers were exposed. Kabul came under siege. The city lay in a pale bowl of light, and every movement seemed magnified. April insisted it was a troop of Jack's basketball players who attacked the compound wall one windy, hot afternoon, but Lindstrom said they'd disappeared.

"Gone up north to fight the Russians, just like they told me they would."

Jack was sitting in the garden late that night as Burling returned from his office to the Residence, where all remaining personnel had retreated in precaution. Lindstrom spoke up as Burling approached, answering an unasked question from the darkness of the overhanging branches above a bench.

"They killed the American ambassador," Burling said, "so they ran."

From the tip of a brass pipe the shape of a cigarette, an ember glowed in front of Lindstrom's face. "Keeping you up, is it?"

"I'm the guy that's left behind."

"Me, too," Lindstrom said, exhaling a plume of blue smoke. He stood up slowly, a head shorter than Burling but possessed of a taut strength, like a wrestler. Burling saw that he was wearing a sidearm, as if in the aftermath of the attack he had returned to his former life as a marine. He peered up into Burling's face. "You know what I'm talking about?"

Burling took a step backward on the uneven path. "I need to get back to Amelia."

"The *mujas* didn't kill Wes, your buddies in the government did."

"I was there, Jack."

"Then you should have seen it for what it was: a cluster fuck."

"The *mujahedin* wanted to grab Godwin. Taraki's people tried to stop it and shot him by mistake."

"You don't wonder how the government forces knew what was about to go down?"

"I wonder about a lot of things. Apparently you have a theory about this one?"

"It's just stoned thinking, Lucius. You go on back now. Tonight might be your last chance for a while."

Burling stared uncomprehendingly at him in the dark. Strangely, there was no sound of birds or bugs here at night. The dry air was luminous and still. Far away he heard the pop of gunfire. "Why, what's happening tomorrow?"

"I'm a married man, too," Lindstrom said, "so I know how it goes. The mysterious rhythms."

"I don't know what you're talking about."

"Man, you really don't, do you? You don't keep track of that shit at all."

From an open window of the Residence came the sound of a television, the volume unnaturally loud. An American newsman was talking about hostages. "What are you smoking in that thing?" Burling asked.

"Thai stick. Grass soaked in opium. Very mellow, but I wouldn't recommend it if you want to make love to your wife."

Burling tried to hide his astonishment, but the effort made him seem prim. Lindstrom's vaguely Asiatic eyes held two counterimages of the match, like tiny blazing question marks, as he lit the pipe again.

"We've been married for twenty years," Burling told him. For some reason, the contemplative menace in Lindstrom's face made Burling want to reach out to him. Or maybe, he thought, it's because we have April in common. "There's just not the urgency now."

"Between the two of you, no."

"What's happening tomorrow, Jack? I really want to hear."

"Half of the staff won't show up," Lindstrom told him, squinting as he waved the smoke away with his hand. "The masons you ordered from north of the city won't come to fix the wall."

"Your players told you this?"

"A month ago or more."

"And you neglected to pass it on."

"You didn't want to hear it. You were so sure you had this thing nailed."

A sound of boots on gravel startled them, and a flashlight raked the wall behind the trees: the duty marine checking the perimeter at the beginning of his watch. Above the wall the sky was a dirty yellow from the streetlights that hadn't been shot out. "So you wouldn't let April ride in the car with us that day. You made her come to the gym with you and said it was because she was going to show your players her jump shot."

"I wasn't joking," Lindstrom said, but Burling thought he sounded evasive, in the way of a petty informer. "They didn't think a woman could do it. I said, how do you think she got a scholarship to Georgetown?"

Jack's pride in his wife was affecting, but it made Burling wonder what still existed between them. "What would make you think they'd understand a thing like that," he asked, envy stirring, "when you see the women here?"

"You don't give them any credit, Lucius, that's your problem. All they wanted was to get their people back, the ones Taraki was torturing."

"Why won't the masons come tomorrow, Jack?"

"Because they've gone off to fight, man, just like they have since the British—shit, since Genghis Khan was here. If they don't show up tomorrow, that'll be our signal to get the hell out."

THE MORNING AFTER, JACK PROVED TO BE RIGHT. THE masons didn't come, and by afternoon the rats had chewed a tunnel through the wall from the open sewer running outside. Burling and two marines tried to patch it with a rotting bag of mortar they found in a shed, but the rats seemed to like it—for the salt—and made the hole larger than before. Like the siege of Krishnapur, no one in the embassy cared anymore—except Burling.

In the three days it took to get dependents out, he worked with a calm insistence, as if he'd been waiting for this all his life. He felt vaguely guilty at how much he relished it, and how much the work left room for nothing else.

Late on Friday afternoon he left Godwin's office, which he had taken over, to bring his wife the news. He had kept his own family here while others got out because that only seemed right; now it was their turn. The gift of what Amelia wanted, to leave him, he bore sadly through the Residence gate. The sun was sharp from the west, and marines had taken up positions around the ornamental garden where he had kissed April, then learned that her husband had been perfectly willing to let him be kidnapped or killed. Crossing that threshold, breaking into their lives, had set something real and true in motion inside him. He had begun to believe that he was meant to understand things, about women, about the whirl of borders where he had been sent in his country's service. He saw more clearly the factions involved in Godwin's murder, the role of the northern tribes, even the future as it involved the United States, its enemies and allies, perhaps a Third Force, and how these things fit together in the puzzle of nations. Kissing April had even allowed him to set aside his anger at his wife, given him the distance he needed to treat Amelia with compassion, as he should. But even as he thought fondly of pleasing her, longing, hard as a stone, rose up in his throat. It's all turned around, he thought. I actually want her to go.

Burling found his wife and son on the path near where Lindstrom had predicted the future. Jack had the information, all right, because that was his role, but Burling was meant to parse it, to *understand*. Godwin's death, his plan to work with the *mujahedin*, seemed ordained.

"Mom killed it," Luke said. They were huddling above a lank brown body, its coarse hair matted with blood. The boy was twelve, and his round eyes and freckled face couldn't decide whether to be impressed or horrified. He hadn't known his mother, a savior of birds, would beat a rat to death with a shovel.

"I am finished," she said.

Her voice seemed unstable, and Burling wondered if she'd been drinking. He could smell something strong but not quite sweet in the air, pungent and headier than alcohol. Then it came to him: the smell of Godwin's car.

"I know," he said to his wife. He felt mourning coming on, prematurely: the strength it took to hold up against it steadied him. Being a man entailed equal measures of risk and resignation. He touched her on the shoulder. "It's all pretty horrible, but you'll be out of here tomorrow."

"You're not coming with us," she said.

"I can't, Amie."

"You don't want to."

"We're going home?" Luke asked, disappointed.

"I am done," Amelia said.

LATER THAT NIGHT HE WAS BACK IN THE EMBASSY, arranging the journey up north. Sleeves rolled up past his elbows, blue pencil touching the map. Godwin's office smelled of rugs, books, and furniture polish. The pool of light from the desk lamp ringed a pleasurable solitude. Amelia had changed, or misrepresented herself, while he had simply stayed the same. What had been an adventure when they married, what had drawn her to him, she despised in him now. His sense of purpose was a burden. That was why he'd turned to April. It was not what he had wanted, but he would have to take it on.

"Burling."

It was as if he had fallen into the map: he wasn't sure how much time had passed. April, dressed in a white *djellabah*, was leaning inside the door.

"I'm sorry, but I just can't call you Lucius," she said, seeing the look on his face. To his surprise, her presence was unwelcome. "It doesn't fit you somehow."

"It was my father's name," said Burling.

"Where I'm from they'd call you Junior. Something else if you were black."

No other person in the embassy would dare to affect native dress, but April wore it as a provocation. Like her languages, the robe was almost a weapon, or a camouflage. Inside the open neckline, he could see the low swell of her breast.

"I haven't seen you since . . . ," she began, then immediately laughed at herself, collapsing slightly to one side so that her knuckles bore her weight on the credenza. A deceptively strong woman, she tossed her fine blond curtain of hair behind her shoulders, as if its luxuriance annoyed her. Not exactly beautiful, Burling observed. Amelia would have turned more heads at the Chestnut Hill parties where she and Burling had come of age. April's eyes were a bit too light, the skin across her wide cheekbones sprinkled in places with the pockmarks of a childhood disease. But her neck led gracefully into her muscular shoulders and long, slender arms, wrists cuffed with tight bracelets; and her breasts, while substantial, looked firm. His father could have drawn her in three or four finely arcing strokes, his pencil describing a long thigh and hip, a cheekbone on the opposite side and above, perhaps the hair and slender shoulder to bring the composition into balance. From her waist to her toes, which were painted and bare, she was perfect. Irritation at her presence dissolved into something warmer, desire.

"You meant since Wes was killed."

"That's what I was talking about, yes," she said, coming around to his side of the desk where he could see her whole length. The *djellabah* rippled across the space between her thighs. "But you were thinking of kissing me in the garden."

Burling's words caught deep in his throat. "I can't stop thinking about it, to be honest."

"You're a good man, Lucius Burling," she said. "One kiss is not that big a deal."

"Since Wes died, things are not . . . No, I don't want to put it on that."

April turned and went to the tray on the windowsill, where a cut-glass bottle of arak, a pitcher of water and glasses, shared space with Burling's African violets and creeping philodendron. "You brought your tray in here," she observed.

Weary with lust, Burling rose. "My plants," he said.

"You're funny."

"I've kept them alive for a long time," he told her, picking up the long tendrils of the philodendron in his hands and rubbing his thumb on a waxy leaf.

"Most men don't keep plants."

"These are easy to care for."

April poured them each a measure of the clear liquor. Adding water clouded the liquid to the color of milk. A smell of licorice rose from the glasses.

"My father raised vegetables," she told him. "He would make them come up out of the ground like a sorcerer. Rocky ground it was, too, but fertile just the same."

"Did you and Jack have a garden in Berkeley?"

She laughed, somewhat ruefully, and handed him a glass. "Jack is more like one of those bitter weeds that grow out of the cracks in a sidewalk. You have to respect his kind of strength. Hack him down, he just keeps growing back."

"How did you meet?"

April sighed and lowered herself on the long leather couch, and Burling stood above her, tentatively drinking. "When I entered the program at Cal, I felt very detached. All the other kids were privileged, very stoned and theoretical. I went down to a gym in Oakland to see if I could teach the girls from the neighborhood basketball. And there was Jack, just back from his first tour. His grandfather's mission had funded the gym."

"I just realized," Burling said, feeling his height and sitting down on an ottoman. Their knees were almost touching.

"What did you realize?"

"That I don't want to talk about Jack."

April smiled, which narrowed her eyes. "We're not going to make it here, you know," she said, watching for his reaction over the rim of the glass, "in Godwin's office."

"Was that supposed to be on the agenda tonight?"

"I'm probably not even your type," she said, bringing the glass again to her lips. They were plump, of a rare shade of pink, defined by clean lines against her pale skin. He thought again how they had felt against his, the slight pressure receiving him, and the hardness of her teeth inside.

He had to take in breath to gather himself. "Why do women always say that to me?"

"That we're not your type?"

"Yes, but why?"

"Because under most circumstances, you wouldn't even look at a girl like me."

"I would find it impossible not to."

"That's sweet, and I know you're not lying, right this minute, but if I had come to your office, the summer I interned at State, you wouldn't have been any more than polite."

Burling took a quick gulp of the arak to steady himself. She wouldn't have found him at the Department of State, of course, but she would certainly be aware of that. Jack would not have been reticent on that score. "Why do you think so?"

"Because you're a sophisticated man. Worldly. Handsome, but not so good looking that people wonder."

"No?"

She smiled to acknowledge his feigned disappointment. "You move like you played a sport, football or basketball, maybe had an injury or two, but you're careful so as not to hurt anyone smaller than you. You went to private schools, and you're probably rich, or at least well off compared to most people, and now you're being groomed for one of the top political appointments—deputy national security advisor, or number two at CIA."

"Shhh," said Burling, pointing at the ceiling where the microphones would be. Taraki's government had the benefit of Soviet security expertise. "Who says that?"

"Jack. Besides, you married a debutante."

"Not quite," Burling said. "When I met her, Amelia was rebelling against being a society girl. Drinking and going to jazz concerts with men. It's her money, by the way. My family lost ours long ago."

"What luxury!" said April. "To reject what others want more than anything."

"What *do* people want? Amelia and I are about as conventional as can be. The problem is what goes on in my head. I tend to disappoint people."

"Are you going to disappoint me?" April asked, pointing to his nearly empty glass.

"I'll have one more, if that's what you mean," he said, draining it.

April got up. She seemed somewhat hardened now, yet still he couldn't help feeling encouraged. When he envisioned the journey up north, she was already with him in his mind. Up to Samarkand, over the Pass. Translating Dari and Pashto and whatever else they ran across. It was probably a very bad idea to take a woman, but he was making up reasons that it had to be done for the sake of the mission, and he had already begun to believe them.

"I need you to stay with me," he said.

She looked at him over her shoulder, half-angrily, half-wanting. At least that was what he hoped. "I already told you, I can't do that." She said it softly, as if to the glasses she was filling.

"That's not what I meant," Burling said, accepting the fresh drink. They stood close, their glasses resting against each other in salute. "When the charter flight leaves tomorrow, I need you to stay. Come over here."

"Be careful," she warned. "Jack is probably out in the garden right now. He's getting high again, and when he does that he likes to talk to the marines."

"That's why I can't take him with me," he said, setting down his glass on the corner of the desk, "even though he knows the terrain." On a yellow legal pad, he wrote, *I have to go up North, to Mazar-i-Sharif, to talk to the mujahedin.* "Things are happening faster than I thought, and I need someone with languages."

"I came out here to help with girls' education," she said, sounding slightly desperate now. "Just because I speak Dari doesn't mean I understand what these men are up to. And I don't care what Jack says, killing Godwin didn't make any sense."

"Oh, yes, it did," Burling said, sampling the new, stronger, mixture. "Ever heard of Franz Ferdinand?"

"That's another problem. I'm not as smart as you are."

"Now you're patronizing me," Burling said. "You know what I think?"

April raised her eyebrows. "I wish I did."

"You're perfect for this."

SUNDAY MORNING, BURLING'S FAMILY LEFT, BOARDING THE DC-3. Only Luke, young and game enough still for the flight on an airplane to excite him, looked back across his shoulder at his father. Amelia stared resolutely at the seatback in front of her, and their daughter Elizabeth already had her nose in a book about Emily Dickinson. Jack Lindstrom sat in front of them, "headed for an epic druggie meltdown in the States," as April put it.

As the plane took off, leaving a trail of oddly black exhaust, and tilted across the mountains to the east, Burling thought about his children. Another secret thing he cherished was a potent love for Betsy and Luke, but he had probably lost them, too, if he had ever really had them. They were beautiful, but he had thrown off the delicate balance of that beauty through his failure with their mother. It made what he was about to do all the more important, so that someday they would understand, and the pieces could be put back together into a larger, more beautiful whole.

That afternoon he took April on a different kind of plane, a light Cessna of the type they had used in Vietnam. Its spartan cabin shook as the engines choked to life. In the front seats rode the pilot and a young Afghan man named Abdul Hadi who worked as a liaison to the government, but was run as an asset by Burling. In the narrow seats aft, pushed together by the tapering fuselage, sat April and Burling. As the Cessna climbed above the mountains to the north, April smiled at him quickly from behind her shining hair. She wanted to be a part of his world, but what did he want from her? In his office, sharing the arak, he hadn't kissed her again, but the possibility had hung between them like a strong magnetic field. It crackled there now, at the margins. The hard stuff—as Godwin had called it—excited her. He knew that he was taking advantage of that, and yet he didn't, couldn't seem to, stop himself.

"On the way back—" Burling was talking above the engines to the pilot, pointing his finger at the windshield—"we may have to get in down there."

A spine of dry, trackless hills hunched up before them, and the pilot nodded, taking a drink from a flask and offering it to Burling, who politely refused it.

"Is this where the ones who killed Godwin went?" April asked.

Abdul Hadi turned to look at her. He was uncomfortable with her presence, and Burling felt it as a judgment on him. The Afghan might be on his payroll, but where Abdul's ultimate loyalties lay— to the Americans, Taraki, or his clan—was definitely a matter of concern. "She's merely cover," Burling had told him. "When we get to Samarkand, she'll be my wife."

"Hey, Lucius," said the pilot, cocking his head to one side. They looked down at the pocked, ochre dirt.

"Mines," said Burling, nodding. The plane's feathery shadow blew across the expanse. "That's the Soviet border down there."

IN SAMARKAND, THE MINARETS WERE SILENT. THE *madrassah* with its symmetrical blue-tiled façade was empty of life. In the center of town, an old hotel faced a large, shaded square. Its lobby had the stale, dour feeling of a place for English travelers on the Continent; the old British ladies who played bridge in the cool dusty corner by the stairs seemed right at home. On the roof was a terrace strung with multicolored lights, and on the night following their arrival, Burling boarded the creaky old lift with April, to eat "*en plein air*," as he said. He had dressed in khakis and his white linen shirt, as if playing the part of a colonial in a play. His hand spread gently across April's back as he helped her to her chair.

Children ran through the tables while their parents sat smoking over the wreck of their meals. The night air was blue with their fetid tobacco, which smelled as strong as Jack's dope, and the savor of herbs and roasted meat. In one corner of the roof a raggedy band sat on the edges of folding chairs, war medals flapping on their chests in time with the swing.

"Dance?" Burling said.

On the floor, the touch of their hands seemed quite harmless, refined.

"I've never been asked like that," she told him when her cheek was close to his. He could feel the slight tremble returning, and he didn't answer her for fear he would stutter, something he had struggled with as a child. "In southwest Virginia the boys don't typically ask, they just take you."

No one else joined them, and the old English ladies nodded their approval; their milky blue eyes tacked from April to Burling as the couple drew more closely together beneath the star-strewn globe of the sky. The ladies said they hadn't seen a man dance like that since the Blitz, and they fixed April with watery stares that were fond and regretful. The music was flat, an uneasy rendering of the big bands that Burling used to play in the living room at home—his Washington home—in a time that seemed long ago now. The music felt wrong in this dry, spicy air. No scratch of cicadas with their manic crescendo, no scent of honeysuckle sweetening the night. So far from Amelia advancing through the soft, firefly dusk toward the picnic table, flowered apron tied loosely across her hips, leaning over to pick up plates. No Glenn Miller from the open kitchen window behind her. The arid Soviet night had an electric taste of betrayal and he and April glided through it with ease while the people talked about them in Russian and English and the keening of Dari.

"Why did you really bring me up here, Lucius Burling?"

Across the tables, the lift opened and a young Chinese man emerged. Burling knew from the sharp concentration of her eyes that April had seen him. Her body stiffened, which improved their dancing, as if she had taken the lead. Behind the younger Chinese came a short, fat man about Burling's age, his thin hair combed across his scalp. The thought ran through Burling's mind that he wanted to spoil this now, to save himself. Bringing the Chinese in complicated the whole thing beyond what he was able to predict.

"I'm serious," said April. "If you brought me up here just to fuck me, that I can understand. And Jack can't seem to do that anymore, in case you didn't know, so I might just be up for it. But if you pretend there's something else, if you're just putting on a show . . ."

"I don't know how to do this properly," Burling told her, watching the Chinese colonel take his seat. "Even those ladies over there, watching our every move, I don't know how people think about things like this."

"I think you do but you like to think otherwise."

He furrowed his brows to signal that he didn't understand.

"I think that people like you like to *tell* yourselves that you don't understand what people think about in the darkness of their minds, what they do with each other. That way you're protected from the consequences."

"People like me?"

"Powerful ones. You can screw up people's lives and hide behind your 'properly,' your discretion."

"You have me all wrong," Burling told her. "I couldn't do this without you."

Her laugh was thrilling, and warm. "No shit, Chief."

AFTER DINNER, HE AND APRIL RODE THE LIFT TO THE LOBBY, agreeing without a word that they would not go to bed, not just yet, if that's what they were going to do. The old elevator jerked downward, and the drop in Burling's stomach disoriented him: along with the possibility that he would sleep with April tonight came the thought that his rush to fulfill one desire might be a willed distraction from the enormity of what he was about to set in motion with the Chinese. Working with them to arm the *mujahedin* against the Russians was a line of attack that had only glancing support at the Agency, if it had any support at all. If Amelia found out about April, or if the deputy director hung him out to dry when the operation backfired, he would be in the wilderness for a very long time.

He and April sat close, her hip touching his thigh, on a hard wooden bench in the square, framed by short, dusty trees. A public security car trolled the streets around for black marketeers. Up the crumbling steps from the bare little park they could see the brown, implacable face of the hotel, its roof bleeding color and music into the sky.

"I wasn't making it up, when we were dancing," Burling said. "I don't think you understand."

Between her thumbs April broke a pink grapefruit she had taken from the table. The fruit smelled ripe, a bit funky, and her face was sly but reluctant in the shadows. Explain yourself, she seemed to be saying. If you can.

"The first time I saw a Viet Cong dead," Burling told her, "it was early in the war, before the marines even landed at Da Nang."

"Where Jack got his 'million dollar wound,'" April said with fond sarcasm, tearing the peel.

"That was Tet. This was long before that, in the fall of '62. We were there in an advisory capacity, helicopter support. The ARVN had killed this VC in a village outside Soc Trang, and we went up to look at him, because we'd never seen one before."

"Like killing a cougar," April said. She handed him a section of grapefruit, the strands of pink flesh sticking to her fingernails. "When I was a little girl all the cougars, the mountain lions, were supposed to be gone from the hills behind my father's house, but he and my brothers swore they were there. They wanted to kill one to prove they existed."

"Did they ever get one?"

"They never did, but that didn't stop them from believing it. If they ever had killed one, I don't know what they'd have done."

The security car moved soundlessly behind the trees, a cigarette glowing inside, showing dark figures slumped against the seats. The Chinese colonel, with whom Burling was to meet next morning, came down the steps and looked this way and that.

"When Wes was murdered," Burling ventured, "the first thing I remembered was that Viet Cong. Two of the men dressed up as police, or maybe they *were* police, we don't know; anyway, they were dead, too, one of them lying there on the ground beside the car. No one had closed his eyes yet. I looked at him, and he had that same sort of meditative look, almost thoughtful, and he was terribly slender, just like the VC, and I thought again that we were in trouble, now—how'd you put it?—now that we know it exists."

April got up an inch and sat down, the way women do to shake off a subject from themselves. Above the trees to the west the sky was the color of amber, liquid and dirty from the marketplace stalls.

"What exists, Lucius? I ask you why you brought me up here, and you tell me a story about dead Viet Cong, about the soldiers of God. You tell me it's real. What is real?"

"Sacrifice."

"For you? For me?"

"Love."

"Who were the Chinese on the roof?" April asked him.

THE NEXT AFTERNOON THEY TOOK OFF AGAIN, THE PILOT flying low above the ruinous desert country to the east, shaped by wind, through the jagged peaks and chilly, verdant valleys to the landscape of rocks that was home to the *mujahedin*. The flat, rocky ground came up to meet them, the pink horizon rocked back and forth, and April grabbed Burling's hand with a disarming strength that reminded him sharply of the night before. At first she had led him, for which he was grateful, but as soon as he felt her with nothing between them, all the impediments around them ringed like forces held at bay, he'd begun to believe he was truly in love. What a fool I am, he thought.

"What is it?" she asked, drawing back.

The wheels banged across the slabs of the landing strip, jolting him out of his dream. The airfield had been built by the British after the war, part of their own misadventure in this remote, empty place. The plane shimmied as the engines and brakes dragged it down, then choked to a stop before a rusting Quonset hut. A hundred yards along the tarmac sat a Chinese military plane, with a Land Rover parked beside the tail. When the pilot opened the hatch there was no sound but the wind.

A rumpled guard roused himself from his seat against the corrugated steel of the hut, scratched his new coils of beard, and dragged his rifle out to see Burling's papers of introduction, his *bona fides* from Jack. Somewhere a piece of metal banged against itself.

"How did the Chinese get here?" April asked.

"Overland," Burling said. "The borders are pretty porous up here, but they can't fly that plane into Samarkand."

"I don't see them, though."

"I know. Neither do I."

April tried to ask the guard in her limited Dari, a language of which she was proud for the very obscurity of it, but the guard was like a man waiting for a storm: as Burling's papers flapped before him unremarked, he kept looking at the featureless sky. Abdul Hadi climbed from the plane and watched her with dark-eyed contempt.

Where had he been last night? she wondered.

"What on earth possessed you to learn a language like Dari in the first place?" Burling asked as they waited. "Apparently even the natives don't trust it."

She could see that Burling was trying to place the guard.

"They didn't tell me that at Georgetown," April said. The guard uttered a few rusty, atonal syllables she didn't understand. "They were more about Pashto, the language of the rulers."

"Did he say that they were coming?"

Abdul nodded before she could open her mouth, and suddenly her irrelevance coursed through her like a shock. The guard seemed to be suppressing an emotion, although it was unclear if the twitch around his mouth was mirth or rage.

"He speaks the languages, too," she whispered fiercely to Burling. "Apparently some that I don't."

"There are a lot of them," he said, "but I don't trust him as far as I can spit. Come on. Roy!"

He hailed the pilot and turned toward the plane, but before he took another step they had begun to hear the sound of a small band of men riding down from the hills—not a sound exactly, but a sudden disturbance in the ceaseless wall of wind, the creak that is made by tack flailing the muscles of lathering horses. The pilot, smoking by the wing of the plane, reached for the holster on his hip, but Burling made a damping motion with his hand. Shapes emerged from the brown pack until each was an individual rider and animal, bearing down across the hardpan in a clatter of hooves and drawing up, veins bulging in necks dark with sweat. April watched them with her mouth half open, her hands raised slightly from her hips as if she were about to appeal to them for something. Mercy was the word in her mind. The air had stopped in her mouth. Saliva seeped from the insides of her cheeks, but her throat was bone dry. This was the first place she had been where she knew that being American didn't matter.

The leader, who rode a bay stallion two hands taller than the rest of the horses, dismounted in a whipping of cloth. The loose jacket of April's suit lifted in the wind, chilling her. Her hands were plunged deep in the pockets of her pants, stretching the coarse cotton across her hips and the backs of her thighs. She had always been strong, tough; her physical qualities had served her well while making her different and hiding her mind, her emotions, from men in particular. Burling had seemed to cut through those traits: while he clearly admired her body, wanted her openly like a younger man would, he seemed genuinely moved by her manner, intrigued by her mind. He made love as she'd thought he would, carefully, restraining, controlling a massive emotional and physical force. He moved forward now, a grim smile set on his face. The wind stung April's cheeks. Slowly, he and the leader looked each other up and down. In a moment they were shaking hands vigorously and nodding, the leader looking to his comrades and flashing his gleaming white teeth, pointing and laughing as if he'd won a bet.

"Abdul!" The leader, an uncle to Jack's power forward, gave the man a kind of greeting that April had seen in Kabul, grasping both shoulders, shaking him. "Come."

"You stay here with Roy and the plane," Burling told her, *sotto voce*. "If you see Abdul Hadi come out of that Quonset hut without me, he may have sold us up the river."

"What do we do then?"

His eyes met hers as if to say that no matter what happened, it had been worth it, but she wasn't so sure. Something told her that his own romantic dream would survive, with her as only a memory.

"I want to come with you."

"That would be more dangerous than staying here," he said. "I'm doing this for you, believe me."

"Burling!" the leader said heartily. "We go?"

Together they started toward the hut.

The other riders drew their mounts together, the smallest man holding the reins of the leader's incredible horse. April shuffled back toward the wing of the plane, where the pilot was smoking a cigarette. The *mujahedin*—because that's what they were, "the soldiers of God" whose names she had taken in vain the night before—were nothing like she'd expected: up close, they were scruffy and rancid, with nervous faces and intense, dark, sorrowful eyes—not mountain lions at all, but scary in the way of stray dogs, unpredictable. They reminded her of hollow boys back home.

April said a few words to them in Dari, and they replied with a slur against women. The pilot, Roy Breeden, raised his eyebrows at her.

"They say they want to rape me," April told him, although that was not exactly what they'd said. "I think a stake may be involved."

"Like a Joan of Arc number?" Breeden squinted through his smoke.

"I could go for that maybe, if they didn't smell so bad."

The pilot took a pensive drag. A scar cleaved his upper lip, and when he smiled it made his mouth look like a beak. "These boys might not take you up on it," he said. "They'll be fed grapes by seven thousand virgins if I shoot them right now."

April looked at the *mujahedin*. Suddenly their shifty demeanor seemed more menacing than before. Lucius had used the word "sacrifice" about them, equating it with love.

"What a load of shit," she said aloud. The horses had moved more closely together, and she couldn't see the hard desert light between their bodies anymore. Her own bravado went brittle. This might work with the hollow boys in the gravel lot behind the high school, as the vapor lights wore out from the game, but she'd miscalculated here: she'd never been outside of Kabul. Two other riders dismounted, and for the first time she noticed the rifles lashed across the pommels—long, black, shining automatics like Jack's own M-16. Breeden flipped his cigarette toward the nearest hoof, reached back into the plane, and casually brought out a shotgun—a twelve-gauge like her father's—holding it as if it were as harmless as a broom.

April turned to the men, who had drawn their horses back at the sight of the weapon. "I'm the closest thing to heaven they'll ever get."

"You're a hell of a woman, all right," the pilot observed. "I can't decide if I like you or not."

"Do you think these boys know Jack?"

"Might."

She couldn't tell if he was implying that knowing Jack might not be an asset right now. He held out the carved walnut stock for the men to inspect. The one who'd been holding the leader's reins handed them up to the man beside him, who still sat his horse. Then he came forward and weighed the shotgun like an offering in his palms.

The near proximity of the dismounted men, who gave off a rank odor of horses and sweat, was causing fear, the real thing, to run through her like a current. She was guilty, she realized, not only of coming up here with Burling, but of thinking she could handle this. She had run with the boys all her life, run from her brothers straight to Jack, which had upset her mother and scandalized her graduate student friends at Berkeley, with their stoned existentialist boyfriends who didn't care what women thought, even whipsmart scholarship girls like April Wheeling, who could drink harder and quote Jean-Paul Sartre, Lévi-Strauss, and Fanon better than they could. When Jack went off to Vietnam for the second time, April had finally realized she could want more than boys could give her, but it was hard to break their grip. Beyond the horses, she could see Lucius Burling and the leader coming back across the runway. No Abdul. What did that mean? Trailing them was the stout Chinese man she had seen on the roof of the hotel. The man who'd been holding the leader's horse barked something at his clan, in a dialect she could barely understand. He removed a thick knife, about twelve inches long, from his garment. Fear gripped her heart when she realized what the man had said.

"Roy?"

The man on the horse trained his rifle on the pilot.

"They said we're not leaving," April told him.

Breeden moved his hand to the holster, but the rifle gestured him to take it away. Breeden didn't do as he was told. She saw him unsnap the holster, and the rifle went off above her, a quick burst that cut Breeden down. He was on his knees, screaming obscenities, as the horses crowded around her. At first it made her feel safer, their bellies pressing against her, the familiar sweet, sharp smell. She had a flash of her father, his long legs in blue jeans hiked high on his backside, climbing stiffly up the hill toward his broken-backed barn, winter sun in the bare trees behind it. Then she felt herself being lifted; her feet no longer touched the ground. Through the dust she saw the knife raised above Breeden's head.

book

one

INDSTROM'S PLANE PICKED UP SPEED AS IT SLICED THROUGH the clouds; below the cover, fires burned on the ground. Smoke rose from the crossing of twin brown tracks, and he saw red-brick communes surrounded by fields. The man in the seat beside him—a tall, stiff German with muttonchop sideburns and rectangular glasses that turned an odd purple shade in the sunlight—stirred at the abrupt drop in altitude and slapped himself sharply on the knees.

"Well, now, Jack," he said, angling an elbow between Lindstrom's ribs. The German's use of his first name seemed vaguely insinuating, maybe even coercive. "You are coming to see me, yes?"

The plane settled after floating on a deep breath of air. The German was director of a joint venture power company in Shanghai: earlier in the flight he had invited Lindstrom to his plant, to show him how energy was revolutionizing China.

"I'd like to," Lindstrom answered, and wondered if he would. It was his tendency to view industry with suspicion. "But I have these plans in Nanjing."

"Right, right," the German said heartily. "The missionary business." He dismissed it with a chop of his hand.

The plane crossed the Yangzi River, its lumbering surface flashing bronze in the hazy spring sun. From a dock along this river, almost seventy years ago now, Lindstrom's grandfather had embarked with other missionaries up into the gorges in Hubei for a summer retreat, the whole junket paid for by a brewer from Tsingtao. A man of obvious and violent contradictions, Lindstrom's grandfather hadn't had any scruples about accepting the invitation, although by that time he was temperate to the point of fanaticism. The gorges they'd visited were about to be dynamited by the German and his indigenous partners for a dam.

"I'm really not a religious man," Lindstrom said, "but I've never been able to resist the possibility of revelation."

"And that is why you are coming to China?"

"To see the church that my grandfather built."

"This will be the occasion for your revelation."

Lindstrom was about to reply, but explaining his motives would only draw attention to himself.

"As a businessman," the German said, "one cannot be concerned with such things. Nevertheless, power can be—what is the word?"

"Corrupting?"

The German accepted Lindstrom's trope with a ruthless sort of calm. The plane was cutting through frayed wisps of cloud, and the sun gave off a soiled and monotonous glare. The German's lenses grew darker. "I'm not speaking in metaphors," he said. "In China whoever controls the generation of power can be a force for reform. I must believe this."

Lindstrom let the subject lie. A geopolitical discussion with a power company executive, no matter how endless the potential store of puns, would probably not be that illuminating. Since September 11, everyone possessed a theory about world historical order: doomsday philosophy was epidemic even compared with the 1960s. It rivaled the paranoid epic of the late Cold War. Outside the window, the cruciform shadow of the plane stretched and rippled across the towers and cables of a bridge. The plane moved faster above the water. The fence around the airport approached, and he experienced a pleasurable rush of fear. Beyond the concertina wire stretched a dry landscape of yellow-green grasses and flame-like trees that reminded him of Vietnam.

"You come to my plant," the German told him as the plane jammed down on the tarmac. He sighed like a man who has just made a lot of money from some defect in human nature. "You will see."

As the plane slowed to taxiing speed, the Chinese passengers began to get up and trip over each other in the aisle. Outside, a stairway was wheeled across the slabs. Stooping under the bulkhead, the German pulled on a corduroy blazer that had gone out of style in the seventies but was coming back in now. The new global capitalists were adopting a retrograde camouflage, several sizes too small.

Lindstrom slid from his seat and moved forward past studious men and bantering elderly couples, Taiwanese businessmen in clashing Hawaiian shirts, all silenced by the German's unusual height. Lindstrom shadowed him, grateful for the cover. As he emerged behind the German from the hatch of the plane, heat met them like a curtain, and they flailed for a moment in the new, thicker element. Lindstrom felt himself awakening slowly in an old, familiar place, at once comfortable and frightening. Backstage again, behind the ancient drama of the East, where each person, object, strand of phrase you caught above the diminishing whistle of the engines might be trotted out for use under the great proscenium of communist government.

"You come to see us," the German said pointedly, "when you are done with the church."

They were hurrying now across the tarmac, through the greetings and luggage; every face they passed looked amazed. Beyond a low chain-link fence, a BMW waited, with the license plate letters signifying foreigners, followed by the regional number for Shanghai. Lindstrom felt a wave of paranoia. Behind the Bimmer was a tiny, ornamented cab.

"You're not flying on to Shanghai?" he asked.

The German's shaggy hair lifted in the wind. "Ever since the Chinese government deregulated the airlines, it is impossible to get a flight from Frankfurt to Shanghai. *Impossible*," he yelled above the sound of a plane taking off, as if the word could explain the whole country.

THE TAXI WAS CRAMPED, AND ITS DASHBOARD WAS COVERED with talismans. From the homemade bodywork, Lindstrom could tell that it was an unregulated cab. The driver squeezed them onto the road between two stinking trucks, and the diesel burned the back of his throat as the driver, playing with the knobs on the radio and steering with one hand, overtook the frontmost truck in a torrent of blue exhaust. The truck was filled with reed baskets and great chunks of Styrofoam; its pilot grimaced through the windshield at the pale disk of sun.

The road lay straight as a canal between fields. As the taxi gained momentum, moist air funneled through the windows, thinning the fumes and the odor of hot vinyl seats and painted metal. Bicycles pumping against a flickering background of trees. In the paddies, workers with pants rolled up to their knees spread floods of blue water. Lindstrom checked the pulse in his neck to gauge his excitement and found that his skin had a cold, clammy feel. The air wept huge, grimy drops on the windshield, then held the rest in.

As they neared Nanjing, the spindly poplars of the windbreak gave way to giant Himalaya trees, their peeling branches trained upward like arthritic fingers around the wires. Long strips of bark lay curled in the dust at their feet. Caustic smoke hung thickly above the city, and Lindstrom realized he had not given the driver an address. The taxi pressed into the crowd, buses and bicycles everywhere, ringing their bells. The driver turned and showed him a rictus of rotting teeth.

"Jingling," he said. "Jingling Hotel."

Of course, Lindstrom thought. Where else would a Westerner be going? Still, the prescience wasn't encouraging. In Saigon, if you weren't in uniform, the drivers would take you to where a bomb was about to go off, thinking you were a journalist, or a missionary priest. With his shaved head and quarter-Asian eyes, Lindstrom had often been mistaken for a priest.

The taxi rounded a rotary, hazy with neon. The radiating streets showed wet treads from the watering truck. On the far side, some citizens loitered, staring up through the gates at the Jingling Hotel. A recent joint venture between the Chinese and a Scandinavian hospitality chain, its slick white concrete and gray glass belonged in Helsinki. The unlicensed cabbie couldn't pull onto its driveway, so Lindstrom gave him some *yuan* he had traded for in Tokyo and asked him to wait.

The lobby was filled with garment designers and Overseas Chinese. Security cameras bristled from the capitals of marble columns, and all the porters and check-in attendants had been given English names. Lindstrom held a small argument with a porter for show, then allowed the man to disappear with his suitcase while he checked in under the name on his passport, John Tan, and went up in the glass-sided elevator. Looking down on the lobby, at the double-breasted businessmen checking their watches, he thought of the lobby of the Hotel Nikko San Francisco, where his own desk sat empty now, his brass nameplate removed to the closet where the manager kept the names of all the wayward concierges who had gone out in the world to find themselves, only to return less sure of who they were but much more broke and in need of a job. Lindstrom had been on duty there, eight months ago now, listening to an Indonesian salesman explain, in the code of Asian businessmen, that he wanted a girl, when Alan Rank had appeared in the queue. At first Lindstrom hadn't recognized him, but when they faced each other two hours later across a table in the Nikko's sushi bar, Lindstrom had seen behind the dry tucks of skin around Rank's eyes, through the salt-and-pepper beard, and there was the gangly kid from Flatbush whom he had known on the Batangan Peninsula more than thirty years before. When the pretty Cantonese waitress brought their drinks, Rank had already told him that he wanted Lindstrom to smuggle a dissident out of mainland China.

"Would you believe," Rank said, holding his sake under his nose when they had consummated the deal, "that there are Americans living in China, old communists from Brooklyn like my parents, living in Beijing as citizens? Been there for fifty years."

It wasn't clear if Rank admired them or not.

"What do they do there?" Lindstrom asked. Suddenly the five-star Hotel Nikko, where the rehab gurus placed him years before, had begun to look like a smack bar in Saigon, all mirrors and hustlers and promised games of chance. "Are they happy?"

Rank signaled for the waitress to bring them more sake. "Happy? Why would they be happy? Everything they went there for has gone up in smoke. The girls in Beijing wear the same platform sneakers they do in New York."

"Why do they stay, then?"

Rank looked at him strangely, slightly turning his head. "You know, you haven't changed a bit, Jack. Not many people would ask that."

"But I am asking. Why don't they just go home to Brooklyn, where they can get a decent bagel, or Florida?"

"Because they have lives, Jack. Friends, a system of being."

"Yeah, I wonder what that would be like."

Rank watched the rising bubbles in the fish tank uncomfortably. Whenever Lindstrom tried to broach the subject of his discontent, people looked as if they needed to use the bathroom. Even the shrink the rehab gurus had sent him to had only wanted to talk about the present. All behavioral, he said. What about the past?

"There's this British guy, Jack, I swear he looks like an overweight golden retriever. Got a crease in his forehead from an accidental discharge, says it happened on a transport in Burma. He's the one who got in touch with me, not long after I accepted the position at the Center in Nanjing."

Lindstrom swallowed with alacrity in spite of himself. When you didn't have a "system of being," you needed a rush to fill the empty space. It was not unlike going back on the spike, he thought. "You're saying he's Six?"

"I don't know what that means."

"MI-6, Alan. As in Military Intelligence. James fucking Bond. Don't play virgin with me."

Rank shrugged. "All I know is he likes to quote Shakespeare. Seems to think he's Falstaff, complete with a giant chip on his shoulder for being rejected by the king."

The flutter had quickened underneath Lindstrom's ribs, and he took a swig from the fresh drink to quell it. "This is beautiful," he said, looking around in the aqueous blue light of the bar. Already, it didn't feel like home. "Spooks who've been privatized. I need to know more, Alan. Such as it is, I'd be giving up my life."

Rank's head swiveled back and his gray eyes were sharp. "In our current state of post-9/11 madness, the group feels that human rights have been buried. They feel that China is as good a place as any to bring those issues to light."

"You might tell that to the Afghans," Lindstrom said.

Rank looked at him quizzically. People tended to forget about April, perhaps willfully, about that chapter in his, in their country's, collective life. Al-Qaeda had forced them to remember, and in that sense, Lindstrom felt connected to the world for the first time in years.

"Are they professional?" he asked.

"Very," Rank said, eyes following the waitress as she lay down their sushi on black plates. On Sunday afternoons, she and Lindstrom sometimes met for dim sum and a karate movie—a sad, platonic date. "They say to be ready to go on a day's notice, but no later than June 1. Someone, Falstaff I imagine, will be in touch."

LINDSTROM'S ROOM AT THE JINGLING WAS A STERILE AFFAIR, looking out across the cowering town. He turned on and off all the lights and the television. At the minibar, he recorded his presence with the room service office by fixing himself a glass of Glenfiddich from an airline bottle. Trying to steady his hand, he realized too late that the ice might be bad. A small lapse of instinct, but it worried him. When his suitcase showed up—attended by Frank, Joe, and Miles—he tipped them all way too much, messed up his bedclothes, took his daypack, and went down to the street.

The driver had moved on beyond the hotel, and Lindstrom had a hard time convincing the gatekeeper that he wanted to go out unaccompanied. Then he had to fight off the black marketeers and the other gypsy cabs. His driver was reading a newspaper and drinking a Coke, and this time Lindstrom told him, "Black Cat."

The Black Cat Lounge, Rank had said, was like one of those places—three small, thatch-covered rooms of candles, round wooden spool tables, and sweating cement—that the two men had frequented in some of the grislier localities of South Vietnam. Set up in this instance as an exercise in entrepreneurial activity by Rank's students at the Center for Sino-American Studies, instead of MAC-V, the Black Cat was a mixture of Bangkok and Berlin, dive and cabaret, but its terminal dusk had been startled by the morning. Sharp blades of light cut from the door into the anteroom, which smelled of hemp and rain. Wandering through the requisite beads to the barroom, Lindstrom found a sole American woman in the flush of her early forties, hip on the edge of a stool, discussing a pile of receipts with a Chinese man in a soiled apron and white paper hat. As she slid off the stool, she tried to place Lindstrom's face with a worried expression.

"I thought word had got around," she said, slipping her fingers around the bottom of her throat. Her reddish hair was swept up to the back of her head, and the dangling earrings she wore made her neck look unnaturally long. "They shut us down. The police. This morning. For health violations."

Lindstrom had thought she was talking about his mission, and he swallowed the lump that had risen in his throat. His view of the kitchen did not contradict the police's decision.

"I just arrived in country today," Lindstrom told her. "Professor Rank had said I should meet him here."

"Then you must be his friend, Jack." She removed her hand from its clutch around her throat and extended it formally to Lindstrom. "I'm Charlotte Brien."

"Johnny Tan," Lindstrom said. Her hand was chapped, but strong. "Is Alan here?"

Charlotte Brien looked unhappy for a moment, and Lindstrom wondered if standards of cleanliness were the only reason the bar had been closed. "You must know him from Vietnam," she said, brightening. "That would explain the 'in country.' Alan calls those his 'Namisms.' I sometimes think he has too many 'isms' mixed together, but then I wasn't in that terrible war."

"Neither was Alan."

Charlotte peered at him sharply through the dimness, like a dog catching a whiff of something bad.

"Alan was with AID," he explained. "Hearts and minds. Development stuff."

"I'm with public diplomacy in Shanghai," Charlotte said.

"At the consulate?"

She nodded—somewhat bitterly, he thought.

"Then I know your boss, Burling."

"I'm a cultural liaison. I work very little with Lucius."

"Don't do the hard stuff, right?"

Her green eyes flashed as the cook reached down beneath the bar.

"No, no," Lindstrom told him, surprised that he understood English. "It's a diplomat's expression. Hard stuff, soft stuff. Still, a drink might be good."

"It sure would be," Charlotte said with resignation, feeling her way back onto the stool. She kneaded her temples, and Lindstrom wondered what exactly she was doing here. Her pallor had the desiccated look of a perpetual graduate student, and he considered the possibility that Charlotte Brien was the genuine article, someone who believed you could change a bad country from the inside. In Lindstrom, it sparked a predatory mechanism.

"Sometimes this country makes me nuts," Charlotte said.

"Did you prefer them as Maoists, rather than—what do they call it now—'socialism with Chinese characteristics'?"

"That's what the Party prefers."

The cook poured something clear from an unlabeled bottle.

"Let me ask you something, then," Lindstrom said. Accepting the drink, the heel of his hand stuck to the polished veneer of the bar.

"We can be honest because we don't know each other well. Friends of mine back home in California are offended that the Chinese haven't stayed true to their principles. Since the Soviet Union went down, it's a slam dunk for capitalism, and that bothers them. For me, I've found that being true to your principles can be somewhat . . ."

"Disastrous?" Charlotte looked at him knowingly and held the dirty glass up to the light. "For the young people caught up in the Cultural Revolution, or the Great Leap Forward, or any of Mao's other lousy schemes, it certainly was."

"I was going to say self-destructive," Lindstrom told her, putting his empty glass down on the bar. The cook refilled it immediately. It had tasted like Jameson's. "But that's my own lousy trip."

To her credit, Charlotte let his candor pass. "I'm not sure I understand you."

"To put it another way, if you stay true to yourself, does it crowd out other people?"

For a moment, Charlotte seemed uncomfortable, as if he had given her a line. Then she started to laugh. Her laugh was musical, uninhibited by scorn. "Of course not, Jack. I mean Johnny. Boy, what a guy!" The drink was warming her, clearly. Maybe even unhinging her a bit. "Which one was it again?"

The sound of her laughter warped in his head; the liquor was turning on him.

"Johnny. Johnny Tan."

"Johnny." Charlotte reached out, took his wrist in her hand. "Being true to your nature connects you with other people, with history. Being true to your nature makes room."

She was smiling, but Lindstrom pulled his arm away with a sniff. The predatory reflex came back hard and strong. "How well do you know Burling, anyway?"

"Lucius has been back in D.C. for the past month," Charlotte said. She stared at him evenly, but her hand went to her neck again, and between the pale fingers he saw a spreading blotch of red. "I think I'd better point you in the direction of Alan. He must be wondering where you are."

"I'll leave you then," Lindstrom said.

"It's okay." She picked up on his note of apology, and he wondered if it was genuine. "It's just the wrong time for drinking and spilling my guts." Her unsteady hand was pointing past him toward the door. "Alan's over at the Center."

The wedge of light from the door stabbed his eyes, and his head began to throb. The pleasant melancholy feeling he had carried from the airport turned into self-loathing.

"I'm sorry. Sometimes I can barely stand my own company," he said.

Charlotte smiled across the room, recovering herself. He saw that she couldn't help listening. That, and her ease in this alien country, reminded him of April, before his suffocating presence had made her compassion turn inward and burn itself out.

"Join the club. Two years ago, this was the center of the universe. Now no one even thinks about China."

Perched on her stool, she seemed to preside above the waters of his discontent. He needed to leave before he asked her to go to the Jingling with him.

"The entrance to the Center's just down the alley on the left," Charlotte told him. "You'll come to it before you even know it."

Lindstrom left the bar like a scene from a parallel life.

OUTSIDE, THE *HUTONG* WAS COBBLED AND DUSTY; ITS SAND-colored walls dazzled his eyes. Above the ruin of houses, the muggy air hung like a tent, scented with a sweetness that prefigured decay. A hundred yards farther, Lindstrom found the gate to the Center and pushed his way inside.

The compound was refreshing to his eyes: green muddy lawns and walks lined with bright poppies and marigolds. He sensed a chance for renewal in the fresh, bitter smell of the garden. At one end of the grounds stood an old mission building with a red-tiled roof and walls of porous gray stone. Directly behind it a newer building loomed, and through its windows he could see young

American students in sweatshirts and Nikes, in various attitudes of study.

Rank received him in a room full of overstuffed furniture, lace doilies on the arms of the couches and chairs. It had the empty formality of a funeral home. Rank came forward from the window, shrugging his shoulders in a loose-fitting khaki suit. He seemed to have aged in the three months since Lindstrom had seen him—his high, narrow forehead was creased like parchment, his beard had more gray. On his feet he wore black cloth shoes, which struck Lindstrom as an affectation.

"Sergeant," Rank said absently. He took Lindstrom's hand in a loose-jointed grip while he checked his friend's body for damage. "How is it every time I see you, you look just the same, while everyone else keeps getting older?"

"It's part of an experiment," Lindstrom said. "The doctors want to see if certain methods of torture perfected by the Viet Cong retard progression through the normal stages of life. So far it's been successful."

Rank's reaction was shy, and yet there was something smooth and practiced about him as he brushed off the joke and showed Lindstrom a chair. Rank was eerily comfortable with what Lindstrom had always taken to be a collective sort of grief. He had first noticed it in Vietnam, where Rank was nicknamed Oracle, a spiritual consultant of sorts for the recon marines. He had made them believe they were all on a pilgrimage, that the East would heal their psychic wounds and they would all go back to the world knowing a purer way to live. Rank himself was ambivalent—that was part of his draw—but after Lindstrom got home he'd started to see something vaguely unsavory about him. He'd begun to think that Rank might not be so pure after all, or that his purity had been a catalyst to violence.

"To be honest," Rank said, sniffing reflectively, "I was a little surprised when you agreed to come."

Lindstrom sat down heavily, peering through the curtains at the lawn. "I met your girlfriend at the bar. She reminded me a bit of my wife."

Rank's breath made a whistling sound, and he placed a finger under his nostrils to stay it. "You mean Charlotte? She's not my girlfriend."

"Well, whoever she is, you can't tell me she doesn't remind you of April."

"Maybe a little bit, physically, but only in an approximate way. You're not still on that, are you?"

"It just seemed like one of your tests, Alan, to see how human beings react."

"I can't arrange a woman's physical appearance, Jack."

"That's not what we thought in Vietnam."

Rank grinned, and the trimmed, white hairs of his beard parted, revealing the scar beneath his lip. Inflicted by the one grunt who had thought that Oracle was a fake, it became a sort of stigmata when the man who did it was killed the next day. "In Vietnam it was good to believe those things. It kept your mind open and your instincts sharp. But now we're back in the world."

"It feels more like 'Nam to me."

Rank cocked his head and tugged at his beard.

"My instincts, by the way," Lindstrom told him, "turned out to be better suited to a shithole like Vietnam than to anywhere else. When I got back home I tended to see things that weren't really there. Then I willed them to be true. You look worried, Professor."

Leaning forward, Rank parted the curtains with his fingers. Outside, the lawns were misty and dark. He sighed, and Lindstrom felt his own sense of drama overtaking events. "China is a frightened and tragic country, Jack."

"Isn't that why you love it so?"

Rank's fingers bunched the lace as he gazed at the tower of the Jingling Hotel. When he looked back at Lindstrom, his expression was plaintive. "It's not the same as Vietnam," he said with a tremor of conviction. "Here we're dealing with a communism that's hardened, gotten older, the same way I gather we have."

"You mean they don't believe in anything at all?"

Rank let go of the curtain and settled back in his chair. He studied Lindstrom with avuncular concern. "Is that how you are, Jack?"

Lindstrom threw it off with a laugh. The room smelled of mold. "My grandfather made me believe that you couldn't have a meaningful life unless you gave it away first to some ideal. In his case, God. I didn't find out what bullshit that is until I lost the one thing that was good for me."

Rank watched him evenly. On the wall above his wing chair hung a few courtly, hand-colored prints that resembled cartoons. "You've got to move beyond her, Jack. You've got to take steps."

"Is that what you're doing?"

Rank's teeth shone for a moment, before he reacted to the sound of the latch. "Ah," he said, uncrossing his legs, "here we are."

The door to the hallway opened silently, and through it came the sounds of typing and hushed, earnest talk, the odor of a men's room. A woman entered with a tray of porcelain cups and a large jug of tea.

"Thank you, Suki," Rank said, rising formally. "Jack, this is my wife, Su-ki." The second time he pronounced her name precisely, as if to emphasize his mastery of the language. "Su-ki, this is John Tan. His grandfather built the church in Anhe."

"So this is what you mean," Lindstrom said. As he took in her figure, the blue dragons on the teacups shook just enough to make a musical sound. Suki's beauty made you search for it, as if you weren't supposed to see it all at once, but once it entered Lindstrom's mind it remained there like the sun. She made Rank look ravenous, old.

"You are pals," she said, staring at the teacups. Her idiom made her seem fey.

"Is that what Oracle told you?"

She nodded unsurely and looked at her husband.

"Oracle is a name the men had for me in Annam," Rank explained.

Suki took a deep breath as if about to recite. "My husband has told me that the war was a very important time for his life," she said, looking up as she poured the tea.

Lindstrom blanched his irritation by burning his palm on the side of the cup. "It certainly had an effect on him," he said. "Alan was observing just before you came in that your country is much different from Vietnam."

Rank was checking the strength of his tea, and he nodded, his pendulous nose cupped by steam. It was a signal between them, and Suki turned to go.

"Many Chinese people go to Annam," she said, backing out the door, "but their talent for business is not appreciated there. Good-bye, John. Some time I see you in the States."

"I hope so," Lindstrom said, but he doubted it would happen. He couldn't imagine her in Morningside Heights, serving tea to Rank's students, another object in the old Orientalist's collection.

"Jack," Rank said in a suspended tone of warning. "You're flirting with my wife."

"You really married her?"

"I love her," he said. "We just had a kid."

Lindstrom couldn't conceal his astonishment. When he'd returned from Vietnam the second time, he had known what he'd thought was an older man's wisdom, but it hadn't progressed at all and everyone else had passed him now. "Good for you, man. I mean that."

"I recommend it," Rank said. The steam had moistened his brow. "Since we've been married, I've constructed a little garden of contemplation. Would you like to see it? You may remember I'm an amateur poet."

"An amateur something, anyway."

Rank pointed at the joke.

"When we talked in Frisco, Alan, I didn't know that . . ."

Slowly, Rank placed a finger against Lindstrom's mouth. The movement was mesmerizing; it froze the rest of the sentence in his throat. Just as slowly, Rank drew back his hand to a point in the air by his ear. The gesture signaled attention and Lindstrom felt his whole being draw breath.

When Rank spoke again, his voice was alert. "We'll go, then?"

THE EMPTY HALLWAY WITH ITS TALL, TRANSOMED DOORS reminded Lindstrom of school—of sneaking out of it, anyway, in the middle of the day. In the shade of the building's front porch,

Rank paused to remove a pouch of tobacco from his pocket. A man pushed by with a cart full of soil that smelled of animal urine and loam, the spoked wheels crunching softly on the path; Rank acknowledged him as he carefully lit his pipe.

"When Falstaff—" Lindstrom began—"you know, the Brit came to see me, he said I'd be taking the subject through Shanghai. At first I thought . . ."

Rank exhaled a plume of fragrant gray smoke. "Burling's there," he said, shaking out the match.

"I thought for some reason I'd be taking the dissident south, out through Canton, or Hong Kong, Macao, maybe even through 'Nam."

"It bothers you that Burling might be back in Shanghai."

"Look," said Lindstrom, "I wouldn't have agreed to this if I didn't think I was strong enough to look back. Wanted to, even. But still, he and I have a bad symbiosis. I've often noticed it in men who have loved the same woman. We're like opposite sides of a coin."

Rank bit down on his pipe and the stem made a fracturing sound. "A bad penny, perhaps."

"No shit."

"Well, I assure you that I only know Burling through Charlotte, if that's what you're worried about."

"I take it she's involved?"

"Only marginally. In the event of a problem."

"It could fucking well be a problem for her if Burling gets hip."

Rank scuffed his toe in the path and moved ahead with a lurch. The people—Quakers, judging from the schoolhouse design—who had built the original compound had planted a boxwood hedge that joined the corner of the building to the compound's outer wall; its leaves had yellowed in the heat.

"You have to understand," Rank said, indicating a break in the bushes with his pipe. Lindstrom followed him into a neat, sandy garden, girded by evergreens. Lily pads floated like grease on a tiny, black pool; pocked gray rocks hugged the shore. "The people who run this thing are powerful and very, very careful. They all have other lives."

"And me with only this one," Lindstrom said.

Rank's eyes strayed beyond the stand of trees, caressing the new building where the students still sheltered behind the glass. "When they first approached me, more than ten years ago, they wanted to hide dissidents here at the Center. After Tian An Men, they had more than they could handle."

"But they've gotten others out, right?"

"Dozens, yes. Do you know Wei She?"

"Won some kind of literary prize in England several years ago. It was very controversial."

"The Chinese wouldn't let him come, then before they could arrest him, Wei disappeared. Showed up in London three weeks later, protected by MI-5, to accept the award."

"Then what's the big deal? Yong hasn't won any prizes, as far as I know."

"Indeed not."

"Tomorrow night, then, after I visit my grandfather's church, I get into my Mao pajamas and make like a peasant. Keep my eyes peeled and walk this guy out. It can't be heavier than north of the Parallel."

Rank cleared his throat deeply and walked away a few steps, as if from a problem. Pale, chameleon-like shadows played between them on the ground. "It isn't," he began, turning around in a posture of appeal.

"You know you make a lousy spy," Lindstrom told him. "You just haven't got the cool."

"Did Burling?"

"Burling had something else."

Rank gave him the sly, quizzical look that had passed for philosophical during the war, then moved toward the high, mildewed wall. Lindstrom was surprised to find that he still believed it— Burling had something that he, Lindstrom, lacked. It wasn't just April—neither one of them had really had her.

"This dissident is somewhat more difficult than the others, for different reasons," Rank said, stopping before a bench that was splattered with birdshit. "That's why they arranged for him to hide in Anhe for a while. Your grandfather's church is the most important stop on their underground railroad. It's why I thought of you."

"What do you mean by difficult, exactly?"

Rank made a show of checking his watch. "I think you should go now," he said, extending his hand like an usher. "The same cabbie who met you at the airport will drive you, but still the road isn't good, and it will take you until nightfall to get to Anhe."

"You didn't answer my question," Lindstrom said as Rank brushed past him. They were met outside the garden by the sharp smell of marigolds. "What did this dissident do?"

"Oh, the usual things. It's more where he was that seems a problem."

"Was?"

"Yong went to the States once," Rank said, "as a visiting physicist."

They were almost to the gate, and Lindstrom grabbed his shoulder and spun him around. "A physicist, as in bombs?"

"It only means," Rank added, shrugging him off, "that he had some ties in the government at that time." He swallowed, and the gray whiskers rippled down his neck.

Lindstrom waited while his heart wound down, poking at the bottom of his throat. "Didn't it ever occur to you, Alan, that a physicist might have drawn more attention than, say, a poet like yourself?"

"We needed a point man," Rank said. His hand was reaching in the inside pocket of his jacket, and Lindstrom stifled an urge to defend himself.

"I was the lag man, not point."

"Speaking of which." Rank's hand reappeared with a white linen handkerchief, wrapped around the dark shape of a pistol. "We thought you might need this," he said, folding back the hemmed corners. In the middle of the grease-stained linen lay a familiar blue-black .45.

The grounds of the Center were as quiet and still as a schoolyard in summertime. After a moment, because Rank didn't do anything,

Lindstrom took the automatic in his hand. The feel of the stubbly grip was like the touch of betrayal, the touch of joining, and he thought that this was how he had always been: the world was there and when no one moved to take it, he did, because something was missing inside him. *What does it profit a man?* his grandfather had said.

"Couldn't you have gotten me a Chicom or something?" It was a joke, a communist weapon grunts had coveted in Vietnam, and Rank's failure to laugh was unnerving. Lindstrom dropped the clip out, checked its spring with a growing recognition, and replaced it; the click of the mechanism threatened to let out the unruly laughter that was flapping like a bird in his chest.

"It's your own piece," said Rank. "See?"

Pulling back the slide, Lindstrom peered into the chamber. The bird in his stomach grew calm, as if it had seen the smiling shadow of the hatchet. "What kind of shitty business is this?" he said. The pistol cocked with a grim resignation, and he pointed it at the small white indentation on the tip of Rank's nose. "Is this some kind of performance incentive, two bullets missing from the clip?"

Rank shrunk back against the gate. Lindstrom sighted on a knot in the splintered wood beside him, and back to Rank's forehead. "I didn't know about that."

"You didn't know. You damn well knew I wouldn't agree to this once I found out Yong's a physicist. Did he work at Los Alamos too? Did he maybe steal a laptop from there?"

"I just told you," said Rank. He was almost pleading now.

"You told me what you know," Lindstrom said. "You're just a front man." The .45 had been stolen from his room at the Nikko, not long after Rank had been there to visit. Two days later, the cops had caught the kids who had broken in trying to pass Lindstrom's cash card, and the kids had started chirping about Asian gangs. They were black, so the cops hadn't bought it. "I should have seen this coming," he said.

"To think I once called China the last best hope," Rank replied, giving the heavy wooden gate a push. Outside, the alley baked mutely in the sun.

Lindstrom shook his head and locked the Colt on safety. "Don't give me your cut-rate historical theory, Al. Once you dig up a piece of history as nasty as all this . . ." He found he couldn't finish the thought. Forty-fives were always so much heavier than they looked. As he stowed it in his backpack, he wondered if their design enhanced their tendency to make their own logic. "Living here, you should have learned that by now."

"Wasn't it I who always said you were a moralist?"

"You've been reading too much Malraux," Lindstrom told him, slipping out the door and into the cobblestoned gutter. "He ended up working for guys like Burling, too."

Rank's gray, tufted eyebrows curled in on themselves, and then the gate groaned shut between them; Lindstrom heard Rank walking heavily away. The walls of the alley zigged and zagged toward the street, and a febrile sensation gripped Lindstrom like the onset of a drug. The noodle shop on the corner gave off a thick white steam. He hugged a brief notion of turning around, but his life seemed like a jungle through which he'd just come. Across the street from the Black Cat, the cabbie leaned against a crooked pole, spooning noodles from a bowl held closely to his chin. His face was tinted sickly green by the fiberglass awning of the shop. Raising his eyes, the cabbie recognized Lindstrom.

O N THE MORNING OF BURLING'S DEPARTURE FOR CHINA, his building superintendent arrived at the door at five minutes past eight—as if late, Burling thought, for a party. He was a spry, thin black man with dime-store reading glasses riding the end of his nose. Toast crumbs clung to the gray wires of his mustache.

"Morning, Mr. Shepherd," Burling said, and stood aside by his luggage while the super walked past him, still chewing.

Burling enjoyed their ritual of departure, and he told himself that Shepherd liked it, too. Going through the wide rooms above the park was so familiar to both men that it gave Burling the chance to bid a silent farewell to his possessions—favored things that he'd never had the energy to take overseas since Afghanistan. His yellowed collection of Roberts prints, his mother's somber and tortured antiques, the 78s of the Big Bands and Gilbert and Sullivan stacked by the stereo, holding their music like strata of anthracite: these things were like an inventory of his life that it was time to reduce. Because of the surfeit of potential emotion, he couldn't have managed the departure alone, so he was always left feeling he should do more for the super.

When Shepherd had murmured acknowledgment to the final item on his list, Burling hoisted his bags and he and the old man rode the elevator in silence. At the lobby, Burling restrained the door and Shepherd bumped his wash bucket over the gap, using the mop handle as a cane. His stiff legs shuffled across the marble floor. The entrance to the building gave onto Kalorama Road and across it, rows of embassies resembling French chateaux; seeing the figure of Shepherd silhouetted against them, Burling experienced an odd, reassuring sensation he couldn't explain. Perhaps it was the strength he drew from being alone, his apartment battened down and all crises contained, or from the respectable elegance of a Washington street. For a moment, he imagined that the super sensed it, too, pausing as he did to sniff the scent of blossoms wafting on a mild breeze through the door. Burling set his suitcase down and checked the inside pocket of his jacket for his ticket and the storage voucher for his car. "Mr. Shepherd?"

The super stopped and bent around. "Oh, all right."

Burling had noticed that Shepherd often replied to salutations with the wrong response; it made him uneasy, as if there were something vaguely subversive about their exchange. "I was just going to offer you my parking space, until I come back. I'm still going to be paying for it, and I thought it would be more convenient for you."

Shepherd took his palm off the mop handle and pushed his Redskins cap backward, scratching his bald head, which was ringed with tiny coils of white hair. He seemed confused by Burling's generosity, perhaps even insulted.

"Is something wrong with it?" asked Burling.

The old man's eyes were steady and yellow. His cheeks worked in and out in folds. "Ain't nothing wrong with it, nothing at all. Only seeing as there wasn't a car in it this morning when I come out, I thought you already gone. So I put my car in there."

In a flurry of denial, Burling jogged out the door and around to the alley. Shepherd's Buick was there, next to the ripening dumpster, a pool of water beneath it from the morning's washing.

"For heaven's sake," Burling said, looking around at nothing. "These bastards."

Shepherd was leaning in the doorway that opened off his apartment, watching the pigeons approach his car. "They get your Benz?"

"I don't even know who would want it. It's old."

"It don't matter," the super explained. "That car was top of the line in its day."

"I'll have to get a taxi," Burling told him. "Excuse me, please."

He helped himself through Shepherd's apartment to the lobby. As he went through the small living room he noticed a picture of a black boy in knickers standing close to the leg of a uniformed man. Pausing to look at the photograph closely, Burling discovered Shepherd watching him from next to the television. The screen replayed the weekend's news without sound.

"Is that you, Mr. Shepherd?"

The super grumbled as if the question were another item on Burling's list, and Burling tried to sound less officious. "Where'd you serve?"

"France and the South Pacific . . . almost. I was in San Diego getting drunk when the Bomb saved my ass." Shepherd's chuckle turned into a wheeze. "That's why I keep him up there."

Burling followed the rheumatoid finger to a framed GI photograph of Truman, which hung on the wall above the set. "Good for you," he said, thinking. He was about to tell this man . . . what? That he had been too young for the war? It struck him that Shepherd must be only five, six years his senior, while Burling had always thought of him as old.

His eye fell on Shepherd's breakfast, which lay unfinished on the scuffed pink Formica. Had Shepherd forgotten their meeting? It was so unlike him that he must be slipping, the thought of which filled Burling with sudden, disproportionate grief. He was about to ask Shepherd more about Truman, but he had the police to call and a plane to catch and besides, the super wasn't much for rebuttals. Sometimes they would have a passing discussion on the elevator about the NBA or some international crisis, on which Shepherd considered him an authority and therefore worthy of criticism, but the super always liked to say his piece and be done. Burling might repeat it later, at the Department of State, as the view of the man in the street.

"I'll have to call now," said Burling, and started for the lobby.

"Right you are," he heard Shepherd say.

For the first two flights of stairs Burling felt surprisingly strong, for the last two he was winded. His legs grew weak, and he thought of his car in the hands of some crackhead or gangster in southeast DC, seat cranked back and speakers thumping that terrible bass. By the time he reached the door to his apartment, his heart was racing at a rhythm that seemed slightly unnatural, as if one of the cylinders were bad. He could feel it beating in the top of his skull. Inside, he paused uncomfortably in the stillness.

The windows were closed, and the rooms had already reached that overheated temperature he recognized from returning after an extended time away. He hated coming back to the apartment after preparing himself to leave. The empty rooms, the closed doors cast an eerie kind of judgment on his life. Already the lonely sunlight seemed to have taken his place. The door to his study made a sticky little pop when he opened it, like a Band-aid tearing off a wound. When he reached the phone on his desk, it was already ringing. As he picked up the receiver he had a flash of premonition, like a flare going off in some perimeter of his mind.

"Lucius? I thought I might catch you."

His heart raced as if he'd been awakened in the middle of the night. "Mac? Did you steal my car?" The supposition came out of him unrehearsed, and for an instant he thought it ridiculous, but then he knew he was right. "I have a meeting on Monday in Beijing with . . ."

Gordon MacAllister cleared his throat like a scold.

"But why?" Burling asked, and the unsteady sound of his own voice frightened him. The dark blinds of his study seemed to shutter his solitary life.

"Really," MacAllister cautioned. The phone he was on crackled, passed through a frequency shadow. "This is hardly a secure line. You're forgetting yourself."

The blood rose in Burling's face. If he could only do that, forget himself.

"Burl? You there?"

"Where else would I be?" he said hoarsely. "You stole my car."

MacAllister's laugh, slightly breathy and tapering, filled whatever place he was in. Burling wondered who else was there hearing it. "I thought you'd lost your sense of humor for a moment."

"That's not the only thing I've lost." He'd meant the words to sound sarcastic, but they took on more weight as his throat closed around them. Pathetic. "At least I hope it's somewhere safe. You know I've had that car since 1973."

"And it's like poor Yorick's horse, Burl, a guide to us all." A car honked in the background, and Burling thought he heard the same sound outside. "Of course we'll keep it somewhere safe. It'll have a damn sight more security than that basement at State."

Burling parted the blinds, but outside it was morning as usual: orderly traffic, calm sky. In the circle before the Chinese Embassy a tattered demonstration of Asian students and American hippies that seemed to have been there for years urged commuters to honk in denunciation of something the Chinese had done. While Burling was watching them, a motorcade pulled into the circle and the demonstrators ran to surround it. In the middle car he recognized Huang, a reformed academic from Beijing. Huang seemed to have an awful lot of security for a low-level cultural officer. Once you'd been condemned as a heretic, Burling thought, they could summon you any time they chose.

"I'll meet you halfway, at the Mill," MacAllister said.

"I think that's hardly meeting me halfway."

"I was speaking literally."

"So was I: it's right around the corner from Langley."

"Give me an hour, okay?"

Burling was a man who liked to take a minute to gather his arguments, but MacAllister had hung up the phone before he could speak.

THE MILL WAS A SQUARISH STONE BUILDING HUDDLED UNDER spreading oaks, just off the route by which Dolley Madison had fled the burning city in 1812. Burling directed the cabbie off the divided highway and into the dusty gravel lot, where MacAllister's Agency Suburban rested against a screen of forsythia in bloom. Through the half-open window of the taxi, Burling could hear the weary groaning and splashing of the wheel as it sluggishly ladled water from the sluiceway and dumped it into the pond, around which waddled mallards and large, vicious swans.

"Come on over here in the shit," MacAllister called, looking up at the sound of the taxi door slamming.

Burling left his suitcase by the wheel of the Suburban and parted the bushes with his hand. The hogs grunted and hoofed in their sty, their pungency lurking beneath the sweet scent of flowers. As Burling picked his way deliberately through the guano, MacAllister shifted his seersucker over his forearm and a big smile spread like a shield across his face. It wasn't a trustworthy smile, but Burling found himself warming at the sight of it. *He looks like John the damn Baptist*, he thought, *about to bathe me in blood.*

"If you wanted to play on my guilt," Burling said, drawing closer, "you certainly picked the right place." An unintended bitterness crept into his voice. "I used to bring my family out here every Sunday after church. Luke and Betsy liked to visit the animals."

"I didn't know that," MacAllister said. "Whole set-up seems like a big, stinking agricultural deduction to me, right in the middle of McLean."

They shook hands firmly, and his signet ring pinched Burling's palm.

"You'll be glad to know they're tearing it down. It's a shame," he added. "Tract mansions for Internet millionaires."

MacAllister frowned. When his plane had gone down in the African jungle, burning jet fuel had flared up the side of his neck, melting the bottom of his earlobe and leaving a hot red patch where it lapped at his jawline and cheek. It complicated his expression, so that Burling couldn't tell if it were pity, contempt, or remorse. In a way it was not unlike a birthmark, or a mark of initiation: whatever mixture of leaves the natives had slathered on his burns had saved his life, although the specialists at Walter Reed had never figured out what had made up the salve.

"How are you, Burl?"

"You tell me. I gather I'm being called down this morning."

MacAllister took a step forward and past him like a feint, a rhetorical gesture Burling remembered very well from the Agency.

"If they're tapping you for director," Burling said, "you'd better not be seen with me."

"There's a whole lot worse to be seen with these days," MacAllister said, bending over to flick the birdshit off his bucks. "I just needed to ask a favor, that's all."

"You didn't have to steal my car to do that."

MacAllister shuffled a toe in the white-gray muck and followed a duck on the pond with his eyes. The scorched folds of his neck seemed to call for reassurance. "Give me your opinion: What do you think about our progress in the War on Terror?"

Burling felt the wind go out of him. Just last night, in his filial call to his son, Luke had asked this very question. The years between them and the trouble with Amelia had not been easy on their relationship, but it had sounded to Burling as if his son actually valued his opinion. He looked across the lot and remembered Luke reaching through the split-rail fence to touch the pig's whiskered snout. When the animal tilted its nose, the little boy shrieked with glee. "I think what you want me to think, isn't that how this works?"

"Lucius." Mac draped a comradely arm around his shoulders, where it hung with a dull, stiff weight like a rod. "I wouldn't do you like that." He gave Burling a squeeze and let go.

Burling took a deep breath and felt the tears scurry back behind his eyes. MacAllister took off his bifocals, squinted into the lenses, then let them hang from a bright, braided string around his neck. "You look like you've been spending some time on your boat," Burling said.

"Not enough. Let's walk."

The swans fled before his bucks, hissing and flapping their wings. The two men crossed the sluice on a rickety bridge, and the ground began to rise beneath their feet. MacAllister's limp grew more pronounced.

"Do you remember a Chinese student at Princeton I asked you to talk to, those months when you were home between Kabul and Islamabad?"

"How could I not?" Burling said. He and the young man had walked beside the canal outside Princeton on a gray November day, the air viscous with oncoming winter, sun remote behind the trees. People were cleaning up leaves in the yards of the big Victorian houses on Harrison Street, reminding him sharply of a fantasy he had cherished as an undergraduate walking to the gym, of living in one of those houses with a wife and children, and going up the wide oak stairs at night behind her to bed. The rhythmic sound of the raking rose like wintering birds. "He was fascinated by Einstein, wanted to know where I'd seen him when I was there. Strange fellow, Yong Beihong."

"I am astounded by your memory."

"You can have it," Burling said. Flattering your intellectual capacity was one of Mac's more obvious ploys.

"Shortly after September 11th," MacAllister explained, "one of our illegals in the PRC was contacted by a group that runs dissidents out."

"What kind of group?"

"Religious right, ties to Asian churches."

"I'm familiar with those people," Burling said.

"Well, the paper our man got was the work of a physicist. Seemed under stress, a bit rambling, but it referenced Abdul Khan, and the development of a missile sounded very much like Silkworm."

"The paper was Yong's?"

MacAllister's nod was full of bad implications.

"You're sure it was genuine?"

"Yong's a strange character. He's been in jail or under house arrest on and off for a dozen years, but he's got a long history with the Party. He'd know enough with us back in Afghanistan that things would be touchy with Pakistan. Hell, with Iran."

Burling couldn't resist filling in, a tendency that had plagued him since grade school: "So he makes it look like he's going to pull a Dr. Khan and skip out with China's technology?"

The downward set of MacAllister's mouth suggested a tension between distress and strategic enjoyment. "It's an awful mess, Lucius. As God is my witness, I'm no liberal, but these maroons who are running the Agency now can't tell the Taliban from the Dalai Lama. I just testified to this fact yesterday before the House Intelligence subcommittee. There's barely a single Dari speaker at Langley anymore."

"Dari." Burling watched a cement truck arrive at the construction site across the highway, its egg-shaped mixer turning gradually in the sun. The last time he himself had testified on the Hill was about April's death, and he'd had no trouble evading the truth then because he had thought that the subject was personal, none of their goddamned business. The real lie had come months before—before Samarkand, before Wes Godwin died. He and April wound up together at a scrimmage of the Afghan basketball team. The weather surprisingly similar to this: April had just played tennis, and the hollow of muscle along her thigh swelled gradually closer to his against the hard, painted wood of the bleacher. Between them, he'd sensed a looming intimacy, a boundary about to be crossed. As the scrimmage increased in intensity, players loping up and down the wooden court, Burling had realized that he was about to refer to his wife as a third person. Thinking back on it since, he had marked that betrayal of usage as a greater sin than the night he and April had spent in Samarkand. For him, words were important, and after he had pushed his wife out of the first person plural—the "we" that he and Amelia had made, the extension of his Victorian fantasy—his evasions on the Hill seemed allowable, honorable even. "I take it you want Yong out, or do you?"

"Things are just too sticky right now," MacAllister told him. "I had to go outside the Agency on this one."

A blade of grass tickled Burling's ankle above his sock. He smiled with alacrity in spite of himself. "You didn't answer my question."

MacAllister started down the slope toward the parking lot.

"I have to confess I can't pick the angle on this," Burling said. "Maybe I'm getting old."

At the bottom of the hill, MacAllister waited, sweating, for him to come up. "Getting? We're both old, Lucius, which is why we can't afford to take chances. We've got to think of our kids."

Burling's smile was arrested by a chill.

"I'm not asking for your involvement," said MacAllister, starting toward his car, "because I've got that end covered. I just wanted to make you aware."

"Now you're pissing me off. Aware of what?"

"If this thing enters your sphere, I need someone I can trust."

"You need someone with a reason to keep the thing quiet."

"That's a factor," MacAllister said across the roof of the Suburban.

The car was driven by a young Jamaican man with tight coils of hair and a tracery of scars on his cheeks. He reminded Burling of the Afro-Caribbean men they had used in Cuba in the early 1960s. In the mirror, his venomous features watched Burling slide onto the seat.

MacAllister held Burling's eyes for a moment as the tires spun on gravel and caught on the road. "If you remember Yong's name, you must remember the name of his superior officer?"

Burling watched the signs pass overhead, places—Herndon, Vienna, Front Royal—small towns swallowed by highways and strip malls that might have held memories for him if he had led a more circumscribed life. Such memories, he thought, would have given his children reasons to care for him more.

"You know that I do, Mac."

MacAllister looked out the window. A paver the size of a battle-ship moved down the shoulder of the widening road to the airport, flying the flag of the Commonwealth.

"His name was Zu Dongren."

"Was?"

"Is. He was a PLA colonel." He could see Zu leave the hotel in Samarkand, look this way and that before walking toward a black Lada, parked on the side of the square behind the bench on which he and April were sitting, talking about the Viet Cong, the *mujahedin*. Why did Burling equate their kind of fervent commit-ment with love? "I didn't know Zu had made it off that runway until I met Yong in Princeton. At the time I thought that might have been why you asked me to talk to him. I was grateful to you for that."

MacAllister's face was reflected in the tinted window beside him. Yong had not been able to give him the same, or any, news about April. "You know that if the press got wind of the little deal you had going with Zu then, they'd fry us both for sure."

"Colonel Zu is General Zu now," Burling said.

"You keep in touch?"

"I wouldn't go anywhere near him, but I'm sure he knows I'm there. He's the head of the Internal Security Service."

"What about Alan Rank?"

Burling felt the car sinking beneath him, then rising again, leaving his stomach behind. "Name's familiar. Some kind of academic in Nanjing."

"You were always a terrible liar."

"Ironically, yes, but discretion isn't prevarication, Mac. On this point you and I can disagree."

"Your girlfriend works with him."

MacAllister had been married for forty-some years to the same woman, and his use of the term "girlfriend" was derisive, at least it sounded so to Burling.

"Charlotte and I have been seeing each other in Shanghai, it's true, but I wouldn't say she works with him. The public diplomacy people have some programs with the center Rank runs."

"Well she, Charlotte, had better be careful. Programs are not all Rank runs. He just got a visa for a man named John Tan, applied through some sort of fundamentalist outfit in Georgia that's in with the China Christian Council, the outfit that certifies churches."

"And spies on them, too."

"I didn't know that. To be honest, I was hoping you could help me out with this Tan character."

"I'm sorry, Mac." Long ago, Burling had found a proper way to refer to his fallen position. He breathed deeply and explained. "It's well known in this administration that I don't happen to agree with engagement. They'd like to get rid of me, but they're afraid I might squawk if some reporter happened to notice that the consul in Shanghai hasn't been changed since Bush One. It seems like nepotism. Truth is, I'm out to pasture there."

"You heard nothing at State? NSC?"

In spite of himself, Burling gulped. He looked for space in the field by the road, in the sky, but found none. The stockade fences of a subdivision crowded his sight. "What about your man in Shanghai? Ryan?"

"A group has been smuggling dissidents off the mainland," MacAllister said, ignoring the question, "taking them out using drug-smuggling boats and black market export shipments from Shenzhen. Sometimes they'll throw the poor suckers on tramp steamers headed for New York, give the triads a shot at 'em. It seems to have started as a right-thinking venture, but someone got the idea there might be money in it. We've been trying to trace it back to the source for years, thinking it may be a way in, but every time we open the door, no one's home. Organized crime in Hong Kong, those ancient import-export concerns in Taipei. We've even had the Bureau lean on the Chinatown gangs. Nothing. Where we've never gotten any help is the White House itself."

"It's gossip in Shanghai," Burling told him, feeling the strength of some authority, "but one thing didn't change between old George and Clinton and this one: the White House turns a blind eye."

MacAllister leaned toward him, arm across the back of the gray cloth seat. The car was getting warm, bringing out a smell of cigarette smoke. Beads of sweat had popped out on his forehead. "I'm telling you, Burl, I've never seen it quite like this, and it's worse since last September. They'll do just about anything for money. I've got nothing against banks, but they're a hell of a place to deposit your conscience."

"The world is a fire sale," Burling said, "and the wind seems to be turning in our direction. You don't think that Rank's man might walk into something?"

MacAllister arched his back and took a sporran flask from his jacket's inside pocket. He tipped it back and exhaled. "Yong has disappeared, Lucius, gone from the house where we thought they were keeping him."

Suddenly Burling felt the need of air. He lowered his window, but a yellow cloud of pollen blew into the car. The airport hovered in the distance like a pair of concrete wings.

"Gone?"

"As of five days ago, according to our man in Beijing."

The driver offered him a bottle of water. He took a drink and looked away. An artificial lake marked the outskirts of the airport, the curving roadway lined with weak trees trained by guy ropes and stakes: the terminal expanding again. This had once been a magical place for him, the airport named after John Foster Dulles—who, as JFK said, had been secretary to the Chinese delegation to The Hague at the age of nineteen. If other families had homes in those places on the green signs—the suburbs, the cul-de-sacs and split levels, the flat green patches of backyards in northern Virginia—to remember, Burling, Amelia, Betsy, and Luke had this airport, its raw concrete and polished ramps and soaring buttresses, the mobile lounges prowling the runways like something prehistoric and futuristic all at once, dedicated by President Kennedy in a happier time. MacAllister's driver lowered his window and plucked a ticket from the parking machine.

"Do you think Zu has him, or did he escape?"

"When you get back, pay a visit to Nanjing. Talk to Alan Rank. Or better yet, have your girlfriend do it."

The car's engine ground to a terrible idle, and Burling watched an elegant woman cross the asphalt. Sunlight shimmered on the back of her skirt as she gained the near curb in her heels. Something vaguely reptilian stirred in him—lust, love? He was tempted to think that the world ran on these things more than power or money. But he felt a more sinister force—love's removal, its absence, betrayal—that was closer to him. The beautiful woman had stopped on the sidewalk to dig in her bag.

"Where will I find you if I need you?" Burling asked.

MacAllister was smiling: the look of a shabby operation to be dealt with somewhere else. The driver clicked open the electric locks.

"Don't you fret," MacAllister said, massaging Burling's shoulder. It was meant to be a friendly gesture, but he seemed to feel through Burling's diminishing muscle for his bones.

Taking his suitcase, Burling passed behind the woman through the terminal doors.

LI XIN PEDALED HIS BIKE ALONG THE BOULEVARD BESIDE Temple Park, his shadow fleeing before him on the plum-colored wall. A bus swayed dangerously close, belching smoke in his face, and Li swore through the windows at the forest of torsos and arms. The traffic was bad for a Saturday, and he had to meet his general at the Beijing Hotel in forty minutes; before that he had to deliver his daughter to the home of his mother-in-law in the city's older section.

Qing rode in a child seat that was clamped to the handlebars, clutching a puppet resembling a hawk. As they passed the northeast corner of the park, she raised the bird so the breeze, sweet with flowering trees, caught its wings and lifted them gaily. Later that day, she was to take part in the annual puppet production at the Children's Palace, the hall of culture where the most creative youngsters went after school each day to learn the sublime arts. The hawk was one of two main characters in the play, the other a lowly, scheming turtle. Children all over China would be acting out the same story during the upcoming week, an ancient fairy tale about the resilience of the Middle Kingdom, and Li was proud that his position allowed her to take part. As they entered the dark maze of *hutongs*, over which the painted rings of the Temple seemed to lean, Qing lowered the head of the bird and pecked playfully at his arm.

When Li had delivered her into the hands of his mother-in-law, the old woman's slow face at the ready for another day of spoiling her grandchild, he was surprised to find that he still had time for a visit to the Friendship Store. The thought of English cigarettes, aromatic in their coffin of foil, drew him onward through the cooking smoke, the blood running in the gutter from the corner abattoir, past the warehouse of the vegetable collective with its affable white-coated workers lounging behind their cardboard stand. A PLA jeep sprinted past him, honking wildly, soldiers tottering in the back like barrel staves, either drunk or asleep behind their scanty mustaches and shades. Along the boulevard, block upon block of new apartments rose behind the powdered trees, painted balconies rising for story on story to the colorless sky. In a year the general would pull him fully into his circle; a year and they would leave his mother's house and have their own place. Behind the sliding glass doors that led from the balconies, he imagined Qing's room with her rows of little dresses in the wardrobe, posters of her beloved Mickey Mouse on the walls. The image buoyed his spirits, even as he passed beyond the apartments and beneath the smug gaze of the foreign hotels.

The day was warming, but his years in poorly heated apartments had accustomed Li to wearing a cardigan; now he felt sweaty, unpressed as he flashed his papers to the guards at the entrance to the Friendship Store and moved politely through the fat, perfumed Westerners and Overseas Chinese to the tobacco counter in back. The counter man, protected by his ranks of dark-leafed Cuban cigars, asked to see Li's papers again and read them over with a dubious smile. As he handed them back, his expression seemed to indicate some complicity between them. As if he knew what Li had seen: the young people fallen, not like piles of laundry at all but flesh showing, thin stomachs and pelvic bones, skin unbearably modest in death. Among their bodies, the mangled tracery of spokes and chrome. As if the asshole had seen it . . .

Joylessly he paid the cashier and jammed the pack hard, again and again against the heel of his hand, smoking one cigarette after another as he cycled along the *Dajie*, fingers squeezing the hand-grip so hard that his knuckles turned white. At the Beijing Hotel, he guided his bike past the taxis and government drivers, the vents of his tweed jacket flapping and coming to rest. The goat-faced Manchu, Feng, leaned against the general's beige Toyota Crown, studying the grease beneath his fingernails.

"Where's the Big Fish?" Li asked.

The driver accepted a Kingston and nodded slyly toward the lobby. When General Zu emerged, he seemed to spring from the revolving door, his short arms flapping at his sides. Feng was up the steps at a sprint, offering help with Zu's briefcase, but the Big Fish brushed him violently away.

"A perfect example of how stupid, how grossly incompetent and obsequious these fools are," Zu said as Li reached him.

"Yes, General."

They hurried down the stairs in quick, shuffling steps.

"You don't even know what I'm talking about," the general remarked.

Li helped him into the back of the car and climbed into the front seat next to Feng. He turned to meet the general's dolorous face. "I assume you are speaking of the reactionaries, who see the corruption in Shenzhen as a far bigger issue than it is."

"We have bred a generation of pirates and slaves," sighed the general. The shadow darkened around his mouth. "Some will have to be sacrificed. When the time comes, I must take a stand on corruption."

"Shenzhen is the future of China," Li agreed.

"It's a wasteland," Zu said.

Feng avoided a donkey cart carrying a refrigerator and moved to the center lane, honking at buses and trucks. They went swiftly across the mouth of Tiananmen Square, under the reviewing stand and onto Quianmen, its broad sidewalk a beach where they had piled the new dead, like fish thrown up from a gray, diseased bay. The calm and heavy-lidded, beatific face of Chairman Mao approved the scene.

"You have gotten me started," said the general, shifting his short, bulging torso on the pinions of his legs. "You always make me think of my son."

Li chose not to respond. The general's son ran a factory in Shenzhen, the so-called Special Economic Zone, and Li had seen him, in his Western suits and German car: he had known from the tender way the son regarded his possessions that he was a thief.

Feng skirted Beihai Park, where the old men sat on stumps, fishing the slimy green water with bamboo poles. The general was silent, and Li wondered if he was thinking of the morning they had mustered in the wet grass on the shore. Li could still feel, still hear the squishy boots as they marched, the burning itch on the balls of his feet. A month later, General Zu had been transferred from the Second Department to the Ministry of State Security, a move in which Li had chosen to accompany him. The wily among Li's comrades had envied his good fortune, offered congratulations or made snide comments about Li's ambition under their breath; the jealous were also the ones who had turned down commands at the Square. The duller ones had simply come to Li's farewell party, gotten drunk, and clapped him on the back, as if they were sending him back to Tibet. Thirteen years and nothing had changed.

"We have a more pressing problem," the general said, rapping the window with his hand. Sweethearts in rowboats sculled against the grim background of the Forbidden City walls. "Yong Beihong has disappeared from his apartment."

"*Yong?* I thought I knew all of their names."

"This one was rounded up again several years ago and has been under house arrest. He was a university instructor who made a short speech on the second day of the uprising. He was signatory to one of those reactionary letters last year."

"When did he escape?"

"It has been five days ago now. The officers they had watching him were common city police. When Yong went missing, they looked for him for three days before they informed their superiors."

"It's the work of the mayor," Li said. The general's bottom lip stuck out. "May I ask how long you've known?"

"Do not always think of yourself, Li. I received a call last evening at home. I needed to consider."

"Then clearly you see some connection between this Yong and the American woman you asked to be followed to Nanjing."

The general's mud-colored flesh shifted downward into a frown. The folds of his chin hid his collar from view. "It is only a coincidence. Without coincidence, however, we would be lost. Do you have anything more on this woman?"

The car took a hard turn into a side street, and Li had to brace himself quickly against the door. As they went through the gates of the compound, a group of restoration students trooped into a painted hall. The students' worship of the past, their leisurely study, caused his anger to rise. "I know one thing," Li said. "She's been consorting with evil forces."

The general's lips clamped together, and Li realized that he must have used the patronizing tone his wife had cautioned him against. "Her name?" the general asked mockingly.

The car pulled to a stop, and Feng hurried from his seat to open the general's door.

"I apologize," said Li. "Charlotte Brien."

"That's the one." The general heaved himself out of the car, and together they started down the sandy path. The compound had once been an imperial residence, and later one of Mao's homes. Seeds from willow blossoms filled the gentle air. The water in the pond was milky with them. "I haven't told you this but the smuggler apprehended off Fujian last week had it written in his logbook when he died."

"That's a connection, then," said Li, taking out another cigarette. "After getting into Nanjing by train, she visited an American professor called Rank at the Center for Sino-American studies. She spent two-and-a-half hours with him yesterday afternoon."

The general stopped on the fringe of the path. "He is a Borodin?"

"Pardon?"

"Rank, you idiot!" The general made a spitting noise with his lips. "Your generation doesn't even know its own history."

Li shook out the match. "With all due respect, sir, we were schooled to stamp out history of that sort."

"Borodin was a Russian Jew, an organizer for Lenin and finally here. What I want to know is if this Rank is an American agent, or simply a man with a need to act out his enthusiasms."

"There's nothing strange on his visa application. He's been here before."

Frowning, the general walked again. "That in itself is cause for worry. Tell me more about the woman."

"Yesterday evening, she visited a café run by students. It is partially funded by the U.S. Department of State, for which she works, so that in itself is not suspicious, but local cadres did inform me that this place has offered undue intercourse between Americans and our own students at university. When they received the recent directive, the cadres believed that the place should be shut down. As a preliminary precaution, they installed one of their men as a cook."

"A wise measure," the general agreed.

"Charlotte Brien stayed late at this Black Cat Lounge, drinking alchohol. She was overheard telling the manager that she would be back in the morning to look at accounts."

"The Black Cat." The general had veered off the path onto the still-damp grass, stopping halfway down the slope to the pond. Li saw that he was losing him. The general's move to the Ministry had been accompanied by a slipping of his mind, and it was often Li's function to bring him into the present again. "That is named after something."

Li waited, but after a minute or so the general had still failed to remember what it was. He reached up and tugged at a branch of weeping willow, flicking the buds off the wood with his thumbnail. Li continued to wait for instructions.

"IS THERE ANYTHING ELSE I CAN GET FOR YOU, SIR?"

The stewardess was standing over Burling, offering another tiny bottle of vodka, cradled in her palm. He politely refused, but her presence, the soft skin and warm perfume, the full breasts in her uniform blouse produced a dull ache that made him feel sick of himself.

"You just looked a bit uncomfortable. Something else to drink?"

He picked up the plastic cup that had held his first screwdriver and was surprised to find nothing but ice. Already, the navigation screen showed the plane crossing the Tetons. "You won't take this the wrong way?"

"Of course not," she said, bending nearer with her hands on the back of the neighboring seat. A tiny gold cross fell out of her blouse and hung between them on a chain.

"My wife has passed away . . ."

"I'm so sorry," she said, smiling kindly and touching him briefly on the shoulder. He couldn't make out her accent—Ohio, or Michigan perhaps, vowels trapped in her mouth, where they resounded as if in a small cave.

"It's been many years," Burling told her, "so it's no longer fresh. Lately I've been trying to establish a . . . relationship, you know, but I'm of an older generation."

"You're not old, Mr. Burling."

"Well, you're kind, but in any event . . ."

"You want to know what a woman my age is looking for?"

"Exactly."

"Well, for me," she said, standing up and throwing out her hip, "I just want to travel, that's all. I've lived in London, in Singapore, now I'm based in Seattle. Next year I'm hoping for Tokyo. If a man can't deal with my wanderlust, too bad. I never wanted any kids."

"They keep you guessing, that's for sure."

"You look like a father."

Burling laughed. "I don't know what that means."

"Take it as a compliment."

"I have a son and daughter, both grown now," he told her. "When I was their age, I was like you, I wanted to see the world. As a result they grew up mostly overseas."

"Lucky them."

"I thought so, too, but they didn't see it that way. My daughter wrote her graduate thesis on the trauma of being uprooted all the time."

"I guess the grass is always greener." She looked over her shoulder at the steward, who was manning the service cart. "Looks like we're out of ice again. Excuse me."

Just like that, she was gone, and Burling realized it had only been her job, to entertain his questions. He was ashamed of having kept her so long. As he ate, he wondered about her forthright nature, which he equated with independence, whether that was the kind of woman he should have chosen as a wife. In a way, he and Amelia were prisoners of their own generation, which had not allowed them much room to decide: the summer they met, 1956, all the children of their class in Philadelphia had the same script to follow. The dances and doubles matches and fumbling in the backseats of Chryslers each were scenes in a larger passion play, the final act of which was meant to unite the prominent families of Chestnut Hill and Mount Airy. Even if it was in his, and Amelia's, nature to critique that play, wonder about what Betty Wilson and Whit Greene could possibly have in common beyond the fact that her father's bank held the paper on the Greene's family business— "*What* can they possibly talk about?"—Burling and the lively girl whose father called her Amie performed the scenes like everyone else. He was twenty, home from Princeton, working at the *Evening Bulletin* as a sports reporter. He professed to want to be a journalist, a war reporter or a foreign correspondent or, less likely given his earnest tendencies, a sportswriter, complete with cigar and newsprint staining his fingers. The way he talked about writers attracted her to him. Evenings on the terrace at the Cricket Club, or in the dimly lit study of her parents' big stone house, discussing Hawthorne and Melville, his favorites, or Wharton and F. Scott Fitzgerald, hers, would invariably end in a set piece of double entendres that led his hands inside her blouse. Consumed as he was, like all his contemporaries, with what kind of woman he would marry, what she would say while the dances and exaggerated talk swirled about them, and what she allowed him after, were enough to promise that their life together would take them on an exotic sort of mission, filled with intellect, purpose, and, certainly, sex.

It was agreed among their set that Lucius and Amelia would leave Philadelphia, destined for foreign capitals, Europe, or India. Amelia was a "live wire," as her friends had it, and "easy to know," as Burling's mother said, which was not necessarily a compliment. Already, at seventeen, she had spent a month "away," under a doctor's care, and already, like her vastly successful Irish father, she liked to drink, harbingers of things to come. Her love of literature was more therapeutic than intellectual, but he was never very discerning when it came to psychology, any more than he had much taste for alcohol. Still, he liked to be around it, as he liked the clubs she took him to on South Street, downstairs places filled with smoke and trumpets and the steady war beat of traps, and actual blacks. Sometimes Amelia had pills in her handbag, but Burling demurred. He found that being the sober one gave him a reputation for character that people admired, even if they didn't always seem to like him very much. It was there that he established his demeanor in the presence of alien cultures, and also, gradually, where he understood that he would not play professional basketball. Amelia, who knew nothing of sports, pointed it out to him. His realization that she was right led directly to a proposal, her recognition of his deficiency sealing the deal.

They were married three years later, following his military service, at the church on Germantown Avenue where both their mothers belonged, although the families came from different hemispheres of the same social world, faded blue blood on his side, new money on hers. Amelia's father, the self-made Irish Catholic from a north Philly family of seven boys, of which he was the only alcoholic functioning enough to offer nominal employment to the other six, put on a reception that caused the mostly Protestant members of the club to mutter as they ate his food and drank more than their fill. He died two years later in the nineteenth hole, telling his foursome about the big house he had bought the couple on Macomb Street in northwest DC, and about his son-in-law's job in the Kennedy administration, of which he was ignorant but exceedingly proud.

His only daughter took her father's death to heart. His absence, like the demise of a benevolent despot, exposed the tensions that had always existed between the factions represented by Amelia and her mother, who was scornful and envious of the girl's wild nature, her freedom, which the father had encouraged, and likely her beauty and sexual charms, of which he was also uncomfortably fond. Outwardly, the daughter railed against her mother's false piety and weak manipulations, while at the same time she set about decorating the house in Cleveland Park with a near-curatorial fervor and making a baby with her husband, more than one if possible, to outdo the fragile older woman. It might have all worked itself out. The babies came, Elizabeth in 1963 and Lucius III in '66, but Burling was barely at home anymore. What happened? If you compared the summer of 1956, when the Soviets rolled into Budapest, to 1979, when the same, slightly updated, tanks invaded Afghanistan, what came between was Vietnam.

"You want to make this a history lesson," Amelia said, when he'd returned to take up residence in the guest room of the cavernous shingle-style house. Two months had passed since rebel soldiers—whether or not they were the tribe who had executed Breeden on the border, or the ones who had killed Wes Godwin before his eyes, no one at the Agency seemed able, or willing, to tell—moved dangerously close to the airport that lay on the plain north of Kabul. Burling himself was forced to go, leaving April, or the rumors of her, behind. "This is not about a war or a revolution. I don't care about those things."

"You used to," he said with genuine remorse, for everything. "I realize I'm not entitled to sympathy."

"I never cared about history, Lucius, or politics, either. You forget."

"You cared about books. We used to talk about novels all the time. You loved *Madame Bovary*."

"You're sad," Amelia said. She was sitting in the corner of their former bedroom, under a standing lamp, her delicate ankles crossed, bare legs folded against the flowery skirt of the slipper chair. "Besides, I can't read novels anymore. They require a certain level of trust, certain assumptions about people."

"That's what I'm talking about," he said, warming to his idea. "Comparing 1956 to now is like comparing . . . Flaubert to Joyce, or Jane Austen to Faulkner."

"Nice try, buster," she said, twisting her mouth in a distorted smile, but in her eyes he saw encouragement. Perhaps his eloquence, which he was aware had mostly to do with the depth of his voice and the scale of his bearing, could save him. That morning his newspaper likeness had appeared above the fold of the *Washington Post*, with the caption THE NEW FACE OF COVERT OPERATIONS? and a long investigative piece about April's disappearance, continued deep into the front section. Every story the *Post* got ahold of was going to be their sequel to Watergate. The next day he had to go up to the Hill to twist at the pleasure of the Agency director in the whipping of partisan winds. While Gordon MacAllister was secretly, triumphantly expanding the operation that Burling had begun, the architect himself had been thrown off scaffolding of his own design.

"It's like a funhouse mirror," he said, feeling weirder and more desperate by the minute.

"Only not so fun," Amelia said. "Why don't you go downstairs and have a drink? I don't feel like talking right now. I want to read my stupid magazine."

"I guess I will," said Burling. He'd been standing in her doorway and he turned to go, forgetting the narrowness of the landing and nearly falling down the stairs. The house was an empty-feeling ship of a place, with hidden porches and deep, damp verandas, and yet it seemed too small. The stairway turned at two landings, each set with a leaded glass window of craftsman design. At the back of the dark, narrow kitchen between high oak cabinets, he was startled to find Simon Bell, lately tenant of the renovated story of their carriage house, furtively pouring himself a straight scotch from the dresser that served as a bar.

"Join me?"

The reddish hair on Simon's fat, freckled forearms and the several large rings on his fingers were reflected in the flaking, beveled mirror behind the bottles. Bell had once been a brilliant China hand with MI-6, but in the middle 1970s his superiors had pulled him away from the desk and sent him to Burma. SLORC, the onomatopoeically monikered secret police, had caught him up near the border with China and subjected him to a brutal interrogation, during which a gun had been discharged, grazing his forehead. The groove it left gave him a perpetually thoughtful expression that drew you to his sad-dog eyes, sagging, stippled cheeks and sunburned neck. The purpose of his mission had been disinformation, but in order for Bell to be convincing this fact had been withheld from him. As the interrogation went forward, certain things had not made sense; Bell understood what had happened, and he told his captors so. To show they weren't stupid, the Burmese let him go, but not before beating him again rather badly, on principle, which had made him, as Simon liked to say, "a bit mental." After Burma he'd been posted to a Washington desk job, his wife in London awaiting divorce. That's when Burling had taken him in, to watch over his house. Since Amelia's return from Afghanistan, Bell had begun to feel he was needed, a slightly dangerous condition for him.

"Is there ice?"

"I don't use it," Bell said, carefully shutting the glass door above the bar. He was wearing only boxer shorts and flip-flops. A tiny silver ball suspended by bearings in the jamb snicked shut, and the glassware inside trembled musically. There was already another glass beside his, and next to that, on the gray marble top, a Pelican edition of Shakespeare. "Foreign office chap shouldn't take ice in his drink. You never know what's in it."

"I like ice," Burling told him. "Besides, we're in the nation's capital. You think the water's poisoned?"

"Absofuckinggoddamlutely. I fancy the water here is drawn from the cesspool that flows directly from the bowels of our, I should say your, elected officials. Nothing but undigested fat from stale red-baiting leftovers and the roughage of lefty post-Vietnam paranoia. Did you see what those jesters had to say about you in the *Post*?"

"I didn't read it," Burling said from inside the freezer door. The ice in his mother's old, nickel-plated trays, imported from Philadelphia, was covered with fuzzy crystals and specks of food, as if they hadn't been emptied for years. He wondered what had happened in his house in the months while Amelia had lived there alone with his children.

"How could you resist?"

Burling slammed a tray against the refrigerator door, dislodging shards of schist-like ice that skittered away across the linoleum. "I don't give a damn what they think."

"Bravo," said Bell, raising his glass. Burling retrieved a piece from the ice tray and dropped it into the tumbler, taking a layer of skin from his finger with it.

"Ouch," he said, tasting blood as he sucked at the tip.

"Honestly, Lucius, I felt a bit sorry. The kids must really have caught it today at school."

Burling reached for the edge of the kitchen table and collapsed in a straight wooden chair. Betsy and Luke had already been in their bedrooms, asleep according to Amelia, when he got home from the Agency at ten. They were at awkward ages, and since he'd gotten home he'd found their appearances slightly alarming. Elizabeth's hair was lank and greasy, her eyes unable to focus on him from behind her big pale glasses. Luke's clothes looked worn out and half a size too small. The possibility that his mistakes would touch them deflated him completely.

"I brought this in for Luke," Bell explained, sliding the paperback onto the glass-topped table in front of him. "I thought it might take his mind off things."

Burling opened the book. *Henry IV, Part 2*. "*Enter* RUMOUR *painted full of tongues.*"

"Oh, glory be," Burling said, putting his head in his hands.

YEARS LATER, WHEN HE HAD SOLD THE HOUSE ON MACOMB and moved to his present apartment, Burling found a story Luke had written for the Sidwell Friends literary journal, about those months before his father came home. Thinly veiled autobiography, it told how Bell and Luke and Elizabeth acted *Lear* and *The Tempest* in the living room for Amelia's entertainment that spring. When the weather turned warmer and Betsy was shipped off to camp, where she would spend eight miserable weeks falling out of canoes, dropping balls, and being tormented by thinner girls, mosquitoes, and poison ivy, Bell and Luke moved the repertory company to the deep porch that curled around the front of the house. In the damp mornings, Bell's paperbacks were still on the little wicker table beside Amelia's chaise longue, curling with dew and the dried rings of sweat from her highballs. Sometimes after Luke had gone to bed, his mother and Simon talked on, of Paris where Amelia had gone to the Sorbonne, and the Comédie Française, of which she had been a fan. Simon's voice rose slowly and distantly, like an old-time announcer on the radio, vaguely corny but filling with a timbre that seemed like a wave from another, more confident world: *Good evening, Mr. and Mrs. America, and all the ships at sea.*

In June, they started the Henry plays, with Bell playing Falstaff. This production Burling saw in the flesh, having returned from Kabul at one of the lowest points of his life. He had done something careless, taken a chance with April; in turn, chance, or fate—thought of now in the upper case, ontological sense of the word, a condition of life on which he'd expended a lot of thought—turned bad and collected a terrible debt. Or maybe the *mujahedin* just didn't give a fiddler's fuck what he or Joseph Conrad thought, a possibility that expelled him from the comfort of his thinking, put him outside of himself.

It was a strange place to be, and yet stranger still was how much the scene he discovered in his house on Macomb, after he had a few weeks to get used to it, seemed to match his internal condition of exile: Amelia cueing the corpulent Simon and the thin, shaggy Luke in the scented summer night, her pale hand flitting up and down like a moth within the baggy silk cuff of her dressing gown. She was vaguely alluring, in a fey sort of way.

"Peace, good pint pot," Bell declaimed, leaving his Ballantine ale on the windowsill beside her. Bugs popped against the frosted milk-glass globe of the porch light. "Harry!"

Luke, draped in the pose of a dissolute scion on the railing, put one white Adidas sneaker on the floor of the porch and turned to face the beer-bellied Sir John. Since returning to the States he had adopted a punk affect, fraying Izods and olive fatigues, a safety pin stuck through the alligator's jagged red mouth. The part of Prince Hal—Harry—who drank with John Falstaff and the other braggart soldiers, only to take up his heroic place at their lead, appealed to him.

"That thou art my son," Simon began.

The wicker of the chaise made a crackling sound, and Amelia whispered, "Chamomile," and giggled, tipping the ash from her French cigarette onto the floor. Her third glass of white burgundy leaned precariously on the arm of the chair, and her voice was a bit giddy, but not with the breathlessness that came before one of her fugues. Sitting in an upright chair in the shadows, elbows on his knees, Burling could see the bond that had grown between Luke and his mother in his absence: Luke was her pal, her companion, and also a connoisseur of her moods, a hard thing to be. "You forgot," she said to Simon, "'The more it is trodden on the faster it grows.'"

"I'm improvising." Simon bowed, his forehead glazed with perspiration. "Plenty of precedent for it. Boys these days don't want to hear, 'Youth, the more it is wasted the sooner it wears.' They know all about that already, they do."

"I suppose you're right," said Amelia. She turned to Burling, but her face was a mystery.

"That thou art my own son," Simon continued, "I have partly thy mother's word, partly my own opinion, but chiefly a villainous trick of thine eye, and a foolish hanging of thy nether lip, that doth warrant me."

The wicker squealed beneath Amelia, and Luke forgot his line.

Burling watched from the guest room that night, but Simon padded across the grass to the carriage house alone. Quietly, so as not to wake Luke on the third floor, Burling moved down the hallway to his old room.

"I was wondering when you'd come." Amelia was sitting in the window seat, blowing the smoke from her cigarette through the corroded screen. "I'd like to talk to you, you know."

Burling moved closer. The fine features of Amelia's long face were white from the streetlight. Her cigarette smelled strange.

"What is that you're smoking?"

"It's pot. Marijuana," she giggled. "You want some?"

"I don't think so, no."

"I got it from Luke," Amelia said.

"You've been smoking marijuana with our son?"

"Oh, he doesn't know I have it. I think he got it from Simon."

"Bell smokes dope?"

"Apparently so."

"That can't be good," Burling said, sitting down on the slipper chair. Their room, the canopy bed, the sheer curtains, the pastel Tabriz he had bought in Uzbekistan, struck him as an odd setting for what was taking place.

"Apparently people do a lot of things. We were just such good children we missed out on most of them."

"We weren't always so good."

"Yes, that's true," she acknowledged in an open-ended tone. "Once upon a time I was known as the wild one. I was Sylvia Plath. I was going to draw or act or write poems."

"Just the other night you denied that."

"That was then, this is now. Are you sure you don't want some?"

"I've never even smoked a cigarette."

"So many things have changed, Lucius. For once, I wish you'd come down with us mortals. You'll lower your standards for April Lindstrom, but not for me."

"All right," Burling said, standing up. April's name seared him. A puff of marijuana would not be the worst thing he'd done.

"Here."

When he drew on the joint, the ember was so close and hot that he burned his fingers. "Shit!" He coughed and dropped the thing.

"Poor Lucius." Amelia laughed and came toward him, her arms as wide as an angel in her translucent robe. He coughed, and the blue smoke kept coming out of him in clouds. "You make everything so complicated, don't you?" The robe fell open, and he could see her small round breasts in her nightgown. Whatever his lungs had absorbed had gone straight to his head, and he was aware of only two distinct parts of his body—the top of his skull, which seemed to have disappeared, and a gradually mounting erection, so strong that it almost hurt. He couldn't help remembering April in the hotel in Samarkand. "Most husbands just screw their secretaries, but you had to make your affair into some kind of idea as big as you are, didn't you?"

"Amelia, don't."

"I wouldn't sleep with you for a couple of months because I was having a hard time. My medication was all messed up, Lucius, and I didn't have Dr. Rose there, so I can understand you might want one night of casual fucking, I wouldn't even begrudge you that, but instead you come up with some kind of grand design, a mission that befits a man of your great intellectual prowess."

"Please."

"You find yourself a hippie whore with an impotent husband, a *folie à deux* of epic proportions, and what happens? You don't just get laid, you manage to invoke the soldiers of God—of *God!*" She looked up at the ceiling and laughed in a way that frightened and thrilled him. Maybe this was how it would be now, a world of sensation and vague paranoia. "They sweep down and murder your pilot and knock you on the head and carry your ideal woman away. She's probably sitting Indian-fashion in their tent right now, like Scheherazade, part of the king's harem, telling them stories so they won't cut her throat."

"Amelia, your imagination."

"*My imagination!* It's always my imagination. Until it isn't."

"I was going to say I always loved your imagination. It's what made me love you in the first place."

"Oh, Lucius," she said, clinging to him now. "Your probity and my imagination. How did they turn on us like this?"

"I don't know. It's a dangerous time."

"You mean our age?"

"Ours, the age of the world, if you know what I mean. That was the problem, that I started to think like that again, about bigger things."

"And all I could think of was little ones. Boring, tiny annoyances and slights."

"April." He couldn't believe he'd uttered her name.

"Yes, but not just her."

"She and Jack seemed to come from a totally different world."

Amelia was crying quietly as he held her and now she began to move her hand down his stomach and under his belt. "Is this what she did?"

"No, sweetheart. You don't have to talk like that."

"I can tell stories, too. It's what I'm good at, you know. That's what the children loved about me, before they grew up and started hating me."

"Luke and Betsy don't hate you," he said.

"Elizabeth does. You run off with a woman, and all she is is 'Daddy, Daddy, Daddy.' She was furious at me for sending her to camp when she found out you were coming home. But I couldn't stand her for another second in this house."

"That's normal, isn't it, between mothers and daughters?"

But Amelia had already moved on somewhere else. All along, she'd been pulling him upward with her fingers, scratching him slightly with her nails. "I could tell you a story," she said distantly. "A story of April."

"Amelia, don't. It wasn't like that."

"Tell me what it was like," she said.

"I don't want to hurt you again."

"You did, you know."

"I don't want it to be that way."

Awkwardly, tenderly, he took her wrist and moved her to the bed. For an hour then, while the fallen joint smoldered on the chair, and for a month of nights after, Burling made love to his wife in a guilty, solicitous way, always aware that their romance was stolen from time. He often thought of April, in the high desert, riding with soldiers of God. He even let Amelia tell him stories about her, making love with the men to stay alive. For a month, chance and fate were suspended, but the king's knife glinted beneath the pillows.

BURLING DIDN'T WITNESS THE END OF THE IDYLL. HE WAS summoned to London for a meeting on setting up an embassy-in-exile in Pakistan. Luke's account of it was all that he had; Luke had never shared the details, or his feelings, with his father. The day after Burling left, Amelia swallowed a bottle of pills that her doctor had prescribed to help her sleep, chasing them with scotch. Her bedroom was locked, and Luke could feel the wind from an open window slipping beneath her door. He stood there in his bare feet, not ready for swim practice, imagining the white room beyond. He put his ear to the keyhole, but all he could hear was a car going by outside, birdsong. The firemen had to kick the door in, and Luke stared at his mother's curled-up body, her buttocks slender and slack where the white sheet had fallen away. A paramedic was yelling into her ear, lifting and slapping her limp hand, the soles of her feet. Luke had to step aside as the man's partner, her pockets heavy with equipment, pushed by with the stretcher.

He moved aside until he was standing in front of the book-shelves that lined the upper hall. A strange collection of spines: popular novels adapted for movies, a marriage manual and a few self-help books, an *Encyclopaedia Britannica* with an entry for the Austro-Hungarian Empire that he had plagiarized for school, a Riverside Shakespeare, gilt and bound in red leather—a gift from Simon Bell. The stretcher passed with his mother on it, her hair thick and wild on the pillow, a pencil line of blood drawn from her nose. The bulky woman held aloft a plastic bag.

"We're losing her, Willie," she said.

"Where's your father, son?" A black policeman had come up the stairs. He had taken off his hat and was looking at Luke with kind, gold eyes.

"It's sure as hell not him," Luke said, looking down at Simon, who had come to stand in his bathrobe in the hallway below, gazing up with his hand on his forehead, above his melancholy face.

"No, he's your tenant," said the cop, reaching out a soft hand. "He called 9-1-1. Your dad is Lucius Burling Jr. What happened here?"

The cop was looking at the burned-up chair in the corner.

"My mother smokes," Luke told him.

The cop reached out gently. "Why not we put this away now?"

Luke felt the pages close on his thumb, the heavy red volume being removed from his hands.

WHEN THE STEWARDESS CAME TO CLEAR HIS TRAY, BURLING felt the plane descending. Beneath the engines spread the slate-colored surface of Puget Sound. The sky was draped with low curtains of thin, leaden cloud, and as the wings dipped below them the water flashed like metal. The plane leveled across a neighborhood of boarded-up bungalows, and the wheels gained the runway in a clamor of rubber. When the pilot had parked at the gate, Burling elected to stretch his legs in the terminal and try to reach his consulate in Shanghai.

The airport was an antiseptic, transient place, and all the kitsch in the world couldn't hide it. There was take-out sushi because this was supposed to be a gateway to the East, and souvenirs of the type sold in every airport terminal: T-shirts and key chains and life trapped in pieces of plastic. By an escalator a cube of glass held the ribs of a giant prehistoric animal and its fossilized scat.

"You wanted us to act all the time like we were in some kind of traveling exhibit," Luke had said to him once, home from college. His long hair was dirty blond and his eyes were like rivets, set in liquid irises that were startlingly blue. He was taking a course on the history of the 1960s and the Vietnam War, which his father had apparently caused. It was a phase during which Burling wondered just how far his son's experiment with drugs had taken him, into what realm of madness and bogus chautauqua, and before he discovered photography, the medium that would channel his watchfulness into something around which he could arrange a kind of life. "Like an American family behind glass. Here you have Elizabeth, holed up in her room with Jane Austen or Emily Dickinson. Here you have Mother, drinking, writing O'Neill plays about the ambassador's murder by communist thugs. And here you have Father . . . but wait a minute, where is Father? That, boys and girls, is the most interesting aspect of our exhibit. No Father."

Burling found a quiet corner behind a Wolfgang Puck cart and took out his mobile phone, newly purchased during his leave. A few steps away he could hear a businessman, also on a cell, telling his secretary what a hectic day it had been. Some people lived to display themselves, others wanted to hide. As he punched in the number, he tried to remember how he'd wanted to approach the call. His mind felt poorly arranged. Punching in the number of the consulate, he thought of asking for Mike Ryan, MacAllister's young station chief, but he wouldn't know anything about Yong anyway, and if he did, Burling would have a hard time not arousing his suspicion. The whole business made him slightly dizzy—he wasn't used to Beltway intrigue anymore—and taking MacAllister at his word made him feel like a fool. In the end, he decided on asking for Charlotte, more than anything because he wanted to hear her voice, but she wasn't at her desk.

"She has been out in Nanjing all week, Mr. Burling," the native receptionist told him. "She is supposed to return here today."

"Is Ryan in?"

"A moment, sir, please."

The line hung somewhere in space. He must remember how easy it would be to listen in.

"Ryan."

"Mike, hi, it's Lucius. Anything happening there?"

Ryan's chair squeaked in the background, and Burling wondered if he'd sounded alarmed.

"The dam project, what else?" Ryan had on his serious tone of complaint. "I got so many environmentalists sending me letters, I feel like a freaking congressman." The Bronx slipped into Ryan's voice. "You on your way back?"

"A third of the way. I have a night in Tokyo at the Imperial, then a stop in Beijing to meet with Ambassador Wardlow. Dennis gets about as nervous as the Chinese every time June 4th rolls around."

Ryan's murmur sounded vaguely affirmative, and Burling wondered for the hundredth time what Ryan did in the way of intelligence work. Every week, Burling saw him heading out for his lunches or racquetball with movers and shakers from the growing number of joint ventures in town—the Volkswagen factory, the German power conglomerate, McDonnell-Douglas—but all things considered, China was still a developing country, with the Bomb and a million-man army but little in the way of intelligence-gathering services. Without its nuclear weapons, the Soviet Union had been like Brazil, but at least the Soviets had been good at the game. The People's Republic was just a barnyard of bureaucrats showing their plumage. Burling didn't believe in industrial espionage.

"He wants to tap your expertise," Ryan told him.

"Uh-uh. Speaking of experts, I ran into an old friend of yours in Washington yesterday. Chuck Byrd," said Burling, using MacAllister's work name. "He asked after you."

Ryan must have known Burling was fishing, but he didn't miss a beat. These second-generation believers in America didn't harbor any doubts. "I haven't spoken to Chuck directly in a while. He must be nearing retirement."

"I don't think the word is in his vocabulary, frankly. He wanted me to play tennis, but I told him my elbow was bad. Maybe you and I could have a warm-up game so next time that I'm home . . ."

"You know what somebody told me about Chuck, Lucius?"

"I can't imagine."

"That you saved his life in Africa. Went over a few heads to do it."

"That's true," Burling said. If saving him meant revealing the extent of their operations in Angola, the Agency had been willing to leave MacAllister to die. "It wasn't really my thing, but I went over there and found the village and brought him home."

"He should take it easy on you, then."

"Huh! You don't know the man. He was always brutally competitive, and Africa didn't change him a bit. If anything, as soon as he recovered, it made him more of a terror on the court."

"Charlotte doesn't play, does she?"

Burling swallowed, looking up at the trestles supporting the terminal's roof. "Yes, she does," he said to Ryan, "very well, as a matter of fact. There's a fine clay court at the Residence, you know."

"She'll have to tear herself away from her friends in Nanjing."

"How's that?"

"That Center she goes up there to help with. Poetry readings and folk music, that sort of thing. The place has acquired her a fan club, Lucius. You better tell her to keep her head down."

Burling glanced toward the lounge across the concourse. A waitress moved through the carpeted twilight of tables and chairs. Since he'd left the Agency under a cloud, Burling had concentrated his professional life on human rights, the rights of women and children especially. That's why the first Bush, who had been Burling's boss at the Agency, had sent him to China. What they used to call the hard stuff of international relations brought on a kind of nausea: he'd begun to imagine what a world without the hard stuff might mean. The soft, on the other hand, put him in contact with women like Charlotte, ten or twenty years younger, officers in the Peace Corps, what was then USIA, or AID. Intelligent, competent women, they seemed new to him, equally aware of the power of their bodies and their minds. They flirted while they took an almost daughterly interest in his wisdom. The first time that he and Charlotte ate dinner together, she argued in earnest about things that seemed quaint to him—International Fruit, East Timor. In the glow of that talk, she leaned toward him, their knees touching under the table. Her fervor, he thought, seemed founded in an anger that was alien, a knot that he needed to untie. The loose ends drew them up to his bedroom, where she fucked him like a refugee. He remembered, somewhat uncomfortably, his surprise at her vigor and willingness, but in the morning she seemed pale and deflated, animated by a discontent that had sent her with a young son halfway around the world. This is the way that women are now, he had thought. April had been their avatar, but she was ahead of her time and had suffered for it. Understanding Charlotte Brien had become a kind of project for him.

"It's not something I want to talk about in detail on the phone," said Ryan chastely. "The local street committees there have fingered the place as a danger."

"Charlotte's a sensible woman," Burling said, although he knew her to be impulsive when it came to her beliefs. In that way, she was very poorly suited for her job.

"I'm not saying she's not smart, Lucius. I'm still working on the assumption she doesn't know what she's into."

"That sounds a bit insinuating, Mike."

"There've been some murmurs, that's all I'm saying. If I went any further, I'd be compromising more than a cultural officer."

The lowest of the low, Burling thought. "My plane was just announced, Mike. We'll talk about it more when we're together, agreed?"

In a cavalier impulse, Burling hung up the phone. It had started to rain outside the terminal windows, and the glistening planes looked like emergency vehicles, strobe lights blinking red and white in the puddles on the tarmac. The sky was smoky above their tails. The trouble at the Black Cat Lounge was almost certainly incidental, some street committee tattletale who needed a gold star, but Burling had to work to convince himself that everything wasn't connected. In an odd way, he found that he wanted it to be. He wanted the evidence to form a pattern that would guide him.

L I XIN HAD HOPED TO GET AWAY TO SEE HIS DAUGHTER'S performance, but at two o'clock he received a report from the cook in Nanjing. He looked for the general in his office, but the secretary told him he was taking a walk. Li found him on the path near the place where they had parted that morning, gazing over the lambent, pink water.

"A little background on Yong is in order," the general said when Li had related the story of Charlotte Brien's meeting with the American, known as John Tan. "It makes our problem somewhat more complicated than it has been with the others."

Li's head hummed the way it had near the microwave towers in Tibet. "At one time," the general explained, "when Yong returned from the United States . . ."

"He was there?"

"Yong may not be our most brilliant product," said the general, walking lock-kneed toward the reeds on the shore. "But we invested a great deal in him as a young man, and he does possess an impressive, nearly photographic recall. After studying physics at Qinghua, he was sent to New Jersey to gather information on the training of American students. In this he was not very successful, but he did manage to learn several processes that we thought could be of help to our research in Xian."

At the edge of the lake, Li lit a cigarette, waving the smoke before his face to ward off the bugs. From Wu, a man who'd been transferred, he had heard of the lab in Xian where the army developed the weapons.

"Yong imported a hostile element when he returned," the general added, blinking at the shine from the water. Li had just pressed the cigarette between his lips, but he took it out again. "In the United States he read things, became involved in organizations. Within a year of arriving in Xian, he attempted to subvert the Party in his research institute, and was sent down to an inconsiderable teaching post at Qinghua."

"It did not turn out to be so inconsiderable," Li said.

The general's eyes flattened. It wasn't only his stature that caused them to call him Big Fish. Beneath the black water of his pupils, his eyes were like a trout's, looking up through its own rings.

"Yong showed remarkable resources under criticism," the general said.

Li's cigarette tasted bitter, and he dropped it on the marshy grass, crushing it under his foot. Gnats flung themselves against his damp forehead. A timbre of respect had lurked in the general's tone, a resonance that irked Li. "Only one with American intelligence training could do that," he said.

The general murmured with the same deep tone of respect. "We thought he had been rehabilitated."

"So we released him?" Li heard the slightest lilt of sarcasm in his repetition of the general's collective pronoun.

"There are not so many with Yong's experience, his knowledge. We needed him with the Iranians."

"But then he was arrested a second time?"

"He began to write things, to meet with Western reporters and stir up his students again."

"The weak never learn," Li told him, "because they do not fight."

The general's eyes slid up the hill in the direction of the Toyota, where Feng had unscrewed the cap on the radiator and was inspecting its contents, his jacket shining like liquid in the sun.

"You are fond of quoting," the general said, "but I wonder if you truly understand. You must respect Yong Beihong. He has struggled.

Perhaps the forces of bourgeois liberalism have been too much for him, but I wonder if one can say the same thing for you?"

Li drew himself up and swallowed with difficulty. The taste of tobacco smoke was thick on his tongue. He had never mentioned his material desires, his ambition, to the general, but maybe the clairvoyance that had plagued him since Tibet was like a two-way radio: he would have to be more careful what he thought.

"I have struggled myself," he said, "and I have found my motivation to be for the best."

Without a word, the general turned and trudged up the hill to the path, his black loafers slipping, tearing skids of red mud in the grass. Like many men of his generation, he had studied with the Russians, and sometimes Li suspected him of harboring an incipient Occidentalism of his own, a desire for foreign knowledge and goods; the son couldn't have gotten it from nowhere, after all.

In the garden outside the meeting room an old woman came out of the dingy barracks and offered them tea. "My conference opens this evening," said the general. He sat down at the white stone table and nodded to the woman, who set a cup before him.

Li remained standing, blinking and twisting his foot in the sand. "We still don't know who this John Tan is, General. He has a tourist visa."

The general watched the old woman pour his tea.

"We also don't know why they spoke of the American consul, Lucius Burling." He seemed to be losing the old man's attention. The clinking of bottles and glasses came from inside the windows, where a long table had been draped with pink cloth. "I did discover that Alan Rank was a pacification officer during the American War in Annam," he added, but the general was raising his face to the sun. It burned through the blanket of haze like a cigarette scorching a gray, oily cloth, and the Big Fish caught it on his eyelids, giving them a feminine delicacy.

"Something larger is brewing here," he observed, his eyes still closed. "I know what you're going to say, but I want you to let it develop. You never know what it might reveal . . ."

The general trailed off, and Li swore, barely under his breath: what if Yong got away?

Like a gunshot, Zu pounded the table. The lid of his teacup jumped off, shattering on the stones at Li's feet. "Did they expect us to sit idly by while their little game with the people of the North surrounded us with hostile governments?" The general fixed him with his grave, hooded eyes. "Have you ever been to Kashgar, Li Xin?"

"You know I have not."

"It's a place full of intrigue. You'd like it. The great game was fought there by valorous men."

"I don't know much about it," Li said, "only its importance as a trade route in imperial times, its proximity to Samarkand, Tashkent, and Kabul."

"Geography orchestrates history. British spies tried to sneak into Kashgar from the Punjab in the 1820s. Times have not changed so much, have they, Li?"

"History is a bourgeois diversion. Its end will come."

The general grunted, a short, grinding sound. For a moment, Li thought he'd gone too far. The woman approached with the tea thermos, but the general motioned her away. "You must observe caution in this matter," he said. "I do not want it handled through Ministry."

Li's heart skipped, and he sucked in a breath. "I may take Feng to Nanjing?"

The general nodded. "Keep your eyes in your head," he said, sipping his tea with ceremony. "Before you go, find out more about the Brien woman's visitor."

A migraine was tightening like a vice on Li's temples. His thoughts dissolved for a moment, and in their place a figure cowered against a wall. Something in its posture suggested that the wall had once been a sanctuary, but then his inward eye began to retreat, and around the wall was a mountaintop scattered with bones. The plateau sky of Tibet beat down on his throbbing skull.

"You seem perplexed, son," the general said. "Is there something that bothers you?"

He saw the desolate staging area where he had been stationed in Tibet, the constant eye-watering reek of the convoys, tasted the rancid, thick yak-butter tea on his tongue. The temples in the mountains were haunted with cannibal rites. Altitude, strange whispers flying through the air had left him with migraines. He groped for a lie through the thickening pain and stumbled on a pebble of truth he could grasp. "I argued with my wife last night, so I started the day with a headache."

"Your wife," the general repeated, leisurely drinking his tea. "About what did you fight?"

"Cigarettes. I find it immodest, unbecoming when a woman smokes."

The general found it uproariously funny. His laughter hurt Li's pounding head.

"Newlyweds, yes?"

"Thirteen years," Li insisted. "We were married right before the rebellion."

"The child?"

"A daughter."

The general seemed satisfied. "As long as she does not smoke in public. What's to be done?"

"I don't like the child to see her."

The general nodded, already far away. What did he find in these interminable meetings with history? The future was before him, if only he played it right.

"If there's nothing else?" Li asked.

The general waved him off with a hand.

THE OLD CHURCH LOOMED AGAINST A SKY FULL OF ashes, its white face slackened by rain, and around it huddled low, red-brick houses and defiant square apartment blocks built of poor cement, their gray walls porous and bowed. The front of the church was wide and square, its steeple squat, and the mullions of the arched windows were awkwardly formed, copied from an imperfect plan penned somewhere in the West. To the top of the steeple a cross had been fixed.

Lindstrom stood in an arch in the old village wall, looking up at it dizzily. Through the TV antennas and telephone wires he traced the outline of steeple and eaves with his eye. The lintels above the high windows were crooked, and his vision seemed to tilt: he had to steady himself with a hand on the crumbling stucco wall. A light echo warbled in his ear.

Weak flesh, his grandfather said.

Lindstrom pulled his hand away from the wall; a powder of stucco remained on his fingers. A tinny bell sounded, a bicycle rattled past him over the curbstones, and as he began to walk again he felt a cadaverous presence, lurking in the doorways that opened on courtyards of chickens pecking mechanically in the dust, its pole-thin shadow cast by television screens on the blue walls of interior rooms. On the high curb opposite the church, Lindstrom came upon an old man in a Mao suit, leaning against the wall.

The man watched him with sunken eyes, arms crossed in a gesture of judgment. He probed the subtly Asian contours of Lindstrom's face, checked his shoes. A group of solemn, middle-aged women and earnest young men hurried past, making their way with their brightly dressed children to the gates of the church. They didn't see him, which Lindstrom took as a good sign. The lag man, the bundle of voices, the ghost—he could be anyone now.

Inside the gate, a lone terraced evergreen grew, a rooster scratching in the dirt around its trunk. A smell of soiled hay and chickenshit prickled his nose. Long, crude benches had been set out on the paving stones, and above them the windows hung open to the damp morning air. He hadn't slept much in the taxi, only a rocking, fitful shuteye against the hard, cold panel of the door, jarred awake periodically by potholes or a washerboard stretch where the asphalt disappeared. His senses still carried weird flashes of dreams. A scraping of chairs and a few coughs seemed to turn the church into a musical instrument. Women in blue smocks shuffled into the yard. Before he could reach the side door to the sanctuary, something pricked him on the back of his hand.

Lindstrom jerked back, ready to strike, only to find the curious eyes of a boy staring up at him. The boy laughed with a tentative daring and pulled him through the door.

In the chancel was a rough wooden table, piled with hymnals and teacups. Through the doorway to the sanctuary he saw the first steps of a section of risers where a small choir draped in mail-order surplices nervously awaited their cue. An old lectern served as the pulpit, equipped with a microphone and a large black amplifier that made the air hum. A moment later, a dried-up old woman appeared from the choir and climbed up behind the pulpit on a crate. The pants of her man's pinstriped suit had been gathered at her ankles with twine, and in the crook of her arm she held a Bible in a manner both chary and loving. Seeing the way her hair was held from her face with a pin, Lindstrom thought that she could have been his grandmother, only she lacked his grandmother's watchfulness, her fearful, immigrant's eyes.

This was her home, Lindstrom thought, squeezing the little boy's hand. The pastor's fingers restrained one another before her chest, as if the moment she let go they would splay out and fall on the nerves of the people like a strum. She let her fist down gently on her text, as if to emphasize the power of the Word. The pages made a soft rustle in the quiet, waiting church. *At first I could not believe,* his grandfather preached, *that God was in my head, in my mouth, in my hands. He knew no boundaries, not of flesh or mountains either. I was his child.*

The chancel door opened, and a cough died dully outside. The little boy motioned Lindstrom to a seat at the table as the pastor began to speak, and a man with bristly white hair came through the door, followed by a flock of young women in pantsuits who gathered quickly at the table, speaking softly into each other's ears. The old man remained standing while the women stared at Lindstrom, whispering and fluttering their hands. The pastor exhorted the people, and the people stood, all except for Lindstrom and the woman beside him, who watched the proceedings with her mouth tightly set. When the pastor began reading the Scripture, the woman leaned to his ear: "She is telling them that only private wants make people do evil things . . ." The old man unhooked his horn rims from their perches atop his ears and wiped the lenses one at a time on his sleeve, the temporary blindness appearing to comfort him. Around the table, his flock scratched notes on index cards.

"God will test you," the pastor charged, squeezing her eyes shut and flinging her arm at the people, "in this way: you will not know when the test has been given."

There was moaning through the prayer, and a little girl who'd been hiding under the table checked to see if the old man's eyes were closed.

A hymn followed, accompanied by a portable organ with a single plywood bellows opening and closing on a belt. While the choir struggled through the decrescendo, the woman beside Lindstrom explained that the pastor had once taught English in the primary schools, but had left to spread the Word. The hymn made Lindstrom increasingly edgy. All that standing and sitting, the call and response and the singing in unison, seemed like collective insanity to him.

"God is infinite," the pastor said, shaking her finger at the gallery in the rear, "and you can give something to the infinite."

The sanctuary walls were streaked with rain below the sills, and as the fans turned above the congregation an odor of carrion rose on the breeze. As she warmed to her theme, Lindstrom noticed a young man leaning against the wall by the choir. Barefoot, dressed in black pants and a tweed jacket over a T-shirt, he appeared to have just woken up, sleeping it off perhaps in the shade of the church. His eyes were glazed, and he stood there unnoticed—like the junkies who would wander off the street outside his grandfather's mission in San Francisco—watching the old woman preach. A compassionate pain in his features recalled certain Renaissance paintings of Christ. "There has been recently a clash between religious people and the military in Henan

Province," whispered the woman beside him, "but this is secret news." The young man stared around him like an impromptu player in the Passion, a kind of sad understudy to the leading role. Not the Second Coming, really, but a failed savior Lindstrom identified with, a broken spy in the desert. If Christ chose to come back in China, he thought, they would send Him down to the countryside to muck out a stall.

"The government is afraid of religion," the young woman told him. The pastor smugly rested her chin on her hand, raising the other to the vault.

"It's only theater," said Lindstrom. He couldn't take his eyes off the sleepy little man—the bare feet, the delicate hands picking at his fly. "Who's that guy behind the choir?"

The woman stared at him crossly, as if he weren't supposed to speak. When she finally looked over, the little man was gone. Only the boy seemed to be watching the place where he'd stood.

When the service was over, the woman pushed him before the tiny pastor, who seemed to know who he was without asking. The man with bristly hair towered behind her, something tender and protective inspiring his stance, and the congregation crowded behind him, their eager, saturnine faces peering over his shoulders. Lindstrom put down a picture of his grandfather amid the Bibles and cups. Gradually, the old pastor's fingers stopped working the knotted drawstring of her bag. Her eyes grew strangely demure.

"*Papa*," Lindstrom explained. As a boy, he had learned some Mandarin from his grandmother, but the expression sounded childish in the mouth of a man.

The pastor nodded, then her eyes began to trace Lindstrom's features, matching them against the foggy picture in her hand. "You are called John Lindstrom," she said in Chinese. It was the dialect of his grandmother, and he understood each word.

"Yes."

"The professor told us you would come."

"I wanted to see what he started," said Lindstrom, looking around at the faces to see which one might betray him.

"Xinlian," the pastor said. The woman stepped forward, pushing her big glasses back up the bridge of her nose. "You will come with us, please, while we show Mr. Lindstrom what his grandfather made."

THE STREETS OF ANHE WERE NARROW AND UNEVEN, THE walls broken at intervals by a dwelling or the gates of a compound of uncertain use. With the pastor and old man in front, they turned into the heart of the town. The Christian Boys School, which his grandfather had built along with the church, was now a tourist hotel. Slender pines dwarfed the buildings, and a monstrous rhododendron choked the garden. White sculptures, Greek in conception but imbued with the cruel, exquisite duplicity of the Qing, sat in the dry circular fountains, eaten by rain.

I built that place because I never had an education. I tell you, Johnny, ignorance is the mother of violence. Father John taught me that, and I'm saying it to you now, because if I'd been kept in school instead of working one high desert place after another, moving across this damn country like a nomad, I'd have never ended up in that mill, nor down in San Pedro outside that warehouse neither. Watching that poor young policeman so stupid with hatred and fear. Ignorance put me there. Johnny?

Xinlian squinted through the bars of the gate and tossed her long mane of hair behind her shoulder with her hand. The savor of shallots and excrement clung to the walls. "Of course no tourists ever come here any more. Not since, you know."

"*Xian zai zenmo ban,*" Lindstrom said.

Xinlian skipped for a moment on the uneven paving, and he wondered if he had used a crude word by mistake. Her lips pulled back from her prominent yellow teeth, and she laughed.

"You have the expressions of an old man," she told him. "Who taught you this ridiculous Chinese?"

"My grandmother was from here," Lindstrom said. Behind a gate, farm machinery rested, painted yellow but dented and rusty and caked with orange dirt. "*What's to be done?* was sort of a metaphysical statement for her."

Xinlian's lips came together in disapproval. "It is the church that has taught these old women to think in that way. I hope you don't follow them."

"You don't believe in God's will?"

Xinlian watched the next corner, where a man was having a shave in a blue barber's chair. "I know that people from your country believe that the Christians can be a force for reform, but I am still a communist."

"Don't you think that the two things have something in common?"

The old man and the pastor were turning on the wide, busy avenue, planted on each side with sycamore trees. On the sidewalk a small troop of boys had just sliced up a snake, and proceeded to stir it around at their feet in a thin smear of watery blood.

"Nothing good," Xinlian said.

Beyond the boys, the pastor and the old man turned again, this time to the right. It was later than Lindstrom had thought, and above the tiled rooftops, purple ridges stood out in the distance, fogged by a salmon-hued curtain of light. He had seen the hills early that morning, as the sun rose in the dusty rear window of the car, and from the position of the sun, he judged that they'd led him in a complicated circle, that they were turning south again.

"What do you think of the professor?" he asked. "What does Rank believe in?"

Her lips came together again, and it made her cheeks suck in, as if she'd tasted something bad. A dog came out from the shadows and nosed at Lindstrom's pants.

"When this started, things were different." Beyond the dog, the street wound down an uneven slope. "Now the people whose boats we use are only common criminals. They're only in it for the money."

"I hope you know that's not why I'm here," Lindstrom said.

"Why, then?"

For her, it would be impossible to believe that an American might have nowhere else to go.

Xinlian reached up to pluck a leaf from a tree that hung over the lane. The pastor stopped and turned to say something to her, pointing toward the blind end where a red cross watched over a gate. "She says that he built this place after the church."

Lindstrom nodded energetically, but he felt like a fool. The gate opened into a courtyard that was meant to have trees. The pastor spoke to a man in a white coat carrying bundles of herbs, and he answered her respectfully while staring at Lindstrom. The man pointed at a door, then turned and hurried away, parcels swinging by the string from his hands.

The hallway they entered had an odor of disinfectant and rubber. Mops of torn, bundled rags lined the walls.

"Teacher Chen says you can change in here," Xinlian said, stopping with the old man in front of a door. Lindstrom entered the room, and the door was locked quickly from the outside. Their voices faded down the hall.

He was alone in a long, narrow closet with open cubbies lining the walls, no window, and a toilet and sink facing each other at the far end. Cool, vitreous light seeped through the reinforced glass in the door. Under the sink he found a briefcase, similar to those he'd seen carried by men on the street in Nanjing, and inside it a worn set of denim, pajama-like clothes. A bar of soap and a scary-looking straight razor had been placed neatly on top of the shirt, but he took his own Gillette and unscented shaving cream out of his pack. Above the sink was a fluorescent tube, and he switched it on and stripped to his shorts. As he soaped and worked the shaving cream into his beard, the light wouldn't quit pulsing and buzzing.

He kept coming forward through those streaming watch lights, Johnny, shining his flashlight here, on the padlocked warehouse doors, there on pallets like the ones I was hiding behind. The wet blue barrel pointed forward from his hand. We had men all over the docks, armed with shotguns and truncheons, and some of the men had gone into the warehouse through a window in the back. Father John of the longshoremen's mission had told me not to go, but I didn't hold to his solution in those days. Live and let live, he said. The politicians stand between you. Feel the mercy of the Lord. But I was hardened from working in the whine of the saw. I had no mercy to give. Have mercy, Johnny.

If every soul's home was a building, then Lindstrom's was a prison, or a brig. The drunk tank where they threw the marchers after they had gunned them with hoses; later the VC prison camp, alive with singsong voices after dark. Even a basement apartment with dim, yellow walls, April reading in the window, or working on her languages, saying the strange words over and over: the warmth remained outside.

His namesake, Father John, had been right. The cop and his grandfather, both from the same walk of life, had faced one another with guns on that San Pedro dock. The apolitical man always ended in prison, cold and watching through a window at the world, at its power and largesse. He always failed to understand what had put him in that place. The inmate and his jailer were brothers.

Lindstrom stretched his hairy face with his hand, drawing skin from where it smoothed in an epicanthic fold around his eyes. As the large hanks of hair fell into the sink, he glanced at his eyes in the mirror and found an honesty there which had been hidden by the beard. This operation, unlike the others, had the power to reveal. Whatever happened, his grandfather, Burling, even Rank had led him there, but they were no mystics. They were chained in the scaffolds and altarpieces of latter-day man. Lindstrom, he was the seer: he was the cauldron of voices who could fit anywhere, the new man. He stared into his small Asian marbles of eyes and fell forever into himself. Turned a somersault into his soul and came up, wet and puffing.

His face was smooth as a baby's but for a short streak of blood at the jawline beneath his right ear. He passed his damp T-shirt over his face and stepped into the pajamas. He was reaching for the soft denim shirt when a key scratched in the lock and the doorknob turned with a click.

"Yong is ready," Xinlian said. He could tell she felt strongly about him.

"Just a minute. I want to transfer my things."

"We're next door, but please hurry. You were too long at the church. You can't be seen going into the house after dark."

As he reached down, the blood thundered in his head. He stowed the piece and the knife in the outside pocket of the briefcase and laced up his shoes. He placed the envelope of meth with the weapons, then hid the pack with his street clothes in one of the cubbies.

"You'll be taking the train tomorrow from the station outside town," Xinlian told him. "You need to be in Shanghai by Tuesday morning."

"That's almost six hundred miles," Lindstrom said. "What if we run into trouble?"

"We've given Yong all the details," she told him. "Other than that, you will be on your own."

At the end of the hall, white shapes in squeaky shoes moved through the swinging doors. The room he entered next door was an infirmary, devoid of patients. To the left stood a white wooden table, two chairs, and a long row of high metal beds. In the far corner, three screens of white cloth formed a single private area. Bars protected the windows on the outside, and the hard sun in the courtyard cast a legion of striped parallelograms onto the cracked green linoleum floor. The man with the herbs passed outside without a sound, head bowed like a monk going to prayer, his shadow slim and translucent as it moved across the beds. It bent for a moment, as if reading at the table, before it was gone. On the table was a Bible bound in grained black morocco. A red ribbon marked the final page of the Old Testament.

"A real cliff-hanger," a voice said in English, then giggled like a child.

Lindstrom started. A shadow moved across the screens in the corner, and a small man stood next to them. He giggled more, but the hilarity had already passed. "I am Yong Beihong. Please." He hurried up the aisle in his hospital gown, bare feet slapping the tiles, and took Lindstrom's hand, shaking it vigorously before letting go. He closed the Bible in embarrassment.

"Refinery fire," Lindstrom said.

"You know the Bible, John?"

"Sometimes I feel like I'm in it."

"Yes," Yong said, cradling the book to his chest. "Yes." He smiled a wan, close-lipped smile. "But now I must finish dressing."

Lindstrom watched him walk, bent with his burden, across the canted rectangles of sun. Only in that gray slanting light did he realize that Yong was the man he had seen in the church.

A PHONE ON THE RICKETY TABLE IN THE CORNER OF THE makeshift operations room rang, and Feng, the Manchu who had driven the general's Toyota, put his smoldering Kingston aside and picked up the receiver. As the caller disgorged his information through the scrambler, Feng wrote a series of characters in his notebook in what Li, who had risen from his own table and hurried down the narrow room, considered a sloppy hand. Beside the notebook lay an open catalogue of accessories for cars.

When Feng had put down the phone, he made a few quick changes to his notes, ripped the page out, and handed it to Li, who read with a smile spreading slowly on his face.

"Find out how soon we can get to Nanjing." In Feng's presence, he tried to control his elation. "I'll be with the general."

Feng reached over and picked up the phone. "I think there's a transport late this evening," he said.

On his way down the corridor, Li caught a glimpse of the room where General Zu's windy conference on the military history of China would meet again after lunch. Before each place at the long table a small replica of a terracotta warrior had been placed. The scholars had retired to another building for their meal, but the general ate alone in the small official dining room at the end of the hall. An archer figure the color of verdigris crouched beside his plate. He must have carried it there, Li thought, like a boy playing war in the dirt. He placed the notebook page beside the archer and studied the general's face. As usual during these conferences, the Big Fish was in a pensive, blustery mood, as if he were commanding lost armies in his head.

"What is this?" he said, rapping the paper with his knuckles.

"Considerable fortune," Li answered. "If I may?"

The general made a sweeping motion with his fingers toward the turntable, and Li helped himself to the steaming bowls of food. "The man who visited Charlotte Brien at the Black Cat Lounge passed through customs in Beijing yesterday morning," he recited, spooning noodles onto a plate. "He was the only American en route to Nanjing. Shortly after arriving, he checked in to the Jingling under the name on his passport." Li leaned toward the paper and read upside down. "John Tan. After digging, Washington seems to think this Tan does not exist."

Li shoveled the chopsticks toward his mouth as the general looked up from his tea. "How do they know this?"

"Like the McDonald's," Li said, noodles slapping his chin, "the American government is open for twenty-four hours."

The general's eyes sagged, and a huge hand flew out from nowhere, knocking the chopsticks, the noodles and meat from in front of Li's chin. They landed with a clatter in the corner of the room. "I am not such an old fool," said the general through his teeth, "that you can toy with me like this. I will have you back in Lhasa in a week."

Li's hand stung as if a set of talons had punctured his skin. The shaven hair prickled on the back of his neck. His wife said that he baited the general to stir his own blood, but what she didn't understand was that the old man's wrath, as well as his kindness, had given Li a vision of his country's virtuous future.

The general was carefully righting the archer on the tablecloth. It was cruel that the conduit for glory had to flow through such a foolish old man. "Tell me how they found out," he said, steadying the figure on its small clay feet. The general's moods were like weather up on the plateau: the wildest storm could stampede across the land and leave a mild, bleating day in its wake. "Tell me, Li."

"As I meant to say, General, it was quite routine." Tears stung Li's eyes, but he blinked them away. "Tan's name was just placed on a list of stolen passports. It seems the Americans actually requested our *help* in locating him."

"We are engaged," the general said distantly.

"Sir?"

The boughs of a pine tree rose and swooned outside the windows on the early evening breeze. The air in the room was muggy and stale with the smell of dirty dishwater and hot steeping tea, but the general's voice seemed caught by the rushing outside. He turned his big head slowly and looked Li squarely in the eyes. "You have no notion yet of the workings, the art of intelligence. Some day you should sit in on one of these meetings for which you affect to have no time."

Li dropped his eyes to the unfinished food. The noodles were congealing in oil, and he found their patterns disgusting, like the entrails used to tell fortunes by animist priests. History was the force of destiny that Chairman Mao had written about, not some fortune-teller's version of the past. "I wish to learn," he replied.

"I knew that this smuggling business was beneath them," the general reflected. He motioned for the waiter to bring more tea, and Li accepted some for himself. "Tan, or whoever he is, has not been employed by the American services, at least not by the official ones. There is a shadow group involved, like the eunuchs who conspired against the dowager on the emperor's behalf. This unofficial group used that smuggler of drugs we just got down in Fujian, and they are likely using this fellow John Tan."

"But how do you know?" Li asked, putting the cover on his teacup.

"Call it conjecture. I want Washington station to move heaven and earth to find out who Tan is, and why they would choose him."

The waiter cleared Li's plate, and he breathed a sigh of relief. A spot remained on the cloth, and he picked at it. "Where is Tan now?" asked the general.

"He never returned to his room in the Jingling. In anticipation of the event that Washington cannot find out who he is, I believe I should go to Nanjing, to question this professor, Rank."

The general looked suddenly tired, his skin bruised with dark gray shadows. After a minute had passed, Li said, "General?"

"Yes, yes. Of course you'll proceed," said Zu, waving his hand in dismissal.

"That will be all, then, sir?"

Li Xin had not touched his tea. He jiggled his leg with the impatience of the young, and Zu Dongren saw a casualty standing before him.

"This Tan," the old general warned, "may have training," but the young man seemed not to hear him. Zu fingered the holes in the archer's clenched hands where his bow had once been. He roughed his thumb across the breastplate. "Did you know that the general who was buried in this tomb at Xian loved his soldiers and believed they would guard him in the afterlife?"

From the diffident expression on his face, Li clearly thought that the afterlife was just a palliative. "So I have heard, General."

"Well? Do you believe it? Speak truthfully, Li."

Li breathed in and clasped his hands behind his back like a wet-ear under inspection. "I believe that a general loves his men," he replied. "And I have seen, from the faces on these figures, that these men loved their general. But as I understand it, sir, the warlord who ordered this tomb built was more concerned with protecting his position in the present life than any so-called life after death. He was more intent on exploiting the farmers to glean food for his table, sons for his army, women for his bed." The dedicated ones were always such prudes. "Wasn't the field of warriors discovered by a poor peasant digging a well?"

Zu Dongren squeezed the archer in his fist. "This man unified China," he thundered, pounding the figure against the table. "If we allow more foreign things into our culture, they will be like water running through cracks in a stone. Winter comes, the water turns to ice, and the stone flies apart."

"Only strength can make rock," Li replied, and Zu Dongren saw the dampness of respect in his eyes.

"Strength is one thing," Zu told him, "love and wisdom are others. Wisdom sees the cracks that are already there; it knows that strength can only partially close them. The water is still there deep inside, and it requires warmth to stave off destruction. Be circumspect with this professor, Li Xin."

WHEN LI'S FOOTSTEPS HAD FADED FROM THE CORRIDOR, ZU heaved himself up and, taking the archer in his hand, walked slowly and painfully across the black-and-white tiles of the hallway to the long room where the conference would soon reconvene. He sat in his chair at the head of the table and gazed over the field of greenish figures: archers, foot soldiers, charioteers. He closed his eyes and imagined the whole field of battle. Each face was different as it flashed behind his eyelids, only now the faces weren't of warriors but of children, girls and boys ranked before him dancing suggestively in a way that made his inner being feel like a void.

Come make love, said the girls. We are soft and alive.

Come debate, said the boys. We are young and strong and we know what is right for our country.

Come kill us all. We are dangerous because we might wake you from the slumber of history.

His loins hung dead in his pants. From the end of the building came a footstep on the stair, a door closed with an echo, and Zu slicked back his hair.

What did they know of history, these children? Had they ever looked into Lenin's startling eyes? Had they ever seen the grace in Mao's visage?

When the scholars returned, they would continue to trace the times in Chinese history when force had been necessary to keep the state whole. Nearly all of them, in the undulant flight of their lifetimes, had known the pain of disgrace and restoration. Zu himself had suffered: his Number Two Brother had escaped in the forties to Hong Kong, where he was now a shipping magnate, and his family had been persecuted because of it. Their hardship had stiffened Zu's public resolve, but recently, in private, he had begun to fear that devils, set loose from the souls of the young men and women he had killed, were tormenting him and his family. His own son was about to be indicted for embezzlement, a new crime that carried the penalty of death, if Zu did not intervene.

Many footsteps sounded now in the hallway, like the clatter of marching, and one set of feet stepped more quickly than the others, like an adjutant rushing to the fore. Zu remembered the sound of a charge, exhilaration and fear when you could not yet see the advancing army behind a hill. He readied an anecdote from Korea with which to begin the afternoon plenary. When the first scholar's face appeared in the doorway, Zu saw that his purple lips were sated and dry and the scholar's weak eyes, that had never seen combat, were the color of grease. The general knew that his old soldier's story would go over well.

AFTER TWENTY-SOME HOURS ON A PLANE, GORDON MacAllister arrived at the Imperial in Tokyo late on Sunday night. He dispatched his luggage upstairs to the sixth floor and crossed the lobby to the Frank Lloyd Wright Bar, where he was glad not to find Lucius Burling, whom he knew was staying in the same hotel. Burling had likely retired early, so as to keep his virtue intact by rising at dawn. For a man who had fucked his operative's wife and nearly brought down the Agency because of it, Burling retained a surprising store of moral certitude.

The Japanese, characteristically in MacAllister's view, had torn down the original building, designed by Wright, saving only the bar, which sat like a stage set within a red marble tomb. He felt like he was entering a catacomb, in which the vaguely unsavory figures of an ancient, ingrown culture were enshrined. Behind sliding paper doors, dark-suited businessmen and exotic women leaned across rosewood tables set with glasses of whiskey. The veteran trafficker in information Adrian Fry held a vigil over one of his sweet, milky drinks at the rail.

"Great spot, this," Fry observed, looking around like a critic at the muslin and honey-colored wood as he stood to shake MacAllister's hand.

"Prairie-dog style," MacAllister told him. The scar on the side of his face was beginning to itch, a bad sign. His earlobe was on fire. "I hate the place."

Fry fondled his drink. "Really? I should think you Yanks would love such a monument to your fruited plains."

"Some plains are fruitier than others," MacAllister said sourly.

"You Americans are all too tall," Fry observed.

Like many in his profession, Adrian Fry was a scholar *manqué*: at Cambridge he'd embarked on a course in the history of art, only to find he didn't mix well with the dons. They'd rejected his common upbringing, made fun of his accent, and used him for sex. In the end, he had taken an undistinguished second in history and, after a brief stint at the Foreign Office marked by some irregularities, had descended into the outer circles of the black market in Asia, dealing first in stolen art and later in pirated movies and software. He had kept his ties open to his former employers in London, and his new position afforded a freedom of movement that Six had, in subsequent years, utilized to great advantage.

"If I had known I would find you in such an unpleasant humor, Gordon, I would have stayed in Hong Kong."

"Don't bullshit me, Adrian. You were already here. Otherwise I would have gone straight to Kowloon."

"Who told you I was in Japan?"

"It was Burling always dragged me to this burrow," MacAllister said, ignoring Fry's question as he slid arthritically onto a stool. The bartender was hovering, and he ordered a Kirin. "We used to meet here in the old days, halfway to Pakistan."

"Now, Lucius Burling is a sophisticated man, not your usual American at all."

"He's a dilettante," MacAllister said.

"Had the pleasure of his company earlier this evening, actually. Told me his father took a drawing class with Wright in Philadelphia. Lucius's father was an illustrator of children's books, you know."

"Maybe that's why he's such a goddamn romantic. Thinks this is all just tall tales."

Fry, betraying his broad, malicious humor, shot him a dubious look. "Now, Gordon, don't pretend you're not interested that your compatriot is stopping here."

MacAllister was parched from the flight and he emptied his beer at a swallow. In the mirror, he watched Fry raise his small, sad, intelligent face from his glass. The little man's curly, dyed-brown hair had begun to thin, and gray showed at the temples, which were slightly damp. While MacAllister's profession tended to view homosexuals warily, as a younger man Fry had held his cards closer than anyone, exhibiting something like nobility in his treatment of the possession of information, and MacAllister had enjoyed haggling with him.

"Burling went to bed early," Fry allowed. "What was more interesting was who dined here after him."

MacAllister hailed the barman and ordered a beer for himself and another White Russian for Fry. "I'm buying," he said.

"Queerest thing, actually. Simon was all tricked up as a World War II pilot. Safari suit and one of those veteran's caps. Nearly hid that odd scar he has on his forehead, like someone tried to fold up his face, but I'd know that bloke anywhere."

"Simon Bell?"

Fry nodded, visibly savoring MacAllister's apparent surprise. "Of course it's all to get him onto the mainland."

"Of course." MacAllister finished his second beer. He would let Fry run with the bit a little, see if he knew anything more. Simon Bell trying to get himself into China was a disturbing turn. If the operation was going right, Bell should never have had to leave home. When bad history, politics, or simple circumstance forced you into hiring freelance—even freelance with whom you knew the right buttons to push—you always ended up with marginal characters, drunks and junkies and worse. MacAllister felt the need for something stronger. The Japanese liked scotch, but he spotted a bottle of Maker's on the top shelf behind the bar, the red wax dripping around its neck. He motioned for the barman to bring it. "Any idea who might be behind our friend Simon?"

Fry's hand trembled slightly as he put his glass down in a circle of light. It occurred to MacAllister that Fry might be scared. "I would have thought it was you lot."

"Not one of the twelve steps," MacAllister said.

"Then the bloke you want would be Teddy St. John." Fry pronounced it as "Sinjun." "Wife's family's been on the island for absolute eons, but their money's run out. Lately, Teddy's been expanding his business in the spirit of the day; word is he might be horning in where competition isn't wanted."

"Triads?"

Fry pantomimed a mannered applause. "Biggest smuggler of anything—drugs, software, people, you name it—on Hong Kong is a man called Henry Sun. He may have a suite at the Regency and a big estate in Paradise Bay, but the chap is nothing but a gangster at base."

"What's he got to do with Teddy St. John?"

"Just a few days ago, I heard that one of Teddy's captains was nicked off Fujian by some state security nasties. Tortured him somewhere then took him out to shoot."

MacAllister frowned. The whiskey churned in his stomach. "Where can I locate this St. John fellow?"

"You'll never find Teddy yourself. He's got an office for the investors downtown, very posh, and an air cargo hangar that's legit."

"Where's the other place, the one that's not so legit?"

"One of the outlying islands, I can't recall which."

"Sure you can't. Where will I find him tomorrow afternoon?"

"I hadn't planned to leave until Friday," Fry began, looking up at the ceiling as if he were counting.

"I don't need a guide. I can't get onto the mainland myself, but I need to nip this smuggling thing in the bud. Tell me where to find Teddy on a Monday."

Fry shook his curly head. "Unlike our friend Burling, St. John is not a creature of habit. Too dangerous to be. And you'll never find the place yourself without making a lot of mess. This is not the Cold War, all bugs in the bedroom and poison umbrellas. It's family over here, corrupted flesh—brothers, wives, lovers. Fathers and sons."

"*These from the land of Sinim*," MacAllister said.

For once, Fry looked utterly baffled.

"It's what they called China in biblical times. Isaiah prophesied that men from all corners of the earth would be called home to roost there, when the Son of God came."

"Stop. You're giving me the willies," Fry said.

The barman was standing before them in a white shirt and dark tie, his hands behind his back. "I'll take that bottle to my room," MacAllister told him, handing over his chit. The barman opened the leather bill folder and saw the cash on top of the credit card slip. "A man dined here this evening, wearing a blue baseball cap with gold lettering. Any chance you remember the room?"

The bartender separated the customer copy and wrote three characters in the space reserved for room charges. MacAllister raised his bifocals from the string around his neck and squinted at the numbers.

"*Domo arigato*," MacAllister said, committing Bell's room number to memory. "Adrian, I'll see you in the morning. Breakfast at six."

"God," said Fry. "That's uncivilized, even for you."

WITH HIS BOTTLE IN HAND, MACALLISTER TOOK THE elevator to the sixth floor, then walked up two flights more, the pain in his leg growing more pronounced with each landing. From the hallway, he could hear the TV going inside the room. It took Simon Bell several loud knocks to answer. When he saw who was standing in the hall, he tried to wedge his foot against the door but MacAllister pushed it aside. Bell staggered backward into the bathroom.

MacAllister closed the door behind him and stood before Bell, who was cowering in his boxer shorts against the commode. "Don't jump, Simon. I just want to talk to you."

"What the hell are you doing here?"

Backing into the entry, MacAllister inspected Bell's ridiculous clothes, which were hanging in the closet beside his battered garment bag. "I could ask you the same thing. What is this, some kind of costume?"

"Just piss off, will you?"

Like everything else at the Imperial, the room itself was cramped. The decorations—textured wallpaper, sconces, woodblocks framed in bamboo—were all an innocuous beige. MacAllister took some ice from the bucket in his fist and dropped it into plastic cups. "I know you shouldn't, but will you be drinking this evening?"

Bell emerged in a robe he'd retrieved from the door. On the television an overgrown English schoolboy was dressed up in chain mail, delivering some kind of rousing speech to men arrayed in battle costume around him.

"Jesus," said MacAllister, pouring. "What sort of pornography is that?"

"It's Shakespeare," said Bell, rushing forward to click off the set.

"We happy few." MacAllister handed Bell the drink and sat in a chair with his shoes on the bedspread. "Or at least we few, if not so happy. Adrian Fry just told me something alarming."

Bell's lower lip protruded in a frown. His eyes drooped more than ever, spreading the skin on his forehead so that the crease that ran to his hairline looked as if it had been drawn in red ink. His cheeks were covered with a tracery of veins.

"Care to tell me how in hell your boys are supposed to get out," MacAllister demanded, "if their ride gets shot before they're even to Shanghai?"

"*My* boys? I don't even know this physicist chap."

"You know Lindstrom."

"Only tangentially."

MacAllister looked out the window at the madness of lights that was Tokyo. "You've made a regular specialty out of living tangentially, haven't you, Simon?"

When their eyes met again, he regretted probing so close to the source of Bell's pain. "I never should have let you use Jack for this. It's bad *juju*," MacAllister added in a conciliatory tone.

"Give over, will you, Gordon? That poor captain getting nipped by the Chinky-chonks wasn't my fault. Seems this operation strayed onto someone's turf."

"You're supposed to be an expert."

"That was twenty years ago. It's a gang war over here now. Can't tell the criminals from the entrepreneurs or the government from the army from the mob. Try to untangle who's married to whose brother, and why one unit of the PLA is competing against another to set the price of eggs? It's like a bloodless civil war. You wipe out the bad guys and meet your own brother coming 'round the corner."

"You've been watching too many dirty movies," said MacAllister, biting the cup as he drank. White fissures appeared in the plastic. "What's it mean for Yong Beihong?"

Bell propped up a pillow and sat down heavily on the bed. "Oh, what the hell do you care anyway? You just want to fuck it up. I know how you operate and why you're in this. You probably ratted out the captain yourself."

"Nonsense. Yong Beihong was once one of ours but then he found God, in China of all places. Quit the army and became a professor. Got mixed up at Tiananmen so State Security put him in jail. Then he disappears for a few years. Who knows where he was."

"I'll bet you have a theory or two."

"Now he wants to defect."

"He's seeking asylum," Bell said in a tone of reproach.

"He's shopping nuclear secrets, or threatening to. When did you get so soft?"

Bell appeared to deflate. Seeing his chance, MacAllister swung his feet down off the bed and leaned forward. "Do you want to be responsible," he said, "for al-Qaeda or the Taliban getting their hands on a dirty bomb?"

Bell fortified himself by draining his cup. "Aren't they the same thing?"

"Not exactly. The Taliban's just a bunch of Afghan rednecks gone mad on the sharia law. Al-Qaeda's a different matter."

"You should know," Bell said. Ponderously, he rose and walked to the table, bare feet slapping the carpet, and helped himself to the bottle again, grabbing it roughly by the neck. Even in him, the rate of drinking was worrisome. He seemed at war with himself. "Another?" he asked.

MacAllister held out his cup.

"Jesus, Gordon. You've crushed this damn thing. I'll get us a glass."

"Don't get any ideas of going somewhere."

"Why would I do that?" said Bell from the bathroom. "You're not going to kill me, are you?"

"What would make you think that?" MacAllister planted his feet on the carpet. His bad leg was going to sleep. "You work for me and I need you in Shanghai tomorrow, Tuesday latest."

"*You work for me,*" Bell said, shaking his head. The glass looked small in his fat, be-ringed hand. His impression of the southern American accent was disarmingly good. "Such a fucking American."

"Who else should I be?"

"Christ," Bell said, dropping ice in the glass. "Has it ever occurred to you that we've been dealing with shit like this for a century? Now it happens to you Yanks, and your rage is so fresh!"

MacAllister was taken aback by the strength of Bell's anger. The Englishman's posture began to worry him. "Do you have a problem with this, Simon?"

"Attacks on the 'homeland,' as your people so quaintly describe it. Ever hear of the Blitz? My mother was killed in it, you know. Watched her get crushed by a porcelain sink that fell through from the flat two flights above."

"I will give Yong Beihong asylum," MacAllister told him. Such a display of emotion alarmed him. "What else do you want?"

Bell sniffed and let the liquor come up to the rim. At the last moment, he tipped the bottle back and regarded MacAllister. His eyes were bloodshot and red-rimmed, and MacAllister caught a furtive twitch in the lids.

"I'm going in tomorrow," Bell said evasively, handing over the glass. His heart beat close to the skin of his slack, hairless chest.

He looked close to collapse. "Mouth of the fucking dragon. These Orientals hurt me before, and I'm not a hundred percent I'll come out this time, not sure I even want to."

"I understand that," MacAllister said, relieved that all Bell needed was a handler's pep talk, a sort of Henry V speech for the twenty-first-century spy. "Honestly I do. But we're talking about a man's life."

Bell squinted at him and coughed, or maybe he was stifling a laugh. He poured a measure in his own plastic cup, without ice.

"Maybe a lot of lives," MacAllister added, drinking deeply from his own glass.

Bell downed the drink, and it seemed to revive him. "The mills of the gods grind slowly, but they grind exceedingly fine," he said.

"How's that?"

"I talked to the smuggler this evening," Bell announced, apparently pleased with himself.

"St. John."

Bell nodded. "He's got a ship leaving Shanghai early Friday morning, stopping over in Hong Kong. One of the crewmen can get Yong and Lindstrom off when it docks, take them to Teddy's place in the outlying islands. They can fly out the next day in Teddy's cargo plane."

MacAllister made his bourbon swirl in the cup. He realized he hadn't eaten since Los Angeles, and the liquor was making him dog-tired. "You can get word to Yong?"

"I believe I can make it to Shanghai to pass it on by Tuesday night, that is unless the Chinky-chonks trip me up somehow."

"They might well," MacAllister said. The top of his head felt dead, like a great black cloud was blotting out thought. Holy shit, it occurred to him.

"You don't think we could let Burling in?" Bell said.

"Burling can't be trusted. Simon, what have you done to me?"

"Don't worry, I'm no Hamlet," said Bell, his wide, glistening face appearing close to MacAllister's eyes. "It's not poison."

He could barely keep them open as Bell relieved him of the Beretta in his sock, intoning quietly:

Be not too tame neither, but let your own discretion be your tutor: suit the action to the word, the word to the action; with this special observation, that you not o'erstep the modesty of nature: for any thing so o'erdone is from the purpose of playing, whose end, both at the first and now, was and is, to hold, as 'twere, the mirror up to nature; to show virtue her own feature, scorn her own image, and the very age and body of the time his form and pressure.

"You're insane," MacAllister managed. It was not an insult, rather a statement of fact.

"I might just have to recruit old Lucius in spite of himself," said Bell.

"Can't be trusted. Man doesn't know his own mind," MacAllister said, as his own drifted away.

"That's what scares me about you," Bell said, lifting his legs kindly onto the bed and placing a pillow behind the barely conscious man's head. "You're so sure that you do."

WHEN FENG HAD DROPPED HIM OFF, ZU DONGREN rode the squeaking, cranky lift to his apartment. The long hallway smelled of old dinners, diapers, and soap. A television played loudly through his neighbor's flimsy door. As a general, he had the best apartment in the building, top floor with a narrow terrace running the length of one end. Inside, he left the lights off, feeling the empty stare of the glass doors in the living room before him as he hung his raincoat neatly in the closet. He had left the sliding door cracked, and his wife's cat slipped in, mewling, rubbing against his legs as he sat on a low stool and pried off his shoes. He fixed himself a generous brandy at the kitchen counter, and she followed him into the bedroom on her tiny stocking feet, jumped up on the quilted silk spread, embroidered with cranes, and kneaded her claws with a catching sound like her dead mistress breaking thread. Zu put the brandy down on the vanity, where a copy of the little red book of Mao's quotations sat vainly, like a decorator's prop. He pushed the cat onto the floor and opened the nightstand.

In its scented wood drawer lay his pistol, his black zippered purse of hypodermics and serum that he called his truth kit, some loose change and keys. He pinched up one of the keys with his stiff fingers and bore it across the room to the wardrobe, where he unlocked a carved chest in the bottom below his suits. His escape box. From it he removed a cell phone and a folded piece of stationery, the watermarked crest of a Hong Kong hotel showing through the cotton paper. The cat was on the bed again, but he heard its paws thump the floor as he replaced the chest and key and took phone, paper, and brandy to the terrace.

Although the night was humid and mild, the cement floor of the terrace was cold; the damp soaked through his socks at once. Standing at the railing, Zu shivered and took a healthy drink to warm himself. He was already drunk from the banquet that had concluded his conference, and the city's amber lights seemed to swarm beneath his feet. The scholars who had come to his conference did not really respect him, he knew, any more than he respected them. They didn't care what General Zu Dongren thought of history; they only came to curry favor with a powerful man, and only slightly less so for the food and drink. Well, who cared? It was a perquisite of his position, for which he had sacrificed much, to indulge himself in these pseudointellectual pursuits. A long-forgotten scent of flowering trees wafted softly past his nose, but he couldn't bring the name to mind, nor the last place he had smelled it. His brother might remember: Lizhi had always had that sense. Or was that only what they'd always been told? It was futile trying to isolate the nature from the cause. In the airy house in Shanghai, courtyards ringing with the sound of dripping water, shuffling feet—grunt, grunt, *ayee!*—doing martial arts while his brother wandered by, his nose in a poetry book, whistling opera off-key. The order in which we were born, Zu thought; Father never thought to know us, to see that I was clumsy, brimming with ideas, or that my brother had a wicked head for numbers, and a tin ear. He took another gulp of brandy; it burned a hot trail to his stomach.

With trembling fingers, Zu unfolded the paper, and a matchbook slid and smacked the wet cement. Happy Valley—a racetrack! Tiny hooves beat in his chest as he bent to pick it up, opened the cover, and struck a match to read the number written in his own crabbed hand. The cat bathed loudly on the chaise, licking and scratching, and the face of the cell phone lit up at Zu's touch as he punched the white buttons uncertainly.

"Henry Sun, *m-goy*," he said in Cantonese. One of his brother's whores had answered. Henry's wife, or so Zu had read in the tabloids, had moved rather permanently to their house in Bermuda.

"Yes. Sun here," his brother said in his false English accent.

"Lizhi? *Nay sik-jaw faan may?*" Have you had your meal yet? It was what they used to whisper through the ghostly brothel screens.

His brother made a noise like someone had punched him. "Bloody . . . Get me a scotch, darling. No, no. The Glenlivet. Number One Brother? I thought you might be the police."

"*Ngaw hok*," said Zu. I am.

His brother laughed, and Zu heard that he was drunk. Five years before, when the Return had taken place, giving Hong Kong back to its rightful owner, Zu had thought that his brother might be picked to run the Island, but that hope had faded quickly.

"Dongren," his brother said. "Can't you speak English anymore? *Ying-gwok wa?* Brother Hughes would surely condemn it."

"Am I an Englishman, Number Two Brother?"

Brother Hughes had been their Methodist teacher, killed in '49. He had given them English names—Donald and Henry—as was the custom then.

"You make as if forgetting your English is a part of your loyalty to them," said Lizhi, "but I know it's only part of your game. You can speak it as well as I can, probably better. People tell me I sound like an American now. *Gay ho ma*, anyhow?"

"The same, Lizhi. Always the same."

"We haven't spoken in four years. How can you be the same? I cannot even say that nothing ever changes over there now, can I? With your new Mr. Nobody running the show?"

"It's how it is. *Taai-taai* is dead."

Zu's brother was silent. The cat paused from her washing; hearing the name of her mistress, she slid her paw down from her forehead, her yellow eyes flashed. "*Du bu qi,*" said Zu's brother in Mandarin.

"It's all right," Zu said. "Anyhow, I am calling on her behalf."

"You're right. Things don't change over there," said Lizhi bitterly. It was Zu's wife who had shamed Zu into calling his brother from time to time, until she got sick and couldn't remember to nag him anymore.

Zu waved at the cat to go back to her washing, stop staring at him. He took up his drink from the railing. The lights of the city made a lozenge-shaped gem in the bottom of the glass. In the middle of the glossy pill floated a tiny black temple, like an insect in amber, a shadowbox version of the Drum Tower leaning above the old houses several blocks away. "I'm calling about her son," he said, swallowing the tower with the booze.

"*Your* son, you mean."

"I have a proposition. This is business, understand."

"Oh, I understand." Zu heard the woman whisper in the background. "I understand and I am . . . well, I'm glad to have you speak to me as if we were on the same level. The way we used to when we went out on the town."

"Yes. I do remember that, but we were boys then."

"Your son is still a boy."

"*Bu!*"

No! he thought. The glass exploded on the floor. The cat disappeared before Zu even knew that he had called out in anger; the only sign of her leaving was the door curtain shrugging slowly back to the carpet. A trail of tiny shards led from his socks to the door.

"He is not a boy anymore," he yelled, panting. "He is a man and must be treated like a man!"

"If that's the case," said Lizhi, "what are you talking to me for?"

"I told you, *Taai-taai* is talking. Tonight it is I who am dead."

"Death-in-life, the life-in-death. Take your pick, but I'm not betting. Everyone in Hong Kong knows that dead men tell no tales. If I'm going to help your . . ." Lizhi's voice trembled with anger. "No, no, pardon me—*Taai-taai*'s boy then you've got to give me something in trade."

"*Deem-yeong?*"

"How, Dongren? How do I know? Don't be so prudish. *Taai-taai*'s boy has crossed to this side of the water, and when they do that, I know about it. You want me to smuggle the boy out? It is no problem. He can be at my house in Hamilton the end of the week. It is already done."

"I want to give you something," said Zu.

"You'll owe me."

"No." The cat peeked through the open door, took one tentative step toward the sparkling cement, paw twitching. "I have something for you."

"You don't want a man in the world, not even your brother, to hold any markers on you, do you? I must admire that, even if you are still a Donkey. If that place were run by men like you, even I might come home."

"Heaven help you, Number Two Brother. There is a company, run by an associate of yours, who is taking your business. We apprehended one of their number coming into Fujian, to pick up a load of fugitives along with whatever else it is you sell."

"He's dead now, the captain?"

"*Shi.*"

"Pity."

"It wouldn't have been wise. To keep him alive. The name he gave us was that of St. John."

Zu almost enjoyed Henry's stunned silence on the other end of the line. Then his brother's laughter, amplified by the phone, froze the frightened cat in her tracks. Her ears folded back against her skull, and for the first time she seemed to see the razor-sharp pieces around her. Zu took a step to help her and remembered that he didn't have his shoes on.

"Teddy? What a bloody dog he is. After all I've done for him, you say he's barging in on my business?"

"He's done some things for you, too, Lizhi."

"With your help."

"This was a small boat, Brother. One man. He told my associate that he set off from one of the outlying islands. Hong Kong, but he did not tell us which one."

"Before he went to meet Marx?"

"Do not tease me," Zu said. He was five feet from the cat, with crunching glass beneath the ball of his foot. "In my old age, I have become immune to pain. My life has inoculated me against it."

"Some herbalist must have cheated you. No man is free of pain."

"My son," said Zu, reaching out for the cat. A sliver went into his big toe.

"Your son is safe with me," said Lizhi. "I only wish his father were."

"Don't get too big for your shoes," Zu said. "It's not your place to worry."

"Donkey?"

"Yes?" Zu's fingers touched the silky, yellow hair beneath the cat's belly.

"Why do you want Teddy Sinjun taken out?"

The question made Zu lose his balance, and he lunged for the cat. As he fell, he felt the loose skin of her belly, scooped up in his hand, but his momentum and the reflex motion drove the same arm upward, reaching for the railing, and the cat was off the terrace, flying into the darkness below.

"Dongren? Are you all right?"

"I stumbled. Broken glass."

"We're two drunk brothers talking through the night."

"The cat."

"Comes on little cat paws and always lands on her feet."

Zu sighed. There were pine trees in the darkness, which would have confused her. "You don't understand, Lizhi. You never did."

"And you, my Number One Brother, still have a pole a meter long up your ass. Don't worry. Your little boy will be pitching a tent on Elbow Beach this next weekend, getting his fill of black girls, and Teddy Sinjun, well . . . yellow dogs never land on their feet. When I find him, whatever he's into, he'll end up in the gutter, along with any of his friends stupid enough to take tea with old Teddy of a Monday. Good night, Donkey. I hope we'll talk again."

Putting the phone down on the chaise, the cushion of which was still warm and depressed from the cat, Zu pulled himself up on the railing and peered into the dark, which seemed to pop with molecular flashes. At night, at the beach off Fujian, the phosphorus glowed when you stepped in the ocean. The air beyond his terrace seemed buoyant, seductive; the branches of the pines floated gently like fans. Minutes later, he found himself among them. He couldn't remember riding down. He was swiping through the branches, cell phone still in one hand, calling the cat's name—Empress!—when he heard a voice behind him.

"Old man," it said. A light shined in Zu's eyes. "What are you looking for?"

A young policeman in a pleated cap.

"My cat," Zu said. "A cat belonging to my wife. It jumped from the terrace."

The light's sharp beam swiveled down to his hands.

"I was going to call my son," Zu added, "to help me, but he was not at home."

"How did you come by that?" the cop asked Zu suspiciously. His flashlight shone white on Zu's hands, which were smeared with dried blood.

"The phone?"

"Hell, no. Everyone has one of those. I meant the gash."

"I dropped a glass," said Zu. "It scared the cat. I was talking and she jumped."

A twig cracked above their heads and a sound like rain came down through the branches. A hiss like a flare shot off at Zu's shoulder and a frenzy of claws scratched down his back. The cat was off in a streak around the corner of the building.

"There, you see?" said the cop. "Cats always land on their feet. That doesn't make them more legal, however. Pets still aren't allowed inside the city limits. Is that phone licensed?"

"My wife," said General Zu.

"You don't have to explain, but you'd better get it in before morning. If you can afford to feed it, good for you, but other people aren't so lucky they can even feed themselves."

He doesn't know, thought Zu, starting toward the corner of the building where the cat had disappeared. He stopped to watch the cop swagger off toward his idling car. He doesn't know who I am.

book
two

YONG AND LINDSTROM HAD SPENT A LONG NIGHT IN A stable on the edge of Anhe. Attached by a courtyard to a gray mud-brick house, it stood at a place where the narrow lane from town dropped abruptly down a dirt bank to a thin shelf of refuse, then onto the vast, tilting paddy beyond. In the dark, moist air with the sounds of rats coming up out of the water to worry the trash and roosters crowing to a broken clock, Lindstrom began to feel like an impostor. He had spent so much energy escaping Jack Lindstrom that perhaps he'd become Johnny Tan. When the lady of the house withdrew to her family's side of the courtyard for the night, Yong read aloud from the Gospel of John, how the two disciples had found Mary by the tomb with the stone rolled back, and thought Christ's body had been stolen.

"When I used to quote this passage to the other men in prison, it often had confusing effects," Yong said, "because the families would come to take the bodies of our fellow inmates who'd been tortured to death in the fields."

A streetlamp high on a pole outside turned his bare arms the color of a bruise; the scars left by rope were dark pink around his wrists. He told stories from the end of imperial times, the proud recruits of Chiang Kai-shek in Canton, trained as well as any army in the world, and the ragged, indomitable soldiers who had followed Mao Zedong to Yan'an, to Beijing. Lindstrom hadn't slept well for three nights, and at times he would nod off, with Yong saying something about birds—grackles or starlings who arrived in the rigging of opium ships and had no natural predators in Asia. The black birds from the eaves of the church came to roost in his dreams.

When he woke, it was as if Yong had never stopped talking. "Just listen," he said. "'My hand grasps the killing power in heaven and earth. Behead the evil ones, spare the just, and ease the people's sorrow.' Who does that sound like to you?"

Lindstrom roused himself to the dry smell of chickens. The empty windows were framed with fragile light. "Chairman Mao?"

Or my Papa, he thought. When it comes to fanatics, what's the difference in creed? He could barely make out a wry shadow around Yong's sliver of a mouth.

"Wrong." His giggle was small and unsettling in the gauzy false dawn. "Hong Xuiqan. Messianic leader of the Taiping Rebellion. Younger brother to Jesus Christ. But there's a lesson in your mistake."

The lightness of his tone made Lindstrom angry. "I'm in no mood for parables, if that's what you're after."

Yong looked stunned. "Okay, John," he said quietly.

He was silent then, and the sun rose and slanted through the windows into their eyes, and the chickens trotted out among the bikes and jars in the courtyard, pecking between the cobbles. The old woman in the head scarf shooed them away as she came across with a jug of hot water for tea, and her stooped movements oppressed him with a memory he couldn't pin down. The tea was green and rotten-smelling, but it quenched his thirst surprisingly well. The room was warming, and the hot drink made them sleepy. Lindstrom unfolded the envelope of crank that he had stowed in his case and licked his finger, scooping out a few crystals and chasing them with the cold dregs of tea. His thoughts began to gather in formation under the authority of the drug, and the Bible verses Yong had read scurried about in his head. For years after his mother had left and his father had moved them up from San Diego, then gone to sea, he'd been forced to sit and listen to his grandfather in his windowless room before bed. He'd be reading *True Confessions* or *Argosy* and suddenly his grandmother would hurry in, shooing the magazines away with her hands, warning him that the men's meal was done, the big kitchen was swabbed and the door to the alley below, its asphalt gleaming with oil that reflected the neon delights of the street, was locked; his grandfather was coming up the stairs. Under the mattress went the pulp, and in the old man came, carrying his Bible and a folding chair. Thinking of it, the loneliness came back to him, and he felt the need of companionship. "My grandfather used to read the Bible to me," he told Yong.

"But you're not a believer?"

"Are you?"

"I try," Yong said. "Mostly I fail."

"Mostly I don't try," Lindstrom told him.

"Does it make you sad?"

"My grandfather made the Bible stories seem like punishments. It mostly made me angry."

"I understand," said Yong. "My stepfather the communist was like that."

"I guess that's the lesson you were talking about."

Yong smiled his diffident smile. "I'm going to sleep a while now," he said.

When Yong was snoring, Lindstrom leaned over and took up the notebook he had seen beneath Yong's Bible at the hospital. He flipped through some pages with notations in English—men who'd died, hours spent in the fields, some arcane system for keeping track of time and apportioning food. After Yong was apparently released from the work camp, however, and didn't have the daily struggle to survive, the writing became more philosophical:

I have decided to pose my own version of Pascal's wager, he wrote, *a bet with God. In jail, it was the discipline of praying, which is like meditation, that kept me alive. I had no paper and I had to memorize what I wanted to say. I built a memory temple in my head. When they took a ball-peen hammer, crushing the bones in my right foot one by one,*

I thought of the nails penetrating Christ's feet. God, my Father, I prayed, I am walking in the shadow, reveal yourself to me. But He did not. Like a father, He cut himself off. Is it possible that God was dissatisfied with His Son? Or with the church built by His disciples? Is this why He will no longer reveal His mysteries to us?

I have decided, as they say in the American movies, to take the law into my own hands. What law is that, you may ask. Whose law? Perhaps law is the wrong word. Perhaps you would prefer justice. Law is made by men, you say, and varies from country to country. The United States says it is against the law to imprison a person without charging him with some crime, to punish him in cruel and unusual ways, and yet it supports other countries who do the same things, or it looks the other way while the People's Republic of China does those things to people like me. It looks the other way so it can buy cheap trinkets or so that men like my former superior, General Zu, can help them give arms to the fighters in Afghanistan, the same ones they now want to wipe from the face of the earth. These are the wages of the laws of men. Therefore, one cannot trade one set of laws for another, China's laws for the laws of the United States or anywhere else. When a Pakistani physicist, Abdul Khan, a man like myself who was once educated and paid by his government to build the most terrible weapons the world has ever known, takes his knowledge and shares it with other countries, the world calls him a monster, but when Albert Einstein does it, he is revered, set up as the God of Princeton, New Jersey. Why should one or two countries only have this terrible knowledge? Are they the Chosen Ones, the right hands of God? I do not believe this. Justice is God's law, the law that governs not only one country, but the world. If I place myself outside the laws that separate countries, that cause men to build more and more powerful weapons of destruction, will God reveal his law to me?

Yong whimpered slightly like a dog in a dream, and Lindstrom shut the notebook and slid it quickly under the Bible. In sleep, Yong's glasses were askew and his wan skin gleamed, glossy with sweat.

Leave it to Rank: this isn't just your typical dissident who wants to get out. He wants to chase the great syncretic dream, test God to see if He will heal the schism between the two great forces at odds in the world from the beginning, Word and Thing. It was disturbingly close to certain paths of thought on which Lindstrom had once wandered, before the rehab gurus closed them off to him.

Have I been alive all these years? Lindstrom wondered, helping himself to another dose. Yong had either gone crazy in prison, or he was after something real. Lindstrom had been in his own prison, but now he was living again.

My Chinese brother, he thought.

When the sun was directly overhead, the woman came to serve them lunch. Yong awoke without a stir or a word and accepted the wet towels she gave them. He washed, shaking his head behind the cloth, and brought the cracked white bowl to where it nearly touched his chin. Then he began to ladle noodles and broth into his mouth with the spoon.

After their meal, they went out through a back door into the next street, where an earthen ramp packed by hooves inclined to a path leading eastward across the field.

WAITING AT THE CHINA AIR DESK AT NARITA MONDAY morning, watching the ticket agents go about their work, Burling was afflicted by a longing like love for a matinee actress of his youth. The painted Han women and waistcoated men seemed like members of a struggling company, come out before the performance to greet the audience, show them to their seats. But even at the sight of his green diplomatic passport, they couldn't quite keep up the show. A man whispered in the ear of the beautiful woman who was stamping his boarding pass, and she nodded brusquely as she tore off the stub. They had learned well at school, these actors in the Party's little drama, they kept up their roles, but their eyes kept sliding past him to the crowd of their countrymen returning, carts filled with TVs, refrigerators, clothing, and electric fans. The beautiful woman handed back his ticket and passport with a military flourish, but Burling thought he caught a glint of terror, and sadness, in her large, mascaraed eyes.

He paid his airport tax with the small stock of yen that he kept for the purpose and bought an overpriced stuffed Mickey Mouse for the son of his cook in Shanghai. In the duty-free area, a group of World War II veterans, hale and hearty fellows considering they must be in their eighties, fanned out among the stocked shelves of liquor and perfume. Outside the broad windows, a ground crew fueled the old Aleutian, its engines high on the tail, which with luck would return him to China. Burling ducked through a curtain into the first-class lounge, ordered a Bloody Mary and a caffeinated coffee at the bar.

Twenty years ago, after Amelia died, he and his son had taken a break here from the long flight out to Pakistan, where Luke would spend the summer with him. In Islamabad, Burling was known as the cultural attaché, touring the squalid sprawl of the city, a sunburned colonial figure pricing rugs on the banks of the wide, muddy river, haggling in the shops and the *suk*. His large figure, the full head of light hair gleaming in the sun, attracted notice, as it was meant to. In the course of his wanderings, he would meet behind the teahouses and in private homes with men from Pakistani intelligence, who were moving money and arms to the *mujahedin*. He'd brought in Jack Lindstrom to work himself into the Pashtun regions, down south near Qetta and Kandahar up to the Khyber Pass, Peshawar and Jalalabad, where some of Jack's basketball players had fled the Soviet invasion, fighting a rearguard action like the Continental Army as they retreated, shooting down Russian helicopters from their Arabian mounts. They were raising an irregular army, trained jointly by the CIA and ISI. When Jack was in town, he would stay in the spare room of Burling's apartment.

Every night they shared a magnum bottle of viscous commissary wine. Luke had never seen his father drink much before, and that seemed, to Burling's sweet, distracted son, the central ritual of their strange ménage. It was unclear to Burling how much Luke knew about April, or the horror on the airstrip near Mazar-i-Sharif, or the trouble that ensued when word of it leaked past the Agency. His attempts to broach the subject with his son were always met by a casual indifference, signified by the lock of hair that fell across Luke's forehead, fine, blond hair that seemed to grow longer and lighter with each passing day. Physically, Luke had always resembled his father, though by now Burling's sandy hair was salted with gray. Tall and skinny, but with his father's wide shoulders, Luke became all angles that summer, with biceps and pectoral muscles beginning to swell and the pitched-forward gait of a jock. Partly in rebellion, Burling believed, Luke had not taken to basketball, preferring swimming, which detached him from the world, and baseball, at which he was an average pitcher with a tendency to labor, think too much, and overwork his junk, in situations when the natural fastball that came from his height would have served him just fine. Temperamentally, he had always seemed more like his mother, oversensitive, but as they spent more time together, sharing the brooding atmosphere in the wake of April's disappearance, Burling began to wonder whether Luke's detachment was a mirror of his own.

Luke hadn't been happy to be taken away from all-star season, but with Amelia gone there was nowhere for him to stay. By the end of June, Burling had given up arguing with him or trying to jolly him out of his silences. He allowed the kid to have a glass of wine at dinner, but still their talk skipped across the surface of the trouble they shared. By ten o'clock, when the cook went home, they were still around the table, drinking sweet, silty coffee, arguing about Jimmy Carter, whom Luke and Lindstrom both thought a holy fool, listening to classical—Mozart, or Bach—or if Lindstrom had his way, Led Zeppelin or the Rolling Stones. Luke developed a liking for Jack, which Burling secretly envied. He watched for signs that Jack was leading his son on, trying to turn Luke against him, but could find none. It unnerved him when things didn't go the way he expected.

"By all rights," he told Lindstrom, "you should have killed me by now."

"Waste of energy," Jack said, leaning back with the big rounded glass in his hand. Too late, Burling remembered his son was there listening. "I can't get behind that whole revenge trip."

"I confess it's not the way I'd be," said Burling, although the whole arrangement had begun to feel oddly natural to him.

"All I want is news of April. If you can help me get that, I don't care who you are or what you've done."

"Either you're the coldest SOB I've ever met, or you're a saint."

"I love my wife, Lucius. Maybe you can't understand that."

Burling had to consider whether he could.

As the summer progressed and the wine became habitual, Burling fell back on a sort of game to try to lure Luke back from his distance. Father and son agreed tacitly that this game was preferable to the dark pit of viperous questions over which they were hovering. One morning in July, he returned to the apartment and knocked on Luke's door.

"Rise and shine," he called in his military voice. "A clue awaits you in the kitchen."

From the bedroom, he heard his son groan and his feet hit the floor.

The rug was in the kitchen, still wet from where the dealer had washed it in the river. The cook looked down at it as if it were bleeding on the tiles. She murmured something and went back to the groceries she had bought in the *suk*.

"Luke, good," Burling said, setting his coffee on the table. He went out into the living room and returned through the swinging door with the coarse Afghani carpet from the hall, throwing it down like a gauntlet beside the new rug. "Well? What do you say?"

Luke was silent, as he usually was when Lindstrom was gone. The night before, Jack had slipped out after dark, leaving the sweet smell of hashish behind him, drawn by the promise of a ride to Peshawar, maybe Jalalabad. A rumor had reached them of a band of guerrillas with a woman in their midst, who sat a horse like a man wearing clothing that more closely resembled a burnoose than a burka.

"The rug, Luke, look at the rug."

It was pink and blue with an ornate central emblem, the borders twined with light green arabesques.

"It looks like M. C. Escher."

Burling sipped at his coffee and tapped his foot. "It doesn't have people," Luke added. "Could be Islamic, a Tabriz?"

"Wrong colors," said Burling. "Too bright. No animals."

Luke sat down at the little plastic table. "May I have some coffee, please?"

"Are you sure?" Burling said, pointing at his chest. In a posting in Africa that Luke had been too young to remember, a fever had weakened his heart. Burling worried for him.

"It's only coffee," Luke said.

Burling shrugged. "You know what?"

Luke brushed the hair away from his face. He and the cook were in cahoots, and he accepted the coffee with a wink.

"I stood there watching that weaver, and darn it, there was something wrong with his rugs, with that very rug there on the floor."

"Why'd you buy it, then?"

"Number one, there was dye coming out of this rug, so it's relatively new, but we've established it's not Pakistani."

"We have?"

"Of course. So where did it come from?"

"Afghanistan? They're trading guns for rugs, now? Wait'll the American people hear this."

"You know," said Burling, suppressing a grin, "if you applied your brain to the problem and not to making jokes you might understand where I'm going with this. There was a time when a boy not much older than you might have shipped out to India to make his name figuring stuff like this out."

"Was that the same guy they chopped off his head in Bokhara?"

A stab of pride and regret caused Burling to draw an uncomfortable breath. "We've been over this before. What kind of rug does that leave?"

"Turkish? Azerbaijani? I don't have a clue."

"It's Chinese, of course!"

"Okay?"

Burling struck the table, rattling the cups. "If it's a Chinese rug, how did it get here? How in the hell did one of these merchants from Peshawar get a new Chinese rug, when there's a war going on between here and there?"

"Like I told you, he must have traded it to the *mujahedin*. You should ask Jack about it."

"The border to China is in a military district, Xinjiang," Burling explained. "It's shut up tight as a drum."

"Maybe not anymore?"

Burling raised his mug to his chin and held it there. "In the days of Marco Polo, of the Great Khan and Ulug-bek . . ." He paused to allow the sacred names to sink in. They were meant to be a happy bridge between them. In the days before Wes Godwin's death, before the coup and the Soviet invasion, they had taken their own trip to Samarkand with Jack and April Lindstrom and another family from the embassy in Kabul. It was on that trip that Burling began to look at April from the corner of his eye. Their party was accompanied by the local communist flunky to a historical site in the desert outside town. There, on the crest of a low knob of sand, Ulug-bek, descendant of Genghis Khan and grandson of Tamerlane, had built an observatory for charting the stars.

"I think Ulug-bek was gay, Dad, looking up at the stars while his grandfather's empire got crushed by the Romans or something?"

"In his day," avowed Burling, trying not to show that Luke's answer had hurt him, "why, you could have gone up to Peshawar and through the Khyber Pass. You could have gone to Samarkand, Tashkent, Urumqi, all the way to Shanghai if you wanted."

Luke looked at him over his coffee. There was something new in his face, a leanness, a cant to his head, that suggested he wasn't a boy anymore. It made Burling's throat catch to see it.

"Don't bullshit me, Dad. Is Jack going to find April up there?"

"He's got as good a chance as anyone."

"But don't you think about it? I mean, you were there when—"

"She was taken, yes." Taken. "It's like I told the president, Luke. If there was something different I could have done."

"When I was staying at the Great Spook's?" Luke inquired. "Before we came out here?"

The Great Spook was Luke's name for Gordon MacAllister, at whose farm Luke had stayed for a month after Amelia died. "Took her own life," as they said euphemistically, while Others had "taken" April.

"Yes?" said Burling. MacAllister had become another surrogate father, he thought, one too many.

"It's just that he had a Chinese guy out there, a little fat guy with a face like a goldfish. Didn't speak any English, but he brought a woman with him who did, and they said they were there to look at the Great Spook's new Japanese tractor, but it didn't seem like that was all they were talking about."

"Was his name by any chance Zu?"

"Should it be?"

Burling took a deep breath and looked directly at his son. "He was the colonel who was with me at Mazar-i-Sharif. I didn't know what had happened to him."

Luke held his gaze with a mixture of yearning and reproach, as if his father had cheated at the game of his own devising.

WHEN BURLING WALKED AN HOUR LATER WITH THE OTHER China-bound passengers across the windy runway to the plane, the beautiful woman from the ticket counter was waiting by the rolla-way stairs, her cheekbones raw from the jet wash, dark eyes watering. A futile yet powerful lust swelled inside him. He was suddenly aware of his age and yet how much the desires of his younger self could still overpower him. Had he loved April? Had he ever loved his wife? He lowered his head in shame, cradling the Mickey Mouse against his face to ward off the stinging grit.

The Aleutian resembled an awkward, ruffled pelican, hunched on the tarmac in the wind. Since he had quit the Agency, he had enjoyed flying into other countries with the knowledge that his papers were in order, he was who he said, but now he felt that this sense of identity had been one more illusion: parts of himself were scattered everywhere—Samarkand, Pakistan, Kabul, DC. Ducking to enter the cabin, he heard the World War II veterans banging up the metal stairs behind him, all eulogies and jokes. A man with a *Vanity Fair* obscuring his face was in the window seat beside his. The only thing that showed of the reader's head was a blue baseball cap with the words "HUMP PILOTS" stenciled across the crown in a military script.

That's all I need, Burling thought, reminiscences.

The flight attendant welcomed a passenger aboard, and a woman swayed toward him down the aisle, holding her carry-on bag above the seats. Burling stood aside, ducking under the luggage compartments. When she'd passed, a pair of sad eyes with liverish pouches beneath them was watching him from above the glossy edge of the magazine.

"Lucius Burling," said an exaggerated Southern voice, but Burling couldn't place the owner. He girded himself for some neo-Hemingway bullshit or right-wing political swagger. The rest of the face appeared from behind the magazine cover, which featured a woman in a red bikini holding a cigar, and slowly remade itself into a pursed and somewhat malevolent grin. "Are we neighbors?"

Reluctantly, Burling accepted a flimsy, damp shake. "Simon," he said without enthusiasm. "What's happened to your voice?"

Simon Bell let go of his hand and wiped both palms on the legs of his golf slacks. He looked over the empty compartment with irises the color of eggs.

"Come on, Lucius," Bell said in his ludicrous cracker accent. "Give us a break."

"Cut that out," Burling told him.

Bell grabbed his shoulder with a surprising store of strength and yanked Burling, who was caught by surprise, down into the neighboring seat. After Amelia's death, a brief period had followed in which Simon went totally haywire: he was at his father's house in Costa Rica playing Robert Graves with the wife of a Nicaraguan official with ties to the drug trade; he had just arrived in Aquaba when a tanker blew up. Centrifuges from Holland disappeared from the harbor the following day, and insiders suspected he was working for Mossad against Iran. Then one day he disappeared without a trace from the King David Hotel in Jerusalem, and it was assumed that Six had brought him quietly in. A year later he turned up in Washington as some sort of attaché, wearing a chastened and furtive expression. Burling didn't install him in the carriage house again. Six years later, when Iran-Contra broke, there was quiet speculation that Bell had been a damaged cog in North's proverbial warped set of wheels.

"Be a sport," Bell hissed imploringly. The hair sticking out below the cap was dyed an artificial strawberry blond, which could not possibly still be his natural color anymore—a costume, Burling thought.

"What are you doing here, anyway, Simon? Still playing the fool?"

Bell put down his magazine and swallowed painfully, one hand on his heart. "A matter of some importance," he said, burping silently, "that you don't take me lightly."

"Oh, my goodness." Burling's eyes slid past him in despair. If the Great Spook MacAllister wanted to remind him that someone was watching, who better than Bell—who had nearly moved into his house, his wife's bed, and, like Jack, briefly taken his place with his son—to remind Burling that he could be vulnerable, too.

"Are you threatening me, Simon? Is that what this is about, a little message from our sponsor not to mess around in his sandbox? You know, it's funny, I'd thought your threatening days were over and you were happy at FSI. A friend of mine there says you teach a rather colorful class on the Philby affair. Sorry I haven't had the chance to sit in."

"I quit that months ago," Bell said, watching the last few passengers file toward the back of the plane. His eyes had a moist, confiding sheen. "I was suffocating, Lucius."

"I understand," said Burling quietly, squirming in his seat. Better to draw Bell out, humor him. Once upon a time he had wept real tears before this man. "But sometimes I think I might be happier there myself. Maybe SAIS or Georgetown. A class on something theoretical. My path out here began in study, you know."

A smile spread slowly across Bell's face, bringing with it a candor that was awful to behold. "I can fancy you a professor," he said, "but I wasn't cut out for it. When they found out what I'd done in the field, they started talking about me."

Uh-oh, Burling thought.

The door closed and there was an announcement in Mandarin which, roughly translated, said, "We will take off now," and the Aleutian commenced an alarmingly long, shuddering run before it lifted over the canals and striped industrial towers of Tokyo. The plane banked through a wave of muddy cloud, and the bright white lights of factories glowed like phosphorus among the flooded paddies below.

"What exactly did they say?"

"Oh, the usual lies. I'd been turned by the Israelis or some such rot. Buggered by Oliver North. Then an old friend came to see me." Bell smiled and his finger wagged gaily. "Don't even bother trying to figure out who."

"Simon, listen to me. If you're about to go off on some maverick crusade of your own design, I don't even want to be talking to you."

Bell leaned in and whispered to him greedily: "My employers are not mavericks, Lucius, they're prominent men."

"What's with the accent, then, this ridiculous Hump Pilots thing?"

"Vinegar Joe," Bell announced, rearing back toward the wall of the cabin. A manic integrity invested his frame. "Stilwell. The flight over the mountains from India to Guilin. We helped Chiang Kai-shek tie down millions of the best Jap troops, and our only supply line was over the goddamn Himalayas, tallest mountains in the world."

"I remember it well," Burling said, "but I was eight, ten years old, same as you. I heard about it on the newsreels at the movies."

Bell appeared a bit miffed. His melancholy returned. The stewardess came down the aisle, and Burling ordered a Bloody Mary and coffee.

"Just coffee for me," Bell said.

"I'll level with you," Burling told him. "Before I left Washington, I had a meeting with an old friend. Luke used to call him the Great Spook, or GS for short, as I'm sure you'll remember from your days at our house. I'm wondering if he might be one of the prominent men you say have employed you?"

Simon's eyes shifted away. Below the wing lay a misty country, shades of brown and dark green, and in the towns punctuations of neon.

"Because he said," Burling added, "the GS, how did he put it? That when you hire outside help, you may have to deal with a lower sort, cowboys, loose cannons, the semiretired."

Bell retreated into his mad self-importance and tried to look hurt. He removed his hat and smoothed back the dyed, thinning hair with his palm. The crease from the Burmese bullet, an accident apparently while SLORC was pistol-whipping him, showed white in the unhealthy pallor of his forehead. "In the beginning, Lucius? I was just a consultant on this."

"A pathetic old mole is what you were. Our friend called you up, didn't he? Asked you to penetrate this group, just as a favor to pay for your sinecure. Most of them are probably British, old Hong Kong types or OVC. So you felt an affinity with them, a certain nostalgia for the bad old days. You reported back, no harm done. Now it's gotten beyond you."

Bell was silent. His eyes darting guiltily from side to side, he added two plastic jiggers of milk and three packets of sugar to his coffee and leaned in conspiratorially, stirring. Burling dripped a few drops of half-and-half into his own cup and emptied the miniature vodka bottle into some watery tomato juice.

"That's why I'm here, Lucius. And it's why I needed to talk to you. The friend we spoke of is out of control. Now he wants to take out the same man whom I was brought in to save."

"How do you know it wasn't always like that, Simon? The friend we're speaking of doesn't tend to change his mind. As far as he's concerned, everything is black and white, good and evil. It might as well be 1962."

"Don't try to make me stupid, Lucius. That worked with Amelia to keep her in the dark, but I've been around the world a time or two."

"Amelia went around the world herself, with me," Burling reminded him, but he was only buying time. The implication made his stomach burn with barely controlled shame and despair. "She didn't like it as much as she thought she would."

"A wonderful woman, Lucius, don't you forget that."

Burling tried to reach back for an image of her as his young wife, her brown hair styled like Jacqueline Kennedy, topped with a dainty yellow hat with a pin and square of lace. She smiled with a smug mischief that said she was up to no good, which he knew at the time that she could be, doling out a string of little secrets and favors that he had never imagined a woman would give him. Had he really demeaned her, as Bell said?

"She let us down," was all he could muster in response.

"I want you to know something, Lucius. I know this is awkward. Amie and I never slept together—a kiss maybe, once or twice, a touch. Not like you and April. Amelia may have wanted more, but she was too much of a lady to say, and I was too timid to take her up on the yearning in those eyes."

"That's just a fantasy, like one of your plays."

"If it pleases you to think so."

"We were the last of the good children, Simon. Maybe it was a cage, or maybe it was how it should be. All I know is that the rules changed and we didn't know what to do. Now we have the world that we have because of it."

"Maybe, maybe not. All I was going to say is that I'm doing this in honor of her. You and the Great Spook are not going to turn my last chance at redemption into your own little revenge drama."

"It seems like you might be doing that yourself," said Burling, beginning to see the picture. Bell had lured him into self-reflection, the past tense, but he needed to stick to the present. "What do you know that I don't?"

"The GS, as you call him, had an appointment to keep this afternoon in Hong Kong, but he is indisposed . . ."

"You mean?"

"Sleeping off a big dose of K back at the Imperial. You and Adrian are going to keep his appointment for him."

"Fry? I'm not going to have anything to do with that crook."

"Listen, Lucius. The GS set it up so that the package arriving from the mainland would be taken to the outlying islands, where it was supposed to be transported by plane to safe haven. According to Adrian, however, that plane was never going to leave. He can bring you up to speed on the way out from Kowloon, but basically the Great Spook, or something worse, was going to be waiting for them."

"Them?" Burling lowered his voice to a whisper. "You mean 'him,' Yong Beihong."

Bell shifted his weight backward in the seat and slowly looked away. Through the window rolled the green-black hills of North Korea, cloudy fingers of land pointing into the sea.

"Simon?"

Bell turned to face him again; the sad eyes seemed to have retreated deep into their sockets.

"Is there a character I don't know about?"

"It's not what you think, Lucius. Honestly. They just needed a good exfiltration man."

"Who did?"

"MacAllister, of course."

"Shhht!"

"Lindstrom wasn't my idea, I swear it. I don't even know the man."

Burling felt as if he'd been punched in the gut. His head swam, and the sea of clouds outside the tiny window seemed to rush at him, pink and soft and yet in their beauty somehow menacing, absolutely meaningless but shot with celestial light. "The hell you don't."

"Only by implication, Lucius. Only through you."

"Excuse me, Simon."

Trembling, Burling got up and, head ducking, weaved toward the bathroom at the rear of the plane, beads of sweat popping out on his forehead.

"Sir," the stewardess said in alarm.

"A minute, please," Burling told her, wedging himself through the bathroom door. When he locked it, the light clicked on automatically, and he steadied his hands against the thin plastic walls of the compartment and vomited, twice, into the blue water and steel. Morning drinking wasn't his thing, any more than infidelity had been. He had no retreat, no place or substance or ideology in which to shelter from his relentless analyzing. Was it the curse of an intelligent man, or was he mildly nuts in his own pathetic way? Not crazy in a manly way like Hemingway or brilliant like Faulkner or Pound but just a degree or two unhinged from reality. It was the thing about people again: locked in his own isolation, the strength of his mind, his will, and his physical size, he had failed to connect with anyone. That, his mother had told him, was the only truly important thing in life. She had said it the night he'd announced his engagement, about which he knew she was not completely content, and the tone of seriousness in her voice was unfamiliar, a warning. She was usually a jolly woman, given to kindnesses and harmless chatter. He'd kissed her papery forehead and climbed the stairs to his boyhood bed.

Now, in the wave of nausea that came with the taste in his mouth, he closed his eyes and the image of pink clouds in a lofty blue sky rose up in his mind. He wasn't allowed the traditional benisons in which other men indulged. Or perhaps his escapes, the destinations to which he fled, were only ideas. All the women in his life, his mother included, had said so, in their own particular ways. And what ways they had been, too, sweet, alluring, but themselves a bit strange. The thought made his head spin, but opening his eyes didn't make it go away. For some reason he remembered going hiking with Luke on the Sunday after 9/11. Amelia had given him his children, and he was grateful for that, especially in those days last September. Everyone had their safe place they clung to that weekend, and for Luke, apparently, it was the mountains. Burling went along to share Luke's place because he had none of his own. On a segment of the Appalachian Trail, they had come upon a bearded thru-hiker with zippers on every seam of his clothing, a blue bandanna tied around his head, who had not seen another human being for a week.

"Have you noticed there aren't any planes flying over?" Luke asked him.

"No planes," the hiker repeated, setting down his bulging pack. He pulled the bandanna back from his forehead and looked up at the high fall sky, a few torn clouds spread across it. His voice was distant from lack of use. He had not heard the news.

"Weird, isn't it?" Luke said when they had left the man and returned to the trailhead. "Not to know for all that time."

"It might be good," Burling said.

"Absolutely. The sky probably seemed perfectly, I don't know, benign, like it used to. Now it seems almost evil."

Burling didn't know what to say. As a father, he was caught in another emptiness, between the fables he had told Luke as a child, the pitchy games of adolescence in Islamabad, and the silence that had settled over them since. For the first time it occurred to him that Luke, the semiprofessional photographer, was not carrying his camera, something he was almost never without.

"I could never remember," Luke said, still gazing at the blue vault, "how I felt in the days after Mom died. Then last Friday happened. It was the first time that everyone else seemed to be feeling the same way I did."

Burling realized that his son had been carrying this thought with him, as they walked. "How did you feel?"

A breeze moved through the uppermost crowns of the trees, swaying the branches and turning the leaves upside down. The sweat on Burling's forehead was cold.

"Guilty. Angry. Ashamed." Luke had turned toward the road, and his voice seemed to follow it, flat and curving toward the tunnel through the mountainside. It sounded almost like the voice of the hiker.

"Why ashamed?"

"Don't you know this, Dad?"

With all that you've done? Burling finished the thought.

"When something like that happens," Luke went on, "you feel this horrible guilt."

"Guilt about what?"

"It doesn't have any object. That's what's so horrible about it."

"You shouldn't feel that way, Luke. None of any of it was your fault."

Luke turned, his sunglasses catching the sky. "That's what you said then. You told me not to feel bad because I was there, and you told Betsy not to feel bad because she *wasn't* there."

"I didn't know what to say."

"Better not to say anything, Dad. It hadn't even occurred to us that it might be our fault."

"I'm sorry, Luke. I truly am."

"I know you are."

His son's sweetness, sensitivity, unmanned him. "My thoughts, my ideas are too big for me. I get on board with one and get carried away."

Luke looked up, and their eyes met, or at least he imagined they did; his son's mountaineer's lenses were too dark to see through. The tears felt heavy in the bottoms of Burling's eyes. Luke looked away and up at the empty sky. Two liquid tracks made their way through the film of sweat on either side of his nose. Burling could tell that Luke was struggling to forgive him, or not, but that he couldn't quite bring himself to go wholly either way. In that they were alike, indecisive.

"We better go, Dad. Marina gets worried."

"She's got a baby," Burling said, trying to turn the subject forward. "I'm sorry she couldn't come."

Luke started toward the car. "Hell of a thing, you know, having a baby right now. We thought the Cold War was bad, all that *Day After* shit. Now you have no fucking clue what kind of world your kid is going to grow up in."

As they drove down the eastern slope, the sky didn't change. It didn't change even when Burling got back to China weeks later. It was waiting for him, quietly judging, outside his residence in Shanghai; it followed him as he walked along the Bund. It hovered above him through October, swallowing the ruckus of traffic, the smoke, often swallowing his thoughts. Life was not supposed to be quiet for him. The anxiety first thing in the morning, the moments when the present flew away and he couldn't remember what he'd just been doing. Food was tasteless and music was flat. Those planes that hit the Trade Center towers had been flown from the airstrip where Roy Breeden died, where they beat Burling up and took April into a captivity that never ended. He was the center, the beginning, and possibly the end: the Great Spook had trued the spokes and spun the wheel, and now all was turning around him again.

"I RISE AT FIVE EVERY MORNING," LI SAID IN CHINESE. The American professor, still bleary with sleep, nodded and pinched the imperial collar of his dressing gown closer at the neck, hiding the white hairs that sprouted from his chest. The gown was richly embroidered with dragons, the kind of thing you saw hanging in racks at the Friendship Store; to Li it looked like a garment for a woman.

"Good for you," Rank replied. He pushed his palms down on the desk blotter and nervously tried to assume his position. It's hard in that get-up, Li thought with delight; difficult to maintain an emperor's posture with your young wife standing next to you, so cold in her thin silk robe.

"All over China, people young and old rise for *tai chi*," Li informed him. "I bet your wife has forgotten that."

"Suki was born in Canton," Rank said with a pride that made Li want to strangle him. The wife's nipples pierced the fabric, and her large, red-framed glasses, purchased in vanity back in America, slid down her nose. She poked them back up with a finger that flashed a diamond ring. An unfamiliar lassitude came over Li, and he leaned back in the chair.

"The south of China has always been weak in the face of foreign influence," he told them, smiling at the woman.

"I will make some tea," she said. "After I check on the baby."

Li watched her leave, and Feng, who was standing by the door, gave her a vulpine grin as she passed. Her scent lingered in the room.

"Where did you meet your wife?" Li asked.

"On Taiwan, where I was studying Mandarin. But that's all a matter of record. What can I do for you this morning, Mr. Li?"

Li ignored the professor's question. "It is a difficult language, yes?"

"A life's pursuit," said Rank with that arrogant pride.

"I am curious, exactly what moved a bourgeois such as yourself to pursue it?"

"As a student," Rank told him, "I was interested in Mao Zedong. Many American students of my generation were."

"I studied Chairman Mao's thought in the army," Li said.

Rank pushed his chair back and crossed his legs behind the desk. He picked up a pipe from the blotter. "You and your quarry have something in common, then, don't you?"

His candor surprised Li, but Li caught himself before he responded.

"You're surprised that I would mention the reason for your visit?"

"Don't try to turn the tables on me, Professor Rank."

"Quite the contrary. I invited Tan here. He was coming to talk to my students. My name is all over his visa. Naturally I never expected him to disappear."

"And of course you have no idea where he went."

Rank removed the cold pipe from his lips and wagged his head back and forth.

"You won't mind if we look around?"

"I'd prefer not. The baby . . ."

"Of course," said Li. "He is yours?"

The professor's face grew flaccid. Perhaps this was the way.

"Yours and . . . ?"

"Suki."

"All the same, I think it would be wise if, before leaving, Mr. Feng and I looked around."

Rank stood up and pulled his robe together again. "I really must protest," he said. "This is an American compound. You have no right . . ."

"And to whom will you protest?" Li asked, remaining in his seat. "Charlotte Brien?"

"Charlotte is only a liaison to the consulate in Shanghai. She helps us with our programs."

Programs, Li thought. "Perhaps her superior, then, Consul Burling?"

"That name means nothing to me, but if he is an American consul, perhaps I should call him." Rank moved for the telephone sitting on his desk, but before he could get to the receiver, Li reached out and put the phone on the floor.

"Mr. Feng?"

Li looked over his shoulder, and the Manchu's black eyes were expectant.

"Will you retrieve Mrs. Rank and her son?"

Feng turned to go, but Rank started around the corner of his desk.

"Stay where you are," Li told him. "Remember you are on Chinese soil."

"Mr. Li! This is my wife and child."

Li cracked his knuckles. "I will look for them myself, then, if you don't trust my driver. Mr. Feng, why don't you ask Professor Rank about the Mercedes cars? I'll bet he has one at home. I heard somewhere that Wu Hongda, the one who makes seditious videotapes for Western television, has two for himself."

Feng's eyes were as large as a child's as Li walked past him and down the wooden squares of the hallway in the direction he had heard the woman take. Behind the first door, he discovered the bedroom. Shades drawn, the coverlet half on the floor and the drawers of the woman's dresser hanging open like steps. It reminded him unhappily and lustfully of his own wife's messy habits. Li stuffed two pairs of pink stockings into the pockets of his windbreaker and went back out. The door at the end of the hallway slid open, and the woman, Suki, stood before him, patting a baby that was slumped across her shoulder.

"What were you doing in my room?"

"Your husband needs you," Li said.

Suki clutched the baby to her. The nursery behind her was like no room Li Xin had ever seen. A red train chugged around blue walls. Three mobiles hung from the ceiling, and the crib was a pavilion in itself, with a canopy and decorative woodwork befitting a Buddha.

"Let me see him," Li said.

The woman's eyes, now naked of glasses, became larger, but she turned halfway, hugging the baby closer as she moved. The pudgy chin rested snugly on her shoulder, and the baby's eyes were tiny slits in cheeks that were swollen and flushed from the nursing.

"He looks Chinese," said Li.

"He *is*," Suki told him.

Her presence, the scents and the feel of the silk in his pocket, made a lack swell inside him like a balloon. "No, he's not, either. Give him to me."

The woman stopped stroking the baby and took a step backward into the soft, yellow light of the room. "What are you here to know?"

Her eyes were huge and black, and Li felt himself growing.

"Close the door," she told him, laying the baby down with her hand cupped behind his tiny head.

Li bunched the silk stockings in his pocket with his hand.

"I don't care about your games," said Suki. "You want to know about Alan's friend?"

Li fingered a wooden toy on top of a shelf. A carved bird, wings painted in scarlet and gold—his daughter had one just like it to chase away nightmares, and for a moment he thought of the landscape outside her nursery window, the derelict Japanese Zero left in the field, the new highway span. His apartment was built on the floodplain, and the wind blew down the dried-up riverbed, whistling through the cracks around the poorly fitted windows every night. The hawk is good for her, he thought. He was thinking of his daughter. When he stepped outside his building in the morning to take her into Beijing, he could feel the wind stealing the strength from his voice.

He took a step toward Suki, and she folded her arms across her swollen breasts.

"We already know all about him," Li said. He stepped toward her, and the baby suddenly started to cry. The woman did nothing, but Li heard a scuffle down the hall. The slap of slippers, then Rank pulled the door open just as Feng reached him.

"Put that away," Li commanded, seeing the gun in Feng's hand. "It's in his sleep. See? He's stopped now."

The baby was silent. "Your wife was just about to tell me all about your friend, Tan," Li said. "How that is not his real name."

"He," the woman began, but Rank raised a hand to stop her. Suki took several steps backward and sank in the rocker, throwing giant stuffed animals onto the floor. Against the teddy bears she looked like a child. She raised one hand in front of her face as if to ward something off and began to weep silently.

"I don't know where he went," Rank said.

"His name?"

"It's Tan, as far I know. I told you, he came here . . ."

"Why are you lying, Professor? To protect your handlers?"

Rank made a spitting noise with his lips. "The CIA? Are you kidding me? I have nothing to do with those people. They've made my country no better than yours."

"Professor Rank," Li chided. "You should not be disloyal."

"I'm allowed that," said Rank. "I'm supposed to be allowed that, you see."

BURLING MADE A SLOW PROGRESS DOWN THE SLOPING Kowloon street—jagged, even in daylight, with neon. The doors of boutiques blew rich scents of leather and perfume into the muggy air. The pavement leveled, and before him stretched the harbor, calm and flat in the hazy midafternoon sun. As he approached the Star Ferry terminal, he saw Adrian Fry waving to him from a newsstand.

"Ready to find our friend Teddy?" Fry asked, folding a tabloid eagerly under his arm. His khaki shirt had epaulettes that made his shoulders seem even more narrow than usual; his slight physique enhanced his untrustworthy manner.

"Hello, Adrian," Burling said, brushing past him in the direction of the ticket window. "It's been a while."

"Indeed," said Fry, "how long?"

"I got you out of jail in '99 when you tried to smuggle those blueprints from your mole at McDonnell-Douglas."

"It's all coming back to me now."

Burling gripped the railing leading to the window. "You never did let on what Airbus was going to pay you."

"Nice try, but I'm still not going to tell you who hired me. It wouldn't be good for my health."

"Seems like a different world, doesn't it, giving a damn about a Dreamliner airplane? I guess you know Simon gave our mutual friend some kind of knockout back in Tokyo?"

Fry tugged on his chin as Burling paid for their billets. Before the stalls, Asia-trekkers—emaciated Americans with watery, drugged-out eyes—begged for money and food. "Fitting, don't you think—Gordon getting buggered in his sleep?"

"Jesus."

"Don't worry," Fry laughed. "The chambermaid is not going to find old Gordo trussed up like J. Edgar Hoover, if that's what you're thinking. He just won't remember what happened, and his imagination may get carried away."

"This is a very bad situation," Burling said as they clicked through the turnstile. "I can't emphasize that enough. I'm not sure even a fellow like you wants to mix yourself up in it. You might wind up in there." He tapped Fry's tabloid with his finger.

"I get you, but I've got a bit of a thing for Teddy," Fry explained shyly.

"This would be Teddy St. John, the young HK entrepreneur with his wife's money to spend?"

"Invest, is what I believe he calls it."

"I heard that myself," Burling said. "He came to Shanghai once, looking to meet some American hotel executives who wanted to set up a joint venture. He was a rather sore loser at tennis, I might add."

"Teddy promised me a bit of this venture he's into; it's all rather frighteningly high-tech."

Burling scanned the terminal signs for their mooring. So far, Simon Bell's directions were right on, but that was bound to change, and Burling felt the lack of a proper map. Somehow Bell had gotten him MacAllister's gun—the prized lightweight Beretta subcompact Px4—which didn't give him much faith in Japanese airport security, but he hoped not to use it. He hadn't fired a weapon in anger since Jalalabad. "St. John cut you out?"

A line had formed before their gate, and a sailor in a blue jumpsuit was leaning against the railing, one padded glove holding the chain barring access to the gangway. Burling could have sworn that the sailor perked up at St. John's name.

"In a manner of speaking," said Fry. "Promised him a good thing on licensing if he did things above board. Home office counts on me, you know."

"You wanted a kickback, right?"

Fry's face was perturbed. The hydrofoil's battered white hull rode stoutly at its mooring. The water went flatly and greenly for a half mile out from the dock, ending abruptly at the quay of Hong Kong. On the Island, skyscrapers folded like foil against the riotous foliage of Victoria Peak. "Have you ever been to Hong Kong before, Lucius? It's dog-eat-dog, literally."

"Yes, I have, but intellectual property's a big deal, Adrian. Thomas Jefferson wrote that you can't have innovation without it. It's a crucial part of a free society."

Fry nodded with a schemer's understanding. As the passengers lurched down the slippery gangway, an airplane lifted from the jetty runway into the sun. "That must be why the Chinese don't get it," he said.

Burling lowered his bulk painfully into a seat, which was much too small for a man of his size. "What did Simon tell you about this place, Adrian?"

"Was me told him," Fry corrected. "Teddy has gotten into the smuggling business."

"Bootlegging, like Al Capone."

"You could call it that. Only Capone never smuggled people. Never sold them either, as far as I know."

"That would be Jefferson again."

"Truly a Protean figure," Fry allowed.

The windows of the squat craft were tinted, scratched and streaked with salt spray. A crewman shut the hatch, pressing the humid air against their eardrums. The smell of diesel was choking, and the engine vibrated under their feet as the hydrofoil eased through the shipping.

"Very popular in China, by the way."

"Jefferson was never my favorite, I admit," Burling said. "I prefer John Adams."

"Poor manners, paranoid, but a good family man. I'm not sure that fits you, Lucius."

"If I'd known there was a history lesson this morning, I wouldn't have let Simon talk me into this."

"I was never happier than when I was studying history at Cambridge," Fry told him.

The hydrofoil settled high on its hull and rushed toward the thin shadow of the outlying islands. Fry's dubious eyes watched the masts of the fancy marinas flick by. The English, it seemed to Burling, only deceived themselves about social realities; where human nature was concerned they went straight to the heart. As much as Fry's presence always presented a liability, it also sharpened one's thoughts.

In the hour it took to reach their destination, Burling tacked back and forth between ways of confronting St. John—as a colleague, assuming he had Six's, maybe even the Agency's, blessing; or as a freebooter, Aaron Burr after his betrayal by Hamilton, Sir Walter Ralegh seeking his own twenty-first-century City of Gold. The tradition of freelance endeavors was almost evenly split between greed and liberation, with a treacherous and hazy middle ground; in that gray sea, Burling was set upon by a gathering anger—about MacAllister, about Lindstrom. Pulling Jack out of his "whiskey protection program," as he called it, even though the real addiction was heroin, had to include a coercive finger pointed directly at him. The problem was to tease it out before it poked him in the eye. The pure blue mirage of the islands filled out on the western horizon.

"Does Teddy have any partners?" he asked.

Fry emerged happy from the tabloid's world of common vice and white-collar crime. "You mean on the mainland?"

"Triads, the PLA. Simon mentioned a man named Henry Sun."

"Henry's those two things and other things besides. He's made a lot of money since the Handover. Factories in the Special Economic Zone, making toys and computers for the States. Word has it Sun's not his real name, though, that his brother's on the People's Council in Beijing."

"Do Teddy and Sun share any interests?"

Fry squinted his eyes and shook his head. "Only horses, perhaps the occasional girl. Otherwise they're from two different worlds. St. John is hanging on to an HK that ended twenty years ago. Henry Sun is what made it go away."

Waves were hitting the windows now, obscuring the sky. Burling felt a great distance from where he should be, but he realized again that no one really cared where he was or what he was doing—not his superiors at State, not his children; probably not even Charlotte Brien, who for a short while he had begun to think might offer him something new, a practicality to tie him to earth, take him safely through his waning years, instead of the unstable dreamers he had chosen in his youth and middle age. His misadventure in Afghanistan had cut him off from everything, it seemed. The only people who might care about what he was doing right now—MacAllister, Lindstrom perhaps—also wanted him out of the way. It was something he had to confront, the possibility that he was tied to other people by animus, not love, and that brought him down to the darkest dream of all, the truth that sometimes in the years after April went missing in Afghanistan and Amelia had willfully ended her own life, he had entertained the thought of following them, ending his life or causing it to be ended by the same kind of violence that had been visited on Godwin. He felt enough hatred from the world that he turned it on himself, for surely, as Simon had suggested, Amelia had taken those pills because he had tried to hold her down. The trouble was that he had too much strength of will, the will to live and even live rightly, he supposed. He had to follow this thing to the end.

"Was St. John really smuggling out dissidents?" he asked finally.

"Back in the day he was, after the Square. OVC groups that were getting them out figured they had to use existing channels. Teddy had a thriving business for average people who wanted to try a new life in the States or Australia. Wherever the Communist Party was not."

"How exactly does he move the people out? He has to bring them here first?"

"Listen, Lucius. I'm not going to stand up for my countryman. Teddy St. John is a pimp and a white slaver. If my own daughter, were I to have one, which is highly unlikely, went missing in Shanghai, one of St. John's brothels in Thailand's the first place I'd look. Poor girls think they're going to cook in their third cousin's restaurant in Seattle, and they end up with the door locked from outside and their legs spread in Bangkok. Aptly named, if you ask me. No, if Teddy was moving dissidents, it was only for the money, and heaven help them if their benefactors didn't pay up. Any man deals with him might as well go to the devil. He *is* the devil, in my humble opinion."

"'Any man' in your words means MacAllister?"

"I wouldn't be a bit surprised if Gordon's been mixed up with Sun and St. John for years, although the two of them were into different cargo. Handover changed things, but it's still pretty easy to move in and out of here. The law doesn't really reach the outlying islands."

"How do you know all of this, by the way?"

Fry's forehead wrinkled vertically into a frown, and he snapped his tabloid to attention before him. "I'm not a denizen, Lucius. I just visit this world."

"It might come to visit you if you're not careful."

"You don't look well," Fry observed.

THE HYDROFOIL'S PROFILE WAS SO LOW THAT IT SEEMED AS IF they never moved closer to the island, until suddenly the engines were cut and the beaches and coppery waves began to pull the craft in. They were deposited in the empty concrete square of a housing estate. Fry soon led Burling to a bus that chugged swaying along on a cracked asphalt road between palms. The clatter of the engine didn't allow for conversation, and after an hour the route terminated in an empty parking lot. The remoteness of the place, the encroaching jungle and bright, native colors of the clothing put Burling on his guard. The uniformed driver pinched the shiny black visor of his cap; he seemed to be wishing the white men good luck.

A strong smell of brackish water and rotting fish blew across the marsh from the ocean. Fry was already walking with the few other passengers, laden with string bags and boxes, toward a narrow road that led through the cattails and starveling trees. Burling hadn't dressed for a walk in the vertical sun, and he felt the hot pavement and grit through the soles of his shoes. The road snaked along the edge of a wetland; beyond it stretched the rotting sea. To the leeward rose higher land, rocks and scrub bushes scattered with gaudy red blossoms. Cloud formations moved abruptly against the headland and changed in a way that seemed violent and prophetic.

Robbed of his habit of speech, Fry diminished, until Burling no longer worried about his duplicitous nature. Half an hour and he began to develop a protective feeling for the man. Out of the world of the Savile Row suit and witty talk, Fry became almost likable.

"I don't know about you, Adrian, but I'm parched. How much farther?"

Fry paused and mopped a monogrammed handkerchief across his brow. "I got directions from a shill in Pirate's Market," he said, extracting a flask from his pocket. "Map he drew's not exactly to scale."

"You mean you've never been out here before?"

Fry performed a little step of surprise. "Are you kidding? You see me fancying a hike in a sauna like this? I see Teddy at the club, maybe once at his office, Happy Valley."

Burling accepted a drink and found it to be lemonade. The desolation of the place was beginning to worry him. He hadn't been anywhere this wild for more than twenty years.

"This out here is the underbelly of Hong Kong life," Fry explained. "You look at society—horses, shopping, estates, expensive women—where's the vocational aspect, you ask, the moneygrubbing? But it's there, just like the States. In fact, this is the underbelly of the States. The engine of modernity."

"I thought we'd established that the engine of modernity was innovation," Burling said.

Fry began walking again, as if some kind of movement were proof of his usefulness. "It has to go deeper than that, does it not?" he asked earnestly. "Otherwise why would all the ragheads hate you so much?"

"I often ask myself the same thing." Perhaps the sun was frying the top of his head, but he was beginning to feel that he was being led by this minor fallen angel into his own blackest thoughts. He was no longer typically religious, in the way his mother had taught him, but having once believed strongly in her God of sin and redemption, it was impossible to do away entirely with the notion that somewhere, somehow, your past fuckups were waiting to greet you with an axe, sharp enough to split the hairs on your head. When it came down to it, his best explanation for things included a fallen world. The asphalt was ending; the road turned into the packed dirt of a lonely village street. The smell of water and fish was still heavy in the air, but the streets of the town were surprisingly clean. A few old men and women loitered about, but most of the population seemed to be elsewhere, away or asleep. After several blocks the street grew darker, festooned with streamers and lightbulbs; a man sold Schweppes from beneath a green umbrella. "Is this a holiday or something?"

"They have so many," Fry replied. Beyond the drink seller, ancient stone stairs led down to the river, where a wide sampan crossed the green water, powered by a dried-up old man who pulled his boat along a fraying, braided rope. "They're all fishing, I expect."

Burling paid off the ferryman, and they inched across in the company of an ageless woman with water jars hanging from her shoulders on a yoke. The ferryman's eyes went over him and Fry, who was standing in the front of the sampan, as if measuring them. On the opposite quay stood a whitewashed bank with crates of Coca-Cola stacked beneath the veranda.

"Is that where Teddy keeps his money?"

"Bank of China," said Fry. He indicated the dark green eaves and window trim, the glassless windows protected by iron bars. "Some of these fishermen own a little piece of your American debt."

Several blocks beyond the ferry, the street narrowed into a track. Burling followed single file through houses that looked as if they'd been built by a child. It was the type of thing his father had drawn, fantastic places he had visited in his mind.

"It doesn't seem real," Burling said.

"Most of the world lives this way."

Tiny temples to animist gods lined the path; hair, a picture, a brown egg struck a wet match of terror in the dim shrines preserved in Burling's mind. It was his purgatory, he thought, these backward places. It felt like they could swallow him whole.

"Where in the hell are you taking me, Adrian?"

"MacAllister's errand."

"I was supposed to be on a six-thirty plane."

"It will be late."

Burling began to believe in a spooky omniscience. "How do you know?"

"China Air," said Fry, picking his way along. Among the small houses, their door gardens marked out by rickety fences and make-shift stone walls, he'd acquired a peculiar dignity. "They're always at least an hour late. You'll probably still make your plane with minutes to spare."

"Is there really anything out here?"

This seems like an ambush just waiting to happen, Burling thought, touching MacAllister's Beretta.

The houses opened up, and there were the dry flats of the bay and painted fishing boats stranded on its scummy green bank.

"Teddy's factory," Fry said. "They burn DVDs, pirated mostly. It's sort of a recycling center for popular culture."

"For this," Burling said, "we fought the Cold War."

Fry made a small grunting noise as he negotiated the slippery path. The next group of dwellings was no more than shacks set up on stilts. Dogs dozed underneath in the shadows, beset by flies.

At the end of the shacks was a region of ramshackle warehouses, locked tight but empty as far as they could tell. Burling peered through a rotted board into a dirt-floored space fingered by dusty shafts of light. In places like this, he had once looked for April. He would see her face in strange cities as he walked down the sidewalk. The smell of fish gave way to a thicker, more penetrating smell of decay. Beyond the last of the warehouses was a low concrete building, poorly constructed but new, with thick amber windows that held and reflected the relentless early afternoon sun. Fry peered through the glass, but reported nothing. He went to the entrance. Burling gagged at the rotting smell as Fry knocked loudly on the door.

"God, what is that?" he said as they stood back and waited.

It came slowly to Burling, but the realization nearly robbed him of breath. In his mind's eye, a man's white chest bloomed with blood; a rat lay bludgeoned to death on a garden path; there was a low wattle building where the villagers said that a woman had been held.

"Try the door—with your handkerchief, mind."

"What in the world?"

With his right hand, Burling drew out MacAllister's pistol; with his left he took the handkerchief from Fry and turned the knob. Then he pushed hard on the door with his shoulder; it came open, bottom scraping against the building's concrete floor. The smell was thinner in the cool air inside, air-conditioning gone humid and stale, but it still made him gag as he entered, sweeping the wide low room with the Beretta, air glowing with a liquid blue light.

"There's the first one," he said, pinching his nose with the handkerchief held between his fingers and guarding his mouth with the palm of his hand.

"Bloody hell."

Fry held up in the doorway behind him, pulling his shirtfront up over his mouth. The corpse of a woman wearing white cotton gloves and a lab coat lay on the floor by what had been some kind of pressing machine. It was hard to tell because the smoked plastic cover of the thing had been smashed to pieces and the insides torn apart. Whoever had done it had been kinder to the woman: several small-caliber machine-gun bullets to the chest had probably killed her rather quickly. A mirrored wall had once existed behind her machine, but that, too, had been smashed: reflective pieces were scattered across the white-coated, blood-spattered bodies of other workers that lay on the floor.

Burling spoke without breathing: "You see St. John anywhere?"

The faces of the dead were young and simple, Chinese faces, earnest in their surprise. Fry motioned toward an office built out into the left rear corner of the factory floor, with a drop ceiling and a large interior window, from which the glass was gone. Burling moved along the wall toward it, covering the open door with the gun.

He need not have worried, because no one in that place was going to threaten anyone now, at least not their waking lives. In all, Burling counted fifteen dead, mostly killed where they were standing in their places on the short assembly line. In the office, torn-out cables lay across the empty desks.

"Teddy's been hurt by the competition," Fry said, greeting the outside air with relief. "The bubble burst on him."

Burling, too shaken to answer, was desperately trying to make sense of it, bring the strength of his mind to bear. But just as soon as he began to build a plausible theory of where this fit in what Amelia had once called, mock-seriously, his "grand design," his attention fled and the whole explanation collapsed from within. The building backed up to a deep inlet with moving water flowing from inland. Launches and fishing boats tugged against the pilings for two hundred yards, at which point a silver slick of water, defining a channel, led out toward the sea. Burling first, then Fry, traversed the water on a swinging plank bridge and followed a narrow path upward through gigantic red ferns and squat palms. Crates of empty bottles baked in the sun.

The stench was still with them, but not so thick now.

"You think it was the gangster, Sun?" Burling asked.

"Remember what I said about him and Teddy trading in different commodities? I think Teddy may have strayed onto Sun's turf. I just hope he isn't still around."

A peeling Portuguese house commanded the top of the path, painted a vivid shade of aquamarine, its clapboards preserved at an advanced stage of rot by the maritime climate. The first-floor windows were glassless and barred like the windows of the bank, and their shutters each hung from one hinge, unmoving in the breathless blue air, as if they had weathered a storm. Overlooking the shacks, the stranded boats on the mud, and the indistinct sea, the house had a timeless aspect; it seemed to wait for the next invasion with a stare of equanimity.

A counting house, Burling thought.

The heavy teak door stood open, and inside the first room the corpse of a man, his bloated face vaguely Arab, sat flung backward with the force of the rounds in a rolling swivel chair. On the wall before him was an old rolltop desk strewn with papers. In life, he had worn his head shaved to a shadow, and a vertical white scar ran from his hairline to the knob of bone at the base of his neck. Flies sat on the corner of his mouth, where a breath mint had melted and dried in a white ooze. Burling couldn't look away from the clouded black eyes.

"Bloody hell," Fry said again, shooing the insects away. "That's Mo, Teddy St. John's accountant." Fry turned and stooped forward with a hand on his own breastbone, as if he were going to vomit.

"Just don't touch anything, Adrian." The stench had coated the back of Burling's throat, but swallowing only made it thicker. It was beginning to upset his stomach. Was this really a part of MacAllister's operation, where the final debts were tallied and came due? For all he knew, Simon Bell had set him up and the Great Spook was in Kowloon this moment, having a drink with Sun the gangster himself. With his shirttail over his mouth, Fry was examining a pile of red ledgers on the accountant's cluttered desk.

"He was from Iran," he said behind the linen.

"The accountant?"

"Mmhm. That's another thing Teddy was supposedly into, selling nuclear technology to Iran."

Burling couldn't take the dead man's blue stare any longer. The filmed eyes seemed to interrupt time. Rolling the chair up to the door with his foot, he tipped the corpse outside onto the sharp, livid grass.

"You're telling me an element of the PLA is doing back deals with the Iranians?" The anger he felt toward the dead accountant surprised him. He didn't like to discover that visceral hatred in himself.

"If this was where your dissident or asset or whatever was going to end up, you owe Simon a great debt," Fry said, running his finger across the ledger. On each page was a name, date, location somewhere on the mainland, followed by a debit figure amounting to an average of thirty thousand dollars U.S. The lines beneath represented the last twelve months; the amounts and duration varied on each subsequent page of the book. When the names in the ledger had worked off a total of five thousand dollars, their service in the factory appeared to be over.

"You forget it wasn't me who was supposed to find this," Burling said.

"A message to MacAllister, then?"

Burling looked across the buzzing front yard. Above the palm crowns, the factory's gravel roof, he could see the flats of cracking gray mud. Yong and Lindstrom would never get out now, of that he was confident. Maybe Simon was right: that was exactly what

MacAllister wanted. The Great Spook, the preacher's kid who was always breaking rules the better to prove the world's corruption, had planned one last disaster to make God show his face. But why had he put Burling smack in the middle of it, he, MacAllister, always so sure of his rightness and Burling so full of equivocation, of doubt? Was the Great Spook resentful of Burling for saving his life?

"It's like slavery," Fry said.

They found Teddy St. John in a room that must have been the library in the days of colonial governors. They had taken a while to kill him, and now the fluids that had given him life had dried around him and blended with the cheap oriental. Neither Fry nor Burling took a step inside the door. A terrible law seemed to reign between the high empty shelves, over the desk implements, the bottle and siphon by the chair where St. John had lived out his sentence. It was not justice, really; perhaps it was vengeance, but the arrangement of elements in the room possessed an order that Burling sensed was madness to disturb.

He folded the ledger book under his arm.

In back of the house stretched a long shed with black open spaces for doorways, like housing for migrants or slaves. The rooms, each one with a pallet and crate and some minor belonging, such as could be carried on one's person, smelled more like a kennel than a human habitation. Alone, it would have been horrible, but taken with the ledgers and the deaths in the factory below, the workers' dwellings retained an overwhelming dignity and pathos. Amazing what these people were willing to pay to cross from one world to the other.

"One thing," Burling said. "Did you or Simon make any calls from Tokyo after you put Gordon to sleep?"

Fry's face screwed up as they passed the accountant's prostrate body in the grass. "I only asked for directions from the bloke I told you about."

"You're sure you didn't *give* the directions?"

"You can't put this on me," Fry said, steadying himself as they went down the steep, rocky path. A junk had appeared above the spit of land guarding the channel, its leathery sail like a prehistoric wing. "I know you Olympian bastards would like to, but this is way above my grade, the kind of thing we lower forms of life can only imagine in our worst dreams."

Burling paused with a hand on the railing of the bridge. "You said that Henry Sun has Party connections?"

Fry nodded, his eyes out to sea. "Right after the Handover, Henry Sun and St. John were partners. Dead Teddy up there had all the old money connections, but he couldn't use them anymore when the Communists came. Henry Sun gave him the one thing he needed, a line to Beijing."

"Well, the line has been severed," Burling said. "Is there a place where we can slip one of those boats down there into Kowloon? I have a plane to catch."

Fry had turned morose, but he brightened slightly at the challenge to his art. "It's a bit more downscale, the place that I'm thinking, than you're used to."

Burling was about to make a comment, something along the lines of his being a public servant who got along on the wages conferred by the populace, but he wasn't sure what those would be anymore.

TEACHER CHEN BENT TO PICK UP THE WASH BUCKET. With the handle in one hand, the heel of the other hand pressed on the small of his back, he straightened, hiking up his trousers with a thumb. With a knuckle he pushed back his glasses, which had slid down in the film of perspiration on his nose. Then he took the rag mop from against the railing of the gallery and entered the final classroom on the school's upper floor.

The pupils were gone for the day, and the rows of desks sat empty. On the blackboard was a series of pictures—a hammer and sickle, a shelf of books, a pot of flowers, and a missile, its bulbous body and sharp fins defined in red, yellow, blue, and pretty lavender chalk; in the row below were round Chinese faces behind a stockade. Seeing the lesson presented that way, Chen felt his throat begin to close, and his legs grew stiff with terror. It was the kind of thing he washed from blackboards every day, but suddenly he was visited by the idea that God had not done these things; men had. Therefore God could not control their repetition.

Quickly, Chen wiped the pictures away with his mop. The handle was cut from a crooked mulberry trunk, and the sharp knots dug into his palms as he dunked the rag head in the bucket. He did a cursory job on the rest of the classroom, smearing chalky water across the linoleum floor, and the streaks dried quickly behind him as he returned to the gallery outside. He took the soap from its basket next to the cold-water tap and began to wash his hands vigorously, gazing over the rooftops at the gray, sun-struck town. He had once taught algebra in this very same school, but years ago he had been demoted for a story problem he'd assigned, and after that he was a janitor. At first he'd preferred it for the solitude it offered. In his routine of mopping and scrubbing, he was free in his thoughts. But not long afterward his wife had passed away, and Chen had begun to discover loneliness, which was a brother to solitude but different, in the way that brothers are. With his wife gone, when he tried to remember the great triumph of conviction he had felt when he faced down the Regional Committee—the educational body in front of which he'd been brought—he could no longer remember the assignment that had been so subversive, so crucial to him and so threatening to them. He remembered speaking forcefully to the chairwoman, who had large squarish glasses over which she had stared down in a judicious way as Chen explained that he would sooner quit teaching than have the board forbid him to . . . As he scrubbed his hands with soap, the memory sloughed away. Loneliness settled over him like a sheet. His wife had supported him in his trial: her Christian faith was greater than his, and he might have knuckled under if it hadn't been for her strength. He tried again to remember what he had said to his class, but it was gone.

When Chen had dried his hands, he heard some boys kidding each other in the courtyard below. They used the foul language characteristic of the countryside, the dirty idiom he associated with Mao. Chen could smell the cheap tobacco of their cigarettes. He turned and rested his elbows on the waist-high, concrete railing, his gaze passing over the gables of neighboring buildings, the dusty crowns of the sycamores that lined the main street, to the edge of the town where he made out the cross on the steeple of his church. On Sunday, when the dissident Yong was still hiding there and Chen had sat with his acolytes at the chancel table, the place had had an electricity, a living power it hadn't possessed since Chen's wife had died almost ten years before. The sermon had taken him out of his anger and loneliness, to a place where people died from conviction, not cancer. His singing voice seemed to swell in his chest and join the others in its journey toward God. Yong was gone now, moved on with the mongrel American, and Chen was conscious of having envied the dissident's relative youth. Left behind, he was in danger of succumbing to despair.

Despair, the pastor had told him the previous Sunday, means you're in rebellion against God. The pastor was also Chen's sister-in-law, and she'd said it in the gentle but serious tone that she and Chen had forged together when his wife was sick.

"But being in rebellion makes me feel alive," he told her.

"Rebelling against God and the government, Teacher, are two different things."

His sheepish smile came back to him now as he rubbed his eyes and righted his glasses again. Below, the schoolboys' talk had turned inevitably to fucking. The hands showed six on the town hall clock. The light had dimmed, but the sky behind the steeple glowed like mother-of-pearl. The pastor might be there, along with some of the women of the church—cleaning pews, mending the choir robes, or replacing the vessels for communion, having washed them since Sunday at home. He couldn't remember if it was Monday or Tuesday; he could ask the boys, but they would probably tease him. Most of the pupils in the school now found the story of Chen's rebellion archaic, an example of the craziness of the Cultural Revolution, which they regarded as an excess of history in which they had no part. Those who were old enough to remember it at all believed that such trouble was caused by the West, which was sad, in Chen's opinion, not only because it wasn't true, but because it meant that they didn't know what kind of cruelty their own people could bring upon themselves. Catching a sharp whiff of their smoke, he coughed to signal the boys he was coming, and went down the stairs.

Perhaps he was looking for a fight, a confrontation to kindle the fire that had gone cold inside him, but the boys would not oblige. Their cigarettes dangling from the corners of their mouths, the one boy's hands cupped in front of his chest to show the size of his girlfriend's breasts, they greeted old Chen with the honorific "Teacher," their voices edged with the barest sarcasm as he went past them, into the street.

They've turned me into a mascot, Chen thought, turning his steps toward the church. When history is meaningless, that's what you do. It occurred to him that he had nothing at home for his dinner.

AFTER MILES OF MARKET-DAY TRAFFIC, OF STINKING chicken coops lashed precariously to flatbeds and bicycles weaving through animal carts, Feng turned the car onto a dirt road that led to the labor camp outside Anhe. The extra fuel they had taken for the trip seemed to have water in it, making the engine buck and cough, and the springs on the vehicle they had borrowed from the Nanjing motor pool were nearly gone. For two long hours, Feng had pushed the car onward as if he were driving in a race, and Li rode beside him with one hand wedged against the cracked plastic dash. Every pothole and washerboard knocked against the top of his skull, and his mouth was dry and sour from chain-smoking cigarettes and exhaust that smelled like rotten eggs.

The labor camp, where the local militia was quartered, sat on a hectare of hardpan in the field beyond the train station. Li and Feng left the car in the station lot and crossed the tracks, marching on a narrow path that led along the top of a dike. Some distance away, Li could see the shapes of prisoners, spreading water across the paddy in the meticulous, awkward way of intellectuals sent down to the countryside, watched over by two young soldiers in simple uniforms. The late afternoon was struck dumb by its unblinking witness to drudgery, and the whiteness and breadth of the sky reminded Li of his posting in Tibet.

The *laogai* compound had once been a School of May Seventh, but all that remained were a few leaning chicken-wire fences and a cinder-block hut that doubled as a barracks and barn. Pigs rooted around the well stand, and the furrows of the vegetable garden were blurred with new green. The man in charge appeared to be a sergeant, though he wore the clothes of a farmer and the only deference to his rank was his idleness and the position of his chair in the building's narrow band of shade. On the sleeve of his shirt, the sergeant's emblem had been sewn with the long, uneven stitches of soldiers away from home.

"Is that Anhe over there?" Li inquired.

The sergeant was reading a book, his crooked index finger tracing the characters, lips moving as if he were chewing the words. When Li addressed him, he blinked into the distance, where a long line of trestles marched across the fields, power lines drooping and rising, drooping and rising between them. The wires led to a power plant, and to its right Li could make out an etching of buildings that must be Anhe.

"Who wants to know?" the sergeant asked. His missing front teeth confronted Li as an insult, or a boast.

Li stepped beneath the overhang of the corrugated roof, out of the sun. "I am Comrade Li Xin from the Ministry of State Security."

"And this is a unit of the People's Liberation Army," said the sergeant, crossing his arms. "Why should I give a shit who you are?"

Calmly, Li reached down and yanked the chair out from under him; one of its legs came off in his hand like a joint of rotten meat. "You might care when you ride through the streets of Nanjing in a cage," he said, tossing the chair leg into the yard. The pigs attacked it immediately, rooting it out with their prehensile snouts.

"I ain't heard nothing from there," the sergeant said, picking himself up from all fours.

"Just last week," Li informed him, "three men were executed for stealing money from the pipe factory run by your command."

The sergeant still feigned indifference, then made a feeble attempt at a kick, which Li caught with his free hand. He smiled for a moment at the man's dusty face, then booted him squarely in the testicles. As the sergeant went down, Li let go of his leg and hit him once, twice in the face, snapping his head back and laying him out on the ground with a dull crack. Then Li lowered his arm and walked away to the rim of the irrigation ditch, where he lit a cigarette and sucked on it hungrily. Squinting through the smoke, he searched the rooflines of Anhe for a steeple or cross. From the placement of buildings, he began to map the place in his mind. He brought up a mental picture of the dissident, placing his imaginary figure against a wall, at the end of a blind alley in the maze of narrow streets, but there Li's habitual discipline left him. The smoke turned bitter in his mouth, and he flicked the butt into the slimy trickle at the bottom of the ditch.

When he returned to the hut, Feng was rifling the sergeant's pockets. Li gritted his teeth and slapped Feng on the ear, causing Feng to fumble his plunder: an onion, matches, and a pack of mismatched cigarettes scattered on the ground. Feng was left with a ridiculous knife in his hand, sharpened down like a prisoner's shiv to the thickness of tin. He rolled the wooden handle over and over between his fingers; the sleeves of the silver Mercedes jacket he wore shone like metal, and his goat-like Manchu face struggled to reach back through years of corruption to the ruthlessness that had made his ancestors glorious.

"Aren't you hot in that ridiculous coat?" Li asked him, ignoring Feng's menacing stare. "That thing is boiling your brain."

At their feet, the sergeant groaned.

"Give that man back his knife."

The sergeant's eyes fluttered, and a tremor passed through him from his shoulders to his feet. He grimaced painfully at them, blood lining his gums.

"One of your inmates," Li told him, "a man called Pao, left this camp last Sunday and went to a Christian church in the town."

Bolting upright, the sergeant looked wildly about. Feng drew his pistol and held it on him. "This Pao," Li continued, "reported that a traitor he knew was hiding in the church. Where is he?"

The sergeant felt the dust tenderly with his hands. His eyes rolled up: "Where is who?"

"You don't worry," Li told him. "You let your inmates into town to go with women, or Christians. It's small potatoes to me. I want the traitor."

The sergeant's face was blank, and his yellow bloodshot eyes slid away. From the opposite side of the building came a chortling voice. The pigs gave up the chair leg and clamored toward the sound on their dainty, cloven feet. Around the corner, a young man appeared in a bright orange sweater. He yawned, and his fat cheeks pressed up against the frames of his glasses. When he saw two strangers standing over the sergeant, he tried to back away without being noticed, but Feng was on him like a shot, dragging him before Li in an elaborate show of loyalty.

Li asked the man's name.

"My name is Pao," the inmate said.

Li nodded and smiled: it was good to let them think that you already knew everything. He was about to continue with his questioning, but the sergeant was crawling toward Pao. Blood dripped from his nose, and when Li saw what the sergeant was after, he experienced a surge of affection. On the ground near Pao's feet, next to the three-legged chair, was a gilt-edged book, by the look of it one of the fancy editions of Mao's *Quotations* that were sold at tourist tables in Beijing. The gold stamping of the title had been rubbed invisible with use, and a thin red ribbon marked the place where the sergeant had left off reading. Pao leaned over to pick it up, but Li put a hand on his chest.

"If you had studied this, Pao," he said, whisking off the cover, "you wouldn't be at Christian meetings where troublemakers are."

Behind his glasses, Pao's small black eyes narrowed in confusion.

"Don't tell me you don't know what I'm talking about. You wrote a letter to your sentencing board, hoping for clemency if you ratted on the traitor Yong Beihong. He was your teacher at Qinhua. He signed a traitorous letter to Deng." Li turned and helped the sergeant to his feet. "When we arrived," Li told him, "you did exactly as I would have done, defended your command. I was once in the army myself."

The sergeant's mouth moved; a reservoir of blood had pooled between his lip and gum.

"Here, I'll show you," Li said. "It'll be good for this fat rat to hear."

He flipped through the book until he found the page number he remembered from his own edition, and began to read aloud: "*He has showed strength with his arm; he has scattered the proud . . . in the image . . .*" The words stopped his throat. They weren't Mao's at all, but something entirely other, a rhythm that echoed from an ancient mouth. The shadow of a dark time passed through him, like a cloud across the sun, and the great, stepped monasteries of the Tibetan plateau rose like mares' tails in his mind. He read on, silently now: *He has scattered the proud in the imagination of their hearts. He has put down the mighty from their seats, and exalted them of low degree.* Li turned the thin page in a fury. In his inward eye, the saffron-robed monks flocked together like bald, fledgling birds. They stared nearsightedly at him from their circle.

"A *Bible*?" he demanded, shaking the book before the sergeant's eyes. "*Low degree*? You think this . . . black magic is for you?"

The sergeant reached for the book, and Li hit him in the stomach.

"I was on the plateau five years," said Li, shaking. "All this magic is the same. It makes men into cattle for the priests to slaughter and eat. They eat men, I'm telling you."

The sergeant hugged himself and tried to vomit, but nothing came.

"There is a meeting today?"

Silently, the sergeant shook his head.

"Pao? No Christian meeting?"

Pao shrunk against the filthy wall of the building, and Li spat at his feet.

"Sergeant, pull yourself together and call your men in from the paddy."

The sergeant turned and walked, clutching his middle, toward the irrigation ditch. Pao watched Li with a timid hatred.

"This crap is for women," Li told him, throwing the Bible to the ground. "Are you a woman?"

Feng, who had moved away from the building to keep an eye on the sergeant, began to laugh. "He's a pansy, boss, a faggot."

The sergeant blew a whistle to the group in the field. The pigs moved toward Pao in a welter of pink flesh, circling around him and watching Li with their mild, glassy eyes. Blond lashes gave their faces a juridical look. Feng took a quick step to shoo them, but the pigs sidled closer together, murmuring threat and affirmation among themselves.

"You like the pigs?" Feng said to Pao, swaying his hips and pointing his pistol at the sow.

Pao lowered his eyes in shame.

"You sodomize them?"

Pao stared at Feng in horror. "W-we raise the p-pigs here for f-food."

"W-w-w-why aren't you eating them, then? W-w-w-why don't you s-slaughter them?"

Pao opened his mouth to speak, but his head only bobbed. In the field, the crouching workers raised their bonneted heads, then began to move in a narrowing delta of blue cloth and hoe-flash toward the camp. Pink-and-purple clouds piled up in the sky above Anhe.

"Leave him be," Li told Feng. From far off, he could hear tractors burbling on the road. "Take that gun off the pig. Do you have any idea what it's worth to this unit?"

Feng lowered the gun. Pao had started to cry. Li took a picture of the dissident Yong from his pocket. "Was this the man you saw in the church?"

Pao waited for a moment, then nodded; taking off his glasses, he wiped his eyes with the tip of a finger. The workers were arriving in the yard. Li addressed Pao loudly enough for the gathering prisoners to hear:

"You're a Christian?"

Pao's chin moved up and down slowly.

"This Yong is one, too, or so they tell me. But I'm curious, if your religion is so great, why would you turn in a fellow member?"

The tears had dried on Pao's cheeks. His stammer was gone. "He didn't stand at the Prayer of Confession."

Li was surprised and a bit shaken by the cold current that had entered Pao's voice. He was out of his element here, far from the crowded, familiar *hutongs* of Beijing. In the countryside, where he had been sent as a teenager by the Red Guards, he had always been scared, out of place. His parents had left their family village long ago. Easy, earthy country customs excluded him.

"You stand like a landlord at a public confession?"

"Yong Beihong used to be a good Christian," Pao said. "Humble. He quit his big job in the army making weapons just to teach us theoretical physics at Qinhua."

Li laughed bitterly and turned to face the workers. With their starved eyes and big heads wagging above their scrawny bodies, they looked like a troupe of giant puppets. Li shook his head. "What Pao doesn't tell you is that this Yong Beihong spent a year in America. He is an agent of the West. His Christianity is only one more plot against our sovereignty. Sergeant! Ready your men. Make sure their rifles are cleaned and in order. How many are you?"

The sergeant came toward him, walking bowlegged to protect his sore balls. "Usually five, but two are returning from leave. They will be here soon."

"Stay here with one man on guard then. Feng and I will take the other three and Pao with us. Feng! Take these men out to the car. One can sit in front next to you, one in the trunk. How are their weapons?"

Feng raised his thick eyebrows as if Li had made a joke, and cocked his head in the direction of the guards. Li walked along the short line to review them, and saw why he had counted only two in the field: the other soldiers, like their sergeant, were out of uniform. The weapons they carried came from all stages of the struggle—a Remington, a Springfield '03, and two bolt-action rifles of Chinese make. The Remington, in the hands of a young soldier with a harelip, was a farmer's gun with a rusty barrel, more like a tool than a weapon.

"You," he said to its bearer. "Stay here with your sergeant."

The Springfield, on the other hand, appeared a source of pride to its owner, a rangy boy with a bulging Adam's apple. The prisoners watched as Li examined the weapon and chambered a round. The bolt locked with a reassuring sound.

"Put Pao in the trunk with the gas cans," he said. "This man rides up with me."

IN THE CHURCHYARD, TEACHER CHEN FOUND THE PASTOR and three women of the congregation filling their buckets at the pump. Each of the three women had a sweater buttoned over her everyday clothes and her hair combed back tightly as a sign of respect to the Lord. Even on a weekday—this exaggerated piety.

The pastor was not pious herself. She wore a newly hemmed pair of Chen's trousers that had given out at the cuffs, and she filled her bucket with a capable grace. She never smiled when she saw him, but her eyes crinkled in a merry way.

"Good evening, Teacher."

"Good evening."

The three women nodded in unison.

"Not enough cleaning for you over at the school?"

Chen smiled and nodded; he felt absentminded. One of the three had brought her grandson with her, a little boy in blue sweatpants and a natty brown blazer, a white shirt fastened tightly at his neck, whom Chen had been teaching to count. The boy came forward and pulled at his hand, but Chen's feet were like clay.

Many in the congregation, the little boy's grandmother included, had not been happy when the church decided to hide Yong Beihong. But the pastor believed in Yong's struggle, and Chen had stood beside her, because she was family and because of the faded memory of his own dissent. Now Chen wanted to talk to her, share the wages of the faith they had exhibited together, but she wasn't alone. He would have to make do with the gentle church humor she adopted in the presence of the women, her mixture of chiding and compassion, the voice that skimmed the sparkling surface of deep waters as they carried their cleaning buckets into the church and worked side by side in the pews.

"Eight . . ." the little boy shouted.

Chen had turned on the public address system and retrieved the microphone from the locked cabinet where the communion wine was kept. In the front of the sanctuary next to the pulpit, the boy held the mike like a little television performer and recited the numbers; his high voice sprang out periodically in the empty, vaulted church. He had made it to eight with only minor difficulty, but now he was stuck. In the fourth row of pews, Chen tried to come up with a rhyme.

"Nine!" came the sharp little voice without prompting. Chen and the pastor clapped, and the microphone rubbed against the wool of the boy's blazer. There was a loud screeching noise, and the boy looked in fright at his hand.

Feedback: at first Chen thought it was only that. He had wired the system himself using purloined components, and he knew it had shorts. Then he heard the sound again. A car was braking outside in the street.

"Who on earth could that be?" the pastor said.

The boy's grandmother stopped dusting the pulpit and looked up in alarm. In the street, a car door slammed, then another, and another.

"Not the troublemaker again?" the grandmother said.

The pastor made a damping motion with her hand. Chen recognized it as a family gesture—his wife had used it with their son—and for some reason a chill passed through him, as if a ghost had come into the church. "We had better go see who it is."

The women trooped out through the chancel, and Chen watched them go with a mixture of solicitude and irritation. His wife had left him behind, caught between the young, who were happy-go-lucky or greedy and callow, and these old ones, so cautious and petty and weak. The pastor's spirit grew stronger and yet more remote with each year, until her peace was walled off from the rest of the world. Chen took the mike from the little boy's hand and clipped it onto its stand. A man's voice rose in the courtyard outside.

Chen glanced at the Bible lying open on the pulpit, pages spotted with mildew. Reverend Lindstrom had brought it with him from America, and since then the Bible had registered hundreds of names, the Christian markers of birth, marriage, death inked with care on the first blank pages. The pastor often held it up during sermons, telling the congregation that they and this Book were the church, not the building itself. Chen traced his own family—his wife and son who never visited him now because he was afraid his father's history with the Regional Committee would hurt his career in Shanghai—then closed the cover to protect the old paper from the moisture and dust. The feel of the hide on his fingers made him shiver again with the ghostly chill. He was suddenly angry at his wife for having died, and his face grew hot with shame.

As he entered the chancel, the door banged open against the outside wall of the church, and a man appeared in the doorway holding a pistol; he wore some kind of silvery jacket that produced a shiny aura around his shoulders and arms. Chen was grabbed by the elbow, and the barrel of the pistol poked his ribs. The man's face, when Chen saw it up close, was a Manchu's, with drooping moustache and pointed goatee.

"You," Chen said, trembling.

The Manchu looked like the devil. He shoved the old man toward the door, and Chen banged his thigh on the corner of the table. The Manchu laughed at him. Chen held the doorframe with both hands as he started down the steps, a small knot of pain in the muscle of his leg. The three women were huddled with the boy against the wall of the courtyard, under the tree where chickens roosted at night. Around them stood three militiamen from the camp outside town. Beyond the wall, a slick of orange sun trailed across the paddy like a wake. Some of the militia came to the church or the school to pick up girls, but he had never actually seen them holding rifles. The pastor was talking to a stranger who sported a sharp city haircut, but she was not looking at him. As she spoke, she looked at Pao, the literal one, in his vain orange cardigan; a frown of pity furrowed her brow. "There is a family in town called Yong," she was saying, "but they only have a daughter, Mr. Li."

"Found another one inside," the Manchu said.

The man named Li turned and squinted at Chen. His eyes seemed serious, but not in a scholarly way: it was a kind of intelligence Chen had never understood. Perhaps shrewd was the word, or sharp—the kind of smarts that always ended in hurt. "And you are?"

"Chen."

"A member of this . . . place?"

"I am a janitor at the secondary school."

"And you have never heard of Yong Beihong, either, I suppose?"

"I don't believe he's a member of the church, do you, Pao?"

Pao jerked as if he'd been stuck with a pin, a faint whiff of gasoline emanating from his sweater. True believers were always the same, thought Chen—communists, Christians—Pao was only a different version of the student who had informed on Chen himself.

"I told you he was here," Pao said indignantly, "three days ago for the worship."

"Yes," Li smiled. "He did not stand for his confession. However, I think I have a medical reason for that. When Yong was first picked up for his crimes, he resisted the police and one of his feet was shattered. Perhaps he didn't stand simply because it hurt him."

Pao's face began to twitch. Against the wall, one of the three women scolded a militiaman whose mother she knew. It's all so confusing and horrible, Chen thought, looking into the sun. The older he got, the more the human variables kept changing their relation to one another so that a solution seemed either nonexistent or infinite. The possibility of infinity had led him toward God, but he was equally capable of getting lost in the numbers themselves, the constant division and carrying over, the day-to-day subtraction of himself. He decided to focus on the pastor so he wouldn't let Li see his fear. Her almond eyes were hardened and angry, but her cheeks looked the same as always, leathery and creased with soft wrinkles, the corners of her mouth curled up with the assurance of her faith. Maybe it wasn't walled off after all, Chen thought—only lost to him, a memory occluded by pain. Their eyes remained together for a moment, and they shared an invisible smile. Perhaps he could recover his will, even find the kind of faith that eluded him, if he took his cue from her. He watched her short, gray figure standing before Li and thought she was truly Christ's ambassador here; an ember of warmth, like a promise, began to bloom in his chest. The pain in his thigh shrunk as small as a pebble, and seemed to disappear. It came to him that God was here, present right now if he would only accept Him; He was here in the courtyard, in the old wooden church; He had not concerned Himself with Chen's trial, or his wife's death, or his vision of bombs, but He was here now—Chen was sure of it—and something inside him leapt at the chance.

"This building is a magnet," Li was saying, as if reading from a text, "a perpetual shelter for evil forces. It has harbored foreign agents and internal enemies of the state. Feng, get the extra gas from the car."

Feng, the Manchu, stopped fiddling with his pistol and came forward, showing Chen his teeth. "You want to burn it?"

"You heard what I said."

At first the Manchu had sounded surprised, but he jogged eagerly out of the gate. Tears popped in silent rhythm from Pao's eyes. Li addressed one of the sad company of militia, a gangly chap who carried an antique-looking gun. "Take these people outside," he commanded, indicating the three women and the little boy. "Send them home. They're not needed anymore."

As they left, the Manchu passed them hauling two five-liter cans, which he carried up the chancel steps and into the church.

"You must not do this, son," the pastor told Li. "This church is sanctioned by the China Christian Council. We've done no one any harm."

Li's laugh went outrageously upward—striking God, thought Chen, in His face.

"Am I your son?" said Li, pointing to himself and laughing in an exaggerated way. He leaned in close to the pastor. "A whore like you has lots of sons, right?"

A swirling of winds came down, pushing Chen forward toward Li.

"Bastard sons like Jesus Christ?"

Chen staggered, and the pain returned like a hot piece of coal to his thigh. Li pulled a revolver from the back of his belt and slowly cocked the hammer with his thumb, aiming at Chen's chest. "I don't think so," he said.

Chen saw Pao considering grabbing Li's arm. Would God act through a snitch? The tears had dried in snail trails on Pao's cheeks, and his hand hovered inches from his hip. His guilt must seem like a forest.

"Go ahead and shoot me," Chen said, feeling suddenly alive. For God to step in, there would have to be a breach. "I'm old. I can barely remember my own name. Go ahead."

Li appeared to consider it.

"You do not know it," said the pastor, "but what you are doing will return to you."

"Don't put a spell on me, witch," Li said, swinging around. Chen stepped quickly between them. Li's face was red and sweating. "I've been cursed by the best and come down without a scratch."

"Come down?" the pastor asked.

"From the plateau," Li said. "Every other type up there is a medicine man. The cannibal monks make their drumheads from human skin."

"That is all propaganda," Chen told him.

"Propaganda?" Li pointed the pistol at his face. "What *you* preach is propaganda. What you believe is propaganda. I believe what I see."

"God is invisible," the pastor told him, "but He is here."

"Yes," said Chen.

The gasoline odor was stronger now through the open windows, and the liquid pinged and gurgled from the cans. Li didn't notice Pao slip past the evergreen and disappear around the corner of the building. Chen couldn't imagine what he was doing—there was no way out there—but he kept his eyes pegged on Li's gun so as not to give the little rat away.

"Your God had better be a tidal wave," Li told them, "or a hurricane to put out this fire."

"He is all of those things," the pastor said, backing up a few steps. Could she be expecting a miracle, too? You would almost think so from the way she folded her arms across her chest. "God is in all of us, even you, Mr. Li. Perhaps you most of all. God is in all of us, and this church is the bride of His son, this building is His house. It's your house, too, whether you know it or not. If you burn it, you will burn the dwelling place of your own eternal soul."

"Don't curse me. I told you."

Inside the church, a can dropped to the floor. Feng shouted, and Li pointed his pistol from Chen to the pastor and back again. A shot cracked, and a window of the sanctuary shattered; Chen turned to see if the pastor was hit.

When the second shot fired, it seemed very far away, the noise coming through a tunnel and followed by a roar that pulled all remaining sound toward its center. Feng appeared at the chancel doorway, backing out. His face flickered, and he seemed to be marching in place. The cuffs of his pants were on fire, and he jumped from the stairs and rolled around in the dust at the bottom.

"The rat," he pointed. "Pao."

Cool air was sucked past Chen's ears toward the fire. It stirred dust in the courtyard like the prelude to a storm. In the heart of it, Pao appeared, staggering, his pants and sweater on fire. His mouth was open, and he clutched something dark against his chest. He gazed into the distance, over Chen's head, then fell forward slowly in an arc, chin striking the bottom step, body sliding to the ground, feet shaking over the treads behind him. Flames continued to eat his clothing.

Feng got up, trousers smoking, and walked to the body, beating the flames out with his hands. The fire rose up in the windows of the church, making the glass seem to melt in the muntins; the heat on Chen's cheek was intense. Feng was extracting the large black cover of the missionary's Bible from Pao's rigid hands. In the middle of the leather was a small hole ringed with ash.

"Mr. Chen!" shouted Li.

Pao had been going for the Bible at the moment he was shot. He had known the church would burn now and that it was his fault. The only way to save it, and himself, was to carry the Bible out. Perhaps God had instructed him after all. Perhaps He had used Pao all along as His instrument, and the logic of it was simply beyond Chen's capacity. Through the door to the chancel, he could see blue flame spreading like liquid across the wood floor. The walls were not yet on fire. The cover had ripped off in Pao's hands, but the Bible itself was still in there.

"Help Feng drag that rat away from the building," Li said.

Chen pressed himself against the wall of heat as if he might break through to something—coolness, water, relief, perhaps the angry mind of God. He entered the penumbra of fire like a new and welcoming element. The corpse was heavy, and sweat poured from his forehead and shoulders, bathing his cheeks and his chest. The water flowed freely, and it made him feel younger; his arms were strong, and he remembered working next to his father in the paddies, how the sweat made you part of the day. Feng held one shoulder and Chen took the other, but Pao's right foot was caught in the treads. The fire scorched Chen's lungs as he struggled to free it. Sweat baked on his face. Pao's ankle had been broken in the fall, and Chen turned it with a grimace; the feel, the sound of gnashing bones hurt his teeth. As the foot came loose, a window shattered above him. Glass rained down like ice. Shards burned the back of his neck, and Feng dropped his side of the body and swatted at his cheek, then began to back away.

Chen crouched alone, holding onto Pao's foot. When he tried to stand up, the heat overwhelmed him. When he looked up from the body, the figures of Li and the pastor seemed very far away, as if he saw them through water. Li motioned with his little toy gun, and Feng ran around the shore of the lake of heat. Only the pastor stood still. Her eyes had always been like smooth water flowing over stones, her faith like fire behind the melting blue windows of the church. She had always stood closer to whatever this force was than he had. She had stood so close, he hadn't been able to touch her. The closest he had come was her sister, his wife.

What had he wanted when he came here today, from her, from God? He'd told himself that he wanted an answer, but to what? How could you ask for an answer when you couldn't remember the question?

You didn't really want an answer, he thought as the heat knocked him down. You wanted a reward.

He had wanted a reward for something he had done out of love for his sister-in-law and his wife. He'd agreed to hide Yong for the same reason he had faced the Committee—not out of courage but of love. Out of love he had hidden the dissident, and now the church was burning, and he was responsible as surely as Pao.

There's your answer: no answer at all. Equal integers on both sides of the equation. You and Pao are the same. You cancel each other out.

The fire roared around him as he crawled up the stairs toward its throat. He'd thought to get the Bible, but now he knew it was a dream. The air inside the chancel was wavy and gray, and he was drowning in heat. Through a doorway of fire, the pulpit stood alone in the blaze, the pages of the Bible blowing back and forth as if in a gale, the microphone raised like a finger in protest on top. A strange sound, a sort of voice swirled around his ears, and he realized that the PA was on. A child counted in the heart of the fire.

One, two, three . . .

Four. A rafter crashed slowly in front of him, knocking the pulpit away in a hail of white sparks. His eyes stung, but he couldn't close his eyelids; heat melted his sight.

Five, six. No more tests, God, I promise. It hurts. My palms are burning. I can't get up. I am here on my knees before your altar. As a child I have come to be judged. Please!

He tried to cry, but it was only a feeling, something trying to escape. It didn't hurt when his cheek hit the floor. It was intimate, now, between him and the infinite. He had taught the boy to count, and the boy had said his numbers on the public address system.

Eight nine ten, the boy said. Is that cheating, to rush to the end?

It's not the end, child. There are many more numbers to learn.

How many, Teacher?

Many many. More than you can know.

More than . . . When can I start?

Soon, child, soon.

The word was like the mouth of a tunnel.

Soon.

THE SUN FELL FROM ITS ZENITH IN THE WHITE SKY BEHIND them as Lindstrom walked to a cadence on the tufted grass track behind Yong. The path had been swinging gradually south for an hour, and now the molten ball hung like a yolk above the rooftops of the town. In the paddy, zephyrs pooled the bright grass. Lindstrom tried closing his eyes, but the dying sun burned at his cheek, and he saw it through his eyelids: *Refinery fire. Fuller's soap. You can't banish this God from your mind. He's in the forest, the vineyards, on the docks, in the paddies, the village, the town. There's no hiding, Johnny Lindstrom. You're His child.*

He marched nearly asleep, as he had in Vietnam, night thoughts coming to greet him. He and Yong were both impostors, he thought, inauthentic, disciples of everything and nothing at all. Because that's how it goes: you reject a creed and pretty soon you're an agent of nothing, of death. You look for adventure, and adventure grabs hold of you. He tried summoning the hope he'd felt reading Yong's notebook, grace afforded by big thoughts, but it had shrunken out of reach, a pebble deep inside him, only worrying his soul. He thought of asking Yong about the weapons he'd worked on, but instinct told him that was one conversation he should save, no matter what the conclusion.

"That sun," he said. The handle of the briefcase was slipping absurdly from his hand, and he put it down, stopping to retie his shoe and to check their surroundings.

"It will be down soon," Yong said.

Lindstrom shivered in spite of the lingering warmth. The .45 was cocked and locked in the briefcase, the path before and behind them was clear. The meth was tempting, but he held it off for the moment. At a distance he judged to be just over five hundred yards, the track they were on joined a road. The road abutted a factory on the southeastern corner of the town and cut in a straight line across the paddy. Another mile and it came abreast of a railbed, raised above the paddy on a flat bed of gravel and grass. The rails gleamed dully in the lowering light. "Who uses that road?"

"Teacher Chen said there's the station." Yong's tone was as calm as the air crouching over the field. A buffalo dragged a stooped farmer on a changeless and lumbering progress across it. Something about the buffalo, its quaintness or futility or its absolute refusal to be anything more than it was, made Lindstrom want to shoot it in the head.

"I hate this countryside," he said.

"The militia has a camp in the fields beyond the station," Yong told him, removing his jacket. The T-shirt underneath was stenciled with a waving giant panda, a ridiculous remnant of some international event of goodwill.

"Come on," said Lindstrom. The light had dipped, spread; the creased, purple mountains came out in relief. What light remained clung to the corduroy surface of the road. "It makes me nervous being out in the open like this."

Yong turned to agree, and something flashed in his glasses like the glint of a knife. Lindstrom's hand moved quickly to the pocket of the briefcase, but it was only a scatter of blackbirds, riding gently on the grass. In Vietnam he might have clicked on full auto and made the rice boil—the catharsis of recon by fire—but the sound of a single shot in this dingy, pinkish dusk would have traveled for miles.

Another ten yards, and the path hugged the railbed. A fetid breeze sprang up, scurrying down the tracks and over the embankment, blowing the birds from their perches in haphazard gusts. The red blazes on their wings blinked like poppies for a moment, then the birds became part of the gathering night.

"Something's burning," said Yong, sniffing. Above Anhe, the narrow, silver band of light was blotted by smoke.

"Slow down. Let me go ahead."

The cross on the church's steeple stood out against the smoke, like a needle in the skin of the land. Heat lightning crackled against the misty mountains behind it. The road ahead curved and turned sharply into the underpass. The tunnel smelled of urine and creosote; bats started from the timbers above. Lindstrom thought he heard dripping, but above the paddy level, the land had been dry.

"It's coming," Yong said. The ties registered the clack of a train.

At the opposite end of the tunnel, shapes like ragged scraps of paper blew around in a pale square of light. A few pieces of gravel dislodged from the embankment, skidding into the road. The interval between each clack on the rails seemed interminable. Lindstrom brought the Colt out of the briefcase as more gravel came down and the train speeded up in an agony of acceleration.

"We must hurry," Yong whispered.

Pebbles bounced off the concrete tunnel wall. The pounding of the train grew louder, carried down through the concrete, and the gravel washed into the road. A heap landed on top of it, then gathered itself into the shape of a man. His shoulders were buttoned with poor epaulets, and an absurd cocked hat made his head appear too small. The man gathered up his AWOL bag; then, as the engine came directly above them, a second soldier clambered down from the railbed, losing his hat in the slide. Yong pushed at Lindstrom's elbow as the hat rolled across the road and into a discarded tire. The train seemed to slow as it passed overhead. The first soldier retrieved the hat with the bayonet of his rifle, flipping it up in the air to his buddy, who caught it and beat the dust off on his knee. Then he put the hat back on his head and the two soldiers started down the road, jostling each other like kids. Steam from the train poured down over the exit to the tunnel, and the clacking lengthened again.

"What sort of camp did you say it was?" Lindstrom whispered.

"A labor camp, for people like me. It's left over from the Cultural Revolution."

"What were they doing on the tracks?"

The soldier on the left was just passing out of sight.

"Probably in Anhe with their women," Yong said.

Lindstrom put the pistol back in the case. The air beyond the tunnel was freighted with moisture, and Yong's face shone blue and sweaty in the twilight.

The station building lay a short distance down the tracks, its vapor lamps bleeding their corneal glow into the white smoke surrounding the platform. At the near end a clock face, laconic and bug-specked, stared away from the lighted square windows of the train.

The soldiers reached the station parking lot at a brisk pace and climbed the wooden steps to the platform. Beyond the building, huddled shapes moved along before the engine, yellow torches tracing short streaks of light in the haze. They stooped and stabbed with long poles like some strange Elysian fishermen, their dark blue jumpsuits wreathed in smoke. The ember of a cigarette glowed at the head of the line. All at once, Lindstrom heard a car's tires banging hard on the washerboard road.

"He's coming fast," Yong observed. Through the tunnel behind them, headlights scissored the paddy.

"That truck," Lindstrom said. In the lot by the depot, a truck was parked, its stake bed mounded with agricultural lime. "Don't run, walk quickly and get in the cab."

As they moved, the train whistle sounded. For the first time, Lindstrom noticed Yong's limp.

"If we don't make the train," Yong began. The car came through the tunnel, springs crying in the ruts. "We'll have to walk to Nanjing."

The interior of the truck smelled of old dust and oil. The seat was still warm from the sun. The overloaded car careened into the lot, skidding to a stop near the stairs.

"Who are they?" Lindstrom whispered.

"They may be state security. Those are usually the ones who have cars."

The back doors opened, and the pastor from the Anhe church got out, between two militia. A tall man in a metallic-looking jacket got out from the driver's seat and went around to the back of the car. Air expelled from the brakes of the train, and the couplings groaned and clanged. A short, dark man came around from the passenger side and took the pastor by the arm. He spoke to the militiamen sharply, and they shuffled toward the trunk as the train cars moved into the night, wheels screaming on the rails. The two militia and the driver leaned into the trunk, and then the arms and legs of another man appeared. The short, dark man led the tiny pastor across the empty tracks as the three men lugged the charred body up the wooden stairs.

The observer, Lindstrom thought, *forever alters the thing he observes.* April had once read it to him from a book.

You. You think I'm responsible for this?

AN HOUR LATER, THE BACK OF A BICYCLE RIDER APPEARED ON the shoulder, rack laden with some dirty, blood-red vegetable, and Lindstrom swung the stolen truck into the center of the road, watching as the headlight fell on a pale, determined cheek, then a nose and barely discernible mouth, lips set in a grimace at the truck's wicked stench. As he passed, the clatter of the engine and the whine of the driveshaft beneath the rusted floor seemed to blow the rider sideways toward moon-shadowed fields. The rider seemed for a moment to pedal in place, against a blue background, then his bent figure left the cracked mirror, and Lindstrom saw only blackness, then shreds of cloud across a squashed white moon, and later a few pale stars. His head lolled backwards and sideways, and he ground his teeth and slapped his neck to stay awake. He dipped his finger in the envelope and covered his gums with the crystal.

Two hours out of Anhe, a car approached, moving fast, the headlights first, smeared like breath in the mirror, then the sound of the engine straining. It slowed beside the truck, and the man in back on the passenger side met Lindstrom's averted eye. His round face, the cropped black hair unruly at the crown—Lindstrom knew him from somewhere. The round-faced man was pointing at him, then ahead. The car honked, a broken, plastic sound that woke him fully, and he realized that his foot was to the floor—the truck keeping pace with his headlong mind. When he pulled it off the pedal, the car shot back in front of him. His heart raced with the engine throbbing underneath his foot. A woman's head was beside by the man's, barely showing above the back of the seat. If her hair had not been gray, he would have taken the Anhe pastor for a girl.

The broken taillight of the car bloomed a hundred yards ahead, and the truck closed ground. Slowly, Lindstrom pumped the brakes, which made the old rig shimmy. The wheel skipped back and forth, and it didn't seem connected to the tires. He touched the pistol beneath his thigh. The taillight played tricks on him until he couldn't see it anymore, and the blacktop rolled like the sea beneath the truck. A silent rain smeared the windshield, and he was searching the dash for the wiper switch when he realized he was crying. In the field to his left, he saw the shape of a water buffalo tethered to a skeletal tree. The animal stood impossibly still. Lindstrom squeezed his eyes shut, and sparks jumped from the meth. Life poured from the animal's throat, and the clouds in the moonlight were like the flank of a scaly, silver fish, soaked with blood. He was twisting and dancing in the seat.

A traffic rotary appeared in the headlights, and he double-clutched quickly as he slammed on the brakes. The pedal was soft. He tried to remember the previous minutes, but his mind stepped backward into a wall. His left foot nearly caught in the wires under the dash as he mashed the clutch in and downshifted. The truck groaned on its springs as he swung the wheel right, and the tires roared as if they were being torn from the rims.

A squat building, a toilet or bath, appeared directly in front of him, maybe twenty yards if he were lucky, between the hood and the cinder-block wall. Yong's head struck the side window as Lindstrom yanked the wheel the opposite way. Lime flew from the bed. Yong snapped upright and murmured something confused in Chinese. Lindstrom had missed the curb around the rotary by inches. On the far side, the dust spread out level with the road. The car from the station was stopped there, blocking both narrow lanes. Its fenders were dented and tan, its design a mean approximation of some poor American product of the late 1970s. Behind the hood, two men were holding rifles, Springfield ought-threes from the profile, something of that vintage, single-shot. The men had put on Sam Browne belts with ammunition pouches on them. The round-faced man was chambering a round as the truck went toward the center of the rotary. The taller man brought the stock to his shoulder.

The truck was moving slowly now, with not much room to ram.

"Get down," Lindstrom said. "Now!"

The first shot whacked a side rail of the stake body and ricocheted off.

"Lead a little, fucker," Lindstrom called out. The ricochet tapped out a crazy tattoo on the metal and silenced itself all at once. He waited for the pain. "Come on. Lead."

Sure enough, the next shot starred the windshield, salting the dashboard with glass. Yong was already down on the floor. As the truck rolled forward, presenting its flank as a target, Lindstrom brought it to face them, peering through the wheel as best he could. They'd get a few shots at the engine, but their ammunition wasn't jacketed, and the only other thing to do was go around the circle and run. The truck had bulk, not speed. The second shot rang on the door but didn't seem to go through it, or at least Yong didn't cry out.

"You hit?" Lindstrom yelled, bringing out the .45.

"Not unless it doesn't hurt," Yong said.

Lindstrom let the truck coast straight. He got two shots off through the open window, but both were high. The men at the car ducked their heads anyway. Lindstrom jammed the accelerator down.

The old truck bucked, and the men's heads came up, long enough to see it bearing down, or rather, crawling toward them, making a hell of a lot of noise. If Lindstrom had had the time to shoot or kick the shattered windshield out, he could have popped them both, frozen there behind the car in the headlights, but he could only see them through a fist-sized hole. The rest of the windshield was snow. The round-faced man was struggling with his rifle, and he chucked it away and pulled a revolver from his belt. The taller man got off a shot that passed through the cab, taking out the rest of the windshield and showering Lindstrom's lap. He put a hand in front of his eyes as the bullet hit the back window with a sound that stopped his ears. He yanked the wheel left to get a shot off before he thought of the old woman, maybe still in the back of the car. It was too late and he couldn't see where he was going anyway, too little speed to change direction and still break through the car. He fired once, blindly, but he never saw where it went. The truck hit the rear door of the car with a thud and scream of metal, jerking the wheel from his hands and slamming his hip against the door. By reflex, he had braced himself against the seat and pedals, and the truck moved forward to the sound of crying metal, tearing off the side of the car. He could feel the back wheels rearing up and then pawing the ground. He gritted his teeth and shifted into first. He couldn't risk a search for reverse. A shot hit the passenger door with a ring, and another whistled over the roof. He found the .45 beside him on the glass-strewn seat and squeezed off a shot that seemed incredibly loud in the cab. The truck had stalled.

The pop of the rifle came from farther away than he'd have guessed, and the bullet went buzzing over his head. He hit the ignition, and the starter turned over with a dreadful whine. He cranked again and heard the engine cough. The synchro-mesh in the transmission was a memory, or hadn't been invented yet, and the gears clashed, which at least meant the motor was turning. As he jammed the lever, holding the stalk at the base, into what he thought was first, two more shots, first the rifle then a .38, judging from the sound, hit the door and the hood of the truck in succession. They were firing from closer this time.

"John?" Yong moved and glass fell from his shoulders.

"Stay where you are. I'm going to try to break on through."

There were moments, he thought, when the very worst positions were comforting. Just curl up in a ball and let them come on. He was compelled to wonder if this was what he liked, what he sought instead of something else that other men wanted, but simple survival made him raise the pistol again. Seven minus five, he thought, two left. He waited for the next two shots, one of which hit with a ping, and fired in the general direction. He brought himself up with a hand on the wheel, and something stung his knuckle. Through the passenger window, he could see the taller man, raising the rifle, no more than twenty yards from the car and coming on. The man's hand came up to the bolt, and Lindstrom ground out the clutch as he sighted as low as he could. The scream of metal commenced as the truck raked the car, and Lindstrom squeezed the trigger, but the .45 didn't respond.

One missing, he thought. My performance incentive. The man with the rifle was taking his time, and Lindstrom ducked and pushed down on the throttle. The car swung out of the way. He heard the rifle pop again, but the shot missed. The lime made a target as bright as a flare, so he ducked his head again as the truck gathered speed. The next shot tore the mirror from the passenger side. Yong blinked at him and fumbled with his glasses. He shook shards of glass from his hair. Lindstrom shifted into third, the highest gear, and pointed the truck down the road. The headlights were gone, but a half-moon was low in the sky. The night had lightened.

"Is it safe to come up now?"

"I think so. You might look back and tell me what you see."

Yong scrambled up onto the seat, his hair whipping in the wind through the broken windshield frame.

"I'm not sure," he said, "but it looks like they are shooting their car."

AT NEARLY NINE O'CLOCK, BURLING'S PLANE FROM HONG Kong descended through dusky air to Beijing and landed between barbed-wire compounds, trees planted in dust. There was the familiar empty feeling of communist airports, as if a big flight of people had recently left, waxed floors and ads for RJR China. At the quarantine, Burling handed over his passport and, before he could protest, felt himself being shoved toward a small room with sweating blue walls. It was finally happening, he found himself thinking as they pushed him through the doorway, the punishment, but why? He was a failure in many things that mattered, it was true, but hadn't he tried? He felt the Mickey Mouse removed from his arm.

The air in the tiny room was stifling, and he became aware of his breathing. Before a small, barred window a man and woman in customs uniforms sat on either side of a gray metal desk, playing cards in the breeze of a fan. A matron in knee-highs watched them from the corner. The single bulb that depended on a wire from the ceiling threw the exaggerated gestures of their game out the window and onto a rhombus of light on the dark ground outside.

Excuse me, he thought. Are we alive?

A scuffle was going on behind him in the corridor, and after a moment's hesitation—you should always ignore them—he hazarded turning his back on the room. In the doorway, a man in a V-neck sweater was attempting to disengage Burling's stuffed mouse from the arms of the agent who had pushed him. The two Chinese tugged back and forth on Mickey's limbs.

"Hey," Burling said. "You're going to break him."

The man in the sweater whipped around and found himself holding the mouse. His face was red, more from anger than effort.

He had a bandage on his forehead and a streak of what looked like soot on his neck beneath his ear. The Chinese cooked with charcoal, and often you would see it on them, like Good Friday ashes, but this man looked like he'd been through a fight. "I am," he began, then started over. "No, I beg your deepest pardon for this commotion. I am Li Xin." He looked down as if the mouse had just jumped into his hands. "Please." He thrust it toward Burling.

"*Milou shou* is very popular," Burling observed.

Li's face grew dark. "This customs man wished to sever the stomach of your mouse. He thought perhaps that you might be a smuggler. I told him that you were an official of the American government, and that could not be so."

"I'm coming in, not going out," mentioned Burling.

"Please," Li lowered his chin. "We'll go."

But Burling stood still. The security checkpoint had now been abandoned, and his passport was not in his hand. "I'm passing through Beijing for a meeting with Ambassador Wardlow," he said. "I don't . . ."

"A friend of my minister," Li told him, moving out of the doorway. "The customs official has your passport. He will return it to you in the VIP lounge."

Burling allowed himself to be escorted down a long hall and into a room decorated with boxy rosewood furniture and deep rugs with blue and pink fishes swimming in oceans of red. He set the Mickey Mouse down on a chair. "I was supposed to be met by a car from the embassy," he said, "but that was before I missed my original flight."

"Please." Li held out his small hand, indicating a couch. "We know all about your delay in Hong Kong, and we have eagerly awaited your arrival, so that we may be of assistance to you."

A man in a white waiter's coat came in with a tray of glasses filled with green or orange liquid. Burling sat down and accepted a kiwi juice, which he balanced on his knee without drinking. Li took his orange juice with overt appreciation, a practice the Chinese liked to use to make you feel ungrateful.

"This is kind of you, really," said Burling, "but I have made it through this airport before like a regular citizen."

Li's eyes traced the stitching on the Johnston & Murphys Burling had purchased at home. "We will wait for a moment. These are cowboy boots, yes?"

Burling raised his trousers to show the height of the shoes. "Just regular oxbloods."

"Ox blood?"

Burling tried not to laugh. "Cordovans. Oxblood refers to their color."

"Ah." Li nodded. "Where I was raised, men had actual blood on their shoes."

Burling restrained an unkind observation. "Where was that?" he asked, but Li was pensive again, as if he had already revealed too much. He had said "my minister," and the customs officials had been scared of him . . . State Security, Burling thought, or Second Department, neither one of whose attention he wanted to draw.

"I must apologize again for the lack of hospitality," said Li. His manner was shy and dishonest.

"Mickey doesn't hold a grudge," Burling told him, which brought a flicker of a smile to Li's lips. "He does, however, have an appointment with a little boy in Shanghai tomorrow morning, which he doesn't want to miss."

"Of course. I myself have a daughter who wishes to crush *milou shou*."

The customs agent appeared in the doorway, Burling's passport laid out on his tray.

"Ah," said Li. "Your passport has now arrived. My minister, General Zu Dongren, would be honored if you would join him for a banquet honoring the participants in his seminar on the historical period of the Japanese occupation of China."

"But Ambassador Wardlow . . ." He would have finished, but the general's name made his breath feel like fire in his lungs. There would not be two Zu Dongrens.

"The ambassador will also be attending," Li said. "The general is particularly interested in the attempts by the American government, by General Joseph Stilwell and his successors, to utilize the forces of the Communist Party to fight the Japanese fascists."

"I believe they abandoned that plan early on," Burling said, tucking his passport safely away. He felt the need of its security acutely. "But I'm not an expert, of course."

"Of course. General Zu has also invited a delegation of former American pilots, who supplied the Nationalist forces in Chongqing."

"They were on the first leg of my flight," Burling said. From behind a cloisonné screen, he could hear outdoor sounds—cars arriving, voices sharp on the night. Suddenly he thought of Luke again, of his sunglasses holding that sky. "Where are they now?"

"They have been conducted immediately to their hotel. The general has heard of your experience in Asia and would very much like including you among his guests. He has discussed this with Ambassador Wardlow, and you will be welcome at the State Guesthouse tonight."

"General Zu is too kind," Burling said. He wondered just how much MacAllister had planned of this and how much was outside his control. The only thing to do in a situation with so many loose ends was to pull one and see what unraveled, even if it turned out to be your whole life. "Please tell him that I am honored by his invitation, that it is an unexpected pleasure to accept."

"We will go, then."

At the doorway, a man in a silver Mercedes jacket had appeared with Burling's luggage at his feet. Burling set his untouched juice on the end table and got up to follow.

"Don't forget your mouse," Li said.

THEY CAME INTO BEIJING ON A LONG ROAD LINED WITH alleys of trees. In the center were two lanes of asphalt with no yellow line; beyond the first row of trees was a thoroughfare for bikes and then another row of trees, like a French park, trunks whitewashed at the base. The driver pressed the car to a speed un-safe for the narrow space, his mirror barely missing the oncoming buses and trucks with their dull yellow lights. Even Li rode with one arm stiff against the dash.

As the road began to curve, the trees seemed to move toward them as if the car were standing still, and Burling turned to the window to break their hypnosis. In the dusty lane beside him, girls rode sidesaddle on racks behind the men and children sat like little Buddhas on their parents' handlebars. Beyond the trees, the city had begun to assemble itself beneath the white haze. Beijing—its ramshackle houses and sandblasting wind—had always seemed bleakened by power to Burling. Like Kabul and Samarkand—these great historical capitals often retained a feudal soul, villagers living in fear of a dragon. The humble people who dwelled in the shadows of government only saw its retractable claws, the tip of its tail left outside while the beast napped fitfully in its sanctum. Yellow street-lights filed ahead into the early amber dusk.

The surly driver honked, and women yoked to carts of burlap jumped from their path. Burling felt sick to his stomach again as the car debouched from a rotary onto the wide carriageway.

"We are now on one of the roads that was built along the foun-dations of the old city walls," Li explained. "I am sorry, but your plane was delayed so we must go directly to the restaurant. Later we will take you to the State Guesthouse where you will be staying."

"Thank you," said Burling. He wondered if they knew why his flight had been delayed, but better to treat the whole thing as a rhetorical exercise, bide your time while you discovered what had brought you to the dragon's attention.

"The Peking duck is the best in our city," Li told him.

The car slowed and went through a gate into a parking lot crowded with tan and black sedans. The steps to the restaurant were covered in deep red carpet, and the dining room beyond was pan-eled in shiny, fake wood and brocade. Under the bright chandeliers, Simon Bell and the Hump Pilots sat scattered at round tables with a handful of American diplomats and Chinese men and women in

Western dress. Li escorted Burling to a table with Bell and two pilots, an elegant woman whom he recognized from Shanghai, and a man of Napoleonic stature whom Burling vaguely recognized to be Li's minister, General Zu. Li guided Burling forward with a proprietary hand.

"Consul Burling," said the general. A large, fleshy palm levitated from his side.

"An unexpected pleasure," Burling told him. The way his thoughts were running, he had expected to shiver, but the general's handshake was solid and warm. His expression, however, seemed vastly preoccupied, perhaps even annoyed. It was almost certainly the man from the runway at Mazar-i-Sharif.

"Of course you are welcome," the general said.

"I hope I haven't kept you waiting."

"It is the general who has been waiting to meet you," said Li.

Burling readied a suitably flattering response, but General Zu had looked away.

"Somewhere out there a poor duck is giving its life," said a hearty American voice. Burling turned straight into the grip of Simon Bell. "So that we may eat well."

Simon gave Burling's bicep a squeeze as both men sat down. "Bruce Travers," Bell told him. "We met on the plane to Hong Kong."

Burling nodded to the two other Hump Pilots, burly Rotarian types with lapel pins on their lightweight summer blazers. After Bell's introductions, he tried, unsuccessfully, to make out Ambassador Wardlow among the guests. The Chinese at Burling's table all seemed unhappy, and he was about to introduce himself when he saw their eyes shifting toward the corner of the room, where General Zu stood with Li at his shoulder, surveying the tables from beneath his drooping eyelids.

"I would like to offer a toast," the general said, ending the phrase on an upward beat, "to friendship and scholarship. The pursuit of the latter depends on the former."

The audience clapped when Li delivered the translation. The general commended technological and educational exchange, and welcomed the American consul from Shanghai as well as Ambassador Wardlow, whose head Burling now picked out at a table in the opposite corner. Through Wardlow's coiffed white hair, he could see the pink scalp, as if he'd been boiled. General Zu looked at Li with impatience as Li rendered his words into English, and the military men took the opportunity to drink, while the intellectuals listened attentively to the struggling Li. When the general finished, there was a lull like the drawn breath in the stands of a football game, when the crowd is not sure if the ball has gone over the line, then the scholars began to drink and there was a general eruption.

During the drinking, the general went around pointing his glass at each guest. When he reached Burling, he made a show of taking a bottle of wine from the center of the table and filling their respective glasses to the brim. With the tepid wine spilling onto his hand, Burling nodded at the general's somber eyes and drank.

When they had emptied their glasses, Burling sensed that the general intended to reestablish a bond between them. In Samarkand, the idea had been to find a way to arm the *mujahedin* through the finger of Afghan territory that touched the autonomous region of Xinjiang, in far western China. After Burling had made the connection, MacAllister had taken it up, communicating with Zu or others like him through men like Yong Beihong. As the minister of state security, Zu might want to stop Yong from getting out for multiple reasons, even if the information about China's nuclear program was only a bluff. Zu wouldn't appreciate a dissident's successful defection, even a relative unknown like Yong who had never attracted individual attention from the Western press. A more likely, and slightly more sinister, motivation would be that Zu's cooperation with the Americans might cause him to lose face with those even higher placed than he in the Party and the State Council, thus thwarting his chances for advancement, or bringing about his demise. In this, he and MacAllister were alike. Together, they had armed groups that now posed a threat, and Zu had the Uyghurs to worry about, the restive ethnic minority in Xinjiang, who more and more subscribed to a pan-Islamic vision sympathetic to the Taliban.

Rationally speaking, it would seem that Zu and MacAllister had the same goal, to stop Yong Beihong from escaping from China, or at least not get very far out of the country, alive. Which left Burling in a familiar quandary, able to analyze the hard motivations involved as well or better than anyone, yet still unable to ignore the human cost. And just as he was resolving to leave, to get in touch with MacAllister and tell him to go to hell, Burling was surprised from his thoughts by an invitation to offer a toast of his own. He tried to defer to Ambassador Wardlow, but Wardlow returned Burling's glance with a mischievous shrug. He seemed to be saying, this is your fuckup, not mine.

"I can't hope," began Burling, wiping the wine from his lips with his napkin as he rose. The glare from chandeliers splintered his vision. "I can't hope to match the general's . . . what was it? Iambic pentameter?"

The woman at his table from Shanghai, and Bell with her, laughed spontaneously, while Li searched for the Mandarin word. After a moment, the woman helped him and the scholars all signaled their appreciation of the joke, while the warriors looked confused. The general's expression was ponderous.

"It must be his martial background, which allows him to offer epic toasts," Burling added, and the general's jowls shifted slightly. "In my family, it was always Uncle George, himself a military man, a veteran of the Great War, who was known for his eloquence, a trait that has, unfortunately, passed me by."

As Li gave the translation, Burling watched for the general's reaction. His several chins had shifted downward in numerous folds on his chest and as he listened, his head bobbed slightly like a buoy absorbing a swell.

"For his part, Uncle George attended the Moody Bible College in Chicago and traveled to Persia as a missionary . . ."

Burling paused again to await the translation. When Li pronounced the word "Bible," which only had a cognate in Mandarin, the general's head came up and Burling was staring straight into his moist gray eyes. Up to now, the story was true, but what could

Uncle George do that would cause a reaction—what parable did you compose for the dragon, the khan, to keep yourself breathing through the night? In a way, that was what diplomacy always came down to—stories that staved off inevitable violence and death. As Amelia had it, your life was only a story you told yourself, and when it turned sad or you didn't believe it anymore, you were in trouble. Burling had always argued against her version of things, but now he wasn't so sure. After all, intelligence was stories, too, albeit mostly lies. Li seemed to stick on the last word—"missionary"—perhaps the character had disappeared from the sanctioned history books.

"But Uncle George was restless," Burling went on, "a dreamer. Perhaps that's the gene that lodged here." He poked his own chest—a Chinese gesture—as Li caught up.

While Li spoke, Burling slid his eyes in Wardlow's direction to see how his words were going over in that quarter. In most cases— the signing of a trade agreement, the groundbreaking for a joint-venture plant or hotel—Burling knew what to say to bring the assembled together, to give them a good feeling about the profits they were about to accrue, as if they were somehow a sign of good works; but here, he had no idea what the goal of the conference, or meeting, or whatever, was meant to be, except his own discomfort. Dennis Wardlow, a recent Bush appointee, offered no help.

"Persia and missionary work were not enough for Uncle George. He developed an interest in linguistics and, later, antiquities. He pressed onward into Afghanistan, Turkmenistan, looking for the Silk Road, the lost Indo-European language he had heard about in Persia, and the cities of the Great Khan. What were his politics, you might ask?"

At the translation, the guests looked to one another as if for the answer.

"You might as well ask, what were Marco Polo's politics, or those of Columbus? These explorers served a government—though in the Admiral Columbus's case, not his own—they served a king or queen who desired greater dominion, riches perhaps, gold . . ."

Against his intention, the last word got a laugh. A powerful spirit overtook him.

"But men, I would submit, men like Columbus who descend from what they understand to be a mountain in the center of an ocean that ends in the abyss; men like Columbus and Uncle George, for whom penetration into Asia was like going undercover into the land of the Infidel . . ."

General Zu was watching him now, with an even, an interested, not inhospitable sharpness of eye. His jaws worked inside his sagging cheeks. Burling had meant to discover what the general wanted, but he was revealing more of himself than drawing General Zu out. He shouldn't let Zu know what drove him, why he felt he had fallen so unbelievably far, but he couldn't stop himself. He needed to complete the connection.

"When Columbus discovered the New World, he believed he was sailing to Cathay, to meet the Great Khan, described in such detail by the Venetian Marco Polo, and on to the court of the emperor of China. Instead he set an irretrievable process in motion, the founding of America. What I'm saying is that my country was actually discovered by mistake by a man who wanted to visit yours."

He knew this would garner a laugh, and a good one was indeed forthcoming. Bell's wink said that Burling had extricated himself and should stop now, but Burling had no intention of doing so. He pressed willfully toward the edge of the abyss.

"Inspired by Uncle George, then, I might say in a sense that I have discovered, by mistake, my own country by intending to see yours. Some of the Hump Pilots gathered tonight, I would bet, had a similar experience years ago."

A few murmurs of recognition went on while Li spoke. When Zu received the translation, he nodded and raised his glass. Was he, too, letting Burling know he should end it?

"It is a commonplace to say that the world is shrinking, but Columbus lived in a very small world himself, or so he thought . . . Therefore I would encourage us, in our deliberations on the subject of history, to look inside for our secret motivations, and thereby not shrink, but enlarge our shared world."

The general stood up and took Burling's elbow, steering him around to each table, where their glasses were emptied and filled, emptied and filled until Burling lost track of the number. The company seemed generally divided on whether he was an ass or a master rhetorician. By the time he and Zu had circled back to their own places, the chef was wheeling out the duck, heralded by applause. To the pilots, the general explained the process that resulted in its glistening, brown skin, its tender meat, and Burling found himself relating to the bird.

WHEN THE MEAL HAD BEEN SERVED AND THE TABLE WAS BUSY with their food, the woman from Shanghai, Madame Yang, leaned toward Burling across Simon Bell.

"Your uncle," she began.

"George," said Burling, a sea slug quivering on the ends of his chopsticks.

"He was a missionary in what we call Iran?"

"He was really a teacher," Burling told her. "George was never ordained."

Madame Yang nodded thoughtfully, and Burling tried to remember where he had met her before. Her English, what he'd heard, was graceful and delicate, as if she'd been educated overseas, or in a mission school.

"He was distracted in his studies by a beautiful woman," Burling added, "of whom my grandparents did not approve."

Madame Yang barely smiled; she was more serious than he.

"Most Chinese philosophers," she said, "the Greeks, also, were called teachers. Not to mention Jesus Christ, as I'm sure you are aware."

"Fisher of men," the chief of the Hump Pilots said.

Madame Yang smiled openly now. It seemed to Burling that she judged the pilot on a different scale, a more charitable one. Women had always expected more of him than he was able to deliver. She helped herself to some fish from the turntable, spooning it on top of a rice cake. "It seems that he is in the kitchen tonight."

The chief thought for a moment, then looked at the other pilot. "This lady knows her New Testament," he said.

General Zu was arguing with the two scholars next to him, but the rest of the table took her comment with polite laughter, all except for Li Xin. "There has been quite a history of Western missionaries in China," he told them. "I understand there are Christian congregations even now, with Americans and Europeans assisting them in the printing of Bibles and other tracts, meeting in the more remote provinces."

"My church in Macon contributes to that," the second Hump Pilot said. "Last month we viewed a video in adult education regarding a minister in Florida, whose relatives had been here in the twenties. The film was called *A Resurrection in China*."

The general was listening now. "To be perfectly candid," he spoke through Li Xin, "I do not talk now for the Party, but from my own experience. The presence of Western missionaries, like Western music or films, has always been a source of anxiety for us."

"But Christian worship is sanctioned," Burling said. "There is a China Christian Council—"

". . . and even a Chinese Catholic Church, yes," said Madame Yang with a note of sadness, "but it does not recognize the Pope."

"Neither do I," said the pilot from Georgia. Bell and the chief pilot laughed. Madame Yang appeared lost in devotion.

"We are a nation of two billion people," the general told them. "We must maintain order, you see."

"I reckon that's what you had in mind in 1989," said Bell, obviously drunk.

It took a moment for the table to absorb his comment. While they did, the general took his wine with melancholy. His irritation showed only in the downward turn of his mouth. "You ask Li," he said in gruff, halting English. "He has a good thing to say about that."

"I believe," Li began, fumbling with his food like a child brought out to perform.

"Your schooling," the general prompted.

"I was about to say that my education, like many people in my generation, was interrupted by the Cultural Revolution. For several years I raised pigs in the countryside."

"No harm in that," the Georgian Hump Pilot said.

"We do not want that chaos to happen again," Li informed him.

The Hump Pilot shrugged and let a chastened laugh escape from his lips. Satisfied, the general nodded. "There," he said, and with that, silence reigned at the table.

The Georgian pilot looked nervously at his fellows as another course came around. As they ate, Madame Yang engaged the chief and the Georgian in stories about their families back in the States. She had a daughter studying English in Madison, Wisconsin.

"More Catholics than you can shake a stick at up there," the chief said.

Tea and compote were brought for dessert. Dinner ended with handshakes and hopes for productive exchanges in the morning, and the group moved in waves from the banquet room into the lobby.

In the men's room, Burling stood at a urinal next to the pilot from Georgia.

"I think my mind must be going," the Georgian said. "Fellow seated next to you . . . ?"

"Travers."

"That's him. Bruce Travers. I am sure I remember Bruce as a tall kid, bad skin."

The chief pilot came in and took his place on the other side of Burling.

"Travers was always scratching himself," the Georgian said. "We called him Itchy. Didn't we, Bob?"

The chief undid his fly and groaned with relief. "What's that, Riley?"

"Didn't we call Travers 'Itchy'?"

"Yeah, we called him that. Did he deny it?" asked the chief.

The Georgian zipped up and went to the sink. Burling was too tense to have any luck.

"He didn't deny it," said the Georgian, washing his hands, "it's just that I swore I had heard that boy got himself killed in a hunting accident, years ago now."

When the pilots had left, Burling stared for a while at the wall. A toilet flushed, the stall door opened, and Li Xin walked over to the sink.

"Have you enjoyed yourself?" he asked.

"Very much." Burling washed his hands and Li offered him the towel. "Do you know where the pilots are going next?"

The awareness that Li had been listening crackled between them.

"One of the pilots, a Mr. Bruce Travers, has retired from your aircraft company in the United States. He wishes to tour their joint venture factory in Shanghai. So he will . . . how did you put it? . . . discover himself there before rejoining his party in Kunming."

"I'd like to host him for dinner," Burling said. "The factory manager and I play tennis often. Will you and the general accompany the other pilots?"

"That will depend on the general's plans. We must take you to the guesthouse now, for you to receive a good night's sleep."

As he and Li stepped out under the portico, Burling saw Ambassador Wardlow's white head through the passenger window of his embassy Jeep. The engine ticked and whirred in the silky Beijing night, and Wardlow's face appeared like a well-fed apparition inside the tinted glass. The window slid down without a sound.

"Consul Burling," drawled Wardlow. "Sorry we didn't have more of a chat. My mouth was too full of that excellent duck."

"Tomorrow morning," Burling began.

"We had enough of it in Washington, didn't we, Lucius? I'm sure you're itching to get back home."

Itching? For a moment, Burling thought Dennis Wardlow was telling him something. The face of the driver shone in the dashboard's circus lights, and bugs swarmed in the high beams like snow. In the absence of reasonable connections, the world was overdetermined, as it had been in biblical times: he might as well divine the future from the little green numbers on the Jeep's stereo. Burling could feel Li's impatience on the red steps behind him.

"The general seems like an interesting fellow. I'd never met him before, had you?"

"Here and there," Wardlow said. "We don't move in the same circles, if you know what I mean. I'm surprised you hadn't made his acquaintance."

"I wish I had. He seems like a genuine student of history."

"An enthusiast."

"I was heartened by his openness about Tiananmen. I'd like to talk to him more."

"Well I've got to be going, Burl, sorry. We'll chat next week."

Burling put his hand on the top of the window. Why would Wardlow think he knew General Zu?

"I was hoping we could keep our meeting tomorrow, Dennis. If only to go over a few things I ran into on the flight."

"You and me and the general," the ambassador promised in a hearty tone, "the very next time you come through Beijing."

"The Hump Pilots," Burling said, his fingers tightening on the window; the glass felt flimsy, as if he could snap it right off.

Wardlow contemplated his own hands, working each leathery knuckle as if it were a knot. "So . . . Those fellows are something, hey? Real American heroes." He turned his shallow blue eyes on Burling. "Give my best to . . ." Then he nodded at the driver, and the Jeep roared forward, its brake lights blooming like roses as the vehicle paused behind the row of waiting cars. Whether by accident or design, Burling was definitely being left to twist in the wind. The beige Toyota that had carried Burling and Li from the airport pulled up, and Li held the door.

As Burling got in, he saw General Zu get out of the car in front of Wardlow's and stop at the Jeep. The general spoke a few words, laughed once, and saluted good night. Then the general walked toward the Toyota—whether waddling or goose-stepping was hard to decide—and slid onto the seat next to Burling.

"My car," he said gruffly in English, pointing at Li and the driver in front.

Burling wondered if it was too late to get out and beg a ride, a room in the Ambassador's Residence. He had the feeling he should escape from this man.

"The general wonders if he can share the ride to the guest-house," Li explained.

"I don't want to keep General Zu from his family," Burling said. "Perhaps there is another car that could take me?"

"I . . . ," the general began, and his face grew sad, like a great stuffed bear.

"The general's wife died this last year," Li explained, "and his son now lives in Shenzhen. He would enjoy the company and would like to hear more about your uncle."

"George. Of course. Tell the general that I, too, am alone."

The general murmured and nodded as the car lurched; the tolls of a disastrous calm went through Burling. His daughter Elizabeth was right: China's plangent mixture of mourning and menace made him feel right at home. He watched the embassy Jeep move in front of them onto the avenue. The streetlights gleamed across its black paint, its luggage racks, gold pinstripes, and honeycomb wheels. Although he normally hated seeing showy American cars on the mule-clogged thoroughfares of the developing world, it seemed to Burling that the black Jeep was bearing something—the last vestiges of his illusion about his ordered relationship to things—away from him. When it disappeared into the traffic, he did feel entirely alone.

LINDSTROM LET THE TRUCK COAST TOWARD A BRICKWORKS with piles of new bricks in the yard, each pallet covered with straw matting. He steered around the back as best he could and pulled in behind the building. When he turned off the ignition, the engine gave a great buck and cough, then expired, as if never to start again. In the distance, perhaps five miles off, the stacks of a chemical factory rose from the fields, its red lights winking in the moonrise.

"That's Nanjing," Yong said.

"How do you know?"

"Xinlian brought me in a tour bus," Yong said, "full of Japanese. We came into town by that factory, I think."

They jogged across the field behind the brickworks, where soybeans grew. Lindstrom felt their figures pasted on the sky. His knuckle ached and throbbed. The bends of a drainage ditch gleamed in the silvery light, and they made for it, moving as fast as they could through the furrows. Sliding over the lip, they dropped down into the water, almost five feet below.

"How did you come to Anhe?" Lindstrom asked at length, as they sloshed along side by side. The crop was different now, a kind of wheat, and it hid their heads from view.

"They told me the church would hide me, that you would come."

"Did they select it because of me?" Lindstrom asked. The ditch smelled of still water and clay. Night insects chattered above them.

"I know what you're thinking," Yong said, "but the church had hidden others. You don't have to blame yourself."

Ahead, the ditch shallowed. "It's a specialty of mine. And right now I want to go into Nanjing and cut Alan Rank's throat."

He felt Yong stop beside him. "Foreigners have been coming to China for many years, John. It pleases them for some reason. I don't know why. It is as if my country is a scroll on which they want to write a story about themselves. Sometimes they write in ink, sometimes in water. Other times they write in blood. The Chinese people just want to be left alone."

"Rank told me you'd been in the States," Lindstrom said. "He told me you were approached there by the Agency."

Yong started walking again, shoes sucking in the mud. "Yes, I was in the States, in Princeton, New Jersey. I met a man who wanted to know about the general I worked for. I imagine every Chinese student who travels to America is approached by such people. The only ones who entertain their advances are already working for the equivalent authorities at home."

"And were you?"

"I might ask the same thing."

"If you did, I would tell you that I worked for them once, twenty years ago in Pakistan, and earlier than that, for their army counterpart in Vietnam. I didn't start out wanting to do it, I was even against the war. But once I was in I believed what the old hands told me, that by assuming a cover you realize that everything is cover, that everyone is acting and nobody really knows who they are. I had always been a chameleon, so the whole thing was like a flash of reality for me. It felt good. In the process, they said, is the possibility of breaking through to the other side, of finding out who you really are."

"I went to Princeton as myself, John. When I was young, my mother and father were both Christians, converted by missionaries like your grandfather. I argued with them because I loved the sciences, the physical laws. I saw what they called their divinity in them. I couldn't help that people wanted things from me. I couldn't help that I wanted to please my mother, to do well in school, in the army, to get ahead. They used me, both sides against each other, because I was smart and I wanted to please them. It turned me against myself. But I'm going to have the final say."

The ditch was only a wash of gravel ahead, like a small river delta. Nearer the factory, ghosts of night mist hovered just above the fields.

"The man you met in Princeton," Lindstrom said. "Was he small, dark, balding?"

"No," Yong said when they were on the flat again. His voice was breathy with their faster pace. The telegraph poles that marked the road were far away now, the land before them sandy and barren in the darkness. "This man was tall, and fair. Very . . ."

"Polite?"

Yong nodded. "Like a mandarin."

The factory's cyclone fence approached. After walking along it for several hundred yards, they reached a traffic circle at the intersection of the road. A sign pointed east toward Anhe. A few tractors came down it out of the striped moonlit sky, weak headlights glowing, people piled into the wagons behind. Next the shape of a bus, heaps of baskets and furniture lashed to its roof. Lindstrom studied the windows for signs of the two men from Anhe, but gave up. His cartridge was empty; he was really a citizen now. In the center of the circle stood a grim-faced memorial to the liberation of Nanjing by Mao's army, lit by a single shaft of light. Beyond it, the Yangzi River Bridge rose like a dragon from the river's milky fog.

"I know him," said Lindstrom, walking around the fence and joining the side road with the workers from the night shift. A stream of cyclists pedaled toward the factory gates. "Come on, we need to steal some transportation."

Between the fence and the road was a wide band of packed dirt and ashes where a sidewalk might have been. In spite of the glory of the bridge, every road in the country was half-finished, every project abandoned. Ahead, an unfinished building lay outside the cyclone fence, dried mortar dripping over the top of the block wall. Beyond the building was a rack of bikes. It was a country full of raw materials—earth and water, people, souls. A good place to be a citizen, if you wanted to be made into something new.

"His name is Lucius Burling." Lindstrom picked a bike several from the end. "I worked for him in Afghanistan. When we get to Shanghai, we might have to look him up, that is, if we get into trouble."

"You know," Yong began, his small mouth biting off the words. He stopped, and Lindstrom looked around, but there were too many faces to watch. He felt Yong's hand on his elbow as he threw his leg over the saddle. "I may not turn out to be what you require. If you were coming here to somehow seek redemption by helping me escape, I am not a good man for that at all, not a hero or a savior or a scholar, which was what our country produced in spades before the Europeans came. I'm not even a character, as you say in the States."

"Let's just get to the train before morning," Lindstrom said.

"I am a coward," Yong told him, looking back and forth as his countrymen passed him, "and I have played every angle I have to survive. Can't you see this? I have no idea now where I stand with these people, with anyone."

"Tell me about it," Lindstrom said.

T HE CAR SPED THROUGH EMPTY STREETS TOWARD THE Daoyutai guesthouse, and Li turned around in the front seat to interpret for General Zu.

"My Uncle George was lapsed, as we call it," Burling said. On the sidewalks, people took the air in impromptu groupings of stools. "As I told Madame Yang tonight at dinner, George came back to the United States on a visit, and fell in love. It was hard for him to be a proper servant of God after that."

"I have recently visited a Christian church near Nanjing," Li said. His feelings about it were hard to appraise, but Burling could guess. "This church was built by a missionary named Reverend Lindstrom."

"A missionary?" Burling hid his shock by watching two men fixing an overturned bike by the curb. The first man held an electric torch on the black gears and chain. The bike looked like a dead animal. The general's body shifted on the seat beside him.

"You have heard of Reverend Lindstrom?" Li asked.

"No," Burling coughed, hoping his hosts would mistake it for a laugh. "I often run into the descendants of China missionaries at home. I'm always surprised at how many there are."

The general grunted something and met Burling's eye. "General Zu says, 'We know.'"

Burling joined in the compulsory laughter, but he wondered what exactly they did know. Clearly they knew about Jack; perhaps Wardlow even suspected that Burling still worked for the Agency, and that Lindstrom was part of some harebrained covert op. State had been left out in the cold on China policy starting with Kissinger, and they bore a grudge. Perhaps Wardlow had mentioned Burling's former employers to the general just to get them off his back. He could imagine Wardlow saying, "Lucius Burling is an old China hand," which was a lie, but would signal the necessary grounds for suspicion. "China hand" to the Ministry of State Security would be synonymous with "spy."

"It is unfortunate," said Li, "that the reason for my visit was not a happy one. The church has been burned by the local militia; they suspected the congregation of sheltering smugglers."

"Smugglers," the general repeated in English. "Very bad."

"Undoubtedly," Burling agreed. "It is a problem for my country, too."

"They smuggle people, as you know," Li said. The general watched him with care. "Sometimes the motive is money. Other times it is something else. In your toast tonight, which the general enjoyed very much, you spoke of secret motivations. The general wondered what these might have been."

Burling saw the trap he had laid for himself: indeed the world was a double mirror, hard and simple on one side, on the other elaborately framed. It kept spinning around, and you never knew which side reflected the future, which the past. In the immediate present there were no analogies, no chance for embellishment. His face in the windshield of the car looked drawn. "I was speaking historically," he said.

The general spoke gravely to Li. "Are there historical incidents where human beings were contraband?" Li asked.

"I suppose in my own country . . ." The hole he was digging looked deeper and deeper, but there was nothing else to say; he wanted to open the door to candor. "Before our Civil War, black slaves from the South were sometimes smuggled to freedom."

"Freedom," the General repeated. He seemed to recognize the sound of the word, but he pronounced it with suspicion: the Minister of State Security would have ordered the march on the Square; General Zu would still be in prison like Zhao if he'd opposed it. Freedom was something that scared the Chinese; indeed it scared most men, as it should. The cost, after all, was more than the average modern man, even American, was prepared to accept. The months since 9/11 had proven that.

"The general wonders," said Li, though Burling had not heard him speak, "how a country such as yours that has enslaved human beings may speak so highly of its values while it encourages an indecent act such as smuggling?"

"I don't make any such claims for myself," Burling said.

The general made a noise as if he were clearing his throat. For some reason, it made a cold fear creep up Burling's midsection. "Your ambassador . . ."

"The values of the American business community have made Dennis Wardlow rich," Burling cut in, "so he has no reason to question them."

"You do not like Ambassador Wardlow."

"On the contrary, Dennis and I are good friends. Whenever he comes to Shanghai, we play tennis together on my court. The president of the United States believes strongly that a man of his commercial abilities is important to a constructive relationship with our Chinese friends, given the times."

"But you believe otherwise?"

"I guess you could say that I believe differently about the times."

The general nodded and murmured again. "Because of what you said in your toast, the general had hoped you might help us, as a friend," Li interpreted, stressing the last phrase. "Men have already died as a result of this smuggling group, and others may soon."

Burling felt his head clouding. "I'm sorry to hear that people have been harmed. Not long ago a whole container of human beings arrived dead in one of our ports."

"It was the general's sad duty this afternoon," Li said, "to inform your Ambassador Wardlow of the expulsion of an American professor from Nanjing, a subversive called Rank. Professor Rank has admitted to involving himself with these smugglers."

"I wonder whom we'll expel in return."

Li watched him from the front seat, Burling's sarcasm wide of the mark. "Maybe you will be next, Consul General."

Burling tried a laugh to hide the fear that was gripping his shoulders now. Could it be that he was under a silent arrest? Could

Wardlow, MacAllister, or that little shit Ryan have shopped him to General Zu? After all they could hold him up for days at the Daoyutai on some hospitable pretense while they all followed whatever path they wanted to with Yong.

"I'm afraid I'm not much of a bargaining chip," he said.

"Perhaps you can help us in another way. Before Professor Rank leaves us on Friday, the general has requested of Ambassador Wardlow if it would be possible for you to speak with him, confidentially of course, as an officer of the American government."

The general's expression was the ponderous frown that Burling had noticed during his toast.

"It is a question of protocol," Li continued. The driver braked hard turning into the guesthouse, and the guard at the gate jumped out of the way. "A woman from your consulate has been observed visiting Professor Rank frequently. Do you know anything about that?"

"It's rather difficult since you haven't even told me the woman's name."

"Forgive me," Li smiled. "Charlotte Brien. I believe she is some sort of cultural agent?"

"Attaché," corrected Burling. Agent was a better way to put it, he thought: Charlotte, an agent of culture. Somehow it must have led her to where she was now, away from him toward this Rank and his scholar's adventure, but Burling had never quite understood what Charlotte meant when she used the word. For her, as for April, come to think of it, "culture" seemed to have an anthropological connotation, strongly imbued with leftist politics, while Burling had always known it to mean the fine arts.

"Is this now ringing your bells?" Li asked.

Burling smiled in spite of himself. "Charlotte Brien is a dedicated and intelligent cultural officer," he said. "The professor you speak of must be attached to the Sino-American Center in Nanjing. Charlotte has spoken of him often, though not by name. They arrange for cultural exchanges and fellowships together. I'm sure his expulsion will come as much of a shock to her as it does to me."

The general watched Burling's face as Li interpreted for him.

"Speak to her, please, Consul Burling, and to Professor Rank as well. You have been away for a month and . . ."

Burling bristled. "Mr. Ryan, my vice-consul, is a capable man, General Zu." The car swung into a circular drive and moved slowly under a lighted porte cochère. "And quite a good economist to boot."

"You will understand if we cannot share implicitly your assessment," Li said. The general's tones had sounded impatient. "Having never seen a market economy function, we cannot judge your Mr. Ryan's skills."

Men in Mao suits stood on either side of the doors, like figures guarding a tomb. Shaggy pines grew against the pale pink bricks, their drooping branches laden with candles. Gradually, Burling understood the general's subtlety, what was really an elaborate joke. A certain American economist, of whom the propaganda organs had made copious use, had recently argued that the market was impossible to understand for people who had never seen it at work. Burling allowed himself another smile. If he was under arrest, at least it was amusing.

"Please tell the general I have enjoyed his conversation, as well as his erudite humor, all evening," he said, opening his door. Li hastened from the front seat to help him. "As for speaking with Professor Rank, I will have to, as we say in America, sleep on it."

"The general hopes it will be comfortable for you," Li said. He closed his door and spoke through the open window. "As you may know, President Nixon stayed here."

"I believe I read that it reminded him of San Clemente." Or was it San Quentin? "His summer home," Burling added.

"The driver will take you to the airport in the morning. Good night."

In his relief, Burling didn't ask where he would be going. "Good night, General. Good night, Mr. Li."

The car backed up and gunned out of the driveway. Burling heard its engine nearly to the gate. The compound struck him, as he stood in its pine-scented darkness, as being much like a country-club prison, one of those places in Florida where corporate grifters played golf. Fifty yards down a grassy slope lay an ornamental lake, its water absolutely still, its islands occupied by summer pavilions. Only on the far shore could he make out a guard's perch atop the lighted wall.

In neighboring buildings, or so he had heard, dissidents who'd served out their sentences were held incommunicado, many with medical problems from torture and labor camp work. Going up the stairs to the porch, Burling tried to imagine the dimensions of such a life, but it was beyond him. On some level, he thought it might be a relief. A nagging guilt made him lower his head as he passed between the guards. In the dim, cold foyer a man in uniform collected his passport and gave him a key.

Climbing the wide curving stairs to the upper story, he thought of MacAllister, the hearings that would ensue if their old operation were opened to the world, the evisceration in Congress and the papers, with the State Department leaking whatever they could to fuel the fire. His reputation, so important to Mac, would be ruined, and, depending on the political calculus, he might even be sent to some prison like that, with the junk bond traders and corrupt politicians, although he would no doubt be pardoned like Nixon had been. But was his reputation, or Zu's for that matter, worth a man's life?

In the upstairs hall, Burling imagined Tricky Dick, whom he had met many times, walking down this same corridor rubbing his hands, having just met Mao Zedong, with whom he'd tried to bond as a man of the people, harassed by intellectuals. Through an open window, he could see another segment of the wall, barbed wire gleaming along the top. Had Nixon felt the walls around him even at the moment of his triumph of opening China; had he already known that they would get him? What is it that leads a man into these circuits of power and deceit; does that energy fill the space that opens when he hesitates, or knows not how, to love?

A sudden breeze sucked the curtains through the window where they flapped in the night, and Burling felt something leave him. A powerful searchlight on the guard tower swept the dark grounds. Every country, he thought, has its typical jails.

book
three

YONG AND LINDSTROM GOT TO SHANGHAI ON AN afternoon train, riding in the hard-seat compartment with a nation of grandmothers, babies, and young men in blue shirts and sports jackets, come to the city for work. The passengers shared around pork buns and tea. As they climbed down onto the clean station platform, Lindstrom felt sorry to be parting from them. To pass the time as the crowded car rolled down the swollen river valleys to the coast, he had entertained a fantasy of staying in China forever.

From the station, they walked across wide streets and a barren park to the address that Yong had been given, in a neighborhood of buildings that reminded Lindstrom of the Upper West Side of Manhattan. The apartment, which belonged to a woman named Mei, had been in her family for many years. She had grown up there during the Cultural Revolution, when her father was denounced as a descendant of landlords, touching off a spiral of trouble at her school. When Yong and Lindstrom arrived, she was starting the dinner fire in the small, dark kitchen off the hall. At first she didn't seem pleased to have them there, but Lindstrom chalked it up to fear. She made them dinner and told them of three times and places where Lindstrom was supposed to go for further instructions.

The first meeting point, where Lindstrom went in the morning, was the No. 1 Department Store. He loitered in Ladies' Garments for an hour, affecting nervous indecision and a stutter before buying a printed scarf. Mei had said that the woman he was supposed to meet worked at the American consulate, which meant for Burling, and when she failed to show, Lindstrom walked the mile to the old French Concession, where the American compound was. He watched both entrances for several hours—the pedestrian gate to the office building, the vehicle gate to the residence next door, watched over by a black marine. The little house in which the man stood guard was the prefabricated kind, bolted together from aluminum studs and thick plates of smoked glass; the pieces could be brought from the States in a transport plane and carried to location on the back of a truck. An identical one had stood by the entrance to the embassy in Kabul, and Lindstrom, who had befriended the marines there, having just got out of the service, knew the security equipment that the guardhouse employed.

In the first three hours that he watched the consulate, only some Chinese staff and a thirtyish man in horn-rims carrying a racquetball bag went in or out. At one o'clock Lindstrom left his place on the bus bench and walked the perimeter of the compound, looking for a breach in the high stone wall. Barbed wire was visible, but there were probably shards of glass too, stuck in the mortar by whatever nervous Frenchman had built the estate. On the street behind, he found an elementary school with some playground equipment placed conveniently close to the parapet. Along the upstairs porch of the school building, a class of young children—he had never been good at their ages—the little boys dressed in sweatpants and white shirts, the girls in frilly, short dresses, were being led by their teacher in a course of calisthenics. One boy kept leaving the line and doing what looked like a modified break dance to the end of the veranda. A future Yong, Lindstrom thought.

As he rounded the block by the loading dock, the familiar construction reminded him of a feature of the embassy in Kabul. When the U.S. built a diplomatic compound, usually adding an office building on the grounds of an existing estate, they often dug a tunnel for security between the two, which would allow him to access the Residence simply by getting to the loading dock. The number of deliveries and the attitude of the guard at this end would make infiltration relatively easy.

Having satisfied himself that he could make a quiet visit to Burling if that became necessary, Lindstrom reconnoitered the Residence guardhouse once more, glancing through the dark glass at the video monitors, and took a different route back across town.

THE SECOND MEETING POINT WAS AN OUTDOOR EXHIBIT on the margin of Renmin—or People's—Park, which he entered down a short flight of foul-smelling steps from the sidewalk. The exhibit consisted of two rows of locked glass cases set upright on concrete footings, shaded by flowering chestnuts that must have seen the treaties that marked the first Concessions. Even his grandfather, getting off the boat from Frisco in 1921, might have walked beneath their buoyant pink cones along the Nanjing Road, a Bible under the arm of his dark ministerial suit, learning the ropes from a mission administrator who carried a parasol.

The history enshrined in Lindstrom's mental image was exactly what the sidewalk exhibit had been designed to erase. In the glass cases, streaked with birdshit and sap from the branches above, five-year plans for factories were tacked beneath photos of long ranks of women at sewing machines. The women kept the bobbins winding, their arms crossed and uncrossed in successive frames like organists playing toccatas. The seamstresses smiled to themselves as if they possessed a universal secret that could be stitched into clothes.

Over his shoulder, Lindstrom cast periodic glances at the steps, but judging from their dress, the citizens of Shanghai, on their way back from shopping or lunch in platform sneakers, bell bottoms, or double-breasted suits, were not much interested, having mostly abandoned the ideological fount of their government for better ways of turning a buck. As he was peering more closely at the women, who could have been walking down Sixth Avenue in New York, a young man in a conservative suit rounded the case at the end of the row and descended the steps. He looked at Lindstrom a moment too long, and Lindstrom reached around to unsnap the sheath on the back of his belt. The exhibit had clearly been chosen for its unpopularity: the lines of sight from the street weren't good, and beyond the inner row of cases was a thicket of evergreen bushes that provided a protected, if thorny, escape. The wind blew refuse from the park into their bottommost branches, where soft-looking paper hung like rags.

Stopping with his back to the first display, the man removed a pack of cigarettes from his shirt pocket and cupped a match with his hands. He wore an encrusted school ring and a gold wedding band. Lindstrom sidled closer, easing the knife into his hand. When the cigarette was lit, the man looked up at him.

"You're American, aren't you?" His voice had the lilt of the Valley, California anyway, but on second glance his round Asian features bore much more than a passing resemblance to the man in the car at Anhe. He broke into a big, white, even-toothed smile. "I could tell from your shoes."

Lindstrom had to restrain himself from looking down.

"Rockports," the Californian told him, suppressing a smile. "My Dad wears them. He's retired. You must be with an NGO. I know you all don't want to wear Nikes or whatever. Which one are you with? My wife deals with them all the time."

Lindstrom also considered the possibility that this might be his contact, gender notwithstanding, and that the wife was the one Mei knew. The NGO question was curious, perhaps leading, although there were plenty in town.

"Come on, dude," the man sniffed, letting out a quick, nervous laugh. He started reaching for his pocket again. "I know you're U.S. What's your deal?"

Lindstrom covered the ten yards between them in two steps and grabbed the man's wrist from his pocket with his left hand, twisting it quickly up the center of his back. With his right hand, Lindstrom brought the knife around and touched it to the bottom of the Californian's chin.

"Hey, what the fuck? What are you on, dude?"

"Who do you work for?" Lindstrom asked.

"Morgan Stanley, for Christ's sake."

"What do you do for them?"

"Influenza futures trader."

"What?"

The man jerked and Lindstrom started to break his wrist. "Hey. Ow! It's sort of a joke."

"What is?"

"You're breaking my arm."

"I don't like jokes at my expense," Lindstrom told him. "What's the punch line?"

"That is the punch line. You're hurting me."

"And I'm going to keep right on hurting you until you tell me the joke, 'dude.'"

"Ease up, will you?"

Lindstrom relaxed his hold enough so the young man could speak.

"Every May," the man said, his voice still exhibiting strain, "the biotech companies come here to test the cattle, the pigs, to see what flu we've got in store for us next winter in the States."

"Go on."

"Well, there are about twenty-five different strains going on every spring, so each company chooses which one they're going to develop the vaccine against. You know, the flu shot. Company that guesses it right wins the equity lotto. I trade futures on that."

"Jesus Christ," Lindstrom said. It was far too absurd for anyone, especially a communist agent, to make up. "Get lost, right?"

"You're not going to mug me?"

"What do I look like?" said Lindstrom. "Some kind of gangbanger?"

"I thought you worked for an NGO."

"Try three other letters. And if you say a word about this to anyone, I'll be waiting for you down at Morgan Stanley and you won't get a chance to get the flu."

The Californian looked at Lindstrom, first in disbelief, then— weighing his options—in astonishment. He turned on the heel of his low-slung kid loafers and ran up the steps, into the blast from the suburban-bound buses. Lindstrom's nose filled with sulfur and diesel and soot. He'd been told to wait an hour for the woman, but it was forty minutes into it, and he'd made too big an impression, so he left the exhibit and sprinted across the street, between the trams.

On the opposite corner stood a wide-hipped church building of porous gray stone, reminiscent of Paris or Saigon. The Gothic windows, fenestrated with scalloped rosettes, were obscured by frosted glass to which construction paper, decorated in the crabbed hand of children, had been taped. The paper caught and seemed to hold the little sunlight filtering down through the dun-colored air. One of the windows in the old apse stood open, and as he passed, the flat, resonant sound of a dulcimer sprang from it, the strings struck with something like joy by the long rubber mallets he had seen displayed in the windows of music stores. Standing in the shadows of the buttresses, each carved with a different saint, he could see the mouth of the street where he and Yong had spent the previous night.

How was it, he thought, that some people were able to give themselves completely to an idea—futures trading, or textile collectives, or Jesus—and all at once they smiled like lunatics, cured of the chronic anxiety of being themselves? Was it dangerous self-delusion or absolute bliss? To him, connection with an organized system—economic, religious, political, or military—was always a net. His own weakness was a feeling of invincibility that the rehab gurus had shown him would lead back to heroin—to think that he was strong, smart enough to evade the strings of whatever system he entered. He was beginning to see that he was caught and the men who ran the systems were reeling him in. He looked up at the terrace of the building and thought he saw Yong.

WHEN LINDSTROM ENTERED THE APARTMENT, MEI WAS starting the dinner fire again. Had she been doing this every night for years, and he and Yong had simply joined her routine? Her loneliness, the homely repetition of her life, made Lindstrom feel hopeless and comforted all at the same time. She struck him as beautiful and sad. Down the hall, he could see the headboard and ironed covers of her father's rosewood bed. He had died and Mei never seemed to go into his room, but Lindstrom had snuck in there during the night and found the old man's calligraphy set and an opium table blackened by smoke. On the corner of the table was a pack of matches with a single Chinese character written inside.

The living room was fitted with shelves and a desk, a bed for the daughter, which Yong and Lindstrom had shared, and a nightstand, all in cheap blond wood. The furniture looked like it had come from a dormitory room. The daughter Mei slept below them on a mat on the floor, snoring lightly, and her proximity had kept Lindstrom's mind suspended, denying him sleep. The clacking of the rails, the sway of the train car, had been in his head.

"No show," he told Yong. His voice sounded almost triumphant. The rehab gurus had told him that he thrived on the negative, but the positive had always seemed mindless to him. "Pretty soon we may have to throw ourselves on the mercy of our mutual friend."

Yong looked up from his Bible, uncomprehending, and offered a drink from the bottle of water on the nightstand.

"The man from Princeton," Lindstrom said. He found he was sweating, but he declined the drink. The water was nasty and sulfurous, and the glass he'd had with breakfast had only made him thirstier in the middle of the day.

"Why so impatient?" asked Yong. "They gave us three places, maybe they knew she wouldn't go to the first two. The reporters in Beijing always did it that way."

Lindstrom collapsed on the daybed in his shoes. "You know this woman we're supposed to meet must work for Burling, don't you? I think I may have run into her in Nanjing."

Yong was about to say something, but Mei was coming from the kitchen, bearing two cups of tea.

"John." She dipped her head shyly, and her bobbed hair fell in a point across her cheek. Last evening, when he had introduced himself, she'd struggled with the final consonants of "Jack," and asked him for his "given name." Her sensitivity to language charmed him. Late into the night, she'd smoked cigarettes and argued with him about Hemingway, in a precise British English accented like chimes. The possibility that she had risked her life for a bit of literary talk had given Lindstrom a giddy, insupportable hope. When he saw her now, her open face shining from the steam, the day was erased and his fresh excitement returned. "Any news?"

"I'm afraid not," he said.

"I didn't hear you come in. I will get another cup."

"You weren't considering a martyrdom, were you?" Lindstrom asked Yong when she had gone out.

Yong gave him an indulgent look, the kind the gurus had given him when he started to talk his way out of his problem. "Is that what you want me to consider, John?"

When Mei returned with his tea, she was carrying a book.

"I found it!" she said—*For Whom the Bell Tolls* in a Chinese translation.

Lindstrom was amazed to see the book in this place.

"I wish to get your opinion on something," Mei said, sitting down at the desk. She opened the book to the epigraph, pushing it across the table toward Yong. "You will understand this better than I."

Yong took the book, and Mei leaned her elbows, which were dried and cracked, on the blotter. In the failing light, her chin and neck reflected the chessboard's red-and-white squares. She couldn't have been much over thirty, April's age when she'd disappeared.

"No man is an island," Yong read.

Mei turned to Lindstrom. "Do you know this book?" she asked.

Yong was flipping through the pages, and Lindstrom wondered how the *mot juste* had fared in translation. He couldn't help laughing at the thought. The rehab gurus were wrong: if he could just keep this feeling, things might turn out all right.

"When I first encountered that book," he told her, "I was eighteen, maybe nineteen, shipping out to Vietnam. I believed it was the truest thing I'd ever read, the frankest depiction of the world. A couple of years later I even gave it to the woman I married, as a way of seducing her. In the book there's a great scene where a man and a woman make love in a sleeping bag and the ground beneath them moves."

Mei nodded happily, resting her cheek on her palm, and checked her tea. The setting sun cast a dagger of light across the daybed and table; she had a wistful look in her eyes. Lindstrom had not been able to make love to a woman in longer than he cared to remember, but he found himself searching her face.

"Do you not still believe this?" she asked.

Her question caught him off guard; he hadn't thought in such terms for so long. "The book is about the Spanish Civil War," he said, taking the paperback from Yong. "That's probably the only reason the Party allows it to be printed."

"It memorializes the war against fascism," said Mei.

"Only what it leaves out," Lindstrom told her, "what it has to leave out, is that while men like Hemingway, and his character, Robert Jordan, were risking their lives fighting Franco, believing that their Russian comrades would come to their rescue, Stalin was selling them out. It's what that whole bloody century was like, proof that a man can't act the way Hemingway makes you believe, because he is always caught in a larger net."

"But isn't that what the epigraph means?"

"It ends up feeling mostly ironic to me."

Mei frowned. "You don't believe that Robert Jordan acts morally?"

"He's a good man," Lindstrom said, "but he has the luxury of falling on his sword at the end, which of course is the only logical response to what he sees."

Mei's dark eyes looked sad, but when she spoke her tone was angry. "If what you say is true, that things are connected in a bad way, the opposite also must be, that they are connected in a good one."

"She's right," said Yong, baiting Lindstrom with one of his diffident smiles. "It is possible for a man to act in the right way, at least to try, even in a fallen world."

"Spoken like a true double agent," Lindstrom said.

Yong looked at him warningly. "In a way, you know, every Christian is a double agent. He must serve God while living in the world as it is. It seems impossible sometimes."

Lindstrom couldn't help it; he felt a few strands of the net snap inside. "Is that what you were thinking when you agreed to let your old master at the Agency get you out?"

Red-faced, Yong stood up from his chair. "I told you before that my faith is weak," he said. "But I don't know what you're talking about. If you thought you weren't connected, too, you wouldn't be so angry, right?"

Yong turned and stalked away toward the kitchen. Mei watched him go doubtfully. "Did Beihong do something to make you angry?"

On the balcony, her father's birds beat their wings against the bars of their cages. A parakeet squawked at the lackluster breeze.

"Yong's been turned around so many times he's meeting himself where he thought that the bad guys ought to be," Lindstrom said.

"You know Yong very well," Mei observed.

LINDSTROM RETURNED AGAIN TO THE APARTMENT A LITTLE after eight o'clock. Yong was sleeping on the daybed, and Lindstrom found Mei in the kitchen, standing over the brazier's hot coals. She was slicing a yellow onion into an enamel pot of briny-looking water.

"I was beginning to worry," she said.

Lindstrom peered into the water and felt as if a balloon were inflating in his throat. "I'm sorry."

Mei sniffed and shook off the apology, wiping her nose with the back of her hand, which held the sharp, curved knife. "I fell asleep after dinner, and when I awoke you were gone. What were you doing out?" she asked.

"I wanted to check the place where I'm going tonight, in case I have to lose a tail in the *hutongs*."

"You should not go out so much."

"I had to be sure."

"And you are sure now that you can lose this 'tail'?"

"It's the one thing I know I'm good at," Lindstrom said.

She stopped cutting and stared at him credulously.

"When I lost my wife," he explained, "it made me feel like my own shadow, that's the only way I can describe it, like the person who really defined me was gone."

"Reflected light," said Mei.

"The people, we called them the gurus, at the drug rehabilitation place where I was sent, they tried to make me believe in what they called the before and the after. Give yourself up to a higher power, they told us, and this great paradoxical thing will occur. You'll get yourself back."

"And this didn't take place?"

"My wife disappeared in Afghanistan and never came back," Lindstrom said. "It was just like my mother: one day she took off and my father never spoke of her again. He just gave me to my grandparents to raise. So the guru could never make me believe in an after. The wheel just keeps turning, you know?"

Mei put the knife down and dried her hands roughly on a cloth that was hanging on the back of the single chair. He imagined her eating there, day after day, in the grimy kitchen, a book by her place. "I know what you are talking about," she said, taking her cigarettes from the oilcloth on the table. "When I got married, I was very young and silly and I believed that I would find myself in him. So I gave myself away . . ." She paused to light her cigarette, and Lindstrom knew, without thinking, what had happened.

"He was killed at Tiananmen Square?"

Mei nodded, and smoke came out of her mouth in harsh little gusts.

"I don't know why that just came to me," he said.

"So I came back here. Then my father died." She turned and went to the brazier, where the soup had begun to splash and sizzle onto the flames. Her hand felt for somewhere to put down her cigarette, and Lindstrom held out his fingers.

"I know that this is going to sound crazy," he said, taking it and dragging on the awful tobacco. He hadn't smoked for several years. "But sometimes I know other people's thoughts before they share them."

She looked at him, black, lustrous eyes glazed with steam. "Why does this happen?"

"You mean . . . ?"

"How do you know other thoughts?"

Lindstrom took a pensive drag and handed the cigarette back. "When I was really frightened, in Vietnam, I learned to imagine how the enemy did things. I had to in order to survive. But then I began to understand why they were fighting."

"But I'm not the enemy, John."

"No. Of course not." Lindstrom smiled at her. "In this case, I think it means I'm falling in love with you."

She put the cigarette on the edge of the counter and turned to her stirring. "As if that might change things," she said.

Lindstrom touched her elbow, which was moving back and forth with the motion of the spoon, and held it there. "You never know. It's certainly better than trying to believe in an after."

"I have been waiting," she said, arching her neck. A line of soft, curling hairs coiled downward at the top of her spine, disappearing beneath her collar. She moved her arm back so that he held the soft inside of her elbow in his hand, damp skin and the sharp knob of bone. He squeezed a bit and felt her blood pulse beneath his fingertips. From the living room, they heard Yong rise from the daybed.

"He must get out," she said, looking over her shoulder. She turned and gently removed her bare arm from his hand. "He can change things from the outside. No matter what we feel, we still must believe in that."

"I believe in you," Lindstrom said.

HE LEFT THE HOT APARTMENT FOR THE THIRD TIME AT HALF past ten, carrying a plastic bag of trash. He descended the open stairway, its animal smells and piles of briquettes on the landings, down to the entry of the building. An old woman with a deeply furrowed face and a red armband registered his presence as she wandered, muttering, among the parked bikes near the gate to the street. Lindstrom nodded at her, wondering if she could smell the rice wine on his breath, and turned unsteadily toward the court-yard. As he went across the paving stones, he heard the woman—a bound-feet detective, Mei had called her, one of the nosy old women with a natural proclivity for scandal whom the local street commit-tees had turned into a snitch—go into her apartment by the stairs and close the door.

The last appointed meeting place was a crumbling temple only a stone's throw away from Mei's building—each one getting closer, Lindstrom thought. Mei had directed him through a small passage-way at the corner of the courtyard, where the refuse cans were kept. He dropped his bag into the nearest one and squeezed past them, soiling his shirt against the filthy wall. All his anger at the situation, his entrapment by Rank, was focusing as it had on other missions on his personal hygiene, the filth of the country in general and the unhealthy food, the fact that he hadn't had a shower since he left San Francisco. The thought of a bath in Mei's tub, in water that smelled like natural gas, was too much for him.

At the far end of the passageway he found a second, locked gate for which Mei had given him the key—a skeleton copy that her fa-ther had taken off the superintendent years ago when he was lying drunk in the entryway after the wedding of his son. Locking the gate again behind him, Lindstrom found himself in a different Shang-hai—the Old Chinese City. Gone were the wide boulevards that felt like Paris and the modern glass and concrete that could have been in Singapore or Hong Kong. Here the narrow *hutongs* snaked beneath sagging gables made of wood, the windows on either side so close to each other that he saw a woman pass a jug of water across to her neighbor above him. The smell of soft-coal smoke and cooking oil was even stronger than in the courtyard of Mei's building, the heavy air so full of soot that he felt tiny grains on his tongue. He walked without hope, past families eating late dinners on the sidewalk, blaming himself for his position and wondering if he could walk away now that he knew how compromised Yong was—a spy for Burling. Alone, he might be able to get out, even get on a plane, but now he also had Mei to think of: leaving Yong with her would be the same as if he gave her to the goons on the Anhe road himself.

Mei. Saying her name, the compression of his lips, then the opening, made him feel a great affection for the lives he saw as he passed the open windows: old men smoking at low tables and the clicking of chopsticks on bowls. He arrived at the temple exactly at eleven, walked the perimeter of the courtyard, and sat on the porch beneath a heavy, peaked roof, a pillar running up his spine like a stake. In the narrow, cobbled street leading from the far corner, paper lanterns hung from the balconies, red dragons cavorting across their accordion folds.

If I could change into a million selves, he thought. It was a Chinese poem his grandmother had taught him. He recited it drunkenly, feeling the fumes of the wine blow out through his nostrils: *I'd send one to climb each peak and gaze far off toward home.*

The lanterns cast a dim reflection onto the dark water of the temple pool. In the still light, men played mahjong at stone tables set around the edge. The rhythmic sound of tiles put him slowly, unwillingly, to sleep. His last waking thought was of a sweet but unknown scent; footsteps crossed the courtyard like sounds in a dream.

He bolted upright minutes later, slapping himself on the back of the neck. His watch read eleven fifteen. From his pocket he retrieved the envelope of meth. The last few crystals sparkled like quartz in his palm. What he really craved was smack now; behind it, maybe he could find a way out. He licked his palm, which tasted of sulfur and salt, and swallowed in a dry throat. A long time passed, or so he thought, before the rush asserted itself; tiny fissures spread into his back from the pillar. *If I could change . . .* He was breaking apart—like the Buddha, the dead. The cracks ran up from the ancient stones into his head. From their perches around the courtyard, the temple animals gazed at him, crawling around pillars, waddling like armadillos along the walls of the pool.

Terrible faces, lolling tongues and eyes and teeth from the pages of his grandmother's book—they danced before his eyes, took great, plashy steps in the puddle of his heart.

Pulao! A child's voice called him. It's been a long time. You who are so fond of crying, you whiner on the handle of bells. The woman was not coming, and here was Lindstrom again, in another broken-down temple like the ones in the deep Central Highlands, head popping with speed. A boy came out from a neighboring house and began to place lanterns, unlit, around the perimeter of the court-yard. Setting out a short line on the side by the pool, the boy went along with a tallow, carefully lighting each one. The smells of wax and kerosene cleared Lindstrom's mind.

The boy began the line next to the temple, and Lindstrom slid around in the shadow of the pillar, out of the flickering light. When the boy came around to the front with his candle, Lindstrom saw that his young face was feral: an angry red birthmark spread from the right side of his forehead down to his jaw. In the flame of the tallow, his eyes were mild and searching, like the eyes of Chiwen, the gargoyle from the ridgepole of a house. He went on with his task until the whole courtyard glowed like a stage in the round. Beyond its ring of footlights, the darkness rose and seemed to go on forever, the tortured fields of the People's Republic writhing under the night. People began to pause on their late evening errands, and the boy rang a bell that startled Lindstrom to attention.

He looked up. So it is that the gentle Chiwen always brings out Chaofeng, the one who loves danger, the wild, leering beast peer-ing over from the roof of the temple at your squirming, craven self. Scared of Burling, scared of dying, scared of taking the thing to its ultimate end, scared of love, scared of knowing. Timid and cautious in spite of your undeserved reputation as a badass. A coward. He felt eyes on his back and turned to see the figure of Jiaotu, the mea-suring mascot of professors, the moderate one, watching him with amusement from above the temple entrance, which was barred.

Chaofeng is baiting you, he said. Jiaotu held several objects like playing cards in his slender, callused paws. Patience.

In the courtyard more people were lingering; a motorized rickshaw driver lounged on his seat. A man in a Mao cap stepped into the low square of light, followed by a monkey on a leash. The monkey had long, silver hair and an iron collar fastened around its neck. In one hand, its master held the end of the leash, a dozen feet in length; in the other, a small gong and baton. The master beat out a cadence as the monkey marched around in a circle, watching its torturer, while the audience pointed with delight. Cigarette peddlers worked the growing crowd. An unsanctioned spectacle such as this would have to have protection, but what would it look like? He didn't know the culture well enough to find the triad who must be in attendance, the one who could get them a place on a boat for a promise of cash. His pillar, supported by Bixi, the tortoise, poked into his back.

You have the heart of a tortoise, he thought, getting up. You won't make a decision. Each face in the crowd was like one of the Foo Dogs—watching, considering, savoring—each was repellent, reflecting a piece of himself. The monkey strutted to its box and removed a small replica of a woman's pillbox hat, flowers waving from the brim. Hairy arms hiding its face, the wretched animal pulled the hat over its head, which was inclined like a coquette's. In the intelligent simian eyes, Lindstrom thought he saw shame, rage, despair. He was surprised by the strength of anger rising inside him. He couldn't put it away. Once again, you are nothing but a chess piece, he thought, and Burling . . . only Burling would know enough to put you in this game. The amateur feeling is a part of the cover, that's all. Rank was only a pawn.

The master barked, and the monkey vamped around, a transvestite in its silly woman's hat. As it danced, Lindstrom felt eyes upon him. Had he stepped within the margin of the lights? Was he going to fight back now, take it to the source, to Burling, or cry like Pulao, banging the clapper in the hollow of his guts, turning in a slow circle, tolling out his grief, waiting for the two goons to find him?

The crowd pressed in, and Lindstrom turned to find the boy with the eyes of Chiwen. The boy stared back at him, as if he looked strange. He held a black hat out to Lindstrom, turned upside down.

In the crown were some seed coins, oddly shaped little silver and copper things, old, nicked, and bent; Lindstrom looked closer and saw the broken and unbroken lines commensurate with change.

"The Way," he said aloud. He seemed to be falling forward, and the coins swam around in the hat, like fish in a bowl. The hawkers and the monkey drum were distant in his ears.

"The Dao."

He reached into the hat and grabbed a handful. *I Ching*, he thought, his heart tripping. *Book of wisdom.*

The boy made a sound like a needle scratched across a vinyl record. As if he were the channel for its collective voice, the crowd was silenced at once. A man grabbed Lindstrom's wrist, but Lindstrom pushed him so hard that people fell away before someone caught the man by the shoulders. Lindstrom backed into the circle, holding the coins aloft in his fist. The monkey hissed at him and skittered away on its claws.

"This isn't *yuan*," he told them—money. "*Bu. Mei shi.*" No. Money doesn't matter. He felt his grandfather rising inside him. "You try to see the harmonious way through the cycles of money, but these cycles are moved by the devil."

The monkey made another run at him, but its master yanked it back with the chain, lifting it off its naked feet. The crowd was restive but lacking the will to attack, the faces in the center etched by the hard-edged light of the lamps, the ones at the outer limits blurred into darkness. The effort of speaking made the rush return, doubly hard.

"These are not coins," said Lindstrom, letting them fall from his hand. They rung on the pavement and bounced and spun around like tops. He reeled a bit, watching them dance. "These are signs from the powerful dead."

The people closest to him looked down.

"You want to see the harmonious Way, you want to penetrate the Dao?"

He did. Indeed, the universe was strictly unconscious, the cosmic order if there was one, impersonal. The will of the crowd, of the masses, were its worldly emanation, and this crowd was getting pissed.

For an interval, they watched the scattered coins, something ancient moving inside them, but their minds could no more hold to some retreated mystery than his—Lindstrom's—could. They looked to him, a hopped-up impostor in need of help himself, to tell them what to do.

Kill me, he thought. Kill me now and let it be.

The coins were silent on the paving stones. He thought of Mei and Yong.

You crazy Christ-bit fucker, Lindstrom thought. The inauthentic live while the real ones pass away. Get over it and go.

An old man in a Mao hat crouched to see the coins arranged around his feet. He called out in a gruff, atonal voice: "Qian!"

A murmur rippled through the crowd.

Lindstrom saw his opportunity and turned to run. The only open place was past the monkey, but the monkey howled and turned from him in fright, jumping nimbly to its master's arms as Lindstrom sprinted past.

Qian, he thought, dodging people into the *hutong*. Pure Yang. Something to do with a dragon. Checking over his shoulder, he slowed to a walk, trying to remember his grandmother throwing the Ching at the apartment in Frisco, April and their hippie friends in a circle on the carpet watching the real thing with the serene, detached concentration of the genuinely stoned. The *hutong* turned, and he saw the wall of the temple again at its end. From a doorway, an old man wearing small round spectacles hissed at him.

"Qian."

The monkey's tambourine was jingling down the way. Exploded shadows danced against the temple wall.

"The dragon," said the man, and disappeared into his doorway. Above it hung a little sign with the character he'd seen on the matchbox in Mei's father's room. The hall inside was lit by candles, and in a room to the right another man, younger but wasted, lay on a daybed covered with a rug. An opium table sat before him with a pipe stand in the shape of a dragon, scales molded from brass.

"When the Dao forms images, we call it *Qian*," said the old man, preparing the pipe. When Lindstrom sat on the daybed, the younger man stirred in his dreams. "As for *Qian*, in its quiet state it is focused, and in its active state it is undeviating. This is how it achieves its great acts. Opening the gate is called *Qian*."

Lindstrom took the sweet smoke into his lungs. The old man's voice was accompanied through the open window by the monkey's tambourine.

"*Qian* is the strongest thing in the entire world . . . It is able to delight in hearts and minds." His words attenuated, slowed like a record on the wrong speed. Lindstrom's body felt like rubber and he slid to the floor. Slumped against the edge of the bed, he watched the old man sketch the hexagrams of Yang:

> *A dragon in the fields; a dragon submerged.*
> *A submerged dragon does not act.*
> *If you see a dragon in the fields, it is fitting to see the Great Man.*
> *Hesitating to leap, the dragon stays in the depths, so suffers no blame.*
> *A dragon that overreaches should have cause for regret.*

Dragon . . . Lindstrom blinked and April was standing before him.
"He'll make you a martyr, like his wife," Lindstrom said.
The old man watched him as he put the pipe away.
"Who, Lucius?"
"Who else are you fucking?"
"I'm not fucking anyone," she said meaningly, walking past him. The old man left the room.
"Do you love him?"
April laughed. "Burling? He doesn't really inspire that emotion, at least not what I used to think it meant. It's more like he's asking you to join his crusade."
"That's how he's a fake, baby, why can't you see that? He doesn't love anything but some idea he has. You know he even asked me to

sniff around my players, see if any might mount an insurgency once the shit went down?"

"And you did what he asked, didn't you, Jack?"

"I did it because I thought it would help you, not to push you into bed with him."

"You're like the ocean, aren't you? Whatever color the weather." April's hair was wet and straight from the shower; it made her look desperate, sad. "I only kissed him once, Jack, and I know better than to make something out of it, even if he doesn't. Do you want to hear about it? Maybe that would turn you on."

Hours later, it was the vaporous glare of the People's Park that really woke him. He'd been wandering the Old Chinese City for hours, talking to himself. As he waited to cross at the stone church, the old man's hexagrams came back to him clearly:

A dragon in the fields; a dragon submerged.
A submerged dragon does not act.
If you see a dragon in the fields, it is fitting to see the Great Man.
Hesitating to leap, the dragon stays in the depths, so suffers no blame.
A dragon that overreaches should have cause for regret.

When he reached the entry to Mei's building, he knew that the old man had given him the answer: The dragon was Burling. Lindstrom would have to pay a visit, and this time Burling was the one who would have cause for regret.

LATE THAT NIGHT, MEI CAME TO HIM ON THE BALCONY, where it was cooler and Lindstrom had pulled a mat to sleep. The birds warbled in cages that hung from the ceiling, and the dark, spiky leaves of her houseplants shifted against the louvered glass. The opium was active in his brain, and he remembered soft nights in a hotel in Saigon, where he had gone to get drunk and high before a patrol. He was lying there breathing in his own fear when Mei placed her finger on his lips.

He found a cigarette between them.

"Did you bring your sleeping bag?" Lindstrom asked.

An ember glowed before her face. She took her cigarette out of her mouth and touched it to the end of his.

"I want to make love," whispered Mei, putting her cigarette aside. "I haven't . . ."

"For years," Lindstrom told her.

She nodded.

"You have to understand," he said, "I'm not sure I can."

Mei stubbed out her cigarette on a tabletop of stone. She nestled against him on the mat. "You went to the opium house, did you not?"

"I couldn't hold it together anymore. That biker crank was scrambling my brain."

"You are like my father. Chasing the dragon. You follow the uncertain just so far, but you are not really comfortable with it. You are not a philosopher at heart. You are a doer."

"Dope isn't the only reason I'm not sure I can."

"Think of me as a stranger." Her body felt solid and inert next to his, and yet their surfaces were charged. She worked on his belt in the darkness below.

"You don't want to do that," he told her.

"Be a stranger? To forget who it is that I am?" Her fumbling fingers were bringing him to life. "Yes, I do, John. I certainly do want to forget myself. It's been far too long since I did."

"You're not afraid you'll lose yourself?"

A bitter laugh rumbled deep in her throat. "What would we lose," she asked, her hand on his chest, "if we played at being strangers together?"

Lindstrom rested his head on the floor and watched his cigarette flare above his nose. Boulders seemed to be shifting inside him, breaking loose from the mud.

"Political ideas? Religious faith like Yong Beihong? Do not go away from me," she warned, tugging at him with her hand. "Come, John," she said, teasing him, "what would you lose?"

He crushed his cigarette under his bare thumb. "You want to be a stranger?" he said, rolling up on his elbow to face her.

"I don't want you to hurt me," she said, pulling back.

"Is that how I sound?"

She nodded. "I do not want you to be rough. It is not a pleasure for me."

"I'm sorry," he said. Her fingers moved in a separate tempo, up and down. "*Dui bu qui.*"

"You haven't answered my question," she told him, leaning down and kissing him, softly, on the tip, then taking him into her mouth.

He put his hand under the tail of her father's old shirt and drew her up onto him. "You don't have to do that," he told her, kissing her lips. They were very soft and he kissed first the top, then the bottom, fully taking them in.

"What would you lose?" she said as her leg swung across him. He was having trouble breathing; his erection stood up in fear.

"The dragon," he said.

Her hand covered his mouth; it smelled of nothing at first, and panic rose like dark water inside him. Her palm relaxed, and he smelled cigarette smoke and something else, queasy and spiced with the past. He struggled, lifting his buttocks as Mei held him tight.

"What would you lose, John, if you never went back?"

Something dark was stealing up behind them. Old thoughts of April that had tortured him for years, of April with the *mujahedin*. He felt for the knife he had placed beneath his mat. He listened carefully, peering at the shadows, but the apartment and the street outside were silent. His erection was suddenly strong. Sitting up, he rolled her gently over, kneeling between her legs. Her eyes were soft, but her mouth was victorious, her face slightly blurred as her body curved upward with pleasure.

"It is okay if you think of your wife," she said as they settled together and Lindstrom began to move. "I am not thinking of my husband."

She smiled, and he drew almost all the way out and paused for a moment, gathering himself. Now who was reading whose thoughts? He felt again the soft, smooth insides of her thighs.

"I was worried I would not think of him," she said, arranging herself, "that it would not be all right."

"But it is all right?"

"It's all right not to think of him, yes. It's better, in fact."

"Not to think."

"Weren't you worried you wouldn't think of your wife, John?"

He was almost too far in the rhythm to answer. "I was worried I would think of her."

"No." She grabbed at the small of his back. "You were not. You were not worried. You were only worried you would not think of her. I was worried . . ."

"Don't worry," he said, moving down on her chest.

"What were you worried?"

He held her.

"I lost her," said Lindstrom. "I lost."

"Her. Yes."

EARLY THURSDAY AFTERNOON, CHARLOTTE BRIEN hurried with her son across the paved square at the edge of Renmin Park, then waited at the corner to cross the busy street. On the far side, through a matrix of tram wires, stood a building that had once been a church, its stout gray buttresses fixed in the sidewalk like a washerwoman's arms. The light changed— Shanghai being the only place in the People's Republic where you could actually count on drivers stopping for lights—and Charlotte started off the curb, holding tightly to Liam's hand.

Liam didn't budge. "*Mom.*"

She swung around, and the nail that had been nervously working her cuticle scraped up over her knuckle. "Ouch! Liam, I told you. You are going today, and that's all there is to it." A bicycle dinged, and Charlotte skipped back onto the curb. "Wonderful. Now we missed the light."

"Ow!" Liam shook off her grip with a violence that frightened, upset her. "You're hurting me."

"I'm sorry, honey."

"I don't need you to hold my hand."

"All right, fine, but you're going to the Palace."

Liam rolled his eyes. "It's stupid."

"What is?"

"Me being in this show when I'm just going to leave."

Charlotte looked through the shag of dark hair at Liam's long, freckled face. Deep black eyes, like his father's, stared back at her. "You like Mrs. Wudun, don't you? Why would you want to leave her hanging, the best voice in the show?"

Liam shoved his hands deep in the pockets of his baggy jeans. He kicked at the sidewalk with the toe of his Vans. When Charlotte had first met Liam's instructor of drama at the Children's Palace, Mrs. Wudun, she had thought her too hard, perhaps even mean-spirited. She had tried to see, through the class, into the heart of the country, but the children were strangely bemused.

"I just don't want to, okay?" His fidgeting seemed scripted, his words dramatic with twelve-year-old torment. For a moment she wondered just how far his play-acting had gone.

"What about what I want?" she asked.

Liam was leaving the next day for Virginia, where he would spend the school year with his father and stepmother at their home in Great Falls. Liam had told her that the house was enormous, with a Ping-Pong table, a bar and a jukebox in the basement, and a pool in the backyard. He'd be going to Potomac School with a bunch of rich lobbyists' kids and South American dictators-in-training. How an attorney on the right, that is, correct, side of the so-called green movement could afford all this Charlotte couldn't imagine, but it was just the kind of buttoned-down shape all the things Dan had once professed to believe in had taken; it reminded her of his inability to carry things through.

"Can't moms have any wants?"

Liam shuffled his sneaker again and gave her the patronizing look of his father. She had never thought that Liam could equal the rebellion she had staged against her own parents, but it was strange what your children could come up with to defy you: with his urban youth language and devotion to rap, Liam was turning into a sexist, an objectifier of women, before her eyes. "How should I know?" he said.

The light turned green again, and Charlotte grabbed him fiercely by the arm. "I don't care what you know or don't know," she said, pulling him off the curb. "Mrs. Wudun has done a lot for you and I won't have you being ungrateful. Now march."

She had actually said "march."

Liam shook her off and shambled, several paces behind, across the unmarked asphalt, the flow of hair hiding his eyes. At the steps of the Palace, Charlotte gathered his thin, bony body against her, and he didn't resist. Stepping back, she took his limp arms in her hands. "There are just some things in life, Liam, that if you don't do them now it will haunt you forever." Her own words sounded cloying, but she sensed in them an absolute truth. Yong and the horrible American she had met in Nanjing had been waiting two days in Mei's apartment, while Charlotte stayed away because she hadn't heard from Rank. She'd missed all three of their meetings. It was time to do something herself.

"I know Mrs. Who-dun-it's gonna haunt me whatever I do," Liam said, shaking the hair from his forehead. His growing Adam's apple bobbed, and he smiled enough to show the gap between his front teeth. His father had promised him braces, too, the son of a bitch.

"You'll thank me some day," Charlotte told him, letting her face betray a twinkle of irony. "Now get going. I have to meet someone."

Liam stepped up one step, creating the small stage between them on which he performed. "Mr. Burling?" he sang, voice cracking. "Loo-shuss?"

He vamped, and Charlotte wanted to stay, follow him into the soft glow and fanciful music of the Palace. She could watch, for the hundredth time, the hawk abuse the turtle in the rehearsal for the puppet theater; the moral, if that's what it was, always struck her as needlessly violent, but she supposed it was no worse than the movies he'd be seeing at home. It acted as a sort of Romulus and Remus for China, with a nationalistic edge.

"No, sweetheart, it's not Mr. Burling. It's a friend of his."

Worry played across Liam's features, making them once again childish and soft. A man in an open-neck shirt came toward them, his face like a wolf, and Charlotte shuddered. Since she'd gotten back from Nanjing, she'd had the sensation she was being followed. The man looked her up and down but kept walking on.

"Mom?"

"Yes, honey. Sorry."

"When I go . . ." Liam paused, his eyes averting to the buses and pedestrian flyover, blocks down the street. "When I go back to Virginia, are you and Lucius moving in together?"

"Sweetheart, no. You don't think?"

"You see him a lot," said Liam timidly. "He stayed over."

"How do you feel about that?"

"I don't want him to hurt you."

"Oh, Liam," she said, smoothing his hair from his forehead. She couldn't help laughing at how innocent he was. "Your Dad and I were young, and then we changed. It happens with people. Nobody set out to hurt anyone. Besides, Mr. Burling is very different from your father. He and I are more alike. You'd better go," she said weakly. "We'll talk more about it tonight."

"At the Tower, right?"

She had promised to take him to the restaurant on top of the Jinjiang Tower Hotel, the only revolving one in China.

"I promised you, didn't I?" she asked.

He nodded without a word and ran up the stairs to the Palace.

THE LIGHT WHERE CHARLOTTE AND LIAM HAD CROSSED turned red, and the people thinned out; she slipped her way into the torrent of bodies and damp, slapping arms. Carried along, she could smell the sweating bodies, the harsh soap the women used. Fences ran along the curbs to prevent pedestrians from crossing, but two young men dashed out and vaulted the fence, dodging four lanes of bicycles, buses, and cars.

She and Lucius alike? Hard to think about now. Her little voice of truth or consequences, so often muzzled, had been urging for months now that Lucius was right for her, a silent-generation mix of conscience and pragmatism, a Steady Eddie in her mother's words, but Charlotte couldn't escape the feeling that life with Lucius would be like retirement at forty, well-appointed but sustained by a fixed income of affection and interesting travel. And then there was his baggage. He had enough for ten trips around the world.

At the steps to the pedestrian flyover, an unkempt man came toward her, holding a baby. Charlotte had to squeeze against the railing. She was only thinking of Lucius to take her mind off what she knew she must do. Buses rang below, throwing sparks from the wires, and she tried to hold her breath as she climbed, looking down with a stitch of fear at the soot-blackened roofs of the trams. Perhaps if she could do this one thing, get word to Lindstrom that things had gone bad, come up with a solution, that feat would be enough to hold her for a more conventional future. She had joined the foreign service, after Dan left, to escape a life in which she saw herself as nothing but a glorified secretary, with a young son in a series of two-bedroom apartments in Arlington, kilims, a library of independent films, and the smell of homemade macaroni-and-cheese. But she had not been sure then that government work was for her, and soon she had begun to chafe against the constant political pressure to dissemble. She had made it down the far stairs and was trying to turn into the flow on the sidewalk when she felt something sharp poke her back.

"Turn the other way, keep moving," said a man's voice very close to her ear. His breath sent a shiver through her body. She turned her chin to look back, and the knife cut through her blouse; the side of the blade was cold on her skin.

"Don't look. Walk in front of me," he said.

"Jack?" She was trying not to shudder.

He came up beside her, holding her arm. His cheek was close to hers, the jawbone apparent, serrated beneath the sallow skin. His voice had a thin sound, a flavor that struck her as rancid. She could have sworn he'd been doing smack.

"You know it's Thursday," he said.

"Well, that's right." She tried to muster her courage, but he was hurting her arm.

"I've been twisting in the wind for two days here."

"The thing is, that I wasn't supposed to come until I'd heard specific news."

"From Alan?" Lindstrom whistled through his teeth. In her peripheral vision, she saw his eyes survey the end of the street, where traffic flowed onto the Bund. In the harbor beyond it, bulky white ships sat firmly at anchor; Lindstrom's eyes seemed to widen when he saw them.

"How'd you find me, anyway?"

"I've been on you since you stopped by the consulate this morning." The knife felt almost cozy against her hip now. "Your kid doesn't like his piano lessons much."

Charlotte watched the muscles flex and relax in his face. When she'd met him in Nanjing, he'd reminded her of the speed-freak charter captains Dan had represented in Boston, men whose boats had been confiscated for running small cargoes of pot or avoiding the draft. The intervening days had dulled his eyes and slackened his posture, turned him into a Chinese peasant who has migrated to the city for work.

"I knew that someone was following me. I thought I was just being paranoid."

"I tried to go see Burling last night," Lindstrom said, "but the consul wasn't at home."

Charlotte shivered. "You were there?"

"I was hoping Lucius could help me out of this little jam I'm in. At least the old fucker had some pills in his nightstand. Where his gun should have been, I might add."

"The Percocet's mine and it's old," Charlotte told him. "The gun is in a shoebox in the closet."

"Shit. You got any more? For a while there last night I thought I was Confucius or something. Mixing crystal with opium is messing with my head."

"I've got some Valium," she said, poking her fingers through the lint and laundered paper at the bottom of her pocket and coming up with two tiny pills. Beneath the cloth, her legs were chafing. "My version of the cyanide pill. How did you get into the Residence, anyway?"

"You were just about to come to Mei's apartment, weren't you?"

"Alan was deported," Charlotte told him. "After they almost beat him to death. I didn't know what else to do."

"Jesus." They were walking much faster than the crowd, and Lindstrom held her back. His overlong fingernails dug in her skin. "We're not protesting whale hunts, you know. You get arrested, they don't let you out with a squeeze and a slap on the ass."

"They've all agreed to keep it quiet, but I heard from our vice-consul. I didn't know what to do."

"They're rolling it up?"

"I don't know what that means. All I know is some agents, State Security or something, came to Alan's apartment. Almost tortured him right in his office with his wife looking on. That's what Mike said."

"He's Company?"

"That's the assumption, yes. And you?"

The green strip of park spread out ahead, along the water. "Where the fuck is Burling, anyway?"

"He called Mike Ryan Tuesday to say they'd kept him at a banquet in Beijing and now they seemed to be stalling about his plane. What I don't understand is why they'd care about him."

Lindstrom yanked her around the corner of the Bund, under the gaze of the traffic cop's raised pagoda. She realized that he must have put his knife back where he kept it.

"He's the center, that's why. He's the sun and I'm the moon."

"It's ironic, don't you think?" she said, freeing her arm. The crowds had crossed to the park on the other side of the Bund. She injected a patronizing tone into her voice, thinking that it might be the right way to gain the upper hand. "All your life you've just gone from one place to another, trying not to hurt anyone."

"Did Burling tell you that?"

"You think I'm some bleeding-heart Dorothy Day type who fell for Alan Rank. Well, I'm not. I had my own reasons for trying to help Yong."

Without warning, he pulled her toward a building, into a doorway. Bad move on my part, she thought, stumbling on the steps.

"I'm going to let you in on a secret, baby." The tip of the knife protruded from the sleeve of his shirt.

Right here, she thought; he's going to kill me because he can't get to Lucius. They just go right through us, with words, with their dicks, with knives. A giddy courage overtook her. "I'm dying to hear it."

"Ineffectual lefties like our friend Alan don't dream up shit like this. Nor do secret fucking societies made up of Southern Baptists and Overseas Chinese. Not to pull out agents, they don't."

Charlotte met his crazy eyes.

"That's right. Average people like to call them spies. Yong was one, and so was I. We were in the same network, even, just on different sides of the border. Lucius Burling was our handler."

"Oh, my God . . ."

"This is an Agency operation, but what kind is anyone's guess. How were we supposed to get out of here, anyway? You were supposed to tell me, right?"

"Alan said it was better that you didn't know until you got here. There's supposed to be a smuggler, a sort of triad, I think. You were going on his boat with some others, ordinary people who pay to get out."

Lindstrom looked at the harbor as if he couldn't stand her face. A pleasure vessel steamed across the channel. Loading cranes rose from shipyards on the opposite shore.

"I met him last Friday at my son's rehearsal," said Charlotte. "There was a sign and countersign."

"Oh, my."

"Why," she said, her voice cracking, "do you keep making light? This scared little man, like a barge captain, begged me, begged me to hide him, and the next day Alan said he was tortured, walked into the ocean, and shot."

Lindstrom breathed and pushed the air down with his palms; it was a movement she had seen old people doing in the park. "Was there ever a backup? Anyone else Alan mentioned? How did you get into this, anyway?"

"A year ago, when I was back in D.C., I was sitting at our booth at the Asian Studies meeting, trying to sign up these brilliant graduate students who have no hope of getting a tenure-track job, and up walks Alan and picks up a folder. 'Ah,' he says in that reedy voice of his. Of course he was too old to be interested in the Service; those meetings are meat markets, so I thought he was trying to pick me up. 'The propaganda wing.' Then he took me to this dinner party out on River Road. A Chinese man in a glass house was cooking dinner for his guests, who turned out to be the ones who fund this operation, or at least I thought they did."

"They wanted you to keep an eye on Burling, right?"

"They said he might still be with CIA."

"It's hard to leave," Lindstrom told her.

Burling's face, looking white, a bit drawn, appeared in the back of her mind, wrinkling his nose at Liam from the window of the consulate Jeep as he left for the airport a month ago. Was he really a good man, after all? Did she belong with freaks like Lindstrom, or was she slumming?

"Can we cross the street, please?" she said. "It smells like piss in here, and I'm getting a headache. What if someone comes out?"

He appeared to relent. "It's my own fucking character. I just keep learning the same lesson over and over again."

They waited for the signal to cross, and Charlotte tried to remember the gray afternoons last fall when she'd meet Alan Rank at the Black Cat Lounge in Nanjing. It was as if they were having an affair, except that Alan was the first man she'd ever respected to whom she didn't develop an attraction, and their talks had felt to her like the beginning of a more serious life. How badly she had been mistaken. In the absence of her comforting illusion, she found herself thinking that it was Lindstrom who knew something true.

"What is it?" she asked. "The lesson you keep learning over and over again."

He had stepped off the curb without her. On the back of his head, below the band of the Mao cap, a short white scar showed through his hair.

"There isn't one," he said as she hurried up beside him. "A lesson is exactly what we're trying to avoid."

She put her hand on his arm as they walked across the grass. A seawall ran around the edge of the harbor, and she felt the draw of its height from the water.

"All these fucking boats," said Lindstrom, doing a push-up against the railing. Something between them had changed. He watched a tug push a line of laden barges toward the river's mouth. *"Water, water, everywhere, and all the boards did shrink . . ."*

"Water, water, everywhere, nor any drop to drink."

"You know the 'Ancient Mariner'?" he asked.

"My Dad worked for the stevedore's union in D.C.," she told him. "The albatross provided a convenient, if not real original, metaphor for him to use at rallies."

Lindstrom nodded, his eyes straying down the quay. "My grandfather, the one who had the church in Anhe? He was a Wobbly who worked on the docks in San Pedro. A mission preacher there converted him after he shot a cop during a strike. That poem was the only secular one he'd retained from his days on the road. He said that China was his albatross, a kind of purgatory for him."

"I know how he felt," Charlotte said.

Lindstrom turned to check the narrow park around them. On the lip of an ornamental pond, two men sat reading, pink lilies floating motionless on the water before them. One man's finger ran across a newspaper, and the other was watching a pretty Cantonese woman in an orange shift, arms out to catch her toddling son. The child was shrieking at his newfound ability to walk.

You'll never catch him, Charlotte thought. She was scared to ask Lindstrom what he saw, and the effort of silence pressed into her. How silly she had been to think she could ever know these people, this place. The last of the barges passed, its gunwales strung with tires. A breeze stirred the water. She averted her cheek.

"Do you see something, Jack?"

He watched the park with the same analyzing eye she had seen Lucius use—it was the only time she had ever seen men look that way at other men, the way women do at women. She had seen Dan use it in the House cafeteria, during the First Hundred Days.

"Someone is watching," Lindstrom said, putting his hand on her forearm. "Don't *look*, Charlotte. You wouldn't notice him, anyway. He was down by the gangplank of that pleasure boat, smoking an English cigarette. Now he's under the trees."

"How do you know it's an English cigarette?"

"I worked in a hotel, remember? In a country like this, imported smokes are always a giveaway. Only high-level bureaucrats, the very rich, or Security forces can get them."

"What do you think he'll do?"

"He wants you to lead him to Yong, so when I leave, you can stay here a while. If he follows me, I can always take care of it. I'd rather know where he is anyway."

Charlotte's heart felt squeezed, and she took in a little hiss of breath. "You know, I'm actually scared."

"That's the appropriate reaction. Let's you and I walk this way."

Her skin stuck to the painted iron railing, and she knew that she'd been sweating. As they walked away, the ocean breeze met them, smelling of salt and dead fish. The park had emptied, and across the Bund the streets of the old French Concession were tented with afternoon sunlight.

"I have to pick up my son in an hour," she told him. "At four. I promised I'd take him to a restaurant tonight."

"He's keeping his distance," Lindstrom said.

A coin hitting the sidewalk rung inside her with a bright little fear. He was suddenly ten feet behind her, stooping to pick it up as she walked on ahead. Gulls screamed above a fishing trawler, and across the harbor the new glass buildings reflected a gunmetal sky.

"You said that Burling's getting back tonight?"

"At ten o'clock, I hope."

Lindstrom led her around another fountain so he could glance back at the man. "Go out to dinner like you planned. Don't make anyone, especially Ryan, think that anything is strange. What time will you get back to your place?"

"Mike told me that the driver has to pick Lucius up at the airport, so we have to be back by nine. We were going to spend the night at the Residence, so Liam can get an early plane."

"At nine o'clock, go up to Lucius's bedroom. If things are quiet, turn on the light and leave the room. Don't come to the window. I'm going to go back and get Yong. He's going to seek asylum in the consulate."

"But what if Lucius turns him over?"

"If Burling is running this thing, which he must be, then he wants to get Yong out. Of course he wanted to do it quietly, but now he won't have any choice."

"But why did they want me to watch him if he's running it?"

"Can't you get behind this, Charlotte? They keep pulling the rug out from under you over and over until you're standing on the final one, the bottom. Then you understand that the people you've known in your life, *connected* with somehow, is the only pattern there is, no good or evil. You just have to read the pattern. Burling's the only one who knows both me and Yong and even Alan, indirectly. The guys you met on River Road don't even know they're being run. That's the whole fucking point."

In the harbor, a buoy clanged. Over his shoulder, she saw the man who was following them. He was sitting on a bench in the mulberry grove, children and birds at his feet. "My God," she said. "He looks like Saint fucking Francis."

"If things aren't cool, you stand in that bedroom window, lights on, right? Then leave and walk around the consulate block."

The water lapped below with little slaps. Far behind them a man coughed, and he touched her softly on the elbow.

"Time for me to go then," Lindstrom said.

On the Bund, a few Mercedes and Bimmers of the new rich crawled along, tires squeaking softly on the tracks of the tram. On the opposite side, a street slithered back into the Old Chinese City. Lindstrom leaned in as if he were going to kiss her. "If he chooses me, stay here for half an hour. If you're sure he's on you, though, you can go back the way you came, pick up your son."

She turned to look at him, to see if he had smiled, because those even white teeth she now found reassuring, but he was already headed across the Bund, dodging cars and flipping his Mao cap on as he went.

When she brought her eyes back to the sidewalk, the State Security man was coming toward her, lighting another cigarette with his hand cupped around his nose and mouth. The match lit up his eyes and forehead, which were strangely mild. He looked almost kind. When he passed her, he was dragging and squinting at the smoke, and his eyes looked through her toward Lindstrom. Suddenly, she wished he had chosen to follow her, but she knew it was a crazy thing to want.

LI XIN HAD LEFT THE OPEN QUAY AND FOUND A BENCH beneath the mulberry trees, where the packed earth was stained with purple berries. Sitting there, smoking, watching the Americans talk, he felt less exposed. A woman in an orange dress ran after her toddler into the grove, lifting the little boy to pluck a berry from the branches and showing Li the firm skin beneath her arms. The boy brought Li the berry, with a grave look on his face as if this were serious work he was doing. His mother nodded and smiled at Li with her open face, damp at the temples. The bold concentration on the little boy's face reminded Li so much of his daughter that he had to restrain himself from squeezing the plump little arm. Li took the boy's offering and thanked him with a nod. That broke the elastic of the toddler's courage; he dissolved into giggles and ran to his mother, overcome by a sudden bashfulness. When Li stood up, he felt dizzy with longing. The leaves smelled sharp and the berry was tart on his tongue. The woman left, looking much like his wife from the back, broad and taller than he. The memory of her clotted in his chest. He lit another cigarette and watched.

Charlotte Brien had rested her hand on Lindstrom's arm as they crossed the grass, but then they leaned against the iron railing, separate, facing first the park and then the harbor, then the park again, their movements stiff as young people courting. Shanghai, unlike Beijing, was a city of excess and display: in the streets, people touched, shook hands robustly, the fashions showed the women's legs, the skin of their chests, and their firm, supple arms. When Lindstrom and Charlotte Brien started to walk, several kids had just come running and laughing into the grove from the opposite side. They mobbed the tree trunks and jumped for the berries, knocking into Li and landing on his foot.

"*Bu!*" Little *qing wa*, little frogs. He picked a child up and moved her to the side as he swiped away the branches. She gave him a cross look such as his daughter often did. She was spoiled as could be, but Li was powerless to stop it. "Shit."

Lindstrom had parted from the woman and was making for the street. Li ground his cigarette out in the grass. Keeping the fountain between him and the two Americans, he moved beyond the shade of the mulberries, into the vacant sun of the late afternoon. Lindstrom walked like the Sherpas Li had seen in Tibet, as if his head were in the clouds and he knew the ground beneath him without looking. Li gave him fifty meters, halfway across the Bund, which was choked with private cars. Passing Charlotte, he didn't look, but her feminine presence, a pastel light, such as the light given off by the flowers in the fountain, stayed with him as he waited at the curb. He could still hear water falling and children laughing under the trees.

Across the Bund were the buildings, high and brown with windows fitted into muntins shaped in strange arabesques. Their brown fronts curved around the corners in a way that excited him. In alcoves high on the walls, statues of bare-breasted women leaned over the sidewalk, the folds of their stone robes embracing their hips. When Lindstrom passed from the boulevard into the Old

Chinese City through a decorated gate, Li was relieved, but soon the houses there bore down on him, too. He was constantly dipping his head, or excusing himself as he tripped on enamel pots filled with peeled onions and shallots. The spices smelled slightly different, rank and phlegmatic, and the heavy gables hung overhead, windows thrust out, sashes peeling red paint. He missed the space, the dry air of Beijing and his hometown outside it. Washing blotted the sky.

Lindstrom followed a deliberate but circuitous route, moving like a cat through the *hutongs*, first hoving to the walls then tacking out across the puddled cobbles, slicked and bubbly with soap, then against the stucco again. He never turned around, and Li began to feel that the American didn't know that he was being watched, that the telepathic feeling Li had experienced on the road from Anhe, the buzzing in his head when he had suddenly known that it was Lindstrom in the truck, had been one-sided. Now Lindstrom, blind, made quickly for the place where Yong was hidden.

After more streets that looked oddly the same, Lindstrom passed through a courtyard before an old temple. He stopped and bent down, picking something from between the paving stones. Li had to shrink back in a doorway, where he frightened a rat. Its nails skittered back along the floorboards, and he felt the blood thump hotly in his ears.

Lindstrom went around a row of empty mahjong tables and stepped onto the coping of a pool, staring down at the tea-colored water. Carp passed beneath the surface like liquid orange flames. A sound wave warbled in Li's head, as if he himself were underwater. Leering animals perched on the lintels of the temple; from beneath the surface, he looked up at Lindstrom's face: head shaved, eyes shining, cheekbones flared like a lizard. It contorted, and its hands slid down its sides, its body stiff, the neck lengthening to change its form.

A salamander. Or agama.

Tibetan lizard with the head of toad.

It shrugged, and something dark left its claw. A bright coin spun above the water and hung below the surface for a moment, then sunk to the fish. The lizard leapt from the coping and went quickly across the square. Li brought out his revolver from the holster on the back of his belt. In the center of this maze of rotting buildings, touched by blood and bad religion, the lizards from the temples of Tibet were coming down to greet him, the *Bull-Headed Spirits of Death*. Li covered the temple porch with his pistol, then moved along the peeling wall, under the tall shuttered windows. Two *hutongs* led from the back of the temple at angles, each seemingly deserted. He was turned around and couldn't judge in which direction the Bund would be, which the open, throbbing light of the harbor, the quay and children's laughter underneath the gentle trees.

Apart from one's hallucinations, in reality there are no such things existing outside oneself as Lord of Death, or god, or demon, said the saffron-robed monk. *Act so as to recognize this.*

"Cowardice is death in life," the general told him.

Li moved along the *hutong*, shaking with anger and sorrow for himself. Behind the dusty windows, ground-floor rooms seemed vacant, teeming with grainy light, the stairs inside the entries leading to a dull, gray emptiness above. The sounds of life, pots clanging and a dulcimer, plucked in a careless tune, filtered through from far away. These were the rooms of his childhood, simple rooms, the cool hand of his mother, the familiar smells of her cooking, the candles burned before the shrines to her gods. Unlike his brothers, he had not made fun of her ignorance; instead he had harbored his plan. He was not good at school, but he knew how to read people; in the army he was good at petty soldiering and figuring out what his superiors wanted. He measured his steps, heart beating in the top of his skull.

The *hutong* narrowed, ending at a T. Li poked his head around the corner and quickly pulled it back. What he'd seen was like a dream. Swinging his arm around again, he found the pistol pointing at another courtyard, full of noise and pinkish air. Paper lanterns hung around a rectangle of tables, and a tall bride in a white lace dress, hair fixed with white netting, went around with a glass of wine in her hand. The groom in a dark suit huddled with his friends beside a small, electrified band. As he moved through the guests, a shyness overcame Li. Out of place and alone, a stranger passing through happiness, secreting, protecting, defending the ambition in his heart. The distant memory of his own wedding, the fear and anticipation, his wife's simple, determined joy and ultimately his own impassiveness, embittered him. A man in a Mao cap seemed to wait at the edge of the crowd, nodding his head in time to the music.

Li drew the revolver from the pocket of his windbreaker, and an old man wearing a war medal pointed at him. The old man nudged the people seated near him, but the guests ignored him, watching the bride. Li felt his past and future crowd around him.

The secret of life is revealed by a teaching presenting itself as the science of death, the monk said.

As Li reached the bandstand, he saw Lindstrom turn and leave the square at a run.

A swarm of cars, bikes, and people; a smudge of yellow light glowed above the end of the street into which he had fled, a street of modern, regular buildings. Li's stiff shoes hurt his feet as he hurried down the sidewalk. Bikes were locked within the open gates, but Lindstrom wasn't there. The street turned a shallow angle, and Li saw the back of him, the cap and gray pajamas, passing into the farthest entry. Just outside the gate, an old woman sat on a folding chair. Footsteps echoed in the concrete stairs.

Taking out his pistol again, Li began to climb, the knuckles holding the revolver scraping against the plaster wall. This was it, the place where his suffering ended—one, two, three steps, his neck craned left to see the next landing. The place where his greater devotion would be revealed. Yes! That was it, not the *science of death,* but . . . A huge hand was covering his mouth. He tried to bring his weapon around, but another hand, this one holding a knife, slammed the pistol against the wall. Again. Again.

"Let it drop or I'll break your neck. I don't want to kill you," the American said. His warm breath smelled like soldiers in Tibet who took dope. "I'm not kidding," Lindstrom told him. "Let it go."

Li's legs went out from under him, now his crotch, and then his head hit the edge of a stair. His vision squeezed together and began to tear away from his consciousness, and came back again. His body felt like pieces of itself.

"We are all brothers," the American seemed to be saying again and again. The voice was oddly friendly, calm, without anger. It sounded like the monk:

My Papa planted the seed, so we're brothers, I'm telling you. That's the secret: We're one and the same. Give me the gun because I need it, then I won't cut your throat.

The hand let Li's head settle gently against the steps.

Come on, brother, give it up. A blade was cold on Li's cheek, then a tug, like a stitch, and a smooth, stinging pain woke him up, warm liquid leaving the side of his face.

It'll feel like that, except it won't stop, it won't clot like in other places. Heart's blood, I'm telling you. I've been there. I was looking for my wife. They tied me up and threw me in a hole. Told me she'd been with them, adopted their ways. When you know you're going to die, that's when you know who to trust, and let me tell you, brother, this whole thing we're in is a lie. Flip the coin, it doesn't matter which way it comes up. It's a lie, full of death, just pretending it's life.

The gun left Li's hand, and he rested his hurt cheek on the cool cement.

"You're not going to talk now, are you?" Lindstrom said.

Li made a noise to indicate he wouldn't.

"Okay, then."

His groin ached, and he seemed to have wet himself.

"I know," Lindstrom said. "It's the kind of pain that keeps you awake but just won't kill you even though you think you want it to. Don't be fooled. You'll want to live again in a little while, and then you'll want to kill me."

Li lay there for a long time before the street committee woman came and helped him up. He had vomited, and blood had dried on the side of his cheek.

"Mmm, triads," she murmured kindly, daubing his cheek with a warm, wet cloth. "Black market's no good."

She sent him limping back into the unfamiliar street.

THE RESTAURANT, LIAM TOLD HER, WAS LIKE A PLANETARIUM his father had taken him to in the District. The circular dining room banked by curved windows; jewelry and silverware twinkling in the intimate light of the table lamps. The hostess seated them in a spacious booth next to the windows and offered two menus like broadsides, encased in black leather. Stories below, the canopy of trees looked tattered in places, revealing a lower world of streets lit by puddles of light, inhabited by dark vehicles pushing their weak yellow beams. Riding from the Children's Palace to the restaurant, Charlotte had sensed again that someone was following.

"Are we really moving?" Liam asked.

"Look at the stairs we just came down, honey. The elevators were right there a moment ago."

The next time she saw him, he was going to be a jaded private-school teenager, but for now he still retained his capacity for wonder. "It's like being in a spaceship," he said.

On the stage, a decent swing band was putting down late Benny Goodman, and a few lithe Western European couples glided around the lighted floor. The waiter brought bread, and Liam chewed thoughtfully as he pored over the menu.

"Order anything you want," Charlotte told him. She was going to have a demi of wine. "Tonight the rules are relaxed."

Liam peered across the top of his menu, considering just how far this rare dispensation might extend. The complexity of the food and the dining room's shadowy elegance quieted him. At table after table, the faces she saw were familiar types in Shanghai: well-heeled Western investors with their big, soft, groomed heads, or the quick, nervous ones, eyes implacable with greed; the little Hong Kong moguls, dark and tyrannical; the good-natured, can-do Taiwanese.

They reminded her of insects—the men like stag beetles and the trophy women, tall and pushed up and made up like dragonflies, sucking their glasses of nectar. She was in a strange mood, fueled by a reckless and indulgent fatalism that scared and invigorated her. One of the women, with a centerfold body and the face of a child, sauntered by, trailing a wake of sweet, gagging perfume, and Charlotte watched Liam's face for some evidence of interest, but he was too busy gazing out the window, where the harbor sat like a band shell of light beyond the bright, electrified strip of the Bund.

Lindstrom was out there, waiting for her. Her feelings for him weren't sexual, but still the idea of him made her head swim. Liam's cheeks ballooned and collapsed like a frog's as he sucked his Orangina through a straw.

"Are Dad and Maureen going to have any kids?" he asked suddenly, eyes still fixed on the power plant, sparkling in the distance. His dark eyes with their beautiful lashes met hers. "Like, brothers and sisters or something?"

The waiter arrived and stood above them, hands clasped behind his back.

"You'd have to ask your father that. What are you going to have?"

"Does Lucius have any?"

"He has grandchildren," Charlotte said shortly. "The man is waiting, Liam."

Liam shuffled through the pages and ran his finger down to a combination of shellfish and beef. She hadn't looked at the menu, so she ordered the same. Surf and turf, her father's favorite, his idea of having made it in the world. Her glass was already empty, and the waiter poured more. He held the bottle up to the window and spied through it, then added the last drops. "*Encore une fois?*"

"*Mais bien sûr,*" she replied. The only nun she had ever really liked at school was French, and when Charlotte joined the State Department—making it first through the written foreign service exam, for which she had studied for a year, then the cold, impersonal oral assessment, at which a Scandinavian Amazon from Minnesota, a veteran of two tours in Moscow and one in Intelligence and Research, had nearly made her cry—she told the man who interviewed her that she imagined herself being posted to a Franco-phone country, West Africa or the Caribbean. She liked the sturdy and sisterly, statuesque women who powdered their necks on the Washington metro in summer.

"Is Shanghai close enough for you?" the gray little man had asked.

"Will I see Lucius before I go?" Liam wanted to know.

Charlotte was watching over the sill as a black car pulled up across the street. The height of the building, the distance between her and the idea that had carried her here, brought a lump to her throat. She pulled back and faced her son, anger simmering beneath a motherly mien she was struggling to maintain. Liam liked Lucius Burling, and Lucius had, she was forced to admit, been a leavening influence on him during a precarious time. "I'm a better dad to him than I was to my own kids," Burling had said. So why was a good man for Liam not a good one for her?

"I told you, Liam. Lucius and I, we . . ."

"Broke up? Like you and Dad?"

"Not exactly."

"You're going to live together then, but you're not getting married. You don't want to mess up a good thing."

Charlotte smiled and reached for his hand. All at once, she found that she was terrified of facing Lucius, because he would know about Lindstrom and Rank, her . . . betrayal? But that was absurd. There was nothing to betray. Leaning across the white tablecloth, she held Liam's hand tighter as he tried to pull away.

"Those are all clichés, honey, things you hear people say on TV. What's happening with Lucius and me has more to do with . . . context."

It was a stupid thing to say to a child, and Liam knew it. Before she could begin to explain, he had already started to brood. The waiter intruded with her second bottle of wine, a full one.

"*Pas des demis?*" she inquired. "*Peut-être une autre . . . domaine de . . . ?*"

The waiter smiled inscrutably. "*Cela parvient avec les compliments du gentilhomme au comptoir.*" He pointed his corkscrew, but the band had stepped up the tempo and she couldn't see through the twining bodies on the floor. "*Un Américain*," the waiter added approvingly, popping the cork.

A woman in a pleated tulle skirt spun away from her partner, and Charlotte saw reddish hair, a face with the drooping eyes of a clown, peering in her direction; the waiter nodded, and the man, who looked like he had raided the wardrobe of a seventies cop film, raised his glass.

"*Non*," she said, waving her hand. The face of her benefactor was bluish with sweat in the light of the bar. "*Je ne peux pas accepter . . .*"

"Mom? What's going on?"

A beautiful Chinese woman, probably a prostitute, sat next to the man. She was playing with the straw in her drink. On the floor, a similar woman was dancing with a corpulent guy in a suit, her head on his shoulder and a bored expression on her face, eyeing his diamond college ring. If the man at the bar were only a businessman wanting a night of love, she didn't kid herself he would even look her way.

"I have to speak to that man, Liam. He's a friend of Lucius Burling."

Liam's eyes became large, and he turned around to gawk. He knew that Lucius had worked for the Agency, and his fantasies were peopled with mysterious strangers. The books that he liked were all about mythical secrets and spies. One of the characters had now come to life and was crossing the dining room.

"Don't stare, honey. He must be staying at the hotel."

"You don't remember," said the man, arriving behind the waiter's shoulder. His Oxbridge accent surprised her. He wore a checked jacket and a shirt with broad lapels, open at the neck. A pinched scar ran into his hairline. Charlotte raised herself from the bench and extended her hand. "Simon Bell. I gave a lecture to your China class at the Foreign Service Institute. It wasn't memorable, I realize . . ."

"Oh, no." She had attended seven months of language study with the same overcaffeinated Taiwanese, but she would have remembered a guest speaker. "Of course I remember. I was Charlotte McCarthy then. Now it's back to the original Brien. This is Liam."

"Hi, there, son," said Simon Bell. He was bigger than life. "Mind if I join you?"

"You're a friend of Consul Burling?" Liam asked, glancing sideways at his mother.

Bell grinned at Charlotte and nodded as he swung himself onto the bench. "Absolutely. Lucius and I . . . well, as it happens . . ." He slid the wine glass from Liam's place so the waiter could fill it. Then he settled in as if he were about to relate a long story. "I just saw Lucius up in Peking."

"It's *Beijing*," Liam told him.

"You're *right*," Bell said, pointing dramatically. "I'm just old-fashioned."

Liam was tickled. He beamed at his mother as if she had hired a clown.

"Why, if that isn't . . ." Bell cocked his ear toward the dance floor, where the band had begun strains of a song Charlotte recognized as a favorite of her father's. "Liam, would you allow me to dance with your mom?"

"I guess so."

Simon Bell put out his hand, and Charlotte took it, smiling reassuringly at her son.

"Where did I really meet you?" she asked as they assumed the position at the edge of the floor. "You didn't speak to my class at FSI."

"No. I don't guess they'd let me." Bell's bulk was belied by experienced feet. "Do you recall Dr. Wu's house? You came with Alan Rank."

The rhythm got ahead of her, and Bell had to take her in hand. Perhaps the reckless, importunate feeling had been a sign.

"You mean the treehouse, on River Road? You're one of them? Oh, thank God. Do you have something for me?"

"You're being watched," said Bell. "Right now, and not just by Liam. I took a considerable risk even following you here."

Charlotte stiffened in his arms. It helped their dancing, and they moved around the floor like a practiced couple. "Who are 'they'?"

"First Bureau, Second Department, hard to tell. Usually Shanghai section concentrates on Hong Kong and Taiwan, half a dozen of their assets right now in this room. Nanjing tricks with you Yanks and my fellow Europeans, but that's an odd bureaucratic arrangement left over from I don't know when."

"Why are they down here, then? Why did they hold Lucius over in the capital?"

Bell chuckled indifferently. They had settled on an easy foxtrot, back and forth without thought. When they moved near the tables, she could hear the near-hysterical tones of Asian men doing business, smell their whiskey and cigars. "I think it's personal, actually. You can't reason in terms of agencies or governments here. You have to look at individual interests."

"You mean political, or economic?"

He didn't answer, and a shiver ran down her back. The pinky of the hand that held hers sported a ring with what looked like a patriarchal cross, inscribed in black.

"I was supposed to watch Lucius," she said. "I wasn't supposed to have to do any more."

"Believe me, I sympathize." The song was winding down, and Charlotte's terror rose with the disintegrating notes. Stepping back, Bell removed a monogrammed handkerchief from his pocket and glanced around the restaurant, wiping the back of his neck. His breath had a rattle, and she looked away from his eyes: the whites were like uncooked eggs, the eyes of angina, malaria, of a hardbitten life in the developing world. It was new dusk outside now, and in the big pale mirror of the window Liam looked dwarfed and bewildered; their food had not arrived.

"I was supposed to enjoy a similarly limited role," Bell said, watching the bass player adjusting his pegs. "I tried to get Lucius to tell you, so I wouldn't have to come, but he put on his Puritan cloak. I knew better than to push. I've got a ship for Yong and Lindstrom to get . . ."

"Out? Thank God. Jack was starting to talk about asylum, taking Yong to the consulate, but a ship . . ."

The drummer muted the high-hat with his fingers. Bell folded the soiled handkerchief neatly and presented his hands. "It's not so easy as all that, I'm afraid. You need to tell Jack that Gordon MacAllister, or maybe someone worse, maybe triads mixed up with MacAllister, will be waiting for him on the other end, on the dock in Hong Kong. They mean to kill Yong, and him, at least as far as I can tell. They already gunned down a dozen or more on an outlying island."

The drumbeat came down, and the saxophone started a song that seemed undanceable at first.

"But . . . Oh, God." The tempo asserted itself, and they fell back into step, Charlotte sliding her soles across the wood. "I know it sounds silly, but all I wanted was something that was free of all that—politics, and money . . ."

"Very likely that's all Jack wanted, too," Bell said, pulling her closer. His spicy aftershave tickled her nose. His physical repellence was almost endearing. "Whether he decides to get on that boat and live it out with whoever's on the opposite end, that'll say a lot about him. About things."

"He has courage, if that's what you mean."

"He does at that. Mental courage, which is tougher than the physical."

"I think he has that, too. Physical, I mean."

"He may well. I'm not a judge. For some people, myself for instance, not getting involved with things—the web of institutions—is a weakness. For Jack it's a strength. What I meant to say was that if Jack gets on that boat, it'll prove that this was not about Yong, that it was all about Jack from the beginning."

"But isn't that true about each of us, too?"

Without warning, Bell let go and spun her, and she found herself turning in time. Her father had taught her to dance in their family room, pushing the coffee table out of the way to make room on the linoleum floor, dark paneling and ship's-wheel lamps turning. Later, she and Dan had twirled, tripping, in the shallow, rocky water of the Shenandoah River, bluegrass plinking through the trees. In each case, she, her father, even Dan, had been trying to let go of themselves, to reach beyond their own needs, and failing. Could anyone ever succeed? She let herself settle back against Simon Bell, like falling onto an unmade bed. He glanced away toward the elevator doors, and his step acquired the slight bounce of a beginner.

"Lucius was generous to me," he said, "so of course I ended up wanting his wife, his kids, who seemed to love him all the more for his neglecting them, while mine just packed me off to Burma and didn't seem to remember who I was when I returned."

Charlotte wasn't quite sure where this was coming from, but she gave him a cue: "So you fell in love with Amelia?"

"With her loyalty, actually, to her husband, in spite of what he did—rather batty, really, under the circumstances. You can't imagine what it was like."

Oh, yes, I can, Charlotte thought.

"She had real class, that woman, and a zest for life. Being with Lucius just smothered it. Anyhow . . ." He dipped her slightly, almost a pantomime, and brought her back gently to his cheek. "The boat is leaving Shanghai at oh-six hundred tomorrow, bound for Hong Kong and Seattle with jet engine parts. There's a sailor who's a friend of the Georgian bloke who set this all up. He'll meet them on the quay before the old Russian consulate at oh-three hundred sharp. They have to get in the hold before the captain and the rest of the crew come aboard. After that they're on their own."

The song was fizzling out.

"After we leave here, I'm to give Jack a signal," Charlotte said as they walked off the floor. His wet hand stuck to the back of her blouse. "But now I'm afraid that if he comes anywhere near me, they'll jump all over him. I know they've been following me."

They had reached the margin of blue light cast by the bandstand, and she started down the short stairs to the tables. Liam's face looked like it had as a toddler, on the verge of disintegration. A huge plate sat before him, untouched.

Simon Bell put a hand on her shoulder. "So much in this life is about getting even, Charlotte. With our wives, our parents, trying to make it up on our kids. My own son calls his stepfather Dad. Calls me by my Christian name. Only time I saw him with his daughter I could tell just how shitty a father I thought I had been by the way he was spoiling her."

"What are you talking about?" Liam asked.

Bell reached down and slowly ruffled Liam's hair. "Not you, me lad. Your mum's a rare one."

"Don't," said Charlotte. "Anyway, it's not true. I'm all about getting even, I'm afraid."

Bell reached down and plucked a steamed wonton from its dish and popped it into his mouth. "Sorry. Haven't eaten all day. One that's on me's got those awful mustaches, Manchurian. They don't have a whole team, so he may be yours, too. And if Lindstrom decides on the boat, he's looking for a South Korean bloke with a Bible and a red neckerchief. More than one stowaway he found rather risky, but what can you do? Wish me luck, then." Bell lifted her left hand from her side and kissed it lightly on the knuckles. His lips were unnervingly tepid. "Thanks for the dance."

"Simon?"

Bell raised a thin eyebrow, almost invisible in the dim.

"You're sick, aren't you?"

"Just tired, my dear. Sun never sets, and all that."

"Please. My father looked that way, only he wouldn't tell anyone. Then he was gone."

Bell's bad teeth made his smile lipless. "Ironic, isn't it? You think of yourself as the white cells—you know, lodged in the organism, fighting disease—then it's those cells that turn on you." His eyes raked the ceiling, its black geometry of pipes. "They wanted to try me with a transplant, but you need a family member for that. Odds aren't good even then. Hullo!" he said, looking at his watch. "I must be going. Is that what you call a 'runcible spoon,' Liam?"

Liam looked at his cocktail fork suspiciously. "I don't know," he mumbled.

"Just one of those things I've always meant to look up. Cheers."

He turned and lumbered, heavy and awkward once more, up the stairs. She tried to think of something more to say, but the band was starting up again, and Simon's face turned briefly to take in the music, the dancers and lights, before he disappeared past the potted palms into the elevator lobby.

INSIDE THE ELEVATOR, THE FEELING OF THE DRY SKIN ON the back of her hand remained on Bell's lips. His body was cold. Charlotte was honest, and that had impressed him. Besides his on-cologist at Georgetown, and his ex-wife, she was the only one he'd told about the cancer. In dire straits, people either became the most elaborate liars or they turned as transparent as glass. The liars you could touch, and Simon Bell had touched many; the honest ones like Charlotte were rare and inaccessible, and the world was not kind to them. The elevator dropped, and he thought of Amelia, on the porch of her house, the slow eddies of a waltz lapping out through the living-room screens. Discordant laughter from Luke's television drifted down from the top of the stairs. Why did men like Burling, the byzantine egos who left trails of wreckage behind them, still con-tinue to get all the girls? Bell was sixty-eight and still he didn't get it.

"Dance with me," he whispered in the hush of the lift.

He had turned out the porch light, and Amelia's white hand appeared like a moth in the darkness. Her forehead was hot as a child's on his shoulder, but her palm was surprisingly cool. When the music was over, he held her, probing with his chin for her face. He closed his eyes, and she was kissing him, hard, like a creature coming up from the depths. He felt the knobs of her back, her sharp shoulders beneath the gown. A profession of love built inside him, and he murmured the beginnings, but she pushed him away.

"Amelia."

"It's nothing," she said, hands held up before her, face turned to the dark street below. The screen door slammed, and he heard her slippers scuffing on the stairs.

"Nothing," he said, the elevator doors gaping open on a polished marble floor. Sick, he understood her better, loved her more than he ever had before.

Going through the lobby, he found a Chinese man walking beside him: Mr. Li from the general's banquet. "You will come with me, now, Mr. Travers," Li said.

This was where the connections ended, where you became none other than yourself, a dying man. Luke, Amelia, Lucius Burling, Charlotte Brien . . . Because he was dying, he would be able to keep the interrogators hanging much longer than he ever had before—a Hunger Artist of spies. He was trying to remember the story, how Kafka's Artist had gone from starvation to victory, as Li held the back door of the Toyota. Bell felt the hand touch the back of his neck, and he knew what was coming, but he was not quick enough: Li's thumb and forefinger groped beneath the lobes of his ears, and then Bell's forehead was banged against the chrome gutter running along the edge of the roof. The blow didn't hurt, exactly, except on the top of his forehead, but as he sank down onto the seat he felt the tingle and itch of the cut, the warmth of blood rushing to the surface of his skin.

It wasn't unlike a good bang in the scrum, and he figured that once he got out of close quarters he'd be able to see his way. Then Li slammed the door into his shin, and tears popped from his eyes. So it wouldn't be like that, after all. This was cricket: cheap shot town. This was the gentleman's game played by ruffians, not the other way around. The dark head of the Manchu was looking strictly forward, and Bell felt the numb despair of his public school days settle around him as he lifted his broken ankle with his hands.

Just don't identify, he thought. Let it happen not to them, but to you.

April Lindstrom had identified, or tried to understand, what her captors were after, or at least that's what Burling had said, in the days when he had opened up to Simon. It had not been easy on her, according to those who knew.

Li got in beside him, and a gun poked his kidney. Bell had drunk two vodka-and-tonics at the bar, and he hoped, above all, that he would not soil himself. The pain of the broken bone was shooting for his bladder, but real pain was so much better than the stealthy traitor cells he couldn't feel.

As the car tore away from the curb, he raised his hand to his forehead. It would be good to see what direction they were traveling, but already his brows were soaked with blood. Just the small downward tip of his head made him dizzy and nauseous. His knees rushed up at him, and a blackout curtain fell across his mind. The car's motion became like a dream, and he heard sirens and saw tiny fires, his mother lying on a bed of broken glass in the parlor of their house on Russell Square. Her eyes were so true, so kind that he would have changed places with her for all the world, but the rumble of the engines was fading away and darkness coming down.

THE GENERAL HAD TURNED UP THE WINDOW UNIT WHEN Li returned to the room. Li was glad he was wearing his jacket and sweater. Only the bedside lamp was on, and a light in the bathroom, the door of which stood slightly ajar. Music played from the television set.

"I'm afraid you have gotten ahead of yourself," said the general, leaning back against the pillows. A tumbler of scotch sat beside him on the bed. "You let the business with Lindstrom spook you. You're lucky you're not dead."

"It's not that," said Li, removing his jacket.

"You have blood on your sleeve."

The general pointed, and Li looked down at the dark red dots on his cuff. A bad smell remained in his nose. "That pig." The hard consonants made his groin ache. "You will excuse me, please, General?"

The Big Fish grunted and waved him off with his hand.

Li went into the bathroom and pulled his sweater over his head. In the wool, he could smell the pig's cologne. Also gasoline, but he had stood next to Feng in the room down the hall as they brought Travers to in the shower, and Feng always smelled like cars. The water ran pink from his cuff as he scrubbed the good white fabric against itself. He found himself thinking of the pastor from Anhe. To survive the ancient magic of the lamas and come home to be cursed by a four-foot-high preacher from an ignorant provincial town! And Lindstrom her changeling, letting him live to some evil purpose? The whole business was bad luck. Li's mother had told him that this was a dangerous year.

He hung the damp shirt over the towel rod and splashed water onto his face. The fancy etched mirror above the sink was losing its backing in places, and when he blinked at his reflection he thought he saw an old face with a hideous scar. In a fright, he backed out of the bathroom, tripping over the threshold, clutching his sweater to his chest.

The general steadied his drink as Li stumbled against the bed.

"You need some rest, son."

Li held up the sweater before him, trying to find the tag. He could smell his own underarms. He thought he saw spots on his sweater, dried spots from the barracks in the countryside, or from his own cheek. The air-conditioned air smelled like a paddy, dead water and animal dung. "I can't sleep," he confessed. "I close my eyes and I see the Anhe pastor. Her hair has turned white."

The general took a dubious drink from his glass. "I told you that church woman didn't know any more than she told you. You said yourself when you asked her about Lindstrom, she thought you were talking about the old one."

"The Reverend," Li said, "but that was an act. She's a witch. I have seen it before in . . ."

"Enough!" The general struggled upright against the pillows. "I won't hear any more of your crap about magic."

"You should have seen her watch that fire, General. It was as if . . ."

Li tried to come up with a metaphor. The building itself had gone up nicely; by the time he had the pastor in the car, only three walls were standing, the front and two sides; already the roof had been swallowed by flames.

"As if what, Li?"

"The old man was burning, he was screaming inside the church. Feng tried to stop him, but the old man was crazy, he just walked right into the fire. She watched him, General. I would swear that she smiled."

The general's face was unbelievably calm, and Li felt something like love for him. The pig Travers had said that the general was in this for personal reasons having to do with the corruption of his son, but that could have been gleaned from any rag in Hong Kong, and Li knew it was a lie calculated to distract him. He knew that Western intelligence agents had excellent training. The idea that Henry Sun was the general's brother was beyond the pale.

"Anything else?" the Big Fish asked.

Li hesitated. "The witch just looked up, as the tower fell into the fire. I took her to the car, and she nearly stumbled on the sill of the gate. She wouldn't look down. She was invoking . . ."

"No more, Li," the general cautioned. "It's only bad history you're feeling. Some men feel its flow more than others, and you are gifted in that way. Why do you think I keep you around?"

Li clutched his sweater hard against his bare chest. "Lindstrom also did something," he said, "in front of the Jade Town God Temple."

"You shouldn't let it scare you, son. Remember he's the grandson of a priest. Sooner or later they all mistake themselves for their gods. Their Bible even has a prohibition against it."

Li looked at him incredulously. How did the general know that?

"How are you getting along with Travers? Do you know his real name?"

The sweater was scratchy against Li's bare chest; indignation prickled his skin. "He's an Englishman, not American. If I had the proper facilities, I could be more successful."

The general rested his head against the headboard. "I told you we don't want the local authorities around."

"But General," Li interrupted before he realized what he was doing.

The Big Fish watched him from sodden eyes. "Go on."

"We could utilize the street committees, there are resources that could help us find Yong. We could pick up Charlotte Brien."

"Feng's still watching her?" the general asked evenly.

Li's heels came together on the carpet. He could no longer control his shivering.

"Put your sweater on," the general said, retrieving his drink from the nightstand. "Surely you have another shirt."

"Not a good one," Li told him.

The general swung his short legs off the bed and went to the window, lifting the dusty venetian blinds. Dusk went on forever on the boulevard outside. "I'll have a hand with Mr. Travers myself," he said. The blinds fell with a clatter against the air conditioner box. The general turned, took one step, and nearly fell forward. Li dropped the sweater and hastened to help him, taking the general's full weight on his arm.

"All right, all right," said Zu, shrugging Li off and finding the bed with his hand. He sat down, and Li shrunk from the sweet smell of liquor. "There's a clean shirt of mine in the cupboard for you."

"Thank you, General."

The bed slats creaked as Zu sat on the edge, breathing heavily as he put on his shoes. Then he took his black kit and his bottle and went out, closing the door quietly behind him. The clean shirt was loose around Li's middle, but it fit at the shoulders surprisingly well.

THE ROOM NEXT DOOR HAD BEEN FITTED AS A SAFE HOUSE when Nixon visited Shanghai at the time of the Communiqué, and it didn't appear to have seen much use since. Stepping in from the hall, Zu wondered if anyone outside of a few hotel staff and the security detail from that trip thirty years ago even knew the room existed, or if they avoided it out of superstition. The Nixon visit did have an air of myth about it, as if it had been a sacred ceremony, a marriage held in secret; in a way what Nixon and Kissinger had started was coming full circle on this night, Zu thought, an ill-fated elopement, a bill coming due. It was time for them to stop treating China like the stepchild of the world.

The air inside the room was dead, and the place smelled of toilet water, mildew, and fear. The white figure on the bed didn't move until Zu was above him.

"What is your name?" Zu asked in English, leaning over to place his truth kit and the bottle of scotch on the carpet. From that angle, he could see the man's heart flutter beneath his hairless chest.

"Bell." The word came out in a whisper. Pink foamy spittle had dried at the corners of his mouth. "Simon."

"Drink, Simon? If you will share the bottle with me?"

Bell's eyes had been staring at the ceiling, but they slid in Zu's direction. Zu had seen that look before, in a man who was dying in his arms on the Yalu River plain—like the evening sky, still blue but without any light. Bell wouldn't last long.

"You'll have to pour it in yourself," he whispered. "Your terrier broke most of my ribs."

"Yes. I am afraid Li was angry, for which I apologize."

"Li."

"Yes." Zu pulled the bottle up by the neck and poured a measure in the Englishman's mouth, some of which dribbled over his lips while he prepared to swallow. He coughed, and tears fell from the corners of his eyes. "Li has become personally involved, superstitious. People from his background often are."

"Background?"

"Li is a peasant."

Bell chuckled and coughed, trying to raise his head. "One more round, if you will? Something inside me's quite broken, and it eases the pain."

Zu held the bottle back.

"Jesus." Bell looked disappointed and rested his cheek on the pillow. "Now you're going to play snooker? At least your young chap just went ahead and beat me. The stuff about your son didn't seem to get him going, but you should have seen him when I told him about your brother. He really gave his all."

Zu was taken by surprise. He quickly pulled up a chair and clamped the bottle between his knees, which helped to discipline the tremor in his legs. "You understand the situation," he said, "whether or not you truly explained it to Li, which I imagine you did not. If you had, he would certainly have killed you."

"Because he felt betrayed?"

"Li's father was killed in an unfortunate accident. I seem to have taken his place."

"Don't think he didn't try—to kill me, that is. Only my ribs got in the way. What about that drink now?"

The general handed him the bottle, and Bell managed to suck down quite a bit without raising his shoulders from the bed. He would have told me, Zu thought, thinking of Li, but perhaps that was before the last few days. He worked the black kit to an upright position between his feet. "You know where Yong is, yes?"

"Actually, no. I hope I won't have to convince you of that. He was a spy for your old pal MacAllister, am I right? This is where I seem to have lost your subordinate."

The general smiled at the dying man's insistence. Leaning over, he unzipped the kit and removed the vial of serum and a fresh hypodermic. Bell's right eye, the one that was visible, grew when he saw the works, and an animal smell emanated from the sheets covering his lower body.

"As you well know, Mr. Bell, our country has been sharing intelligence with the Americans since the days that Kissinger visited this very hotel. He was a visionary man, as was his counterpart Chou Enlai. We can speak frankly here because this discussion will not leave this room. In that way, we are like Secretary Kissinger and Comrade Chou, two men who appreciated each other's refinement and intelligence, who may not have agreed on everything but who respected each other's interests."

"Are you saying you respect my interests?"

Zu drew the serum into the shaft of the hypodermic and inspected it in the light.

"Because right now my interest would lie in a tolerable final few hours on earth. Are you sure you're not using Li's devotion to you?"

"Surely if you know Mr. MacAllister then you understand what Li cannot, that Yong Beihong would never have escaped house arrest without my approval."

"Now it's my turn to wonder if you're bluffing."

"Yong presented me with a problem and a solution all at once—a sort of poem, was how my brother put it."

"Listen. I don't have anything against needles," said Bell, "but the stuff that's in that will probably kill me, you know. And I don't need it to make me talk."

"I didn't think so," Zu said, holding the plunger between his fingers. "What Kissinger, not being an American, understood, and what an Englishman such as yourself can easily . . . grasp, is that leaders must make decisions their people will not understand for many years. Even now, the Americans do not understand our relationship and will not until the huge amount of money involved, which is tantamount to power, becomes clear. That is all they understand. They rage about so-called human rights and the rights of Christians and the Nationalists across the Strait because they have always had a weakness for these hollow ideas. It nearly led them to ruin in Annam, and the blowback from what we did together in Afghanistan has recently come home to roost. Their arrogance will lead them to ruin in the very world they claim, because it is a lie. When their pockets are full, they do not care." Zu sent a squirt of serum flying from the tip. "Where is Yong, please, Mr. Bell?"

"I thought you just said you didn't care."

"Oh, I care," Zu said, raising Bell's arm by the wrist. Bell offered no resistance, and Zu had the unpleasant sensation that he didn't know where Yong was after all, or that if he did, he was too far gone to remember. "Yong has outlived his usefulness," Zu told him, looking for a vein. "Yong was like the dye they would put in your bloodstream if you were in a real hospital now. Letting him escape revealed the whole network of smugglers, all the way to

America. It even got my old friend MacAllister to infiltrate them for me—at least I expect that's your role?"

"I did this on my own," Bell said.

"That is estimable."

"So what about Burling? I agree with you about the Americans, by the way, but where do you think the consul general of Shanghai fits in?"

"You know him?" Zu asked, hesitating as the vein emerged, a blue Y at the crook of the elbow.

"Burling is everything that's good about Americans and every reason they're suckers, too. Please don't do that, by the way. I think I may be having a heart attack."

"The address, Mr. Bell, and then the hospital. I will handle Consul Burling."

"Li didn't seem as sanguine."

"Your meager resources are causing you to repeat yourself," said Zu. He drove the needle into the vein. By the time it was empty, he already knew he had acted too hastily.

"Superstition, was that Li's trouble?" Bell's lips relaxed, and the tendons on the side of his neck disappeared.

Still holding the needle, Zu Dongren had to lean down to hear him.

"And yet . . ." Bell's eyes opened wide, looking at the far wall. They seemed to see nothing, or something beyond. "It's the only thing that stands between you and . . ."

He raised his palm up and shook it once as if to suggest a possibility, then the hand fell back on the bed.

L I FOLLOWED ZU DOWN TO THE PARKING SPACE BEHIND the hotel where a black Mercedes, its rounded fenders shining like glass, crouched in the space where an hour before the dusty Toyota had been. Feng was so excited that he seemed to double over, coming up to the general as they crossed the putrid alley, then turning back on himself like a dog who sees his leash. It was a good thing the general didn't see Li's expression; Zu was too busy watching Feng stroke the tan leather, the ersatz wood trim. The starter rasped between the high concrete buildings, and the sound clashed like a cymbal in the hollow of Li's chest. The alley stank and he was chilled and sweaty, but no matter how much Feng played with the climate control, blowing hot then cold air on his face, Li couldn't get comfortable.

"Confiscated," the general said, patting the seat beside him. He looked past Li, who had turned around to face him as the car pulled out quickly into the street. "Belonged to a corrupt official, a trader at the Stock Exchange."

The car was so quiet Li couldn't hear the engine, and he had the eerie feeling that the general could listen to his thoughts. The ride was so smooth, the seats so soft, that he felt suspended at speed, a sensation that made him vaguely nauseous. Soundlessly, the plane trees that lined the street hurtled toward him, the streetlights like a strobe.

"Shanghai requires different camouflage," the Big Fish observed.

"I'll be happy to get home," Li said.

"I was born here," the general told him.

"I did not know that."

"But it has changed."

"For the better?"

"I don't think so," the general said.

A band of silver light lay across the horizon just above the trees. The general directed Feng to the block behind the consulate.

"Stop here," he said, and the three men got out. The evening street was hushed, and the car's exhaust throbbed against the pavement; its bug-eyed lights cast a sleepy, white beam into the gloaming. Feng had left his door open, and a warning bell chimed with musical idiocy, repeating itself over and over again. "John Lindstrom believes he is an avatar of something. That would be very dangerous if he had any power, but he does not, at least not unless he arrives in the United States with Yong at his side. Feng?"

In the engine, a fan shook on. Feng snapped to attention.

"That is the back entrance there. If any American leaves there, you follow," the general said. "Make a figure eight around these two blocks."

The Manchu fumbled in his pocket and started away, looking back once with longing at the car.

"And Feng?" The general stepped forward and touched him on the sleeve of his jacket. An animal not unlike sexual jealousy gnawed at Li's gut, spreading poison in his veins. "You'll recognize this Lindstrom if you see him? I don't want him lost again."

Feng's yellow eyeteeth showed at the corners of his mustache. "I won't let him get me," he said. His black eyes fixed on Li, and he made a cutting motion with his finger across his cheek.

Li felt his arms rising from his sides involuntarily as he moved forward, making them into the shape of Feng's neck. "Devil . . ."

"Enough," the general said, stiff-arming Li in the chest.

"I could have killed him," Li said, his breath coming quickly. "I had plenty clear shots."

Feng took out his automatic and grinned as he chambered a round.

"It wasn't the time," said the general. Removing his hand from Li, he slapped him fondly on the side of the neck. "Get in the car, Li. You drive."

Li got behind the big wheel, and for the first time that he could remember since the Square, General Zu got in beside him.

WHEN CHARLOTTE TURNED ON THE OVERHEAD LIGHT IN Burling's bedroom at the Residence, time seemed to have stopped there, on the night before Lucius had left for the States. Although the bed was made, the room straightened, she sensed their lingering musk in the air, remembered their urgent, somehow tragic lovemaking. Her head buzzed like a furtive child at the smell of his shoe polish, the shaving cream he used. Late evening light pressed at the wrinkled windowpanes. Liam hadn't wanted to go to bed because it was still light outside, and she'd found herself sympathizing with him, out of sorts at the day that won't end, but also wishing for the cover of darkness. She had lain on the bed in the guestroom beside him, something she hadn't done—and he hadn't let her—in years; like the child he still was, though, he'd fallen asleep in the middle of reciting his instructions for changing planes at Narita.

The hardwood floor groaned under her feet as she went to the window. On the lawn below, the black shapes of three kittens stepped across the wet grass. The morning that Lucius had left, she'd awakened, slightly sticky and remorseful, to see him down there, wearing a deep maroon robe with black stripes like a doctoral gown. The kittens, scrawny, bug-eyed things with ears much too big for their heads, tumbled over his bare, spavined feet. They bit his knuckles when he stooped down to scratch their bony heads. Through the glass, she could hear him talking to them.

The image moved her to pity, a thickening feeling in her chest that quickly dissolved into guilt. She'd been glad he was going— this aging man, white hair hanging in front of his face as he scooped up the kittens and held them in his hand. He loved unwisely and not all that well. The kittens, a month older now, their bottle-brush tails held up stiffly behind them, strutted across the thick lawn toward the dark bed of rosebushes. Green canes waved against the high wall, and beyond it was the playground; the school windows reflected the pink-and-orange stripes of the sunset. Empty terraces ran along each story of the building's rear, and all at once she saw Lindstrom, on a deck of the play structure, legs folded under him as if he were meditating. Her breath caught, and her heart skipped around inside her chest. The light made his shaved head glow so that even at a distance of at least fifty yards she could see the dark shadow of his hair and his beard. His eyes, which were one long dark patch beneath his brow, seemed fixed on the window. She took a step back. He retrieved a cigarette from behind his right ear and lit a match in an exaggerated sweeping motion, perhaps to show that he had seen her. Before he'd brought the flame up to his face, Charlotte had already turned from the window and gone to the bed. He would know that meant she had to meet him.

She couldn't write the note there, so she crossed the room again to Lucius's bureau, a high chest of drawers in the Shanghai deco style. Passing the window, she saw Lindstrom jump from his perch. She tried to explain, standing there at the dresser, pen and notepaper spread amid the loose change from several countries, the pictures of Amelia, taken when she was at Bryn Mawr, and Luke and his sister, the one who lived in Philadelphia and hadn't spoken to Lucius since she got her degree . . . What was it about Lucius and women? She started four times with that as her theme—*I'm sorry; I don't care; It doesn't matter; I care*—and finally settled on the facts:

Thursday, 9:15 p.m.

Lucius:

You will have heard from others what I am involved in, and what I need to do. There's a way for Jack to get out and I need to get the information to him or he and Yong will be killed. I know about MacAllister, but I also trust that you aren't like him. If I'm not back here by midnight, please come to No. 10 Jiangxi Lu, the apartment on the fourth floor landing. Be careful. I put Liam to sleep in the guestroom. If I don't

She crossed out the last three words, the pen shaking in her hand. She hadn't thought about not coming back, what would happen to Liam . . . She threw her head back to catch her breath and tried to make sense of her disordered thoughts.

The day Lucius had left, Liam had done one of his white-boy raps on the steps of the Residence for him, and Lucius watched, smiling vaguely, unsure how to react. She was the only one who understood her son's expanding mind, his oddball set of interests. Dan and New Wife would raise him in that rich wasteland suburb of tract mansions, strip malls, and agate-colored pools. But how could she rail against that, against selling out, knowing she had let Yong and Lindstrom down? It couldn't come to that, could it—where the choices were equally unspeakable? But here she was. She must be knocking at the door of something real.

> If I'm not back in time, please explain to Liam and make sure he gets on his plane. In spite of all this, and you may not believe me, I love you.
>> Me

Charlotte sealed the envelope, which had the State Department crest, and took the curving stairs three at a time. Through the leaded glass transom above the front door, she could see Lao, the driver, waiting for her by the consulate Jeep.

LI I PARKED THE BIG CAR ON THE BLOCK BETWEEN THE American compound and the beginnings of the shops and apartments of Frenchtown, where they could just see the gate of the Residence through a troop of sycamore trees, their trunks preternaturally silver in the dying spring light. A water truck passed, weak gouts falling from its rusted pipes onto the boulevard. In the Residence guardhouse, a soldier stood in silhouette before a row of tiny television screens. Li had never seen a real American soldier before. A white delivery van nosed up to the gate, and the soldier came through the little door of the guardhouse with a clipboard. His face and hands were the color of dry leaves.

In the army, Li had been taught that the Americans had used blacks as soldiers in Annam because their economic system had nothing else for former slaves to do. The blacks had proved to be excellent fighters, strong, with terrific endurance, not to mention fiercely loyal to each other in their shared economic oppression, and now the American military was run by them. It made the consulate guard, his uniform shining in the light, take on a supernatural aura.

"These Americans are superstitious," Li observed. He could not take his eyes off the guard, who was gesturing to the driver of the van, pointing back down the street. "Each one carries it differently, but they are all possessed by magic."

"It is a necessary thing for them to endure the hardships imposed by capitalism," the general said in an offhand way. The van's reverse lights came on, and the guard walked back to the guardhouse in a halo of silver. "There are priests in the American military, who incite the soldiers to fight. Only men from a certain religion are allowed in the American intelligence services. It is like a cult."

One that you would like to join, Li thought. For a man of his ascetic temperament, the rich scent of leather was like eating too much heavy food. He ran down the electric window and lit a cigarette to calm his nerves. He heard the sound of traffic, two blocks behind them on the *nanlu* that led from the Old Chinese City to Renmin Park. Moist air rushed into the car. He shivered. "Americans are like Tibetans, full of death."

The general's chin sagged downward into the several folds of his neck. Out of the corner of his eye, Li saw his lower lip curl. "You are starting to think like them, however."

Startled, Li turned to meet his eyes, and the general smiled and began to bellow with laughter. The smoke-filled car rocked back and forth on its stiff springs.

"Do not look so horrified, " Zu said, patting Li's shoulder with his fat hand as Li sat there dragging angrily on his cigarette. "It is a very good sign. In your generation, to succeed, you must understand how Westerners think, and not only on the battlefield. It is why you were sent to learn English."

"You do not think it is a weakness?"

The general gazed through the tinted windshield. "In some men, perhaps. If they want to be like them."

"You know I do not."

"No. Soon, however, you may have to work with them to obtain the advantage, and that may mean that you have to operate in ways that might be thought criminal by officials of lesser intelligence."

The general reached into the glove compartment and took out a shiny new pistol like Feng's. He dropped the clip out and pushed it back in with a click. Then he nodded across the boulevard.

"WOULD YOU GIVE THIS TO THE CONSUL WHEN you meet him at the airport?" Charlotte asked Mr. Lao when he had started the Jeep. "It's personal. I may not be here when Lucius gets back."

Mr. Lao nodded as he piloted the Jeep through the gates and out onto the gray boulevard. Mr. and Mrs. Lao, who was the cook, approved of Charlotte and Burling's relationship, and if Mr. Lao believed the note was personal, he would guard it with all the considerable ingenuity of which he was capable.

"Where will I let you off, Madame Brien?"

"It's such a nice evening, I want to walk part of the way. This next corner is fine."

"No, the traffic. I will take you . . ."

"But you'll miss the consul's plane," Charlotte said. A policeman in white with a crossing guard's belt was directing cars through the next intersection. A red electric sign above him counted down how many seconds until the light turned green.

"I'll get out here," said Charlotte, stepping out as Lao pulled to the curb. "Thank you so much for this." She slammed the door and didn't look back.

The buildings fronting the sidewalk here had deco façades, elegant in their day but poorly preserved. The people were dressed in bootleg fashions from the West, but the women still seemed a bit awkward in their hip-huggers, unsteady on their platform soles. It felt like Paris under a cloud of occupation, its verve a bit hysterical, like the end of an illicit party. In the street, a constant flow of bikes, like an army going by.

She had often wished that she and Liam could live here, in Frenchtown, instead of the ugly socialist-realist apartment block a mile away, and at the same time she'd believed that their experience of China should be based on something deeper than aesthetics. At the first intersection, the road doglegged to the right and the sidewalk gained some trees, the same prehistoric-looking sycamores that grew outside the consulate, their roots like knuckles sunk in the ash-colored dust. In the next block, she thought she spied Lindstrom coming out of the Gongtai Fruit Store, and her heart began to seize, but coming closer she saw that the man was much shorter, his head bald and pointed, the face below his thick black eyebrows a caricature of Lindstrom's hybrid features. Charlotte pushed past the tipped crates of lemons, taking the inside path beneath the awnings then sliding her hips sideways into the flow of the crowd.

It was one thing she had never gotten used to, the numbers of people, of bikes. A block away, the consulate office building—ugly yellow brick with smoked windows—rose above the tiled roof of a hacienda-style estate. At the corner she waited, watching the opposite sidewalk for Lindstrom. The air was swelling with the acrid smell of coming rain. A bus crossed the intersection, blocking her view, and when it lumbered on again, she saw the man with the Fu Manchu mustache whom Bell had described. She looked again to be sure, but the way he was standing, tall and uncomfortable among the other people at the curb, looking back and forth as if he had lost someone, convinced her it was he. When he saw Charlotte, he stared at her openly and leered.

The fear she felt then derived from a wholly different part of herself—not a thrill, which was more a sort of negative pleasure that proved your existence, but the opposite, a feeling of *nothing*, fear of not being at all. When she looked up, night had fallen. The sky was black above the streetlamps' feverish glow.

The crowd eddied around her. She could not even use her elbows as the Chinese did to hold their position. The Manchu was looking down the block to his right, into the flow of pedestrians moving along the stucco wall. He seemed to sense that whomever he had lost was watching him now, and suddenly Charlotte saw Lindstrom coming up the block, head dipped, eyes staring forward, keeping close behind a group of women in flowered silk shirts. Charlotte watched the Manchu recognize him, lurch sideways pushing people out of his way. He leveled the first of the group of women with a forearm to the side of her head, and the woman's hair fanned from the impact. A sack she'd been carrying split apart, and its contents flew into the air. To Charlotte's surprise, Lindstrom turned around on seeing the Manchu and began to dodge through the crowd. Hard against the wall, he found a clear lane and moved like a man breaking waves with his knees. The Manchu followed, knocking people out of his way, a nickel-plated gun now in his hand.

Charlotte froze. What could she do to help him? The light was about to turn, and she slid from the eddy of people at the corner and moved along the sidewalk instead of crossing. Stepping down into the gutter, she could keep herself even with the Manchu, whom she lost and then found again as another bus went by. Midblock, moving out into the traffic, she nearly got clipped in the leg by a bike. A truck's mirror passed within inches of her face, and a huge belch of smoke choked her briefly and made her eyes blur.

When her vision cleared, the Manchu was almost abreast of her, three lanes away. She watched him through the space between the buses, their big wheels turning slowly at the curb. She stepped in front of a Lada's bumper and gained the raised median, only to find that Lindstrom was gone. The Manchu was turning circles on the opposite pavement, looking wildly over his shoulder toward the intersection from which they had come.

"Change of plans?" The pressing, warm, ironic voice. The Lada's driver laid into his horn, a crazed, mechanical bird trapped beneath the hood, and Lindstrom was standing beside her. The Manchu saw him immediately.

"He sees us, Jack."

"That's the idea," said Lindstrom.

The Manchu was stumbling into columns of bikes, flailing for a moment with his arms raised and looking upstream like a swimmer getting caught in a current and pulled. He rode it for a few yards, then seemed to sense a flaw, darted through it.

"This way," said Lindstrom, and they moved along the median together, toward the intersection.

"I saw Simon Bell. Burling's not at the top," Charlotte told him. "It's MacAllister. He wants to kill Yong. That's why he set this up."

Ten yards away, the Manchu stumbled and collapsed a line of bikes that had come to a stop. Lindstrom raised a revolver in his hand. "Fucker's like some kind of devil," he said, but Charlotte couldn't tell if he meant MacAllister or the Manchu, who was tangled up and kicking at the fallen riders around him, the big gun pointing every which way in his hand. "Come on before he gets a clear shot."

He pulled her behind a heavy truck. The canvas covering flapped at their heads, and behind it Charlotte saw a line of hollow-cheeked men, facing one another on benches, chains draped across their thighs. Two round-faced young soldiers, automatic rifles standing on the butts, tried to look grim as the truck moved ahead.

"I saw," she began, but the truck was gone and the light had changed, and the street between it and the sidewalk was eerily clear. "We're going the wrong way, Jack. Not toward him."

Lindstrom dragged her across the empty lane. The Manchu stepped around the hood of the prisoner truck and bore down on them, the barrel of the gun pointing out from his raised hand.

Lindstrom yelled to her and pushed her so hard that her chin hit her knees. Her toe caught the pavement, and her hands skidded before her across the asphalt. Lindstrom's gun above her sounded like a toy. The Manchu seemed to fling his pistol ahead of him, as if he were pitching it to Lindstrom. Then he reached out in the grainy air. Lindstrom raised the revolver and aimed and shot again in one motion, a snake's tongue of flame lapping out of the barrel. The Manchu stooped and fell to his knees as if he'd dropped something precious, patting the oily street blindly with his hands, then his black hair flew backward in a flap and disappeared, leaving part of his head gone. His body fell forward onto the pavement. Lindstrom snatched up the nickel-plated pistol and dragged her roughly to her feet. A bus was moving in front of them; inside, the passengers were walking down the aisle, grabbing handholds and touching the backs of the seats. A woman in the window gazed at Charlotte, puzzled.

"There's a ship," she said. The bus rolled on and its blue exhaust filmed the red placards on the wall. The engine cover was loose, and she had to yell to make herself heard above the clatter of valves and the fan. "A ship is leaving the old Russian consulate dock, or the dock in front of it, at three o'clock this morning. You're supposed to meet a sailor with a Bible in his hand."

Charlotte thought Lindstrom grinned, but then she was tripping on the curb and his grip had left her arm. A black Mercedes screeched around the corner, rear wheels churning out white smoke. She looked around and Lindstrom was backpedaling, running toward the bus. The elegant grille of the Mercedes bore down, the air dam below it dove into the asphalt and the front doors flew open, as if from momentum.

"But Jack," she yelled. "They'll be waiting for you in Hong Kong. MacAllister . . ."

A shot cracked behind her, and she heard the bullet buzzing through the air. A man who was jogging for the bus next to Lindstrom looked around as if someone had tapped him on the shoulder, then felt for a dark stain appearing on his shirt and sat down. Charlotte hugged herself and started to roll. Lindstrom's gun, lately taken off the Manchu, sounded strangely mechanical, the explosion of the shot quickly followed by a clank like someone dropping a pipe very close to her ear. The bullet skidded across the concrete, raising a tiny white puff, and slapped against the stucco wall. Lindstrom ran with one hand on the corner of the bus, the pistol raised and firing back at the car. The second shot starred the windshield in the upper right corner, forcing the driver to cover, and the third quickly shattered the passenger headlight, the figure on that side getting a shot off and ducking. A hole appeared on the bus's engine cover, and a ratcheting sound began. Blue smoke poured out of the grille. Shortly she heard traffic coming up behind the car, and she realized that the guns were silent. The man at the passenger door slammed it shut and waddled forward on his stubby legs, his pistol, which he held on Charlotte, dwarfed by his hand.

"Get up," he barked in Mandarin, palming the gun. His eyes were small gashes, like a fighter whose lids have puffed up and been cut, the lashes like stitches along the edge. He looked like a small, gray, angry clown. She was so terrified she almost laughed. As she got to her knees, she saw Lindstrom peeling away on a motorbike, the rider sitting on the street behind him, then the stream of bikes obscured him from view, massing toward her, avoiding the twisted pile that had been the Manchu, the riders looking down at him and pedaling onward with a vigor that suggested an earnest attempt to forget what they'd seen. The Mercedes screeched forward, and a warm front of air from the engine splashed over her face, smelling of hot paint and antifreeze. The old man yanked the back door open, and Charlotte stumbled toward it, feeling an immense relief that threatened to dissolve into tears. Somehow she knew they were going to hurt her.

THE SEAT OF THE MERCEDES WAS THE COLOR OF CARAMEL, supple and amazingly clean, and a sharp white light, like a star, shone behind the far door. Something hard struck the back of her head, and the lines of the car and the traffic noise blurred at the edges, then came back terrifically clear. She could hear footsteps squeak on the sidewalk behind her as her face dove toward the seat and the top of her head hit the armrest on the opposite door. Her skirt rode up and her legs were jammed beneath her into the footwell, but they felt auxiliary to her, her body tangentially hers. The old man got in and slammed the door behind him, compressing the air in a way that was not altogether unpleasant. In the sudden lull, Charlotte fell toward unconsciousness, the leather sweet and strong in her nose, the interior muffled and quiet, but the car lurching forward threw her back against the seat, and the pain in her skull made her jerk her head upright. Knees pumped in place at the level of her sight through the window, then shot past as if propelled by a rubber band. The old man gripped the back of her neck as she vomited onto her shoes.

"You know what happened?" the driver yelled in English as he dropped the emergency brake. The smoker from the Bund.

The old man said something in Mandarin, and Charlotte began, "I don't," but the old man's hand tightened and she had to swallow her own bile in order to breathe. The car jolted forward again.

"He killed Feng," the driver yelled. "You . . ."

The back of another bus began to loom in the windshield.

"Li," the old man said, and Li slammed on the brakes. He leaned back over the seat, pointing his weapon like a finger.

"Bitch." He tore around a corner and down another boulevard, toward the People's Park. Taillights came on in front of them, and Li braked and skidded around the stopped car, into the oncoming lane; a bike turned close to the windshield, and the rider fell away. A thud like an animal hitting the floor of the car.

"That was Lindstrom back there, yes?" the old man said calmly in English. "John Lindstrom?"

She tried to think, but her head hurt too badly. Had the car been there before Lindstrom pushed her down and shot at the man, killed him, making his head blow apart . . .

"I don't know who that is."

The fingers left her neck, and she saw him form the fist. The side of her head went black in a crescent-shaped pain as the vision in her right eye squeezed inward. The dashboard bent and went straight again.

"Why did you meet him?" someone shouted through water.

Her eyes squeezed shut, and she opened them quickly. The car was stopped again at a large intersection; the vastness of the concrete square before the Park made Charlotte's eyes grow large with tears. Her mouth was open and a question, forgotten like a dream, left a hollow at the back of her throat: *I wanted . . .*

"I am not going to ask you again," said Li, his voice bouncing off the windshield. Across the square stretched a line of concrete barriers and trees. The car sprinted from the light, and the dash-board stayed still while the dusty crowns grew larger and larger until they slid above the windshield, out of sight. Everything had a finality to it, the poignancy of last things; she even felt an odd kind of love for the men in the car.

"You are going to say something?" Li asked, his eyes trained on the windshield, in which things were slowing. He swerved the car right, and Charlotte pressed against the fat, solid body of the older man. The creases on his pants were sharp, and he kneaded her neck in a manner that was almost paternal, feeling for the pressure points behind her ears. The car was deep in the grove of trees when Li stopped and turned and rested the end of his pistol, with its flanged hole, on top of the back of the seat.

"Who are you, please?" he asked calmly.

"Charlotte Brien," she said. "I'm American. I don't know . . ."

"Oh!" said Li, looking to the trees outside for witness. "She's American, what a surprise. Now I am losing my patience. I know what you are, cunt!"

"She's Burling's," said the old man in Mandarin. Li clicked the safety lever off with his thumb. "Why did you meet John Lind-strom?" the old man asked in a kindlier tone. "We need to know or other people will be killed."

"I didn't meet him. I don't know who he is."

He shoved her head against the window. Pain covered her skull like a cap, and it made her suck air and raise her arms, without thinking, to fight. She dove against the old man's chest, punching blindly for his groin. With her feet she felt for purchase, but a space opened behind her and her legs were yanked backward, nearly pulled from her knee joints. Her skirt rode up over her middle as she watched the old man slip away, the sad old vulnerable clown. Then she was on the ground looking up at the trees and Li's head, upside down. He kneeled on her thighs, grinding them into the roots and the dirt. She tried to pull her dress down, but he slapped her hands away.

"What did you tell him, cunt?"

The air was wet on her cheeks, and gooseflesh prickled her bare skin. That word means . . .

"At least the grandpa will hit me," she told him in Mandarin, and swallowed, awaiting the blow, which didn't come. Time, she thought. All Jack needs now is time, whether he chooses to go on the boat or not, whether he even heard the part about MacAllister wanting to kill him.

"There is a dead man," said Li, "because of you. I am going to kill you, very slowly, unless you tell me why you met Lindstrom, what you told him that you got from Simon Bell."

Charlotte gasped, and her mouth filled with grit.

"The Englishman died," the old man said, coming around the car and standing above them. "His heart failed."

Li had begun to run the barrel of the gun around the waistband of her underwear, clicking the safety on and off. She felt herself shrinking, folding up into herself until she barely felt attached to her legs anymore. So this is how it feels, Charlotte thought. She had heard you could detach and that you never really attached again.

"Stop that, Li," the old man said. "Get her up."

Li spat dryly and climbed off her legs. Her right one was asleep and her toes tingled painfully.

"We are better than that," said the general.

Li slapped the lid of the trunk with his palm and turned around. He is having a tantrum, Charlotte thought. A stunted boy.

The general pulled Li aside, and Li watched her carefully as the general spoke in low tones near his ear. Charlotte lay her head down on the hardened rut of mud, staring up at the trees and the pale night sky above the park, breathing shallowly, the night air touching her underwear. She pulled her skirt to her knees. If she had flirted, tried to come on or invite him to touch her, would it have bought Jack more time? There were movies that her father had liked in which the Mata Hari slept with an enemy spy to distract him from the game at hand, but she couldn't go that far. She was not a fey beauty, just a tall, flat-chested redhead who'd never had the wild blood that men had ascribed to her. You're so smart, her mother told her. Pretty only brings you pain. The only notice she had ever got was academic, the only eyebrows ever raised. She had to seduce them on a higher plane.

"Lucius." His name had come to her, and it seemed like a good place to start.

"Burling," said the old man, the general, breaking from Li and walking stoutly toward her across the clearing. "The American consul. What about him?"

He spoke English now, rather well, and Charlotte pulled herself up to a sitting position, palms feeling her way until she was hugging her knees. "He's coming back tonight."

"What does that matter?"

"Jack thought he had devised it," Charlotte said. "This operation."

"Jack?"

"Jack Lindstrom. It's a nickname for John."

"Like Kennedy." The old man's lids were open wider and the eyes behind them ringed and gray, like a snake's. "Jack Lindstrom thought that Burling had devised the operation."

"When he found out Yong was a spy. Because he's CIA, Burling I mean."

The old man's hand jerked out, and Charlotte cringed, but nothing struck her, and when she lowered her arm the old man was offering his hand to pull her up. "Burling is CIA, you say?"

Li was watching them inquisitively, as if he'd just understood something.

"I didn't know either," said Charlotte. Standing up made her head swim. "Until Alan told me. It was the day that Jack came to Nanjing. Watching Burling was all I was ever supposed to do, I swear."

"Was watching Burling?" asked the general, still holding her wrist. It ached from where Jack had twisted it, but the pain helped her act. She was gaining in confidence now.

"Alan asked me to do it. He didn't tell me that Yong was a spy for them, the CIA, I mean, or that Burling was his handler, but he must have known."

Li was looking at the old man in a curious way that, against all reason, made Charlotte feel a sudden kinship with him. They were both, it seemed, naive in their own way. Slowly, the old man blinked his heavy lids.

"You are all amateurs," he said, voice rising to a growl. "Dilettantes. You and your lover Alan Rank."

"He isn't my lover. And you're right, he is a dilettante."

The old man's eyes narrowed, and he let go her wrist. He raised a fat, wrinkled hand, the hand of a tortoise, which was holding the pistol again. Charlotte felt the curtain closing. "What did you tell Jack Lindstrom?" he asked. "No more stories, please."

"I told him when Burling would be back. Ten o'clock. I told him to wait."

The old man lowered the gun. "Li!"

Charlotte tripped on a root as Li dragged her around the hood to the passenger side. The act had kept her going, kept her up, but now she was terrified again.

"This isn't going to hurt you," Li said as he bent her down over the sleek Mercedes hood. Its black paint reflected clouds torn across an oblong moon. "It'll feel good."

A fresh wind sprang up, bringing the smell of the harbor, shaking branches high above. The ship would leave in rain, she thought.

"I have had to go through it myself," Li was saying, "as part of my training."

He pulled her skirt down and slapped her on the hip. She heard a zipper rasp. His voice, she thought, had been changed somehow—softer, almost sorry—but he was going to do it anyway, because it had been done to him. The door on the driver's side was open, and the old man was leaning across the front seat. He'd let it happen, but at least he didn't want to watch. They pass it on, she thought, but they don't want to see what they've done. Where will it end?

The old man emerged with a large hypodermic held aloft in one hand, liquid spurting from the tip as his thumb spread a bit in the ring at the end of the plunger.

"No," she said, falling to her knees. What if Jack went to the consulate after all? What if he did the unselfish thing and didn't get on the boat and now she had given them Burling? "It's not what I said. I was lying about Lucius. He's not CIA anymore . . ."

But the shaft of the needle was already probing the flesh of her hip, and then she felt a deep, bone pain and the ground rushed up to nothing.

T HE CONSULATE JEEP MET BURLING IN FRONT OF THE airport. The moon was up, and a few cold stars burned dimly to the west, above the fields of the city's remaining cooperative farm.

"Long trip," he told Mr. Lao, climbing into the front seat. His detention in the Beijing guesthouse had seemed like one long day.

Lao handed over an envelope and dropped the car into gear. "Madame Brien, she is leaving this for you. She and Liam sleep tonight at the Residence."

"She's there now?" Burling asked, holding the envelope awkwardly in his lap. Charlotte's name drew a cord of discomfort through his veins.

"First I drive her and Liam to dinner," Lao explained. "All the way to New Hotel, we are followed by a car."

"Do you know who it was?"

"I know, and I do not know." Lao glanced over his shoulder with his professional scowl. Burling waited for a colorful aphorism, but none was forthcoming. The driver stared gravely at the oncoming headlights.

"By the way," Burling said, reclining the seat a few notches. "I got a present for your boy."

The corners of Mr. Lao's mouth curled up in the grin he reserved for conversations about his family.

"A father can't spoil his own children," Burling added as the Jeep accelerated onto the main road, "but I've discovered the joys of spoiling my grandchildren."

"Your son, he is going to have another baby?"

The Laos kept track of Burling's family better than he did. "He and Marina seemed quite adamant about it," Burling said.

Lao's smooth face was inexpressive as he piloted the car. Burling had meant it as an opening, to discuss what he saw as Luke and Marina's obsession with making an ideal family against all odds, but the observation might not cross cultures that well, so he let it pass. Looking out the window, he was struck anew by the mountains of construction by the road, the shells of new buildings lit by strings of weak bulbs. Farther downtown a cloverleaf rose like a jeweled knot against the skyline—more like Atlanta than Shanghai. The place looked unfamiliar, and he wondered if it was time to hang it up. The carnage on the outlying island and the business in Beijing had undermined him. Perhaps MacAllister was right: he didn't have the taste for multiple layers of deception anymore. Or maybe his unease was more fundamental: ideology, faith, even power he could understand, but a world of piracy, terror, and endless transactions was beyond him.

The streets of the old French Concession were darkened for curfew. Electrical wires shone like mercury in the moonlight. Burling lowered his window and breathed the moist air, scented with roses from the walled estates.

"Your son, will he bring his family to China?" Lao asked, glancing over at the breach in his climate control. He had obviously been weighing the question for blocks.

"Honestly? I doubt it. Luke got a taste of the world when he was young and decided he didn't like it as much as his father."

Lao nodded silently and slowed, peering through the foggy windshield as he neared each intersection. Burling had tried to explain the defroster, but Lao would sooner build up an inch of ice on the glass with the air conditioner, to the point of driving blind, than he would ever use heat after April.

"Madame Brien's letter," he said.

Burling looked at his lap. The envelope was soggy from his palms. "She wanted me to read this right away?"

"It seem that way," said Lao blandly. He had turned onto the street where the Residence was, and Burling felt the closeness of the house like an omen. The Jeep went through the front gate, and he waved to the guard. Down the curving tunnel of the drive, he could see the downstairs lights of his house burning brightly onto the lawn; the upstairs windows were dark. Loose gravel crunched beneath the tires. As the Jeep rolled through the trees, he had a sudden shiver and a flash of Afghanistan, riding through a village late at night, crunching asphalt broken by half-tracks, a .45 bouncing under his thigh. The Land Rover in which he was riding with Lindstrom came around a bend, and there they were—a column of shadows, crossing the road between orchards. Some had RPGs, and one led a horse, the outline of their Chicoms and rucksacks like some heroic bas-relief. In the backseat the prisoner squirmed, trying to call out beneath his hood, as if like a lone wolf he sensed his comrades near. The ISI man shoved the butt of his rifle into the pathetic man's ribs. The smell of the package in the boot of the Rover mixed with the taste of stale booze on Burling's tongue.

"Did you see that?" he said to the driver.

"Damn cats," said Mr. Lao in Chinese, swerving onto the margin of the drive.

The apparition, if that's what it had been, was gone, but Burling was spooked.

"Liam's in bed?" He could have sworn he'd seen a man, of less than average height. Not Lindstrom?

"Since nine thirty," Lao said, pushing the gearshift to park.

"And his mother?"

The driver didn't reply; he was pulling Burling's suitcase from the back.

"No, of course. The letter."

The mother cat who lived in the grounds came out of the bushes and rubbed at Burling's ankles. She nearly tripped him as he went up the steps, and he had to hold her back by picking up her soft, drooping belly with his toe and balancing her there while he backed through the front door. Lao was waiting with his suitcase in the hallway. The smell of dried wood and floor wax was agreeable; on the demilune table there were hothouse flowers in a vase. Seeing his house again only made him feel more keenly the rootlessness of things.

"I'll take that up, Mr. Lao. Mrs. Lao must be wondering where you are."

Lao gave him the smile that could signify anything, except perhaps friendship. Burling's position didn't allow that. "She know. Good night, Consul."

Burling bid Lao goodnight in Chinese.

UPSTAIRS, HE POKED HIS HEAD INTO THE SMALL GUESTROOM, where Liam's sleeping form lay in a welter of blankets across the double bed. The light from the hall didn't wake the boy, but he pleaded something violently in his sleep. Softly closing the door, Burling remembered leaving Luke that way when he and Lindstrom left for Jalalabad to effect the exchange. Jack had found his old point guard—"a shooting guard now," at which Luke had laughed—up in Peshawar holding a shipment of heroin. From him, Jack had learned of the bombing in Kabul in which the "woman who rode like a man in a burnoose" had allegedly taken part.

"It can only be her," Lindstrom said. "Am I right, young Luke?"

"Don't involve him," Burling warned Jack, crossing the apartment with a bottle in his hand. "He might get his hopes up. Luke loved April too."

"She turned me on to the Doors," Luke explained.

"We wouldn't want to hope now, would we, Luke?"

"That's not what I meant," Burling said.

"We would rather April was dead, or your father would, anyway."

"He doesn't want her to be dead," said Luke quietly.

"It might absolve him of guilt for your mother."

"You son of a bitch," Burling roared, raising the bottle halfway up from his side by the neck. "You're high."

"Of course I am." Lindstrom stood up and threw a bag and a pipe on the low brass table in front of the couch. "How else do you think I move around up there?"

"What the hell is that?"

"Luke knows."

Burling turned in disbelief to his son.

"Jesus, Dad, get your head out of the sand. It's opium, heroin. It's all over the place in Afghanistan."

"The whole country's stoned," Lindstrom said.

"But you're not doing . . ."

"I would never let Luke taste this shit," Lindstrom said.

Burling poured himself a glass of scotch. "I guess I'm supposed to be grateful for that."

"All I care is that my old baller Omar got nabbed up in Pesh with a couple of ki's and he was so fucking loaded he started telling about April."

It seemed that Omar had developed a habit and had stolen the drugs and tried to sell them in Peshawar. Lindstrom's idea was to trade him and the heroin for April, if she was really in Jalalabad, as Omar said.

"Don't tell me this thing is beneath you," said Lindstrom.

"They'll kill Omar, you know."

"He's a cousin, so." Lindstrom pulled a lump of sticky brown hash from the bag and thumbed it into his pipe.

"The tale about April is probably a ruse."

"Maybe, maybe not," he said, applying his lighter intently to the stuff. "Omar'll probably lose a hand. It's a chance I'm willing to take in return for my wife. You don't have to come, but they know you. They know you control the arms connection with ISI. That's going to seal the deal better than anything."

IN THE STUDY, A DIFFERENT WHISKY IN HIS HAND, HE COULD no longer avoid Charlotte's envelope. He switched on the green banker's lamp on the corner of his desk and sat in the chair by the window, tearing open the seal. His eyes flew over the words in denial, then read them again with mounting dread. He looked at his watch. Charlotte's note said midnight. It was now eleven forty.

Burling took a gulp and picked up the telephone, dialing the number for his voice mail with an unreasonable hope. The first two messages were innocuous greetings from Ryan, MacAllister's man in Shanghai, his voice both guarded and ominous. Burling deleted them both without listening through. The third was from the Great Spook himself.

"Lucius? Sorry to miss you. I got tied up at our Tokyo office, but now I'm on a tour of our facilities in Hong Kong. Thought I might drop over to see you. I'm at the Regency on Kowloon side, enjoying the hospitality of a Mr. Henry Sun, whose interests are strongly aligned with our own. The room is in his name. I look forward . . ."

The scotch burned Burling's stomach and spread through his chest. He paced between the desk and the window, still holding the dead cordless phone. He recognized the shaky feeling in his legs as a symptom of fear.

Enough, he thought finally, putting down the phone. Charlotte was in trouble, at the mercy of forces that despite her intelligence she didn't, couldn't, or didn't want to understand. You couldn't say the same for April: she seemed to have held out in captivity for a very long time, even leaving a narrative behind. This time around, if he could warn Yong about MacAllister's intentions, he had to do that, because he remembered their talk in Princeton years ago, when he had felt that in spite of their separate worlds, they viewed mankind in a similar way, as redeemable—through what sort of action was the lingering problem.

MEI HURRIED TO A WARDROBE AT THE END OF THE hallway and began getting out a set of her dead husband's clothes.

"He always wore black," she called to Lindstrom, who was still at the bathroom sink, washing his hands. "People said that he looked like a laborer."

"I bet that helped," Lindstrom said. He dried his hands and arms on a towel by the sink. The feel of the motorbike's handlebars was still in his arms, a vibration that was something like pain; wind had dried the tears in the corners of his eyes so that they crackled when he blinked.

"Helped?" he heard Mei ask, voice muffled by the wardrobe.

Lindstrom went through the living room, where Yong was collecting his things, onto the balcony, where he could check the street below. The illuminated dial of his watch read eleven forty-five, and the line of trucks that had been turning all day through a gate across the way was idled, like an army of elephants, their gray flanks reflecting the streetlamps. He took out the nickel-plated .357 and found two rounds in the clip. The revolver had three. In the kitchen, Mei handed him the clothes.

"I think we've got something going," Lindstrom told her. "I can feel it. When I was at the temple pool the other night, I said a sort of prayer for you."

"You prayed?" Yong's round face had appeared in the doorway.

"Not the way that you do, Yong, to a man with white hair in the sky."

Yong pursed his lips; he was used to being kidded by now.

"I prayed that the things dividing people would be gone."

Mei helped him strip his sweat-soaked shirt. She watched him in wonderment as he took the pistols out of his belt and laid them on the table. "You are so muscular," she said.

"Clean living."

"You are not serious. Where did you get that gun?" she asked.

"The one that followed me out of the schoolyard," Lindstrom said, putting the clean black shirt over his head. "The piece was his. He dropped it when I shot him."

"You had better stop talking," said Mei. "If they got the woman, they may come here."

He nodded, looking at her downcast eyes. He hadn't been able to measure her tone, couldn't tell what she was feeling. He had made love with her, but now that voice was gone. What divided people was themselves: the simple things, fear and rage.

"Listen," he said, pulling on the black jeans.

"Go," she told him, not looking up. Yong was standing inside the front door.

"If they do come here . . ."

"You have to go now, John. They've come for me before, you know, in Beijing, after my husband was killed. I know what to do." She pushed him firmly, almost roughly, toward the door. On the landing, he could see the empty courtyard, the uneven cobbles and the single, scrawny tree. "You're sure you killed one, yes?"

Lindstrom looked back as he put the automatic in the waistband of the jeans. He was unsure what she wanted him to say, and he did not want to disappoint her.

"We're even, then," she said, reading his thoughts. "If they come here, I will say that I did it because of my husband. You left the revolver on the table?"

"They saw me," Lindstrom said. "They won't believe you."

"The truth doesn't matter to them. They would rather blame me for it than admit they let a foreigner into their country."

"A gun will not avenge . . ." said Yong.

Mei turned on him savagely. "Don't you dare tell me what to do, you stray little dog. His heart was pure, and I will suffer for that if I want to. You are nothing but a spy. How many hearts do you have? Go. It's you who let them say that we could never govern ourselves. It's always you who love the foreign culture more than your own."

Yong with his face averted, trembling: "Y-y-you with your Ernest H-heming . . ."

"Don't you say it, yellow dog. I know what I am, as well as I know what I was married to." She came up to Lindstrom and took his cheeks between her two rough hands. "Thank you, John," she said, pressing her lips against his mouth. "You are my Robert Jordan."

Lindstrom smiled, and fresh tears came to his eyes. "He died, you know," he said, smiling. "What do you think that means?"

"At the end of the book, yes. But he knew, like you, that violence was necessary, and love, too. There's no time to explain now all I want to thank you for. Think about it in the future. I know you'll understand."

Lindstrom started to speak, but she was turning him around, and then he was going down the stairway, covering the landings, checking the courtyard, a landing again. He came down the last six steps slowly with Yong right behind him. Yong remained on the stairs, and Lindstrom moved, crabwise, down to street level. The bound-foot detective was not in her chair, and two bikes leaned against the rack, with their little white license plates. The absence of the old woman worried him. The iron gate stood ajar.

He walked deliberately onto the sidewalk, pistol drawn. The dead-end street trapped the sound of nighttime traffic on the boulevard, but the sidewalk by the building was deserted. Yong emerged from the shadows of the entry.

"We'll have to take the bikes," Lindstrom told him. He had ditched the motorbike two blocks away, behind the Children's Palace. "Can they trace it to Mei?"

"Unless we take off the license plates," said Yong, pulling Mei's bike out. "You need a special tool."

"No time. There's something I didn't tell you."

Yong walked the bike beside him. The yellow beams of cars moved across the mouth of the street.

"We can't get on the boat. Your former handler is waiting to kill you in Hong Kong."

Yong stopped walking and stared at him, lights melting on his glasses.

"I didn't want to tell Mei because if they do come here, it's better for her to think there is a boat. But yeah, there's a good chance MacAllister set us up, arranged the whole thing just to nail you."

"What do we do now?"

"The only good news is that Burling probably isn't involved. He's a lot of things, but he doesn't kill people in cold blood."

"How do you know?"

"There was a time when I knew he had the motive and the opportunity and he wouldn't let it happen. I'd much rather take my chances on him in an American consulate than the Great Spook on a dock in Hong Kong."

"I have no choice but to believe you," Yong said.

"Have faith," Lindstrom told him, throwing his leg across the saddle. As his feet found the pedals, he looked up at the windows of the building.

"We are changing places now," said Yong. "Or you are joking."

For a moment, Lindstrom couldn't tell which window was Mei's, and he heard, felt the wall of traffic draw nearer as he began to pedal. When he did see her face, it was fifty yards away and she was only a woman in a window: if she had raised her hand, he wouldn't have seen it through the dark reflections clouding the glass.

"I wish we could change places," he said.

Still, she didn't move. Waving might be a Western gesture, anyway.

WHEN BURLING HAD ALERTED THE FRONT GATE, HE heard the Jeep start. Mr. Lao would not give up his position as driver, but it was just as well. Burling knew he'd been drinking too much to risk a stop after curfew. He engaged the secure line and dialed the number in Hong Kong that MacAllister had left.

"Good morning, Regency," said a polished woman's voice.

"Henry Sun's guest, Mr. Byrd, please."

"One moment, sir."

Burling watched the rhododendrons wave outside the French doors, while Vaughan Williams's "Dives and Lazarus" played through the telephone, the folky, ethereal chords a relic of the old Hong Kong.

"Lucius? Thank the Lord," MacAllister said. "You understand the situation?"

"Not really, no. Seems your friend the general may have Charlotte, though."

"Charlotte?"

"Brien, one of your illegals. Also lately sort of my gal."

"I had no idea, Lucius." MacAllister's accent sounded like a lament.

"You had every idea. I told you about her in Washington. Tell me you don't want to silence Yong permanently, Mac."

"I'm not the only one they'd come after, you know."

Burling clutched the phone painfully. "I'm going to shut it down," he said, though it seemed like something he'd promised someone else to do, rather than feeling much conviction himself.

"I would rather you let me handle it on this end, Lucius."

MacAllister's condescending manner made his cheeks burn with rage. "I'm not going to end it because I care a whit if Yong sells this whole damn story to *60 Minutes*," Burling said. "I'm going to do it because it's right."

"Dishonor agrees with you, eh?"

"You didn't let me finish. I'm shutting it down because you no doubt recruited a woman who is very bright but very prone to helping, and you did it just to keep an eye on me. So of course she tried to do one better and pull the whole hopelessly screwed-up business from the fire. You lied to me, to *me*, to save your ass."

"Not just mine."

"Jesus, Gordon, you act like I'm some acolyte. I understand the business, I even know what's necessary sometimes, but I never thought you'd do that to a friend."

"Lucius." Burling drained his drink while the Great Spook adapted his story on the other end. It took longer than Burling expected. "As it happens, I was calling to try to get you to intervene. I know what you saw on the outlying island. Adrian Fry filled me in. If they make it on that boat, I'll take care of our friends. Don't you fret."

"You won't get the chance to put Yong in the Salt Pit or Jalalabad or one of your black sites," Burling told him. "I'm going to shut it down. I'll probably have to in order to get Charlotte back."

"Nostalgic for Jalalabad, are you? Site of your fucked-up rescue of your own Moslem whore?"

"April was already gone when we got there. What we found afterward confirmed that."

"But she wrote some very inflammatory, anti-American shit before she died, did she not?"

"She was a survivor. I was proud of her for that."

"You're pretty goddamn proud of yourself, too, now, aren't you?"

"I'm not proud of anyone, I assure you, especially not myself. But no one'll pay any attention to Yong if he does get out anyway. Their attention span isn't long enough."

"If you weren't such a slave to the poontang, Lucius, you wouldn't be asking me to wash my hands. You're not telling me a story, are you? Sure that little redhead isn't there with you right now?"

"Lindstrom will be on that ship, too," Burling told him, "if I let him. He might not like you interfering."

"Two birds with one stone, Burl, or two stones, whatever it takes. Jack won't be expecting me. Then you and I can retire without all of this hanging over our heads."

"You really believe it'll just go away, that the world as it is will not be our sentence?"

"I'm not as learned or deep as you, my friend."

"What about some other kind of justice?"

"I'll meet that when it comes, with my conscience clear. I owe you my life, Lucius. You can call this repayment."

"You go to hell," said Burling, slamming down the phone.

I N THE SCHOOLYARD BEHIND THE CONSULATE, LINDSTROM chinned himself onto the platform of the jungle gym and looked across at the Residence grounds. Broken glass protruded from the top of the wall, as he'd suspected. Through the pine trees edging the lawn, the curvilinear windows of the house blazed with light.

A black Jeep was idling next to the front steps, its halogens boring the shadows, high beams teeming with bugs. Burling came out the front door and down the steps. He jogged through the headlights, and Lindstrom saw he was wearing black sweats of a shiny material and a black windbreaker with a seal on the chest. His white tennis shoes flashed as he rounded the hood and got in at the passenger door. It wasn't closed before the Jeep's tires spit gravel and backed up and gunned down the drive.

"What do you see?" Yong whispered from below.

Lindstrom was standing a short jump from United States territory, and suddenly it seemed a foreign place. Seeing Burling, in command and dressed for action, made him feel like he didn't belong there. He had always linked his actions, no matter how ridiculous or hopeful or compromised, to America, judging himself an odd kind of avatar, a mongrel, like the nation itself the violent issue of some missionary's dream. But now he wondered if he belonged there, after all, without Mei. No matter where the rest of life found him, he couldn't imagine going through it alone.

"I see America," he said, illuminating the dial of his watch. The hands read twelve fifteen. He jumped down. "I'm going back," he told Yong.

"Back to America," Yong said.

"No. I'm going back for Mei."

Yong shifted the small plastic suitcase from one hand to another and took a step in place, like a thwarted child. "But you can't do that."

"The fuck I can't. I'd rather stay behind than go over there without her."

"You're not going to . . . ?"

"Go on the boat with her?"

"It's not what I was going to say. You may be making the mistake of thinking she wants to go. Maybe you don't understand her."

"I'll take that risk."

"Not everyone wants to go to America, John. Not everyone wants to be free."

"Don't talk like that about her," Lindstrom said, feeling a sudden murderous impulse. On that, he could make it through. "She lost her husband."

"And you lost your wife. Surely you see this can't go on, these two nations as they are. She doesn't say this to you, but when you're not there Mei sounds like many other young people, 'Chinese government may be bad, but that can change.'"

"She doesn't know anything else."

"That is the most effective way they have to keep us as we are."

"Mei needs to see that," Lindstrom told him, taking off his watch, "not just read it in books. Now get yourself under this structure here and wait." He handed Yong the watch and the revolver. "If Mei or I don't come back in forty-five minutes, jump over that wall. Leave the gun here and watch out for the glass. Don't worry if you break something landing. Just clear that wall whatever you do."

"But John." Yong's hand was on his wrist, where the heavy Submariner had been. "What if she doesn't want to go? What if you go back there and lead them to her or get caught and it turns out she didn't want to go?"

"This is not about me," Lindstrom told him.

THE CONSULATE GATE SWUNG BACK, AND THE SHINY BLACK Jeep with the white lights perched atop its bumper emerged like a prehistoric beast. Li's hand was shaking with excitement as he crushed his cigarette out in the ashtray and started the Mercedes again.

"You are sure she won't suffocate," he said, gesturing toward the trunk.

"She is no help to us dead," the general told him.

Li turned back to the wheel. The car smelled of sweat and cigarette smoke. She isn't much help alive, he thought, but the general's cross look made him hold fire. Burling's Jeep pulled from the driveway in front of a truck, and Li rolled to the corner. The oncoming lanes were empty, the cone-like blossoms of the chestnut trees glowing in the moonlight. Li made the left turn and gunned up close behind the truck. It was a military caisson, and it made him feel safe.

"Patiently, Li."

Adrenaline played in Li's foot; he was so geared up he spoke without thinking: "But the truck blocks their view."

"You sound like Feng," said the general.

Li stole a glance at the folds of his face, but the ponderous frown was impossible to read; he might just as well have been asleep as grieving for Feng. All at once, his scowl reminded Li sharply of his own father, who might smile or fly into a rage from the same fundamental expression. He remembered the Big Fish asking if he believed that a general's men would guard him in the afterlife. Li hated to remember his obsequious response.

In spite of the late hour, the Frenchtown shops were crowded with people. The truck's taillights blinked once, and Li nearly drove the car into the tailgate. The Jeep turned left and traveled north in the direction of Suzhou Creek.

On Nanjing Xilu, the boulevard down which Li had followed Lindstrom and Charlotte to the Bund, the consulate Jeep pulled to the curb before a restaurant. The streetlamps silvered the leaves of the plane trees overhanging the sidewalk. Neon signs lit the trunks like pale fire.

The consul alighted from the Jeep—he, too, rode in the front seat, Li saw—and said something to the driver before striding across the sidewalk through a waiting wedding party and into the ground floor of the restaurant. Li pulled the Mercedes to the curb.

More weddings. The sight made Li's balls ache all over again. Up and down the street, the sidewalk was filled with suits and red roses that bloomed like genitalia in the crowd. He switched off the ignition, and the general hunkered glibly beside him.

Li sat without speaking for as long as he could; he was about to suggest that he check out who else was in the restaurant, when

Burling came through the doors with a pastry in his hand. The consul ambled past the Mercedes, taking quick, awkward bites from the sweet, the sleeves of his black running suit shining wetly in the streetlight. A bride and her friends looked dreamily at him and giggled as he passed, and the bridegroom looked angry. The general smiled to himself as he watched Burling pause before the Exhibit of People's Industry. The consul dipped his mouth toward the pastry and held his hand to catch the crumbs. The bridegroom's friends huddled menacingly, nodding in the American's direction.

"He knows we're here," said the general. "Look at him pulling us in."

"He's a puppet," Li argued. "He doesn't know what he is doing."

"Every man is," said the general, "in his own way."

Not Lindstrom, Li thought, but he censured himself. Burling stuffed the last piece into his mouth and entered the exhibit, wiping his hands on a handkerchief. The crowd had swallowed the wedding party, and now bicycle punks and strolling men and women in Western dress obscured the entrance from view.

"He may not know who his master is," the general added, rousing himself with a groan. Li smelled his sour, old man smell. "But he has been in the game so long that he is good at it, very. We have no choice but to follow. That he is a puppet only means we can reason with him."

"What if he has his car meet him?"

"Then you take him," said the general, "but gently, mind." He placed a big hand on Li's forearm. "Consul Burling is not your friend Lindstrom."

Li got out of the car and jogged with his head low beside the sooted flanks of the buses, then cut between parked cars to the curbing. Glancing back, he saw the general lift himself from the Mercedes and move to the driver's seat. Li couldn't remember if he'd known that the Big Fish could drive. Li stopped at the edge of the crowd with his hand on the warm hood of a car, and his vision, the tunnel of streetlamps and branches hanging over the sidewalk, warped; the globes of the lamps had yellowish halos, and people slid toward him silently; the sounds of the street seemed far off. The city held its breath. Li blinked to clear his vision, but he couldn't get the humming out of his head—Radio Tibet, calling for migraines. He felt Lindstrom around him in the crowd, but the nerve ends in the top of his skull had gone silent, cringing in the face of the gathering pain.

The general hadn't spoken English that well before, either, Li thought, shouldering people who got in his way. When he drew opposite the entrance to the exhibit, he couldn't see Burling. He waded into the crowd and moved at an angle as the people drew him forward. When he reached the entrance, Burling was gone.

"Where is he?" asked the general, appearing beside him. The Mercedes was parked in a new space, its hazard lights flashing. Li thought of the woman in the dark trunk. "There."

Burling's suit was disappearing like a specter through the trees.

"I will stay in the car," the general told him. Li's skull was like a satellite dish, picking up and separating every sound. The general's voice was a low rumble, hard to understand. "I'll turn the corner by the Number One Store and park again. I will see you when you leave the trees on the other side of Renmin Square."

Li glanced at the figure of Burling, darker now, indistinct in the trees. The general blinked his reassurance. "That's an order, Li."

The general's face remained etched in Li's mind like the head of a coin as he entered the grove. Moving cautiously into a bare patch between the pines, he felt the heft of the pistol the general had given him, riding on his belt. A hundred yards away, the slender trunks crowded together, and Li could barely see the consul slip between them.

For the first twenty yards, Li moved from trunk to trunk at a trot, bugs hitting his face, the holster jabbing the small of his back. Moist heat closed in as the trees grew closer together and the smell of dry dust stung his nose. A clearing opened, and he started to run, taking care where roots knuckled through the dirt, but halfway across he felt a presence and slowed down, looking frantically around him. The trunks came at him quickly, suddenly, as if he were standing still and they were moving. Moonbeams fell in a cone from the branches above, like the ancient philosophers' drawings of an eye. He didn't know which way he'd come. Footsteps marched to the pulse in his head.

The whole grove, the whole city breathed around him. The outlines of the general's face had faded from his mind, and in its place he saw Lindstrom's white visage, with the shadow of stubble on his scalp, the soot-colored rings around his eyes. *When you know you're going to die, that's when you know who to trust. Flip the coin, it doesn't matter which way it comes up. Now we're cooking, my brother.*

Li slapped himself hard on the cheek, and the rumble of traffic, the rising buildings of the city around him, made his head ring with his own isolation. A breeze sloughed through the branches, but he couldn't see the moon. The air between him and the boulevard seemed alive, popping and singing in his ears.

You are the eye, he thought, feeling the city rise around him. This is a war, an occupation by ghosts. They tried to cross the river at Wanping, but their armies were beaten back by my townspeople; so they came up the swollen rivers, the Yellow and the Yangzi, from the hot, marshy coast, fish plying the current, gorged with native blood. Shanghai has always been their whore, their swampy cunt, her bastard children come and go, begging money, entranced by her dark, witch-like charms. *I am the future*, she whispers, swaying her arms, *come to me*. Her legs spread, and her long nails touched his back, tracing rivulets of sweat. When he raised his eyes to her, she had the face of the smiling woman pastor from Anhe.

He cried out. He was standing in the dry-rutted mud where he and the general had questioned Charlotte Brien. *You are the eye. You are China.* His erection strained against his pants, and he took it out quickly and masturbated onto the ground. Ahead, the consul moved at an unhurried pace along the dirt road toward Renmin Square. Li felt dizzy and weak in the knees as he stuffed himself into his fly. He was sweating, and the air was still again. Wiping his hand on his handkerchief, he took out the pistol and held it pointing downward as he ran, dancing in and out of the wheel track, gaining ground. The trees opened up, and the fortress-city rose from the delta; a giant disk like a flying saucer turned atop a building, its windows framed by twinkling lights. The yellow moon sat suspended above it like a yolk. One shot from him would break it, bring the whole city down in a torrent of semen and blood.

The consul swung his leg across the concrete barrier and stepped into the flashbulb light of the square. The uncanny brightness hurt Li's eyes, and he drew up, shocked by Burling's paleness, angularity, and height; his thinning hair was nearly white, and sweat shone on his brow. The consul licked his fingers one by one and struck out across the concrete, wiping first his forehead and then his fingers again on his handkerchief.

When Li saw the general again, sitting on a bench behind a newspaper, he felt a flush, as if he had come through something, and he realized that the migraine had passed. The large white face of the general, the cooler air stirring from the harbor, were his reward. He knew that he had felt this way before, after Ti-ananmen Square, but that he had not understood his destiny well enough to see what it meant. He had risked things for the general, drawn close to history, which had only death at its heart; men, like countries, who experienced sacrifice had always been chosen to lead. The general was only Li's conduit: the moon in the grove had anointed him.

General Zu got up and folded his paper as Burling started across the street, toward a Children's Palace on the opposite corner.

"He did nothing in the woods," Li reported, panting as he fell in beside Zu. Remembered, the woods seemed empty, not haunted at all. They were bare, compared to the brightness and noise, the gaudy colors of the night sidewalk.

Zu watched him evenly. "Only a shortcut," he concluded.

Li glanced at his face, trying to see if Zu believed it. His eyes were like slits; the flesh of his chin jiggled with each step he took.

Why would Burling have left his car behind? The cones of light from the streetlamps lit, then shadowed Zu's ponderous face. He was brooding again.

"This is the place where the Brien woman intercepted Lindstrom," Li observed. He felt solicitous; if the Big Fish was the conduit to Li realizing his ambition, he must keep him very close, like a lover. Li offered the general his arm at the curb. "Is something wrong?"

Zu was winded, but he waved Li's arm away. "I must think. *Think*. The terms."

Burling must be leading them to where Yong and Lindstrom were hiding, but the general looked more worried than he should. His mind was weak, and his talk made no sense. Li saw him tap his sidearm under the suit jacket. At the end of the block, Burling climbed the metal stairs to the flyover. The consul was already across it when Zu, still talking to himself, allowed Li to help him up the steps.

"Do not get itchy, Li," he said when they had reached the bridge itself. "This is not to be another Anhe."

Li moved to speak but thought better of it.

"This must be a thing of which no one, no one will ever know."

The tram wires showered sparks as they crossed above the traffic. The general's words only confirmed that Li was about to take part in something that would guarantee his future, fulfill his worldly ambition and his destiny both. A block away, Burling was turning into a side street. When Li and his general reached the corner, the consul was halfway down the block, consulting a leather-bound book.

"That's not a . . . ?"

"Bible?" the general said. Li hadn't thought he had spoken out loud. The general's mouth turned down at the edges. "You see God everywhere now, Li. We are going to have to reform you."

He couldn't tell if the general were joking or if he were reading his thoughts. A calligraphy store occupied two windows on the corner. The works on display signified the arrangement of things. Li looked quickly away because the eye of his destiny was too strong to hold.

"No," the general murmured. "Remember what I taught you about sacrifice. As soon as you believe that it is only about you, then you become like them. Like him." He nodded toward Burling, who had closed his book and was moving again.

MEI HAD BEEN STANDING AT THE WINDOW, STILL, SMOKING a cigarette and watching, when Lindstrom walked into the room. She turned, giving him the look of hatred she'd been saving for whoever would come for her. Her lower lip began to quiver.

"John." She was trying very hard to be angry. "Why did you have to come back?"

"Because I figured it out."

She put a hand on her hip and held her cigarette high in the other, like a femme fatale she'd seen in American movies. "You figured what?"

"Exactly what you said I would. Actually, Yong helped me. He's wise, for all his waffling."

"A liar has to be."

"He said, 'Not everyone wants to be free.'"

"What is that supposed to mean?"

"We don't have time right now to discuss it. Besides, you're coming with me."

"What if I don't want to?"

He took her wrist. She looked away from her smoke.

"Was that an act the other night?" Lindstrom asked her. "Do you only do that for therapy, or was it for real?"

She raised the hand with the cigarette as if she might slap him. Then she lowered it and looked away again. "I'm not strong enough to go, John."

"I don't care. Maybe he cared, the guy with the pure heart whose clothes I'm in, but me, I've never been strong enough to stay. Forget a pure heart. Pure hearts only end up broken. Come with me."

Without a word, she left him and went into the bedroom. Lindstrom watched her from the terrace door. From her father's wardrobe, she took out a rucksack and stuffed it with two large leather books and several paperbacks, some scrolls, an old pistol—a Luger from the look of it—cigarettes and a few sundry items. She was silent as she packed, her life torn across in a day. When she went to the bathroom, Lindstrom walked back to the far end of the terrace and checked the street below. In the darkness outside, a coin was falling, glinting, passing through a net. He blinked, worried at the vision.

"Free," he said to himself.

Mei was standing behind him with her bag. He thought of the cross on his grandfather's church steeple, standing out against the smoke, like a needle in the skin of the land. Heat lightning crackled against the misty mountains behind it. His grandfather had altered forever the human chemistry of this place, but Lindstrom had done something to redeem it. He, not Burling, was the dragon in the fields.

"Free?" Mei asked.

He was turning to go when he saw Burling's large white head entering the end of the street.

"Nearly," he said.

IN THE DARK STREET BELOW, A TWO-STORY WALL OF STONE commanded the far end of Mei's block, predating the Concession-era buildings by more years than Lindstrom could tell. No way out there. Within seconds Lucius Burling appeared in the yellowish light of a building entry halfway up the street. Lindstrom ducked back and into the stairwell, where Mei was waiting for him.

"Let's go," he said, guiding her past the leaning bikes and into the interior courtyard. Over his shoulder, he saw Burling coming through the gate. Burling went up the stairs, and another man, Chinese, walked past the entry and stopped.

"Out the back way," Lindstrom hissed. "On the balls of your feet, now."

They jogged across the courtyard to a narrow alley stinking of trash. "Do you know the Jade Temple?" Lindstrom asked.

Mei's eyes were dark, and she hugged herself in a thin cardigan although the night was humid and mild. The rucksack, made for someone taller, hung far down her slender back. "In the Old Chinese City?"

"Yes. I'll meet you there. I need to make sure we're not followed."

"But you said we were going together," said Mei.

Lindstrom took her hand. "Look. The other night, something happened there."

"I know. You took the opium. I could see it in your eyes, just like my father. You can't do that anymore, not and be with me."

"But the drugs are not important," Lindstrom said. "Because I can handle that. It's the coins. The coins came up, and I let Burling get in the way of their meaning. I'm free of that now."

"You are speaking like my father," said Mei, grabbing his arm, "when he chased the dragon."

"I know."

"He was a wise man," she continued, "but he didn't want to do anything, so I went with a man of action. They both died of the same thing, John. I cannot go through it again."

"The old man who gave me the opium knew I was the dragon, too, but I didn't understand. Now we're going to the only American territory in Shanghai."

"The consulate?"

Lindstrom showed the gun again. They had heard someone enter the courtyard.

"Yong is on the playground behind the Residence," said Lindstrom. "If I'm not at the Temple in fifteen minutes, get him and get inside the consulate any way you can."

Mei jerked her head back and forth, as if she were trying to shake something out of it. Lindstrom turned back and took her by the shoulders. "Go."

Mei left through the trash cans and into the narrow lane beyond. She hadn't closed the gate behind her when she heard Lindstrom's first shot echo off the alley walls.

AT FIRST THE SIDE STREET WAS QUIET, A DEAD END THAT held and played games with the sounds from the boulevard. A few women gossiped by the grille of a shop, but the city night muffled their voices.

Things, Li thought, could happen here and no one would ever know about them.

"Slowly," the general had said, stooping over a little and bending his knees. The newspaper was folded in his armpit. "Go ahead, Li, ten yards in front. You walk past the entry and nod if it's clear."

The sidewalk was littered with sawdust from a woodworker's shop, the street iridescent with oil. The smell of his home, of pork fried quickly in oil, drifted down from the terraces. Across the street, a line of trucks was parked, two tires on the curb. Li passed the gate through which the consul had entered and nodded to the general, then froze.

"Someone's in the courtyard," he said as the general drew beside him.

"You check. I'll go up," said the general, sliding his pistol between the folds of the newspaper and clamping it there with his elbow. He slid his hand into the paper once, checking his access to the grip, then pushed past Li toward the foot of the stairs.

THE BULLET KEENED OFF THE WALL A FOOT ABOVE LI'S head. He jumped back into the entry and fell against the bikes, then fired the pistol blindly just to keep whoever was out there from coming across the courtyard. The shots echoed in empty space. No one answered his fire, which he took as an ominous sign. Shortly he heard the rusty gate again. It sounded far away, outside the building. Getting to his knees, he peered around the corner. He could only see a black rectangle on the far wall, about a meter from the corner. No movement or contour of light. Then all at once an alley appeared in a flash, the curve of a barrel and Jack Lindstrom's face. The sound of the shot came later, as Li was falling backward again, the bullet catching his right elbow, ripping his windbreaker, burning and tearing the skin. He hit his head against the sprocket of a bike, his pistol pinned beneath him. He felt a leak, and a trickle of blood began to run down his arm. Slowly he worked the gun out and brought himself to a sitting position. From an upper story, a light came on that made the courtyard look ghostly.

No. Unless the general came down, took up a position on the open landing, Lindstrom could pin him there all night, which was probably exactly what he wanted. Meanwhile Yong escaped again.

He wasn't going to let this happen. Getting to his feet, he squeezed off another round in frustration. It hit a can with a sound like a steel drum, surprising him with his accuracy. In training, he'd been good at riflery, one of the many small skills that had fueled his advance. Thinking sharply now, he backed away quietly and ran out of the entry, turning left into the street.

He entered through the gate next door and moved across an identical courtyard to an alley that resembled the one illuminated in his mind—cans, bricks. He could see Lindstrom's face in the muzzle flash. The gate at the back of the narrow space was locked, but there was room at the top for him to squeeze over. Tucking his pistol in the back of his belt, he pulled himself up on the grimy bars, using the lock as a step. First one knee, then the other on the top rail, where the pickets squeezed his instep through his shoes. The gate was set into the wall several feet, and he couldn't see around into the *hutong* that ran behind the buildings. There was something familiar about it, though; in a moment he knew it was the boundary of the Old Chinese City. As he landed on the ground, his balls seemed to have shrunk into the bottom of his throat. He checked the *hutong* in both directions. To the right, it ended almost immediately at another massive wall. Moving down it fifty meters to the left, he found the alley where Lindstrom had been, spent shells scattered by the garbage cans like the scene of a killing. Li looked up at the landing where the general must be.

Remember what I taught you about sacrifice, he said. *As soon as you believe that it is only about you, then you become like them. Like him.*

Like you, Li thought. A great despondency went through him. Maybe he wasn't a secret hero after all. Perhaps all the leaders— Lenin, Chairman Mao—were like the general, hypocrites and traitors.

Now we're cooking, my brother.

All at once he felt a terrible kinship with Lindstrom. The horror of it was a hunger, like desire, lodged somewhere in the back of his throat. It drew him through the shadows abutting the Old City wall, saliva flowing into his mouth so copiously it nearly choked him to swallow. After a while he came to a breach, and before him rose the back of a moldering temple. Its stones were damp and slimy with humidity. Its recesses smelled of mildew and piss. The top of his head began to buzz like a microwave dish—the migraine returning. A weak glow emanated from the far end of the building. He could see the rafter tails of the temple porch, carved into slavering mouths. The sweet, gagging smell of kerosene spread from the lanterns in the close, moist air.

Standing by the pillar, Li couldn't remember walking the length of the temple's outside wall. A little boy went around the square, snuffing out the lanterns.

"Boy," said Li, swallowing spit.

The square was almost empty, and the boy started, staring up at the man who had stepped around the pillar of the porch.

"Did a strange man come through here just now, with a shaven head who looks like a mongrel, an addict?"

The boy watched him warily.

"He has a scar on the back of his head," Li said, holding out some *yuan.*

The boy looked over his shoulder at his father, who was putting a chained monkey's things into a wooden box the shape of a coffin.

When the boy turned back, he took the money and stuffed it in his pocket, smiling like an imp.

His house, the boy explained, had been in an uproar since the night before. His father's show had been interrupted by a madman who, according to his grandfather, possessed the harmonic power of Pure Yang.

"He was the Great Man," the boy informed Li.

"Did this Great Man come through here just now?"

The boy shook his head. Li held out more *yuan*, and the boy took the money.

"They went that way," he said.

THE BOY WENT BACK TO PICKING UP LANTERNS. WHEN he was finished, his father had already taken the monkey and his props to their house. The boy's shoulders hunched with the weight of the lanterns, and walked like the monkey, bowlegged, tipping back and forth on his feet, toward the mouth of the *hutong* where his father had gone. He felt guilty for taking the policeman's money when the Great Man was going to kill him. He wondered if his grandfather would say he was interfering with the *ching*. Mulling over these things, he didn't see the Great Man enter the square again from the opposite corner. When the boy saw him, he realized immediately that the Great Man did not know he'd been followed.

The boy called out a warning, and the Great Man was turning, a pistol in his hand, when the policeman's first shot caught him squarely in the shoulder. The boy dropped the lanterns and turned as the Great Man staggered back against the coping. The policeman stepped off the porch and fired again, the sound cracking like a whip across the stones. The Great Man dropped his pistol and looked at his hip and then in the direction from which he had come. The boy thought he saw a woman's face, an outstretched hand, but he couldn't be sure. She had disappeared before he looked again. The policeman stepped out from under the porch with the gun in his hand. His face looked wet, as if he were sweating or crying. Before he fired the third shot, the Great Man fell back toward the water and landed with a splash. The policeman lowered his pistol, looked quickly at the boy, turned and ran away.

WHEN THE POLICEMAN HAD LEFT, THE BOY CAME OUT FROM his hiding place and climbed onto the coping around the pool to try and see the Great Man underwater, but the dark green color and depthlessness frightened him. The surface didn't tremble even though the man was under there.

The dragon is submerged, he thought. His mind was more active than ever from the lateness of the hour. The Great Man remains in the depths, where he doesn't have to suffer any blame.

He had almost reached the doorway through which his grandfather had passed when he heard the water pop behind him, a sound like the fish made when they fed. Tiny bubbles freckled the surface.

"*Ye ye*, hurry!"

Coming out of the house, his grandfather tucked his robe into the white cotton drawers he wore and lowered his bare feet into the pool. Wading in up to his waist, the old man reached down and pulled the Great Man up by the armpits. His skin looked blue. He vomited a bucketful of water.

Lindstrom gasped, and the old man lifted him onto the coping. He struggled to get oxygen into his lungs. His head was bleeding but that was the least of his problems. Things seemed to be leaking from him everywhere. On the side of the pool was the boy from the monkey spectacle.

"Come on," said the boy in the language of Lindstrom's grandmother. "What if the policeman comes back?"

The old man helped Lindstrom up and led him, still gasping for air, from the square. They entered the house and the room where Lindstrom had smoked the night before. The old man gave him a coarse blanket and a lump of hash to chew on for the pain while he cooked the raw opium for him.

"Look at me," Lindstrom said, huddled back against the cushions. The blanket made him warm, and he quaked with the returning waves of pain. Water still seemed to be in his lungs, but he thought it might be blood. "I'm just a junkie. That's what it is."

"Is?" said the man.

"My blood belongs in the syringe," Lindstrom told him, feeling sorry for himself. "It belongs in the needle. All of it. That's what I am. A fucking junkie."

The old man nodded and produced a hypodermic wrapped in plastic. It appeared to have been furnished by the UN High Commissioner for Something.

"All this saving people," Lindstrom told him, holding out his arm. The old man tapped out a vein. "April. Yong. Even Li when he shot me was crying. You can hide in it forever, just like China. It doesn't take away the fear."

He laughed a little. He was feeling cold again. As the needle went in, the rush didn't make him warm. "The coins," he began.

"You can hide in this forever," said the old man as Lindstrom tried to fight the nodding off, "but you cannot be free."

L I PAUSED OUTSIDE THE DOOR TO MEI'S APARTMENT, rubbing his eyes. He'd killed Lindstrom, and now he felt alone. Bereft of certainty. The world seemed empty without the American in it, and Li was left with only hatred for the general and disgust with himself for his own stupidity. He didn't feel like a hero anymore. Was he really only the kind of man who follows orders, retreats into duty and ends up a pawn? The metal doorknob was wet with humidity, or was it dew? The city would soon be waking to a world that felt diminished, governed only by corruption. He had tried to succeed in that world, but he was not made for it, and now he couldn't decide if that was a failure or not. He turned the knob an eighth of a turn and found that the lock was not engaged. The top corner stuck in the jamb, and the door vibrated when he pushed it fully open.

The apartment smelled of stale cigarettes and dishes soaking in lye. It stunk of unhappiness and lack, and no matter how hard he tried he could not remember if that was the smell of his own life, or whether there was something else in his own home on which he could fasten for hope. He remembered the baby's room in Rank's apartment in Nanjing, and his chest burned with envy. At the end of the dark hall was a doorway framed by moonlight. When he was in, Li slid to his left, across from an open bathroom door. The odor of plumbing was strong, and a shirt stained with dried blood hung next to the sink. He heard low voices as he moved down the hall.

A light switched on, and Li found his pistol pointing at a comic opera mask. He started back in fright. The hallway was empty, and the doorway off it filled with yellow light. The mask was hanging on a wall.

"Li looks surprised to see us," the general's voice called, and the American consul looked up from a chair as Li blinked at the light.

"I'm afraid that whoever was here went away in a hurry, Mr. Li, so you can put that thing away."

Li looked at the pistol in his hand.

"Unless it's me you want to shoot," Burling said, getting up and striding across the small room. It was furnished very much like Li's home, and the way that Burling stood in it made Li upset and ashamed.

"The consul and I have been discussing our common history," the general said.

"A complicated history," added Burling.

"I was taught simplicity," Li told them. Was he really defending himself against these puffed-up turkeys? He suddenly missed his wife and daughter very much. "Who told you this address?"

The consul paused by the daybed, running his hand across the pink chenille spread. "You know the answer to that," he said smugly.

"If you are referring to Mrs. Brien, she neglected to inform us," said the general. He was speaking English again.

"Maybe you didn't ask nicely."

Li struggled to hold the consul's cool blue stare. "We asked *you* in Beijing, Consul Burling."

Burling walked to the terrace doors and turned. "As I remember it, we spoke of Alan Rank. Then you held me in Beijing in a series of transparent nets. If you'd let me get back here Tuesday morning as I'd planned, perhaps I wouldn't be here and Charlotte wouldn't be . . . well, wherever you have her. I should probably take this opportunity to inform you that, unlike your sparring partner Rank, Charlotte Brien is an official of the American government."

"Consul. Please." The general motioned for Burling to sit down. "I don't see any governments here in this room. Only men. In any case, it all comes down to the personal, does it not?"

Burling's pale expression turned rueful. "I have always thought it should be that way," he said, "but that requires some choices that most people find difficult to make."

"Mrs. Brien," said the general, taking a chair, "has had a difficult evening. She made contact with Lindstrom before we were able to protect her. One of my men was lost."

Burling looked up in what seemed like distress.

"Unfortunate, yes," the general said. "But given that Mrs. Brien was close to this shooting, I feel that Mr. Li and I will need to keep her for a while longer, for her protection, until we can see if her role has had consequences."

"For her protection," Li echoed.

"I wonder," Burling said, "if these consequences have to do with the spy Yong Beihong?"

The general nodded gravely at the name and took on an expansive tone. "Our agents are like our children, are they not? They have their own ways: they see purity in us, they become corrupt; they see weakness, they develop ferocity. We nurture their will, their intelligence, and they go off and develop minds of their own, even in a world we have made."

From the corner of his eye, Li saw Burling nod and cross a long leg, as if he were settling into conversation. "This is something I often spoke of with a friend of mine," he said. "Maybe you know him. Chuck Byrd?"

You traitor, thought Li. Everything the Englishman Bell had said was true, perhaps more.

"He is in Hong Kong now," said Burling, "awaiting the arrival of a ship."

"The possible arrival?" the general asked.

"I can assure you," Burling replied, "that Yong is either still in China or he will be on this particular ship."

"I wonder if perhaps when Mr. Byrd meets Yong Beihong," Zu said, "he will find a way to ensure his silence?"

A shadow seemed to pass across Burling's face as he nodded.

"If you could guarantee this for us," the general added, "then I don't believe we'd need to keep your Mrs. Brien for protection anymore."

"No," said Burling. "You wouldn't."

"We won't need to keep her?" the general said pointedly.

"No."

"Very good," said the general. Li could tell that he was pleased, but his pleasure only made Li hate him more. His agitation was such that he almost blurted out that he had killed the American. "Otherwise I would prefer to keep Yong Beihong. He was never abused in our care, you see."

A knowing and disturbed smile briefly flickered on Burling's face.

"There is one more thing about which I am curious," the general continued. "When you and I met before the first Afghan war?"

"A proud moment in Sino-U.S. relations," Burling said unemotionally. He seemed very tired. "Of course we couldn't tell anyone."

The general smiled gravely, the corners of his mouth turning down. His fat face nodded slowly. The two older men seemed to share a repertoire of facial expressions, from years of practicing deceit. "I was only wondering about the woman who was there. The pilot died. I never knew what happened to the woman."

"April Lindstrom." Burling leaned forward, elbows on his knees, big hands clasped before him.

"This was a relation to Jack Lindstrom?" Li was shocked by the connection.

"His wife," said Burling, rolling his neck back and forth. "She was held for over a year by the *mujahedin*. We finally tried to make an exchange, but it didn't come off the way we wanted. Men on their side and our prisoner were killed. She'd been held near Jalalabad, in southern Afghanistan. Men we captured in the operation said she was physically well. To my surprise they apparently never . . . well, you know, according to these men."

"They are different in how they treat their women," said the general.

"They don't allow them to be educated," Burling said in a high, plaintive tone Li hadn't heard before. "They make them cover themselves from head to toe. These men said that April had agreed to put on the burka in return for her life. They said she promised to read the Koran. I'm sure it was all a lie."

"One has to resist if one is taken by the enemy," Li said. "We learned this in Intelligence School."

"Trained well, eh?" said the general very loudly.

Li felt they were laughing at him.

"In any event, no one ever saw April again," Burling said. He got up wearily and went to the window a second time, as if he were expecting someone.

"Li Xin?" the general said, watching him.

Li found that he'd been listening to the sound of children playing outside, but that was impossible. They must be long in bed.

"Did you want to ask the consul something?"

Li tore himself from his thoughts and nodded to the general mechanically. He couldn't remember what it was he was supposed to ask.

"Li was curious about something," the general continued. "Ask the consul if that was a Bible he took out in the street."

Li did as he was told. "Are you a believer, Consul Burling?"

"No one has asked me that in such a long time," Burling said, removing the leather-bound volume from his pocket. "In my own way, I am, but this here is just a notebook. Sort of a longstanding habit of mine. I buy two new ones each time I go to the States. I keep my thoughts in them, and save them when I'm done. This one is new, so it only has a few lines."

He handed the notebook to Li, and Li fingered the spiral-bound mechanism. In detention facilities he had taken away things like this because the prisoners could fashion the metal into a weapon. On the first page Burling had sketched a diagram, a sort of star shape with the names "Lindstrom," "Mac," "April," and "Charlotte," among others. Li was surprised at what a delicate artist Burling was. Some questions concerning love had been scribbled at the bottom of the page, which confirmed Li's impression that the book was sacred to him. On the second page was the name of the street and the apartment number where they stood.

"Keep it," said Burling. At first Li was offended, and he pushed the notebook back toward the American. "No, please. As I say, I have another. The little I wrote there I'd rather not read again, anyway. I can always start a new one tomorrow."

Li ran his thumb over the leather and opened it again.

"Anyway, you know all my secrets already," Burling said.

Li stared at the blank white paper ruled with blue. General Zu got up, and Li watched his stout figure with hatred. He would stay with Zu, but when the day came . . . He would wait for his chance, then the truth would come out, the general would be publicly vilified, in the great transfiguring spirit of Mao.

"Good-bye, Mr. Li," Burling said.

Li closed the notebook and shook his hand.

"General Zu." Burling clasped the general's hand and then closed his left hand around it.

"I have been proud to share this little piece of history with you, Consul Burling. It has not been easy, but sometimes it is necessary for harmony to sacrifice the few for the many."

He is thinking of the Square, Li thought. In spite of everything, tears of admiration rose to his eyes.

Burling was nodding. "I already lost one woman to this little piece of history, as you call it. Maybe even two, come to think of it. I certainly don't want to lose a third."

Zu raised his chin in sympathy. "My wife would have said that Mrs. Lindstrom flirted too closely with the other side."

Burling looked spooked.

"A relationship between two countries is much like a marriage," the general observed. "It is first a transaction. Later comes understanding, perhaps affection, even love."

"If it does come to that," Burling said, "love, I mean, one is tempted to think that he knows the whole world through that person."

"One can know the whole world and still not know oneself."

"I guess we understand each other then," Burling said, meeting his eyes in a shy way, "in spite of everything."

"That is very important," Zu told him. "For this reason, I hope that you will remain with us as consul. I would like to talk this way again."

"Thank you for that," said Burling, "but I imagine that my government's indulgence of me may have run out by now. I plan to accompany Mrs. Brien back home. I hope that the two of us might learn . . ."

"To understand each other?"

Burling nodded and paused as if he would say something else, but the words did not come and he left the room stiffly but quickly, passing into the hallway with one backward glance, like a man who is leaving his home against his will. He opened the front door and stepped onto the landing, then, realizing that the door would not swing closed automatically, he reached and pulled it shut in a more convincing way.

"Unlike Consul Burling," said the general, "who will retire wondering if he is really in disgrace, you will die with honor, Li."

A wave of pride came over Li, and he brought himself to a sort of attention in the middle of the floor. Although the feeling of betrayal was still strong, he was suddenly eager to report to Zu that he had carried out his mission, that Lindstrom was dead. The general turned in a way that Li had seen many times, a dignified turn that he might use to greet a foreign dignitary, or a soldier of equal or greater rank. He was going to shake Li's hand, which he had never done, and Li gripped the notebook and wiped his other palm on the side of his leg in preparation. The general raised his right arm, eyes watery and shallow, and Li's arm came up from his own side.

"You will have been killed by Jack Lindstrom," the general told him, and before Li could protest that this was impossible, a pistol made a sharp, cheap sound in the unadorned room. Li looked around for an enemy as he felt an empty space open in the middle of himself. The burning slug tunneled under his rib cage and shattered his shoulder blade. Hot, liquid pain made him cough and gulp breath. Something went out of him. He stumbled forward to blanket the general, although the shot must have come from the hall, and it would be too late anyway, much too late, to save him—but his legs wouldn't hold; blood was filling his throat. He was already drowning as his chin fell against the general's pistol.

On his knees, Li felt as if he would cough up his heart, but the separate pain on his chin made him fight it; the cut, a child's cut, the kind of injury his daughter would suffer, was a greater affront than the knowledge he was dying. That little cut made him cry.

Father, he said, looking up with tears on his face, but the word was only a bubble, rising in the blood. His throat stopped, he buried his face in the crease of the general's pants. His cheek rested on the warm, prickly wool. As the bubble broke inside him, Li felt a hand cover the back of his head.

IN THE ENTRY TO THE BUILDING, BURLING SLOWED HIS STEP and looked over his shoulder into the dimness of the stairwell. The solid shape of the door closed again in his mind's eye, and he imagined his apartment in Washington, waiting. He thought of Mr. Shepherd, washing his car and riding the elevator with the demonic cat that he fed in the basement. Retirement opened like a chasm—not in his future, it seemed, but in his memory. What did that mean—that he was really an old man and just hadn't realized it yet? He was wondering what would fill his days, with most of life behind him, when he heard the shot crack from upstairs. At first he thought his mind might be playing tricks on him, but the second sound was unmistakably a gun. He winced and stood frozen, deciding what to do, and suddenly it occurred to him that there was another world to imagine, without General Zu or Li. A timid smile pressed at the corners of his mouth as he turned to go, nearly tripping on a small, dusty girl.

"Oh, I'm sorry." The sound of his own voice was breathless, unsure. Her face was the color of gingerbread dough. "I should watch where I'm going, shouldn't I?"

In her cheek was a small indent, like the print of a thumb. Her large black eyes stared up at him in terror. What was she doing awake at this hour?

"*Dui bu qi,*" he said again, trembling. I am sorry. "*Dui bu qi.*"

Her terror softened to entreaty, and then accusation. From a doorway across the entry, another girl sidled into the light. She must have heard the shots, too.

"*Dui bu qi,*" he repeated, but the first girl looked to her sister, who came across the entry with a stiff, outraged stride.

"It wasn't me," Burling said, and immediately felt ridiculous. In the door appeared a woman who must be their grandmother, the red handkerchief of a bound-foot detective tied around her upper arm. The girls stood looking up at him, cheeks brushed lightly with flour-like dust, and they leaned in their soiled white nightgowns together, reminding him of boyhood, of young girls' lithe menace and bloom. If he hadn't wanted Charlotte, hadn't been so lonely that first night they'd talked . . . But the future is memory, he thought. There's no escaping.

His pain and bewilderment must have shown on his face because soon the girls laughed at him and turned and ran into their door. Then the grandmother slammed it, and Burling was left in a flush of anxiety and shame.

You are the center.

He couldn't escape the feeling that the whole, terrible business began and ended with him. Li was dead, and he couldn't help equating him with the man they had tried to trade for April, who had lost a lot more than his hand. He remembered the man's face when they took the hood off him in the courtyard of the dark, wattle house, the roof made of branches, and the look that passed between him and Omar. That was when the firing had begun, and the man in the hood had gone down, taking a bullet meant for Burling. Jack had killed the one firing, and others on the way out, while Omar, unarmed, had fled, perhaps with April. Part of Burling's strength lay in the ability to wall off memories like this, that in recollection scalded his chest, but it could wall you in, too. His future, his hell, would be to return to nights like these again and again.

AT THE MOUTH OF THE STREET, HE CONSIDERED FLAGGING A taxi but decided to walk. It was twelve forty-five according to his watch, but the combination of jet lag and anxiety had pushed him through the wall of his fatigue without notice. It was almost diverting to walk in the moist, grainy air of the slumbering city, avoiding the curfew cars by staying in the shadows of the chestnuts—hide and seek, a low-stakes game. The sidewalks and buildings still held the heat of the day at their heart, like a room where an oven has been on, and in time Burling knew that the idea of a walk to clear your head was a notion for a simpler life, in which a decision you made did not connect in a grim web to other decisions. The only thing he'd get out of a walk was fatigue. Fatigue had become a narcotic for him.

A few beat-up cars and bikes and the ubiquitous dirty trucks passed on the boulevard to Frenchtown, stripping their gears and gunning their engines for God-knows-where. The slight wind, which smelled of rain in the countryside, scuttled leaves along the sidewalk, but the storm didn't come. The neighborhood seemed haunted with bad history. As he walked he went over and over what the general had meant about "the other side." It was eerily close to April's mother's own words at her graveside, a ceremony she had decided upon years after her disappearance. The service was held in a small verdant hollow in southwest Virginia, near the mines where her father and brothers had worked and the site of an old healing springs.

"They are full of the devil," Mrs. Wheeler had said, referring to the *mujahedin*. "Their religion instructs them to kill. Once she started in studying on it, April couldn't get free. The Bible says that when you cast your lot with death, you already have one foot in the grave."

"Where does the Bible say that?" Lindstrom asked her. He'd been hovering, nervously smoking, behind them in his mandarin collar and tight, black suit, the pants riding up on his socks as he took a step toward her. He had the thin, hairless legs of a junkie, spotted with sores. He wore black cloth shoes. "My grandfather spent years with people whom you would call 'heathens,' and he lived to be a hundred years old."

"Criminals! Terrorists!" Mrs. Wheeling cried, shaking. Her sister, who used a four-pronged metal cane, came toward her across the clover-stained lawn and put a hand on her arm. One of April's brothers, a burly man with dark oiled hair and a salt-and-pepper beard, looked up from whisking his hands. "He was running from death just like you, Jack. He was a criminal, just like you, leading my daughter to this."

She gestured violently, as if she were casting dice, at the hole where the empty casket had been lowered, around which a grave-digger had begun to remove the artificial grass. Burling thought to reason with her, but her grief was too much for him. On the simple white headstone, April had taken the place beside her father's carved name.

"She read their books," cried Mrs. Wheeling. "She wore their clothes!"

"That was just a story they told," Burling said. "It helped them recruit other men to their cause."

"Cause, you say? What cause? Their only cause was death."

April's brother had raised his wraparound sunglasses up on his wavy hair and was walking toward them, blinking his almond-shaped eyes. They were startlingly blue in the bright mountain air, and while the rest of him was built like the mother—stocky and dark—his eyes were April's.

"Come on now, Mom," the brother, whose name was Horace, said.

"Why is he here?" cried Mrs. Wheeling quietly. "Why are they both here?"

"You invited them," Horace told her. Burling remembered then that he was the pedal-steel player. All of the men in the family played banjo, or fiddle, or guitar. At the service, the tall, fair brother, who had been April's favorite, had played a lament. "They loved her, too, Mom. Everyone did."

"She was too good for this world," said Mrs. Wheeling, settling down and looking timidly at Burling. "I know they say that about people, but it was true. Since she was a little girl, all the times when she was sick with the fever or she hurt herself trying to keep up with the boys. How else would she have survived those abominations? She was already halfway an angel."

"That's true, Mrs. Wheeling," Burling had said.

AT THE RESIDENCE GATE, LESLEY WITHERS, THE DUTY MARINE, a handsome African American whose white uniform shone proudly against his chestnut-colored skin, seemed surprised and a bit worried to see the consul outside his little booth after midnight, but Burling put on his role and saluted good-naturedly. The marine saluted back with a tentative hand and buzzed him through.

"Seen the playoff scores, Lesley?" He poked his head through the open door of the guardhouse as a few scattered drops hit the leaves of the sycamores over his head.

"No, sir," the young man replied in a high voice that reminded Burling of drill. The patch on his arm held the MSG motto, "In every clime and place." "We got ESPN on the satellite, but I been on duty since nine."

"You need a radio out here," Burling told him, leaning a hand against the doorframe.

"Yes, sir. That would be good, sir. Consul Burling?"

"Yes, Lesley."

"Mrs. Brien come through just five minutes ago, sir. She didn't look so good. Like maybe she had been *mugged*." Withers's voice was high with worry. He couldn't be more than nineteen. "Man was with her told me that they had been in a accident, sir, in the car, a S-class Mercedes. It was busted up, too, sir, with a smashed place in the windshield and one headlight gone. But more like somebody had been *shooting* at it."

"Thank you, Lesley, for your vigilance. I'll have a word with your sergeant, after I ask Ms. Brien what happened tonight."

"Then I should write it in the log, sir?"

All at once, Burling realized the young man's dilemma. It reminded him of Li. "Probably better if you didn't, at least not until I hear Charlotte's side of the story."

"Yes, sir." The marine nodded vigorously and backed away toward his bank of gray screens. "That's what I figured, sir. Truth is, that man looked like the mob, but I ain't sure I can pick them out here."

"He might have been a high official," Burling said. "It's sometimes hard to tell."

The marine nodded thoughtfully, but his candor was gone. Burling said good night and walked away down the driveway as the rain began to fall through the trees.

THE FLOWERS IN THE HALLWAY OF THE RESIDENCE WERE dropping their pollen on the polished wood table. Burling knew that it was time to leave. The house already felt like it didn't belong to him. In all his time in embassy residences, he had never felt that way before.

When he opened the doors to his study, it was clear from Charlotte's posture that she had arranged herself deliberately when she heard the front door. Now she stood with her back to him, a bit unsteadily, before the bookshelves, which were filled with the volumes of history and statecraft, a smattering of novels he had cherished as an undergraduate but hadn't read for years, and a few children's books of his father's, without which Burling was lost. As a young man, his father had wanted to be Thomas Eakins, the Philadelphia portraitist who first considered becoming a surgeon, but the devastation Burling's father saw in the First World War had turned him to children's books, for which he had created a fantasy Europe of talking dormice and rooks. How far I am, Burling thought, from his world of Howard Pyle.

Charlotte was still dressed from dinner in her red batik wraparound skirt, which was ripped below her left buttock and smeared with orange dirt. Her blouse was torn at the sleeve, and her elbows were raw. Her dishevelment made him feel a great tenderness, which struggled to contain a reflex uncomfortably close to revulsion. Was that disgust at her weakness what was really meant by sin? Not the lust, or the greed, or the will to power, which fed on the weakness, but the feeding itself? It felt terrible to him right then to be a man.

"I saw General Zu," he explained, pulling the doors shut silently behind him.

Charlotte turned with a stricken expression. A purple welt, as if she'd been pistol-whipped, swelled at her hairline.

"Are you all right?"

Charlotte put up both hands, as if to protect herself from him, and he saw the palms were skinned like a child's. She backed toward his desk and rested them against it.

"You don't," she began, but something stuck in her throat and she slid one hand inside the neck of her blouse, a gesture he'd forgotten in the month he'd been away.

"With what you got yourself into, they could very well have shipped you home dead. I'm only telling you that because . . ."

"Don't try to scare me, Lucius. They scared me much worse than you ever could."

Burling took a breath. "Because this was much bigger than you. It was bigger, and smaller, too, in a way, than you and Alan Rank could have imagined."

She pushed herself off the desk and limped to the window. "You're only telling me that to remind yourself," he heard her say to the glass.

"Excuse me?"

"It's your whole fallen man thing all over again, isn't it?" When she turned, her face was triumphant. "That's what you were thinking just now. That your sleeping with April set this whole horrible thing in motion. My God, Lucius, you take yourself so fucking seriously, as if you're the center of the world."

Burling cringed at the echo of the phrase. "Do I?"

"The world is not a mirror of your own sad little affair. Now you're ready to preach to me about consequences to convince yourself that you're okay. The beautiful thing is . . ." Her laughter was rough, strange, and Burling thought he didn't know her very well. "The beautiful thing is that it doesn't matter now. For once I don't give a flying fuck if I live up to your pattern of behavior or not. Yong and Lindstrom are free. If that just happens to reflect poorly on your virtue, so be it."

"Free? *Free?*" Burling clenched his fists, trying in vain to keep his voice from rising. "You think they let you go with one of their men dead because they thought that Yong and Lindstrom were *free*? Zu traded you for an assurance that Yong would be out of the way, and Lindstrom with him, that is unless Jack really is some kind of demon."

"You didn't do that."

"I didn't do anything, actually, other than bluff. That is, unless you know where they are?"

"Oh, God," she said. "Why?"

"Because I think I still love you, in spite of myself."

"You don't know . . ."

"Yes, I do, and I thought I'd turned my back on it until I met you. You took me out of myself, Charlotte, and damned if I didn't fall for it, believe it could be. But then this. I . . ." He was going to say he wasn't allowed it, that some sort of curse had been laid on his head and he wasn't meant to be with a woman in the way he saw that other men were, but his head clouded and he turned his back and paced to the window again, biting his lip until the tears stung the rims of his eyes. "I thought that MacAllister set this whole thing up the way he did to test me, to get at me," he said, looking out at the lawn, the bare flagpole, "at exactly what you accused me of, my tendency to pattern the world after my own failures, my hope. Mac has always been a master of this sort of game. No ordinary weapons for him, no, he likes to play with things that should be left to God—love, faith, whatever it is that can make people happy, as Tolstoy said. If you can imagine at all what it's like to be a man, and the son of a man, then you may have some idea why Gordon's son hung himself in his own father's barn."

In the window, he saw Charlotte's face close behind him. He was reminded of the first night that they had stayed up talking, opening themselves. How were two people supposed to do that without ending up here, laid out for the emotional autopsy?

"I actually talked to my father about this once," Burling said, falling into the wing chair. "He didn't understand my job, so I told him that I had to predict what people would do, know what would make them turn around. This was very early, when I still had a sense of excitement about it, as if I were learning an art."

Charlotte sat in the chair across from him, her pupils slightly dilated, as if Zu had given her a drug. "What did your father say?"

"He asked if it was infecting my life. He said he felt the same thing when he was drawing people, like he had to see their bones. That was why for a long time he turned to illustration."

"I didn't know he had, done something else before, I mean."

"He even worked in advertising for a while. I was very hard on him for it. I guess that's why when Amelia died, I still couldn't give up the game, the feeling that what I was doing really mattered."

"Neither could I, Lucius. That's why I couldn't walk away from this."

"What a mess we are," Burling said. When he looked up, Charlotte's green-gold eyes were staring at him, dry and tempered by a strength he had never been able to see. "That's exactly what

MacAllister saw. He knew your refusal to give it up would send Yong and Lindstrom right into his hands."

"He's evil, Lucius, whether you want to believe it or not."

Burling got up to pour himself a drink. "The strange thing about him is that he really believes, that's why he tries so hard to prove there isn't anything. He keeps putting people *in extremis* to see if they'll surprise him, but of course they never do. He's what we used to call a preacher's kid."

Charlotte crossed the room and stroked Burling's back, took his glass and had a sip and gave it back to him. "I told Jack what would happen in Hong Kong, you know, that he would be waiting."

Burling didn't answer. He couldn't bear to tell her but somehow he knew it wouldn't happen that way, that she wouldn't get the ending, the shootout of good versus evil, that she wanted.

"Did you know," he said, finishing the drink and taking her gently in his arms. Her body felt unfamiliar, and she looked at him warningly, suspiciously, but let his hands remain on her waist. "Flying back here, I was thinking all the time about how we could be together. I even told Mac that disgrace wouldn't be so bad for me if you would come to live with me in Washington. Of course I didn't say your name, but I guess he knew who I was talking about."

"He probably said it was impossible, didn't he?"

"Yes," said Burling, "but I can't remember why."

"T HAT'S IT," SAID MEI, POINTING TOWARD THE consulate windows. They were standing on the playground structure close to the compound wall. The light in the upper room was on. "You are first."

Without answering, Yong winged the suitcase over the bristling shards of glass. They heard it land in a rosebush with a snapping of canes. Then Yong climbed up and launched himself off the railing of the platform without looking back. He got more air under him than Mei had imagined he could with his damaged legs. He appeared to hang for a moment above the wall, then disappeared. She heard a grunt as he hit the hard ground.

A survivor, Mei thought. The headlights of a car bored into the darkness of the playground, lighting harshly the trunks of the pines at the corner of the school building, then diffusing in a fine mist that hung above the grass. It was a new silver Buick, with little vents along the sides of the hood, like ones she had seen in the dealerships along the boulevard. Its lights went out. The car seemed to have stopped.

Jump, she said to herself, stepping toward the edge of the platform. She took the strap of her rucksack in her hand and flung it as hard as she could. It bounced, and the strap caught on the glass, and the pack hung down over the other side. John's dead. You saw him die. Now they are coming for you again. Suddenly she was terribly angry with Lindstrom. Like her father, like her husband, he had wanted to die. He had sought it out. It was easy for them, she thought. But I want to live.

An old man, thin and wearing a long gown, was coming along the compound wall, his cropped head stooped down in the shadows.

On the other side of the wall, Yong appeared beyond the cover of the bushes. The tall lighted windows of the house threw angular shadows onto the dark striped lawn. He turned back once and gestured for her to come. When the guard saw him, the lights on the house would go on and she would have missed her chance.

"Ssst!"

She crouched down out of sight. The old man had stopped ten meters away. The lenses of his small round glasses flashed up at her, and she recognized him.

"What do you want?" she asked.

The man from the opium parlor hissed at her again and started back toward the car. She had last seen him lingering in the back row of mourners at her father's funeral. Mei felt herself drawn to him hopelessly.

"What do you want of me?" she said to his retreating form.

From the compound came the unmistakable bark of a military voice, a soldier or policeman. She heard the sound of boots crushing gravel.

"Stop!" said the voice. An impossibly large man in uniform veered from the shadows and dropped on the ground like an archer, weapon drawn.

On Mei's side, the lights of the Buick came on again, throwing a tall shadow of the old man's figure onto the curtain of trees along the wall of the school. He had stopped in front of the car and was pointing at the windshield.

The compound lawn lit up with floodlights. Through a hole in the branches, she saw a small Chinese man in a dressing gown standing in the open front door, silhouetted by the hallway's softer light. He looked like a householder checking for raccoons. The marine fired a shot in the air, and Yong stood up with his hands held away from his sides.

"Help!" he cried in Chinese.

"You!" the voice was commanding. "On the outside! Don't move."

The voice sounded terribly foreign to her, but she knew in her head that if she could let herself go, leap over that wall, her life would change. She believed that the Americans were good. They truly represented freedom to her. Lindstrom represented freedom. Dead. The marine fired another shot, and Mei ducked down, shaking on the hard plastic floor of the structure.

This was how she'd survived the Square, cringing on the garbage-strewn asphalt, as her friends fell around her. Smoke the color of blood and the color of infection puffed out from the canisters fired by the tanks. What had been celebration, a party with dancing and drinking, sex and fighting and overheated talk, in which her husband was paramount, and hope like a drug that had gone on for days, was broken into a riot of clothing and torn limbs and hair that flung out against the bluest of skies. She was pinned beneath two bodies, her husband's and a girlfriend, and a policeman stepped on her hand as he walked by, still shooting.

Now she looked across the playground and saw that the back window of the Buick had run down. Slumped against the rear seat, head resting backward so that she couldn't tell if he was sleeping, still or dead, was Lindstrom.

BURLING HEARD THE SHOT AND SAW THE LIGHTS FLARE in the windows of the study. When the small, ragged figure appeared on the lawn with his arms raised, he knew it was Yong Beihong. Charlotte knew it, too; he could tell she'd been watching Yong before the marine saw him.

"Oh, God," she said. "Withers is going to shoot him."

Burling sprinted from the room and clattered down the stairs in his slippers, as fast as his old knees allowed. On the bottom step, the front of the slipper bent back underneath and he wrenched his ankle painfully. When he reached the front door, Mr. Lao was already there, looking with an equable scorn at the scene unfolding outside. The marine had subdued Yong, or rather Yong had bent forward, head touching the grass, and Withers put a plastic strap, like the ones you use on the neck of a trash bag, around his wrists, pulling it tight with a whipping motion. This forced his hands together before him, which made it look as if he were praying. Lao had stepped out of the way for the consul, and Burling limped across the driveway onto the lawn, which was spongy underfoot.

"This one's under control," Withers said with one hand on Yong's back. He was breathing hard, but he never took his eyes, or his cocked .45, off the top of the wall. "He's unarmed and in bracelets, sir. There's another one there by the school."

"I am seeking asylum," Yong said in good English.

"Who's out there?" Withers asked him. His voice was insistent but professional, and Burling didn't intervene. He gestured behind him for Charlotte to stay on the porch. It would not do for the marine to understand they knew Yong. "What's that pack there hanging on the wall?"

Yong, who was used to being questioned, only lowered his head.

"You had better go inside for your own safety, Consul," Withers said.

"There is nothing in my suitcase but clothes and books," Yong told him.

"I should blow the pack, sir, but we don't have the proper team for it here."

"Corporal, radio your sergeant. I will take charge of this one," said Burling. "You take cover there behind the Jeep just in case."

"Lucius," Charlotte said when Burling reached the front door, his hand on Yong's elbow. "What are you doing? Is Yong . . ."

"Mr. Lao," Burling said, talking over her so Lao wouldn't hear. "Would you please take Mrs. Lao and your boy through the tunnel to the annex? We're concerned about a package someone threw on the wall."

Impassive as always, Lao turned without a word and retreated down the hall toward the kitchen and his rooms. His back was like a reproach.

"In here," Burling said, indicating the parlor. "Who was with you, Yong?"

Charlotte went first and opened the tall, paneled doors.

"The girl with the apartment. She didn't jump over."

"Why not?" Charlotte asked as the two men went past her. The room inside was tenebrous and smelled of musty carpets and old, lacquered wood.

"I went first," Yong said, and the fact of what had happened was already clouding his voice. "She's still out there."

"Was Lindstrom with you?"

"Lindstrom is dead."

Burling took the news without much reaction. He realized that he must have already known it had happened. In his walk through the streets he must have known it. It was crazy how these things could penetrate your consciousness and your mind could work on them, the way it can work on things when you are asleep. April had been a great believer in this mysterious power of the mind; he, the rational one, had dismissed it as mountain superstition, but the idea had gotten a grip on him. Part of her power, her passion, and in some ways her undoing, had been this belief.

For her part, Charlotte was utterly practical, and she took the news like she'd been struck. She put her hand before her eyes.

"Mei saw it in the Old City," said Yong. "He was shot by the state security man from Anhe."

"He's dead, too," Burling told them. "General Zu killed him, neat as you please."

"Who *are* you?" said Charlotte, staring at Burling in horror and disbelief. "I don't know who you *are*."

"This is how it worked," he told her, realizing as he began that their moment in his study had been like his stolen summer month with Amelia, outside of time. At first the lines of what he said would be seductive, and Charlotte might want to take part in it or create her own version in which to live. He was certainly partly to blame for all that had happened, and while his guilt made him feel tenderness, even love, for her, he understood that she would have the opposite reaction, and that things were very likely over for them. "General Zu told me as much tonight. He and Gordon MacAllister have played a game together for more than twenty years. Gordon, and I, to a point, were playing it with the Soviets long before that. Afghanistan was the beginning of the end for the Cold War version of the game, but it was just the beginning for us and the Chinese. Zu knew it from the beginning, and his rise in the ranks was propelled by this knowledge. MacAllister knows it, too. The Islamists are the proxy here, strong as they may be in their own right, the body over which the battle is waged. They complicate things, they even distract us, which is very good for Zu."

"I don't want to hear your world history lesson," Charlotte said.

"You had better listen," Burling told her, and the lack of his sometime officiousness quieted her. "Dissidents, some of them Christians, some of them linked to Falun Gong, have been the greatest threat to Zu's rise because of his role at Tiananmen Square. It's all about *face*, reputation. He couldn't let these people continue escaping, defecting to the West. So he set a trap to smoke them out, like a complicated sacrifice in chess."

"My God," Charlotte said, but Yong was silent, watching him. Outside the windows, Lance Corporal Withers and the MSG master sergeant were crossing the lawn with a dog.

"Zu used you as bait, Yong. He knew you'd been turned and that your escape, unlike the others, would draw our attention. In fact, he made sure that it did. Did you actually write something about missiles and Abdul Khan?"

Yong's features seemed to blur. When he spoke, his voice had a quiet dignity. "I was only working out my ideas."

So Mac had been telling the truth. Or rather, Zu had not created the papers himself as part of the trap. This genuinely surprised Burling. "Well, that was a bad one, your idea I mean."

"It was in my private papers. I did not intend to sell our nuclear secrets to the highest bidder. The Islamists kill innocents; they are barbarians. I was merely questioning the existence, the use of nuclear weapons at all. I was forced to work on their manufacture, you see. I was sent to the United States to learn your own secrets about them. This was against my nature, Mr. Burling, as I attempted to explain to you in Princeton, all those years ago."

"We argued about Einstein," Burling said, "about his role in warning us the Nazis might develop the Bomb. I had forgotten."

"I did not forget," said Yong. "I thought that you were a man of great intellect, but that you and your countrymen had made Einstein into a funny uncle, as we would say here, instead of the man who turned the world inside out."

Charlotte had sunk into the end of a couch, dry-eyed, looking at the wall. The unnatural vapor of the security lights leaked through the French doors. The heavy marble lamps were dark on the end tables. The furniture in this room was late nineteenth century, heavy Qing dynasty, décor of invaders and dowagers, eunuchs. Small red wax seals with characters imprinted in them were stuck to the rabbited corners, indicating their provenance. The cushions were overstuffed but she barely seemed to make an impression.

"What time is it?" she asked.

"Two thirty," Burling said.

"There's still time, then." Her voice sounded desperate. "Yong can get on the boat."

"No, I cannot," said Yong.

"What do you mean?"

"Listen to what Mr. Burling is saying. I am only like smoke."

"What can you mean, smoke?"

"He means," Burling said, "that Zu knew that if Yong was allowed to escape, Mac would bring all of his considerable powers to bear, and in the process the whole network would be revealed."

"This is sickening," Charlotte said.

"Why did he kill his lieutenant," Yong asked, "the security man? He was loyal."

A glimmer of a smile moved across Burling's features, like wind on a lake, followed by a wave of sadness, but he didn't know if it showed to them or not. "There is always a wild card in these things."

"Jack."

"That's right. Zu didn't count on Jack, did he? Jack worked on Li hard. I could see it in his face when the general asked me what happened to April."

"It bothered Li when Jack shot the general's driver," said Charlotte.

"He was probably just beginning to understand," Burling said.

"Li was a gifted interrogator," Yong added without irony.

Charlotte stood up. "He or anyone else isn't going to torture you anymore," she said, "not in America."

"I'm not going to America," said Yong.

Before Charlotte could protest, a phone on the table by the door rang sharply. It took Burling a moment to remember it was there. The floorboards groaned beneath the carpet as he moved to answer it.

"We will get you to the U.S. one way or another," Charlotte was saying.

The lawn outside was empty, and the grass was silvered with dew.

"Burling," he said to the phone.

"Lucius." Gordon MacAllister. "I hear you've got trouble there."

"Did Ryan tell you?"

MacAllister's man in Shanghai had been strangely absent since Burling's return.

"Ryan's off on a junket in Shenzhen," MacAllister told him. "We've got a meeting after that here in Hong Kong."

"You won't have to worry about that meeting. It's been called off."

"You're sure you're not telling me a story, Burl?"

"Jack's dead. Yong's with me."

"Well, that's fine, Lucius, just fine. I'm sure we'll find a way . . ."

"To make Yong disappear? I don't think so." He felt Charlotte come up behind him. "Who's Ryan seeing in Shenzhen?"

"Your intellect never fails to surprise me, Lucius. In all the years, there was never anyone smarter than you."

"Just better prepared."

MacAllister laughed coldly. "A real scout."

"I'm the consul general in Shanghai," Burling told him. "I read the briefing papers, even when I'm home. I visit people who study these things. I even listened to Adrian Fry. So when our old friend Zu said, 'Our children see purity, they become corrupt,' I knew he was talking about his son, the one under indictment. And I know your friend Henry is supposed to be his brother. I know plenty of things I don't care to use to my advantage."

"In this case, however . . ."

"That's right," Burling said. Charlotte's hand was moving up and down, softly, on his back. She was beginning to believe he was a hero, now, believe that he was going to do something, but what he was going to do would be a disappointment to her for a very long time. "In this case, I am going to use the fact that you and Henry Sun are spiriting Zu's son away as a bargaining chip, not to get Yong out, which is impossible now, but to ask Zu to assure me of his safety here, to allow him to return to his teaching or his research or whatever he wants to do, in return for the life of Zu's son, which you control."

"You've thought this all out pretty carefully, haven't you, Lucius?"

Charlotte's hand had stopped moving, and her fingernails were digging into his shoulder. He shrugged her off. She could be angry all she wanted, but if they were going to be together, which he found unlikely now, she would have to accept whatever this ending said about him.

"It pains me to say this," he told MacAllister, "more than you can know, but Yong is safer in China with Zu than he would be in America with you."

"Yong is not to be trusted, Lucius."

"If that's true, you should like my proposal."

"Like it?" MacAllister laughed the laugh that held the whole fallen world in the barrel of his chest. It also signaled resignation.

"You'll be in touch with Zu, then?"

"I don't like it, but I can live with it."

"I hope I can, too," Burling said.

epilogue

THE SHIPPING CONTAINER WAS TIGHTLY PACKED WITH cartons, stacked on pallets two high and ten deep to the back of the long narrow space. Each box held a small motor, cushioned in Styrofoam, that weighed an immense amount given its size, but Mei and the deckhand had managed to clear one pallet, raising the cartons up high and pushing them backward under the corrugated roof. Lindstrom lay on a mattress of packing blankets spread across the rough wood slats. It was hot at the top of the container but the door was cracked and there was air to breathe, although it smelled of diesel and stale ocean water and something else that made her stomach churn. She knew the motion of the boat, once they'd entered the Taiwan Strait, would never leave her body or her dreams.

For no reason she understood, whatever agents Lindstrom had expected would molest them when the ship docked in Hong Kong did not appear, though the deckhand came and closed the door in precaution. The air in the container grew stiflingly hot, and Lindstrom groaned from the pain of the bullet that had lodged in his shoulder. Mei gave him the water the deckhand had left for them. She feared she would faint from her own vicious thirst. The other wound, where the shot had passed through his side just above the hip, began to bleed again from the sutures made by a doctor in the pay of triads who furnished the opium seller. Mei could not see the blood, but she could feel its sticky wetness. She daubed it with towels sprinkled lightly with the water and gave Lindstrom twice the number of pills the opium seller had told her. The pills made Lindstrom talk, ask questions like a child for what seemed like a long time.

"You're a good nurse," he told her.

"That is one thing I am good for," said Mei. "I have taken care of my mother, who was sickened with cancer, and I did so for my husband, who was stricken with doubt. He was the most fearful democrat you have ever seen. Then my father, who was angry and in pain."

"Why was your father angry?" asked Lindstrom. Although she could not see him, she could tell his face was closer to her, and she imagined he had propped up his head with his hand.

"He was angry at everything, at growing old, at dying, at my mother for leaving him alone, angry at Mao for what he did to our country, and at me for not becoming a scholar. The dimensions of his anger were very large."

"And your husband, why was he afraid?"

"He was not a man who liked to risk things. People do not believe it, because of what happened to him, but this is true. His mother died when he was young: one morning, early, she vomited blood and died in the kitchen of their house, and Guo, that was my husband, found her there. Guo's father was a military man, who was deeply obsessed with the logistics of the army, and he would travel around to different bases, counting soldiers and equipment, and my husband and his sister took care of themselves, cooked and cleaned the house and worked their small plot, and made the necessary devotions to their mother and ancestors. Guo, especially, did that. The other boys in their village all joined the army, but he was good at school and he won a scholarship. His father was a kind man, though very lonely and absorbed with his numbers, and he did not tell Guo to go to the army instead but to go to school and study mathematics. At university, the other students looked up to him because of his brilliance, and he could talk before people because he could take up his father's military manner of speaking. Still, when it came time to put our ideas into action, he was afraid. He doubted himself, and he did not like to make a decision. I did not have his brilliance, but what I lacked in that I made up for in impatience. I would hold him at night, even shame him and deny him until he found his resolve."

"How did he do in the Square, in front of the tanks, if he was afraid?"

"In the Square, he was magnificent. He was not afraid, and he was not angry. He was calm because he simply believed it was right."

"That must be the difference," Lindstrom said, wincing as he laid his head back on the pillow she had made with his clothes.

"Were you afraid to be sent to Annam?"

"I got into trouble when I was nineteen, and the judge said it's jail or the intake center in San Diego, so I joined the marines. I didn't really have a choice."

"You were hurt there. I can see it on your body."

"I was lying on a slope," he said, his voice distant, "just below this LZ way up in the Central Highlands near Plei Me. Beautiful country, mountains that rose right up to these luminous clouds. A few of us were smoking hash. When the mortars came in, we all got up and ran. I got hit in the back with some pieces of shrapnel. My mind was still running when my body went down."

"But you did not believe that what you were doing there was right?"

"I was never really much of a believer."

"You believe in love," she said, leaning closer so that her loose breast brushed his chest. She wanted desperately to bring him back. Without him, she would be more alone than she could have ever imagined. "You still loved your wife even though she was faithless to you."

"I couldn't give up on that," he said, softer now. "Even in Kabul, I knew that something was going on, that Burling and I both thought we would have her. 'You're actually expecting I'll choose,' April said, and she laughed. 'Well, at least you have each other.'

I was too stupid to understand what she meant. 'I don't want to belong to anyone,' she said."

"Do you still try to understand it now?"

"It was starting to leave me," Lindstrom said, and she could tell from his voice that he was drifting. "The questions don't have the same force they did."

"That is because you love me," said Mei.

"It may be so."

"You love me?"

In the darkness, Lindstrom didn't make a sound. There were terrifying noises of scraping and banging, a clashing of metal that echoed around the container like the inside of a drum. They throbbed in her head with a pain that gathered for hours. After a while she lay with her chin barely touching Lindstrom's shoulder, so that she could feel if he was breathing, her nose close to his ear. She smelled his body and she wanted him desperately, but she didn't have the strength to act on it, like an elderly person must feel, she thought, and gradually she gave way to sleep. The banging and shuddering became the sound of marching feet in her dreams. There was smoke and the clatter of metal on stones.

When the blade of light from the opening door stabbed her eyes, she wasn't sure if Lindstrom was breathing. She scrambled across the tops of boxes, pushing the last row out of her way. The deckhand clung to the door like a climber. Around him the ship's hold stretched to the open hatch above, trapping its square of pale sky.

"He is alive?"

"I don't know." The air had freshened. "We are away?"

"From the port? Yes. They swept the containers and put more on board, but no one else came. I have brought you some rice and dried fish and some water."

"I need water very much."

He handed Mei a soiled plastic bag that was heavy with bottles. "Don't come out of the box until I come down again. In the day you could be seen from the hatches."

He left the door cracked and Mei crawled back inside. As she let herself down into the space where Lindstrom lay, she heard him take a shallow breath.

"Mei?"

"I am here."

"I thought I was dreaming, but then I heard you, so I knew it must not be true."

The fragile sound of his voice made her weak with emotion. The water was still cold, and the deckhand had put soy sauce into the rice with the dried fish.

"How do you feel? Are you hungry?" she asked.

"I think so, yes."

"That is a beneficial sign. Do you need one of the pills?"

"I'm going to try not to now. That's how I got started on junk."

"When you are wounded in Annam, they give you opium?"

"Morphine," he said, taking the bottle of water. She watched the liquid move the muscles of his throat, and she wanted to touch his body, which was stripped to the waist, but she could tell that it was stiff from the wounds. "It is very much like opium. The pain continued, and when they wouldn't give me the morphine, that's when I got on the shit. It was everywhere in Frisco back then."

"What is Frisco?"

"San Francisco. In California."

"Is that where you lived with your wife?"

"Yes, she went there for graduate school. I shipped back there after Vietnam."

"I imagine you were glad to be home then," she said, sitting cross-legged with the plastic container of food on her knee. She suddenly remembered meeting Guo at university, talking for hours with a plate of noodles set between them on the floor. The memory made her feel absurd, like a girl, but she couldn't deny the goodness of it.

"That was a difficult time," Lindstrom said. "Vietnam had begun to make sense to me, not the why but the how, and then I was wounded and back in the world I wasn't good for anything. April's friends were all against the war, but they didn't understand it."

"We learn in school in China that the American war in Annam has corrupted your country."

"For some people, it did," he said, accepting the chopsticks. "They have not gotten over it. To continue to believe in our country after that took some real doing."

"You said that you don't believe in anything, but it sounds like you do."

Lindstrom's lips glistened with sauce from the food, but she thought they twitched, suppressing a smile. "It's a funny word, belief. In English, it can mean that you take something purely on faith, which is how my grandfather saw it, or it can mean that you think something's true. People do some bad things because they believe."

"Can you believe that you love someone?"

"No, that defeats it. Either you love or you don't."

"Do you believe that you love me?" Mei asked, getting back to the question the only way she knew, through a logical game.

"No. I do," Lindstrom said.

"You love me?"

"Yes."

"And you'll show me your country, and we will live in it together, in San Francisco, California?"

"I'll try to see it through your eyes," Lindstrom told her.

Mark Harril Saunders was born and raised in the Washington, D.C., area and holds degrees from the University of Pennsylvania and the University of Virginia, where he was a Henry Hoyns Fellow. He has traveled extensively in Europe, the Middle East, the former Soviet Union, and China. His writing has appeared in the *VQR*, *Boston Review*, the *Virginian-Pilot*, *Washington Post*, and *Huffington Post*, and on NPR. In 2001 he was awarded the Andrew S. Lytle Prize for fiction from *Sewanee Review*.

Saunders has worked on Capitol Hill, at several bookstores, and as a publisher's sales rep. Currently Director of the University of Virginia Press, he lives in Charlottesville, Virginia, and Castine, Maine, with his wife and three children.